FALSELY YOURS

SCARLETT WITHERSPOON

ISBN 979-8-9940754-0-1

Cover Design by Tim Byrne

Editing and Proofreading by English Proper Editing Services

For my husband, whose love and support carried me through every late night and every doubt. Thank you for pushing me to take the leap when I wanted to play it safe, for believing in me when I struggled to believe in myself, and for making it possible for me to chase my dreams and bring them to life.

1

MAREN

I didn't plan on slinging cheap whiskey at the Rusty Nail, a bar that smells like piss and stale beer, but here I am. The neon sign sputters above the bar, buzzing like an angry wasp. Every few seconds, the light flickers across the cracked floor and the cheap whiskey bottles lined up like sad soldiers.

The Rusty Nail is as divey as they come. Serving drinks in cut-off shorts and a faded Rusty Nail tee won't make me rich, let alone lead me to owning a bar one day, but it keeps the lights on and spares me the need to put on a social face. I look around to see if anyone needs another round. The regulars sit slumped in stained jackets, looking like they'd rather be anywhere else. But then I spot him.

A blonde man in a tailored coat sits at the far end of the bar, nursing an old-fashioned like he has nowhere better to be. He leans back with his legs spread slightly, one arm draped over the seat beside him, as if the room exists solely to entertain him.

His posture is casual, but there's an edge to it. He looks refined without even trying. His sharp, green eyes move slowly across the room, uninterested in everything around him, until they land on me. They don't move after that.

He isn't just handsome. He's magnetic. Unsettling.

His stare pins me in place like he knows something I don't. I tilt my head and size him up. I've encountered plenty of guys who stare, but this feels different. For a moment, his expression softens. My heart jumps in my chest, and I hate that it feels familiar. Then he frowns, and his eyes trail over me in an oddly critical way.

I cross my arms and catch my reflection in the cracked mirror. A few loose strands fall from my ponytail. I need a haircut badly. But why do I even care? He's a stranger, yet his judgment, real or imagined, seeps under my skin and stirs up old insecurities I'd rather keep buried.

Mike, my wiry coworker with faded tattoos that run up to his neck, nudges me and nods toward the scattered tables. It makes me break eye contact with the man, and I'm thankful for that.

"Big night tonight, apparently," he says, his voice as dry as the beer-soaked floor beneath us.

"Oh?" I don't look up. I scrub a glass, knowing it'll never look clean enough.

He chuckles, but it lacks humor. "Some guy's thinking of buying this dump, so Jerry wants us on our best behavior tonight," he says, and I catch him rolling his eyes when I look up.

That's surprising. Jerry is stubborn, and I don't see him selling this place. He's been running it for decades, but never renovated it. He always says it's part of its charm. So things must be terrible if he's considering selling it.

I smirk and set the glass down. "Aren't I always?"

Mike huffs out a laugh. "Sure. But maybe don't threaten anyone with a corkscrew tonight. So tone it down."

I laugh. Some drunk asshole snapped his fingers at me and

said, *"Bitch, get me another drink."* I had the corkscrew in my hand before I even thought about it, and held it just long enough for him to rethink his tone. He didn't come back after that. No one said a word, which tells you everything you need to know about this place.

"Noted." My gaze sweeps the room, landing on the mysterious man again.

Mike leans in and lowers his voice. "See him? That's gotta be the guy. Who else around here looks like they've got money in their bank account?"

"Maybe he's lost," I offer, returning to scrubbing glasses.

"Yeah, lost his way straight into staring at you," Mike teases, elbowing me.

How long has he been watching me that even Mike noticed?

"Go over there and see what he wants."

"Why don't you? I'm sure he tips well."

I don't think I can handle his judgment close up. I never care about what people think, but then again, I work with people who don't give a shit about their appearances, either. And it shows.

"Exactly, and you need it. So go over and impress him."

I sigh. He's right. My landlord told me I have a week before he evicts me, and that was four days ago. So if putting on a show for him gets me some extra cash and a raise in the near future, then I'll do it. I square my shoulders and grab a fresh towel, sauntering over like it's just another night. My steps sound heavy, my boots sticking to the floor with each move closer.

As I approach, the man's gaze lifts and a slow, knowing smile curves at the corner of his mouth. Up close, he's almost too perfect to be real. His green eyes draw me in before I can look away. His blonde hair is neatly styled, without a strand out of place, and his features are sharp. High cheekbones. A strong jaw. A mouth that looks like it was made to whisper sins.

His skin is warm-toned and sun-kissed, as if he's just returned from somewhere far more luxurious than here. But considering how crappy this area is, that's basically anywhere. He wears a tailored suit, deep charcoal, that probably costs more than everything in my apartment combined. Power oozes from him, raising goosebumps on my arms.

"Can I get you another drink?" I ask, keeping my voice light. His eyes flick over me like he's cataloging every detail.

"I was hoping for some company," he replies smoothly, his voice as refined as his appearance.

I raise an eyebrow and scoff. "We don't offer that kind of service here."

He chuckles. "No, I don't imagine you do. I'm Adrian," he says, his gaze unwavering, as if awaiting my recognition of his name.

"Maren," I reply, a bit thrown off, but oddly drawn in. He extends his hand, and after a beat, I shake it. His grip is firm, and his touch lingers before I pull my hand back.

"So, what brings you here?" I ask, attempting to keep my tone casual.

"Oh, I'm just...considering my options," he says, glancing around the bar and then back to me. There's something about him I can't quite place. A strange intensity lingers between us. It makes me feel unsettled, maybe even unprepared.

Adrian leans forward with a faint smirk still on his lips. "I really am looking for company tonight. Are you sure you're not up to the challenge?" he teases.

I hold his gaze and force a polite smile. "I'm not that kind of girl. I'm just a bartender."

He raises his glass and takes a slow sip, his eyes still fixed on me. "Yes, surprisingly this one's good," he says, as if shocked I mixed his drink right.

My jaw tightens. Screw him and his backhanded compliment. I don't know if he's trying to get a rise out of me or if he thinks he's charming, but either way, I'm not having it. Screw him and his money.

"Well, if you don't need anything else, then I'll be taking care of my other customers."

I turn to leave, but his voice cuts through the bar. "Wait."

I pause and glance over my shoulder. "Yes?"

He holds his glass between two fingers and raises an eyebrow. "I want another one."

"I'll put your order in the queue," I retort, clenching my teeth.

He shakes his head with a glint in his eye. "No, I want you to make it."

I sigh, but force myself to stay professional. "Fine."

"Make it in front of me," he adds, leaning back to watch. "I'd like to see what you can do."

I take a steady breath, reminding myself I'm behind on rent. I have to show him I'm good at my job, and hopefully, he'll give me a good tip.

"All right," I say, preparing to make his drink.

This is my domain. Behind the bar, I don't have to think or second-guess. I let my hands and instincts take over, slipping into the rhythm I know so well. I measure, pour, shake, and focus on the process as if he isn't here.

While I work, I see his eyes drop to my chest and linger there like it's the most natural thing in the world. He doesn't hide it or pretend to be subtle. My jaw tightens, but there's a flicker of heat that moves through me, anyway. It's unwelcome, but real, and it crawls up my neck, settling just beneath my skin. I don't let it show, but I know he sees more than I want him to.

I'm used to stares. I've learned how to ignore them. But this one feels different because he's actually handsome, and for a second, I hate how good that feels. Maybe he is interested in me. But the sad reality is it's only for sex, nothing more. He would never date a girl working at a shitty dive bar. Regardless, I keep moving and pour the drink into a glass with a smooth flourish.

Without looking up, I set the drink on the bar between us. "Here you go."

When I meet his eyes, he doesn't look away. I fold my arms and offer nothing but indifference.

"You're different from before," he muses, breaking the silence between us.

Different? Who is this guy? I don't know him, and there is no *before*. I've been working here for a long time. I've seen so many people, but he stands out so much that I would have remembered him.

"Come again?"

He chuckles. "I can make that happen," he says smoothly. He's making a promise, not a joke.

I clear my throat and step back a bit. "I didn't mean it that way."

His expression doesn't change. "I want you to come to my hotel room."

I blink, caught off guard by his bluntness. What is wrong with him? I've barely spoken to him, and he thinks that's okay to ask? It wouldn't be, even if we had an entire conversation.

My face goes cold, but I press my mouth into a flat line. "I'm not doing that."

That should be enough to shut him down. His lips twist into a smile that doesn't reach his eyes. "If you don't, then I'll fire you first."

My stomach drops. He can't fire me for not sleeping with him. Does he really think I'm so desperate that he can threaten me?

It just shows he's an entitled, rich asshole. I'm tempted to wave a corkscrew in his face if he wants to play that game.

"You don't own this place," I say, but my voice is faltering now. I try to sound unfazed, but I can already hear the panic in my voice.

"Not yet," he replies, his voice too calm. "But I will."

I feel the blood drain from my face as panic presses against the back of my throat. He says it as if it's a done deal. It would be impossible to find a new job in time to pay my rent. I also can't afford to have him waiting for me to slip up and have a legit reason to fire me in the future.

I narrow my eyes and hope he can't see past my bravado. "I don't need this job that badly," I lie, hoping he can't hear the shake in my voice.

I don't even have a car to sleep in. This job is far from perfect, but it's all I have right now. It's not worth selling myself for, but I hope he doesn't call my bluff. Because if he does, I don't know what I'll say or do. But he's staring at me like he already knows that. I don't know him, yet his familiarity with me feels freaky.

He leans back with a mocking smirk. "Sure you do," he says, savoring how much this unnerves me. "I could make your life hell if I wanted to. But I won't...because of our history."

My stomach clenches. *What's he talking about?* My brain scrambles for context, any flash of memory that would explain this, but all I find is static.

"Why would you do that? You don't even know me."

He leans in, eyes narrowing. "You're really going to keep pretending we don't know each other? I won't walk out the door and pretend I never saw you here."

I swallow hard, nerves crawling under my skin. "You've got me mixed up with someone else. I've never met you before."

I would remember if I met a rich asshole in an expensive, tailored suit.

His gaze hardens, the polite mask slipping to show coldness underneath. "Stop pretending," he says, his voice flatter now. "I'll make sure you regret it...when we get home."

Home. There's no home with him. He seems sober, so he's clearly just unhinged.

I step back, but his hand snaps out and catches my arm. His palm is warm against my skin, and for one awful second, my body hesitates. I don't want to risk pissing him off even more.

He lets out a slow, disappointed sigh, like he's trying to stay patient. "I'm not trying to scare you, okay? I want us to start over."

His voice softens. He meets my eyes, and for a second, longing flickers in them. "I miss you, Ellie."

Ellie? I stare at him, my chest tightening, my heart pounding harder. What's wrong with him? I search his face, hoping for a crack, something to tell me this is a joke, but he doesn't blink.

God, I hope he doesn't buy this bar. I don't want to lose my job because a stranger thinks I look like his ex. Most guys who come in heartbroken get drunk and pass out. They don't fixate on the bartender and call her by the wrong name. I almost feel bad for him. Almost. But I'm not sleeping with him to make him feel better.

I start backing away, heading toward the break room.

"Ellie, wait, let's talk."

"Leave me alone," I say, my pulse hammering. I rub my temples as I head for the back, needing space to breathe.

"I'm not feeling well," I whisper to Mike, grabbing my coat in the break room.

Mike frowns, glancing at the clock. "Maren, we need you to close tonight."

I pause. The pressure builds behind my ribs. "No one else can do it?"

He sighs and looks out across the room. Most of the regulars are gone. The rest are half asleep in their drinks. The neon buzzes like a dying insect.

"I have to get out of here soon. It's slow, so it shouldn't be too bad."

I'm tired of pretending I don't care. I want more than this place can give me. A real bar. But no one wants to hire a nobody like me. I've tried. I needed a paycheck, so I settled.

Mike's face softens. "Is something wrong?"

My fingers grip my coat tighter. "That guy...the one who might buy this place? There's something off about him."

Mike lifts a brow, unimpressed. "Maren, it's a bar. You'll see worse."

"No." A customer looks up briefly at my quick, raised voice. I instantly drop my voice. "He asked me to go back to his hotel room, or he'll fire me when he buys the bar."

Mike exhales, scrubbing a hand over his face. "Jesus. Just... close up, lock the door, and go home. We'll deal with it in the morning."

I glance over my shoulder. Adrian's seat is empty, but I still feel his stare clinging to me like smoke. Shit, I didn't even close him out. Whatever, drinks are on the house.

My gut tells me to run. But I mutter, "Fine," and slide my coat back over the chair like it weighs fifty pounds.

I force my feet to carry me behind the bar, the floorboards creaking with each step. The muffled sounds of passing cars seep through the thin walls, reminding me that the world still exists outside.

I look, and he left a hundred-dollar bill with a note of his hotel name and room number under his empty glass. He's nuts if he thinks I'm going to his hotel room—but I'll happily take his money.

Over the next few hours, the last stragglers pay their tabs, moving slowly. The clink of glasses cuts through the quiet before they shuffle out the door.

I look at the clock, and it's almost 2:00 a.m. I rush out, and the lock clicks shut behind me, the sound echoing on the empty street. The night air is crisp and carries a faint smell of rain. I take a deep breath, trying to steady the nerves that haven't settled since Adrian came in.

I head down the sidewalk toward the bus stop. The street is quieter than usual, the air too still. Like it's waiting for something I can't see.

Streetlights cast long, uneven shadows that slide along the pavement. I glance over my shoulder more than once, paranoia making every shadow feel like a threat.

The clang of a metal gate down the block makes me flinch. I force myself to keep walking. I have to get to the bus stop, get home, and forget this ever happened.

Home. The apartment I picked has cheap rent, but it also has noisy neighbors who drown out any sounds I make. Across the hall, Mrs. Trask, a quiet old woman with sharp eyes, is practically the neighborhood watch. She'd notice if I went missing. *No*—stop thinking like that.

The bus stop is empty, with benches littered with old flyers and a lone coffee cup rolling in the wind. I glance at my phone. The bus should be here any minute. The street stays silent with very few cars passing through this area this late. I let out a shaky breath.

The bus rumbles past me, ignoring my outstretched hand. Now I'll have to get a taxi. Another expense I can't afford.

I turn to check my surroundings, scanning for headlights, ready to call a ride. The street's too quiet, and my gut tells me to move faster. My fingers tighten on my phone.

Just when I think the worst of the night is over, a hand clamps over my mouth. The leather of his glove is cold and suffocating. My body reacts before my mind catches up—I kick, twist, fight—but he's stronger, and his grip doesn't loosen. My breath comes in ragged bursts. All I can smell is spicy cologne.

"Ellie, calm down," he says.

It's Adrian from the bar. I knew I should've left earlier, but I didn't.

I thrash harder, elbowing him in the ribs. He grunts, loosens his grip for a second, and I rip free, ready to scream. I make it two steps before his arm hooks tight around my waist, yanking me back, slamming me against his chest. My phone clatters to the ground. His other hand fists in my hair, jerking my head to the side. Before I can scream again, something sharp pierces my neck. The burn is instant, spreading fast.

My knees buckle before I understand what's happening, and I fall into him. He picks me up in his arms while my arms go numb. I see Adrian's face, and he looks disappointed in me. *Why would he resort to this?*

"I didn't have to do this. You should've just come with me earlier," he says.

My mouth won't form words. My vision blurs at the edges. My eyes close before I can make another sound.

2

MAREN

I stir, confusion clinging to me like a heavy fog. My heart pounds hard enough to hurt, but each beat confirms this isn't a dream. Smooth, luxurious sheets slide across my skin. The silk gown on my body is a stark contrast to the worn, cotton t-shirt and sweatpants I usually sleep in. My hair, normally twisted into a ponytail, spills over my shoulders. Nothing about this feels right.

I force my eyes open, and my breath catches as I take in my surroundings. The room is dim, lit only by the flickering glow of a fireplace across from the bed. The high ceilings and elegant furniture look far more expensive than anything I've ever owned. I have no idea where I am. I remember leaving the bar and locking up, but after that, everything is fuzzy. *What the fuck happened to me? Where am I?* This sure as hell isn't my home.

A noise beside me sends a jolt of fear through my body. I turn my head slowly, my stomach twisting as a dark figure shifts next to me. Before I can stop myself, a scream tears from my throat. The figure bolts upright and switches on a bedside lamp, flooding the room with warm light. My breath catches as recognition strikes.

Adrian.

His green eyes don't widen. They don't flinch. He watches me too calmly, as if having a stranger in his bed is perfectly normal. My eyes drop to where the sheet slides down his chest. He's shirtless, the muscles in his torso flexing as he leans forward. Heat crawls up my neck, and I hate how my body reacts, even now.

I didn't agree to go to his hotel room. *Right?* I wasn't that desperate. I close my eyes and force myself to remember what happened. I closed up, missed the bus, and then he fucking stabbed me with a needle, and now I'm in his hotel room. I scream again, hoping someone hears me.

"Eleanor, what's wrong?" His voice is rough with sleep, but his gaze is steady.

I throw the covers off and stumble backward, my breath coming in short, shallow bursts. "You kidnapped me."

He sighs, his expression tightening with irritation. "Stop being ridiculous and come back to bed."

I take another step back, shaking my head. "Did you undress me? Brush my hair? What the hell is wrong with you?"

He doesn't flinch at the accusation. "Yes. I wanted you to be comfortable."

"You drugged me." My pulse pounds at my temples.

"I didn't *drug you,*" he says, his tone suddenly sharp. "I gave you something to help you relax."

Anger overtakes the fear, squeezing my chest. He's rewriting history so that he's still the good guy. "That's drugging me, you psycho!"

His eyes darken as he stands; he's tall and towers over me. I instinctively back away, my heartbeat loud in my ears. He moves around the side of the bed, and I catch a glimpse of the outline of his dick in his boxers. My stomach twists at the sight. My brain tries to connect that body to the one who sat at the bar, who flirted with me like I had a choice.

"Is your name even Adrian?" I demand.

He frowns as if I've insulted him. "Are you still going to pretend that you don't remember me, or that you're my wife?"

Wife? I've never been married. An icy shiver runs down my spine, but I force myself to hold his gaze. "I met you once at the bar. Never before that."

Adrian's posture shifts, as if he expected my denial. His fingers flex at his sides before he takes another step closer, his voice lowering. "You're confused. You've been away for months, pretending to be someone else. But that's over now."

I shake my head, my breath coming too fast. "I'm not confused. I know exactly who I am, and I'm not your wife."

A faint smile touches his lips, but it doesn't reach his eyes. "You always did have a stubborn streak, Eleanor."

His confidence is what scares me the most. He truly believes it. He's rewritten everything in his head, and I'm just the body he's dragged into the story.

I clench my fists. "I don't know what kind of fantasy you're living in, but I am not Eleanor."

I don't even know who that is. What the hell happened to her? Did he kill her and is now trying to find a replacement? The thought makes me want to throw up.

His hand lifts to my jaw, tilting my chin up. The touch is light, but the frustration beneath it is unmistakable. His thumb brushes my jaw in a way that feels almost tender, and it makes my skin crawl.

"You will be. Did you think I would stand by and watch you bartend in some rundown dive?" Disdain drips from his voice.

I hold his gaze and force my voice to stay steady. "I'm good at what I do."

His tone softens, but the intensity in his expression doesn't fade. "Eleanor, I meant what I said. We can start over. I know I worked too much and asked a lot of you, but you made your point. You've been gone for months, and I've run out of excuses to explain your absence."

I let out a bitter laugh. "No wonder your wife left you. You're unhinged. And you don't even know it—that's the worst part."

He buries the flicker of anger, pain, and regret beneath a calm mask. "I took you back. You should be grateful."

The words send a fresh wave of revulsion through me. "Maybe you should have divorced her instead of clinging to someone who doesn't want you."

"God, I'm so tired of this," he mutters. "Do you think pretending you can't remember is going to make me go soft on you for leaving?"

"What are you talking about?"

"Do you think that will help you avoid punishment?" he continues.

That word hits harder than anything else. *What does he mean by that?* I can't even fathom what that would be.

"Punishment?" I repeat, barely breathing.

There's something different in his eyes now. They're colder.

"Eleanor, you don't get to disappear and act like none of it ever happened. Actions have consequences. You need to learn that again."

My chest tightens. He just said punishment, like it's normal and deserved. I don't care that I'm exposed or that he's watching me. All I care about is putting distance between us. So I bolt, my legs carrying me through the doorway and into the hall.

My breath echoes off the high ceilings as I fly down the grand staircase. This isn't a hotel—it's a fucking mansion. This house stretches around me in every direction; wider, taller, and more lavish than anything I've ever seen. Every inch of it feels designed to keep someone trapped inside. Finally, I see the front door. Relief spikes in my chest. It's massive—the dark wood polished and solid.

I grab the handle and pull it with everything I have. It doesn't move. To the side, a keypad glows softly. I punch in numbers, random codes, anything that comes to mind. Each attempt gives me the same result: two sharp beeps and a blinking red light. Invalid. Rejected. Denied.

I slam my palm against the wall in frustration, then turn and run down another hallway. I throw open the first door and rush inside. The room is furnished, but empty. I sprint to the nearest window and try to force it open. My fingers scrape along the edge, but the window won't budge. The glass feels cold under my palms. It's thick and reinforced; built to hold, not to release.

Outside, a green lawn stretches across the property, manicured and unnervingly perfect. In the distance, beyond hedges and carefully spaced trees, stands a tall, iron gate. The bars are thick, and the height looks impossible to climb. This is not just a house.

It's a compound.

Still, I keep moving. My chest burns as I run through another corridor, unsure if I'm circling back or finding a way out. Then I reach the back of the house and freeze. The windows here stretch from floor to ceiling, giving a full view of the landscape beyond. And it's not what I expected.

Water gleams in the moonlight, dark and endless. Waves crash against a private dock below. The breeze off the water is visible in the trees, bending branches in slow, lazy motions. Boats sit in the distance, but there's no sign of nearby land. *Where the fuck am I?* Chicago has lakes, but they don't look like this. No shoreline like this could ever exist there.

Wherever I am, it's far from the life I know. I'm not just locked inside a house—I've been taken somewhere I can't even identify. Somewhere I can't walk away from. There's no escaping anywhere.

Before I can take another step, the blinds lower over the

windows, one by one. The mechanical hum fills the room as the light disappears. Every window goes black. The house plunges into darkness as I hear footsteps behind me.

I turn, my heart pounding. "Where are we?" I whisper, more to myself than to him.

"Creswell Island," he says, like it should mean something to me.

I turn to face him. "I've never heard of it. Are we still in the U.S.?"

"Of course we are," he says, almost offended. "We decided to move here together. You said you wanted somewhere private. Somewhere we could start fresh."

I stare at him, unable to speak.

"We designed this house together. And now you're pretending you don't even know where we are?"

My throat tightens, and my vision blurs. A sharp sound escapes me—half cry, half scream. Then another, louder this time. I scream until my voice cracks, until the panic boils over, and I can only hear my ragged breathing.

I bolt out of the room and start searching for another exit. There has to be a back door. Footsteps pound behind me before he grabs me, but I twist out of his grip.

"Ellie, stop screaming and come back to bed."

"I'm not coming back to bed. You're insane! This place is a prison!"

He exhales slowly, the sound heavy with disappointment. "I have to make sure you don't leave again."

"If there's a fire, how do you even get out of here?"

His silence stretches for several seconds. He didn't think of that.

Eventually, he speaks again, his voice softer. "This is why you need to stay. You challenge me."

Damn. There is no emergency exit I can use to escape.

I laugh, but it sounds more like a breath caught in my throat. "You want to punish me," I say.

"To remind you of your place," he replies without hesitation. His gaze flicks down my body, lingering before meeting my eyes again. "You always react this way when I bring up punishment."

I want to scream at him. I want to claw my way out of this house, this lie, this moment.

"You're scary..."

He shakes his head. "No, you're scared of what I'm capable of. You've never been afraid of me."

He says it as if it's a truth I've forgotten, as if I should agree. As if the fear of his actions, and not of the man himself, is somehow acceptable.

"I'm not her."

He sighs. "You have until the count of ten to return to bed or face the consequences."

His voice is calm, almost indifferent, as he begins to count. "One...two...three..."

I scramble, searching for another exit.

"Six...seven..."

His hand closes around my wrist, stopping the countdown. His grip is firm, but not rough. His green eyes search mine with something closer to longing than anger.

"Ellie, stop fighting."

A weak flare of hope rises in my chest. "Just let me go. I swear, I won't tell a soul about this."

"Never. You're home now, and you're staying."

He pulls me back toward the bedroom. I don't fight him— not because I'm giving in, but because I don't want to know what happens if I don't.

When we reach the bedroom, he climbs into bed behind me without a word. The mattress shifts under his weight, and then his arm slides around my waist, pulling me back against him. His chest is warm against my back, the slow, steady rise of his breathing at odds with the panic coiling tight in my throat.

One of his hands settles low on my stomach, his thumb brushing the silk fabric, like he can't help himself. I go rigid, every muscle locked, but he doesn't seem to notice or care.

I stare straight ahead, trying not to breathe too loudly, trying not to feel anything. My pulse throbs in my ears. My eyes sting, but I don't cry. I can't.

He exhales, the sound soft against my hair, and I feel his mouth at my temple. "Good girl," he murmurs again, his voice low and almost fond. "Don't do that again. Understand?"

I nod without speaking. The praise sends ice through my veins.

"Everything will be normal again soon. Now, go to sleep," he murmurs.

For now, I have to stay calm and close my eyes. Eventually, I drift off into a restless sleep.

3

MAREN

I wake up tangled in warmth, muscular arms locked around me like I belong here. I've never been around this much wealth before. Everything here gleams. The sheets, the art on the walls, it all whispers that I don't belong. But he acts like I do, like I always have.

For a second, it feels like a dream. Adrian's scent, the heat of his bare skin, the steady rhythm of his breathing—it feels unreal. When I shift to look behind me, his grip tightens, and I catch a glimpse of his face. Blonde hair tousled, green eyes half-lidded with sleep. He's beautiful. If this were any other man, if he hadn't mistaken me for his wife, hadn't kidnapped me, I might have said yes to a date.

"I missed you." His voice is low and warm, curling around me. I'm still wrapped in his arms, cocooned in something dangerously close to comfort. I should pull away. But I stay still, pretending I'm asleep.

He grabs my shoulder so I'm facing him. Then his lips find mine, the kiss soft—my heart jerks. The next kiss is harder. I open to him, and his kiss becomes more passionate. His tongue strokes mine in a slow rhythm, sending a shiver through me.

He kisses like we've done this a thousand times, and I'm the one who forgot.

I should push him away, demand space, scream that this isn't real. But what would that change? He believes I'm the woman he married. He already mentioned punishment, so maybe I should go along with it. If sleeping with him means he'll let his guard down, then so be it. At least he's handsome. That's something he has going for him despite being a madman.

His hand drags over my ribs and up to cup my breast. His thumb grazes the peak through the silk, and heat shoots straight between my legs. I gasp and push at his chest as guilt overwhelms me.

My voice shakes. "I can't—I can't be with someone else's husband."

He blinks like the words don't register. His fingers slip up to my chin, angling my face toward his like he's coaxing the truth out of me with his touch alone. He then tilts his head and studies my face. "I'm your husband. You're just confused."

"I didn't forget. I couldn't forget you..." My voice is small and weak.

"Admit it. You need this." His hand squeezes my breast, his thumb circling until my nipple hardens under the fabric.

"I don't," I rasp. Except I do need to do this. He'll let his guard down, and if it sucks, maybe he'll let me go. But still, betrayal lives in my skin now. He slides his palm down my stomach, slipping under the gown. His fingers spread over my hip, warm and possessive. I tense as he drags his hand up my inner thigh.

He pushes my thigh open with his knee. My breath comes out fast.

"I haven't—" I whisper, my voice cracking.

He doesn't even pause. His mouth grazes my jaw as his fingers move higher. "Haven't what?"

"I haven't...done this before." The confession tastes like acid. Maybe he'll believe it and realize he has the wrong woman. I hate that my first time is going to be like this; with a crazy man I don't know, in a place I've never been. I hate that he gets this part of me now.

He lets out a low sound, half amusement, half disbelief. "You've never been shy with me before."

"It's the truth," I choke out. I guess he'll see for himself.

He shakes his head, brushing his mouth over mine again. "You're lying to yourself. And I'm done letting you."

There's no room for doubt in his voice. He says it like a fact —like I've wronged him by not remembering the life he swears we shared.

I gasp as his fingers slip between my legs. He slides his fingertips over my clit, gently spreading the wetness there, making my hips buck against my will. His finger goes lower, circling my entrance in small, maddening passes. My hips lift and my thighs tremble. I sink my nails into his arms, wanting to stop him, but I don't. It feels too damn good. My body is betraying me and selling me out, one nerve ending at a time.

"You're soaked," he murmurs.

I shake my head, but he ignores me.

"I knew you missed me."

He kisses me again, harder. I cry out, my back arching, as he pushes his finger inside me. My hip is held down by his hand as he moans against my mouth. My breath comes in ragged gasps.

"God, I missed this," he whispers.

He lowers his mouth to my chest, pressing kisses along my breast. His tongue flicks over the peak, wet heat that makes my body jerk. He closes his lips around my nipple and sucks gently, then harder, until I whimper.

He pulls his fingers out of me, then pushes them back in, slow and steady, filling me over and over. Each thrust of his hand sends another sharp burst of sensation spiraling through me.

His thumb rubs my clit in slow, insistent circles. His mouth moves to the other breast, kissing and sucking while he works his fingers deeper. My hips tilt up, seeking more friction I can't pretend I don't want. One hand threads through my hair, gently tugging until I meet his eyes.

"Look at me," he says, his voice low and rough.

I keep my eyes squeezed shut.

"Ellie. Look at me."

I open them. He's watching me, pupils blown, his mouth wet from my skin. "Come for me."

"No," I whisper, but the pleasure is already building. He rubs faster with more fingers. When my climax hits, I shatter. My hips jerk helplessly as I clench around his fingers. A sob rips from my throat, and he doesn't once look away. He keeps rubbing me through it, his thumb circling and fingers thrusting until I'm limp and shaking.

I've never hated myself more. But I lie here, limp, silent, the echo of my pleasure choking me. He made me come. He made it feel good. And that's the part I can't forgive.

My first time isn't supposed to go like this. I always hoped to find a nice guy who would want me for me. Not some guy at a bar who wanted someone easy—I've met plenty of those—and certainly not a madman who thinks I'm his wife.

He lifts his head and kisses me again, softer, like nothing about this is remotely wrong. "Good girl," he murmurs. "Get on my cock. Now."

Panic claws at my chest. This is happening, and I'm nervous as hell. What the fuck am I supposed to do? What if he thinks I suck at it? But if it sucks, then that's what he deserves.

He tears the gown the rest of the way off and shoves it aside. My breath catches when he pushes his boxers down his hips.

His dick is thick and hard, pushed up against his stomach. He doesn't look away while he kicks them off the bed.

My stomach flips. I try to close my legs, but he catches one knee and pushes it open wide.

He presses his cock, hot and heavy, against my thigh, and it's making me wetter.

"You feel that? Only you make me feel this way," he murmurs, his voice rough.

He brushes the hair from my face and strokes my cheek with the backs of his fingers. "You're mine. And I'll take you over and over until you remember that."

"I'm not yours," I whisper again, even softer. I need to give him what he wants, but a million things run through my mind. *Will it hurt? I heard it hurts the first time. Will he be rough? He's not the soft type, so he probably will be.*

Slowly, he teases me by sliding the head along my entrance. I'm breathing in short, shaky gasps.

"I need to be inside you. Right fucking now," he growls.

When he starts to push in, the stretch steals my voice. He moves slowly, easing deeper until the ache turns into a burning fullness.

So this is what it feels like? I've always been curious, but doubted I'd find a man I liked who would also be interested in me. I'm always attracting the wrong men, and I can't figure out why.

"Fuck," he groans. "You're so fucking tight."

If he thinks that, then he should believe I'm a virgin now, right?

He pauses, forehead touching mine, breath ragged as his cock pulsates inside me.

"Relax," he whispers. "Don't hold back."

My hips tilt up in reflex, my breath breaking on a choked moan. I'm in fucking shock.

"There," he says, his voice raw. "This is where you belong."

I tighten around him, my body overwhelmed. My heart beats too fast, dizzying my vision. His hand moves to my breast, thumb brushing my nipple until I can't hold back a soft cry.

"You needed this," he murmurs.

He drives into me, thick and unrelenting, each thrust slow enough to make me feel the stretch and burn of every inch.

"Say it," he grits out. "Say you're mine."

I can't. My throat won't work, but my body is already breaking down.

"You think anyone else could ever fuck you like this?" His hips slam forward, hard and fast, making the bed creak under us.

He fucks me harder now, like something inside him snapped. Each thrust slams into me, and I can't breathe between them. My fingers scramble for something to hold—his arms, the sheets, until my hands fly to his shoulders.

"No one else gets this. No one else gets you."

His hand slides down, thumb circling my clit, fast and steady. "You're mine. Every fucking part of you."

I close my eyes. I can't keep looking him in the eye. His other hand wraps around the back of my neck, pulling my face to his. "Don't you dare look away from me."

"Please..." My voice cracks.

"Please what?" he growls. "Please make you come again? Please fill you up?"

I moan once, breath catching as my orgasm builds again—hotter, faster, harder than before. "I...can't—"

I'm not going to give him that. I won't.

"Yes, you can. You're going to come all over my cock like the good girl you are."

He pounds harder, relentless now, hips slamming into mine, sweat building between us. The headboard hits the wall in rhythm with his thrusts, the sound filling the room with our heavy breathing.

"Come for me again," he commands, his voice rough and desperate. "Now."

It crashes over me, sharp and blinding. My hips buck up, clenching around him in waves. A broken sob rips free as he groans, driving deeper.

"Fuck," he snarls. "This tight little pussy—milking me just like it should."

His rhythm breaks, every thrust more ragged, harder, his hands locking around my hips.

Then his whole body goes taut, a sharp gasp tearing from him as he spills inside me with a strangled moan.

His cock jerks deep, thick heat flooding me. He thrusts twice more, slower now, dragging it out before finally collapsing over me, his breath ragged and hot against my skin.

He chuckles. "You'll be leaking me for days."

The realization hits me like a freight train. We didn't use a condom. I've never been on anything: no pills, no IUD, no backup plan. The thought spirals fast.

I grew up watching girls in foster homes get tossed out the second they showed. Too much trouble, too expensive, another mouth no one wanted to feed. I swore I'd never end up like that. I can barely take care of myself, let alone a kid. And now it might not be my choice. And worse, I'd be tied to him.

He stays there, holding me like he thinks he can fuse us together. When he finally lifts his head, he kisses me again— slow and soft, like he just sealed something between us.

"You belong to me," he whispers. "Don't you forget it."

"I can't do this with you again," I whisper, my words shaking.

He lets out a low laugh, his breath still rough against my skin. His hand cups my jaw, thumb stroking back and forth like I've just said something foolish. "Ellie, that's ridiculous. You're my wife."

The sound of his amusement burns more than the ache

between my legs. He doesn't even hear me. He doesn't see the panic in my eyes or hear it in my voice.

"You didn't use anything," I press, my voice thin.

His smile fades, his eyes narrowing just slightly. "Ellie." He says the name like a warning. "Don't start."

My mouth goes dry. "But—"

He cuts me off with a kiss, firm and silencing. "You know better than to pick a fight in our bed. Get some rest."

I don't answer. I can't. My body feels raw, used in a way I don't have words for. His arms lock around me like he thinks he can make me stay. I stare at the ceiling, letting my body go still. If I move, if I speak, I might shatter.

4

MAREN

I close my eyes and feel his palm smooth over my hair, like he's trying to calm me. He presses a soft kiss to my temple. It feels gentle. I don't let myself lean into it, but some part of me wants to. I've never been held like this.

When he finally pulls back to look at me, his thumb brushes over my cheek, wiping away a tear I didn't feel fall.

His eyes are steady, unblinking. And in this quiet, I realize he isn't done with me yet. What the hell was I thinking, sleeping with a man who kidnapped me because he thinks I'm his wife? It just happened so fast. He started fingering me, and then next thing I knew, he was inside me.

He looks down at me and smiles. The first warm one I've seen from him, and it reaches his green eyes. He'll never believe I'm not her now. He'll never let me go.

Damn him for being so handsome. I'm not the kind of woman who sleeps with strangers, especially not married ones. I've always kept to myself. I don't care to be noticed.

I've been in survival mode for so long that dating isn't even on my radar. The men who come into the Rusty Nail have never interested me. The last time I went on a date was years ago.

Suddenly, his voice dips lower, and the warmth in his eyes drains. "I can't move on from this...not until I punish you."

The chill that runs through me is immediate, and my body freezes. *Punish?* I slept with him to avoid that.

He's not angry or being impulsive. This is something he's planned, premeditated. Something he's been waiting for. I'm going to be punished for another woman's sins.

"What the fuck?"

"I won't do anything to you that you can't handle. You're stronger than you think."

The words are gentle, but they hit hard. They're supposed to comfort, to sound like reassurance, but it sounds like bullshit to me.

I glance toward the door, instinct screaming at me to run. But before I can react, he stands and grips my arm, his hold firm. I stumble as he pulls me with him. I know if I run again, it will only make things worse. Maybe if I stay calm, he'll change his mind.

The house is so big it feels endless, each step sinking me further into something I won't be able to crawl back out of. He stops in front of a smooth panel in the wall that looks like part of the design. It's discreet, intentional.

Then he reaches for a keypad, enters a code, and the panel unlocks with a soft click. The door swings open, revealing a narrow stairwell spiraling downward into shadows.

"Wait—" I start, but he doesn't pause.

He steps through the threshold, pulling me with him like this is just another part of the house tour. The vibe shifts immediately. It's colder here. As my feet touch metal stairs, the sound echoes up behind us. I grip the railing for balance, my heart pounding as I try to understand what this is. At the bottom, we reach another door—gray and solid, built into concrete.

He opens it quickly. The room inside is windowless, silent,

and shockingly clean. The walls are bare and gray, and the floor is concrete. In the corner, a thin mattress lies on the ground, its edges of linen tucked with military precision.

Thick, polished chains hang from the ceiling and are bolted to the floor. A wall-mounted rack displays leather belts, whips, paddles and other restraints—lined up like artifacts in a museum.

Then I see the stripper pole. It's steel and secured from floor to ceiling. Chains circle the base, fixed into position. Near the top, metal cuffs hang from the beam. Everything here is designed for performance, but not the kind anyone applauds.

This room is not only for punishment, but also for his pleasure. This excites him. I don't need him to say it. I can feel it in how he exhales, how his shoulders ease, how his gaze softens as he steps inside. This place belongs to him. It isn't about moving on. This is part of who he is.

He turns back toward me, his posture relaxed, his voice steady. "I know you're scared. It's been a while. But once it's over, we can move on. You know how this works."

My throat tightens. He gestures to the space as if I'm being unreasonable for hesitating. Except there's no trace of hesitation in his expression. No shame. He's comfortable here. He's used to this. Was his wife into this shit, too, and he thinks I am? Or was she forced to do it?

"We don't have to come down here for a while," he adds. "Not if you behave. Not if you're the sweet wife I know you are and can be."

His voice stays soft. Reassuring. And that's what makes my stomach turn. Because he isn't warning me—this is intimacy to him. He thinks this is how you rebuild trust. He believes this is what love looks like. And deep down, beneath the careful words and quiet calm, I know the truth.

I'm fucked.

There is no way his wife would have been okay with this.

Who would be? It's obvious he decides what's punishment-worthy, unless he had rules she had to follow. This is crazy.

"Take a seat, Ellie. You'll be down here for a while."

"I'm not sitting. Let me go," I snap, every nerve in my body on fire. I can't believe I had sex with him. What the hell was I thinking, feeding into his delusions?

He starts walking toward me like he already knows the outcome, and that quiet confidence makes my skin shiver.

I step back, but I'm too slow. He moves behind me and guides me to the mattress, one hand at my waist, the other at my shoulder. His grip is firm, not aggressive, and that's what makes it worse. He's not reacting, he's executing. Maybe if I stay calm, he'll second-guess doing this.

"Don't—" I start.

When the backs of my legs hit the edge, he lowers me—not onto my back, but directly onto my stomach. My chest meets the cold fabric first, and I stiffen. This bed feels like lying on the concrete floor.

He crouches at the base of the bed, reaches beneath the frame, and pulls out thick chains. He grabs my arms, stretches them above my head, and secures them around my wrists. Then he does the same with my ankles, making me spread-eagled. I yank hard, the chains rattling, but they hold. I'm stuck. I'm fucking stuck.

"This is sick! You psycho!" My teeth clench, my fists ball, and I can feel the heat rising in my cheeks. What the fuck is he going to do to me? Just leave me here? Is he going to torture me before he kills me? I don't even want to think about what else he wants to do.

He doesn't respond or react. He adjusts the restraints, making sure I can't move. Every inch of me is exposed and vulnerable. I gasp into the mattress. I'm completely helpless. This is a nightmare.

"You think this is going to fix anything?" I ask incredulously.

He can't possibly believe this will make anything better.

"It will because you're here at my mercy," he says.

He walks to the wall, each step slow and steady, and his fingers skim the rack of tools, pausing, testing, selecting. He picks out a thick, black leather belt, and then returns to me as he kneels beside the bed.

"Don't fucking touch me."

"You wanted this, remember? You said you wanted structure. Rules. Discipline. That's what I built this room for."

"What kind of idiot agrees to that?"

He doesn't flinch. "You're not an idiot. You want to please me."

He lays the leather belt across my lower back, and the cold texture of it steals the air from my lungs. I've never been hit with a belt. This can't be happening. "Don't touch me. Don't you dare."

I don't know how to get out of this situation, but I'm not going down without a fight.

"You're not being punished for leaving," he says. "You're being punished for pretending it didn't matter."

I never left! I'm not his wife!

"Go to hell."

"You're going to get ten and count each one. If you don't, we keep going."

Why do I need to count? He doesn't lift the belt right away. He waits, like he's giving me one last chance to beg or promise to behave. I bite my tongue so hard it almost bleeds.

"I'm not counting for you."

He lifts the belt. The first strike lands hard across my ass.

"FUCK!" I scream, jerking forward against the cuffs as pain courses through me.

I hear his breath hitch, just slightly. I don't have to see him to know he's drinking in every sound, every tremor, every helpless reaction. He gets pleasure out of my fucking pain. He waits, but I don't speak. I refuse to count. I can take it. We will be here all day before I start counting.

The second strike lands lower across the underside of my ass. I cry out, louder this time. I can't stop it. My legs pull instinctively against the restraints, but I can't move. "I'm not counting! I don't care how many times you do it!"

"You will," he says calmly.

He slides his hand over the welt, his fingers lingering longer this time. He's savoring the heat rising under my skin. Then he lifts the belt again. The third strike comes down with precision in the same spot. I scream into the mattress, the sound muffled, but it's still enough to make him inhale softly.

"I hate you," I sob.

"You don't. You love me."

The fourth lands across the center of my ass, and my body arches. My ass burns. I'm shaking. But I still don't count. I won't.

"You want it to end? Start counting."

"Fuck you," I choke, my voice hoarse.

He pauses. I feel his gaze on my exposed skin, and even through my tears, I know he's focused, entirely absorbed. Then he brings the fifth down faster and harder than all the previous lashes. The pain robs me of my breath.

"I'll go past ten if you don't start counting now," he says. He is so calm, so unbothered—and I know he will keep going. I don't think I can handle much more.

"Five!" It blurts out before I can stop it. Maybe he'll get it over with instead of prolonging it. The waiting makes it worse; knowing it's coming, but not knowing when.

He exhales slowly as I finally count. He's not angry that I hadn't at first, because he knows he's in control—and he probably enjoys my fighting, too.

The sixth strike follows, and I scream. I swear, they keep getting worse.

"Six," I gasp, barely able to speak.

Tears roll down my cheeks and soak into the mattress, but I know he's watching them fall. I feel pathetic crying in front of him.

The seventh lands without warning, and I cry out so hard my throat aches.

"Seven," I sob, hating him, hating myself, hating everything.

He leans in close, rubbing my ass, and I wince.

"You're doing better than I expected," he murmurs. It should chill me. But instead, a part of me glows at the praise. The reaction startles me, because I don't know *why*. So I scream into the mattress again. I want to be strong and fight. But the word still escapes as the next one hits.

"Eight."

He pauses, just long enough for the silence to stretch thin. Then the ninth strike lands across the lowest edge of my backside, sending fire down both thighs.

"Nine," I say, louder this time.

My entire body trembles. I'm soaked in sweat and tears, and he's watching it all like I'm his creation and he's the artist. I don't need to see his face. I can feel how much this means to him. He raises the belt once more, and the tenth strike lands cleanly on my back.

"Ten!" I scream, and it shatters what's left of my breath.

Then silence. He sets the belt aside before reaching for a blanket and draping it over me. He tucks it beneath my arms like I'm something worth keeping warm. This is survival. That's all this is. I'll take what I have to, nod when he needs me to, scream if it buys me time—because when the moment comes, I'll be ready.

He leans down and kisses the top of my spine. "You did great," he whispers.

"No wonder your wife left you," I barely get out. The silence that follows makes me wish I'd bitten my tongue bloody instead. He ignores me, but I can tell he's pissed at my quip.

"You've always responded to this," he murmurs, brushing his fingers over the belt marks. "Punishment excites you, even if you're too proud to admit it."

He stands, walks to the light switch, and flips it off. Darkness takes the room.

He pauses, his voice dipping lower. "You need this just as much as I do. You always did."

"You're fucking crazy, and if you touch me again, you'll regret it."

I would kick myself if I wasn't chained up. I need to keep my temper in check. But I'm not going to lay here and be quiet or agreeable. Still, I need to remember this is a survival situation. I'm not yelling at drunks at the Rusty Nail, but I don't think I can forgive myself if I stop fighting this quickly.

He chuckles. "Says the one who's chained up and can't move. Remember—I hold the key."

The door opens. Then closes. He doesn't lock it. He doesn't need to, because I'm not moving. Not yet.

5

ADRIAN

I sit behind my desk and stare at the screen in front of me. The screen flickers gently, casting its glow across the desk. Ellie is curled on the mattress, chained and trembling under the blanket I left for her.

She's breathing shallowly and unevenly, and her swollen eyes make her look more fragile than I've ever seen her. She looks like she might fall apart. Her hair clings to her face in damp strands, and her fingers twitch like she's dreaming. I could watch her like this for hours. I've done it before—because her silence speaks louder than anything she's ever said.

I should feel relieved, but I'm not. My neck is stiff, my fingers twitch against the desk, and the pressure in my pants only reminds me of how much I want more of it. She took all ten—just like she was told.

When she gave in, her voice cracked as she counted through the pain. It wasn't just obedience; it was honest. It didn't just settle me—it shut down whatever had been clawing at me since I saw her in that bar, pretending she didn't belong to me.

The first time I punished her was the night she didn't come

home for a week. She said she needed space because she was overwhelmed. But space is distance. And distance is what always breaks us. She thought it didn't matter, but she would've kept slipping if I hadn't stopped it.

Afterward, she didn't speak. Her eyes were red-rimmed and glassy, and she looked at me like she didn't know what came next. I wrapped a blanket around her and pulled her into my lap.

She didn't resist. She folded into me like she'd been waiting for it. Tucked her face into my chest and just breathed. No arguments. No questions. Just her body against mine, shivering while I held her.

That night, she fell asleep in my arms. I stayed awake until morning, telling myself I'd done the right thing. She needed release. And then comfort. She needed me.

She fought me harder than I expected this time. I thought maybe it was resentment—leftover bitterness. But when she looked me in the eye and said she didn't know me...That wasn't rejection, but defiance. She knew exactly who I was. She didn't want to face that she left without even trying to work it out. And I couldn't let that stand.

The months without her hollowed me out. I told myself she'd come back on her own. But then days turned to weeks, and then months. And time only made her forget.

When I heard from my PI that she was in Chicago working at a bar, I got on the plane immediately. I thought about all the things I would say, reassuring her that things would be different, that I missed her.

I'd booked a honeymoon suite at my hotel—stupidly thinking she'd be relieved I still wanted her, and we'd be fucking all night to make up for lost time. But she wouldn't come back willingly. She looked at me like I was a dangerous stranger instead of her husband.

That's when I knew I didn't have a choice. I told myself I

wouldn't use the needle. It was only meant as a last resort. But I had to act before she slipped too far into whatever lie she'd started believing. I didn't hurt her; I brought her home. But she is still angry at me.

I run my fingers along the edge of the wood, like that will keep me from going back down there too soon.

I lean back and glance at the photo of our wedding on my desk. Her smile is small and uncertain, but it's real. My eyes trace the shape of her face and the scar above her brow. Her hair was pinned back that day, and she kept adjusting the veil like it didn't feel right.

I chose it myself. She said it was too stiff around the crown, but it matched the life I pictured. I told her it looked perfect. She didn't argue—and I took that as agreement. I always made the decisions she couldn't.

I remember how she smiled at the photographer, then looked at me like she doubted herself. That brief glance stayed with me. Even then, she needed reassurance. She looked to me to tell her she was beautiful.

And I want that version of her again. The one who didn't question me, and trusted I knew what was best. The one who needed me before she even realized it. I know she's still in there. I just have to bring her out.

She looks exactly the same as she did that day. Except her hips are fuller now, and her ass is bigger. But she looks tired— in her eyes, in her shoulders. The nights she spent on her feet, trying to live without me, wore her out.

For a moment, I don't move. The screen flickers in the corner of my vision. I can't believe she's back. My cock throbs against my zipper, a dull ache that refuses to fade. I take a slow breath and force myself to stay still. I could go to her, hard and raw with want, but I won't. She needs to see that I can be patient—even though I want to fuck her senseless because of months without sex.

But I'll touch her when she's ready to accept it. That's why I'm going to draw her a bath. Not just to ease the soreness, but to remind her that I'll always take care of her.

Right now, she thinks I only know how to hurt. But pain brings her back to me after she tries to pull away. It always has. And after the pain, I always comfort her. That's how this works —I take her apart and put her back together, because she needs both.

I stand and head for the bathroom. My steps are light across the hardwood, but in this silence, each one echoes. I hear the faint tick of the wall clock, the creak of wood under my heel.

I step into the bathroom and turn on the light. Everything here is clean, modern, and untouched, except by me. I kneel by the tub and twist the faucet. The water flows steadily and hot. The bath isn't just for comfort. It's restoration. And she's always responded to that.

I add the vanilla scented oil she used to love, that lingered on her skin for hours. I swirl it with my hand, watching the surface cloud and then clear.

I adjust the temperature to the exact degree so it's not too hot, but just enough to soothe the soreness.

The water, the scent, and the setting matter the most. You don't just break a woman and leave her. You remind her who she belongs to while she's still aching. You show her how deep your care runs when she's at her weakest.

I stay there for a moment, fingers resting on the edge of the tub, imagining her sitting there with the scent of warm oil rising with the steam, and it makes me smile. I don't have to fantasize anymore. I finally have her back where she belongs.

I stand and pull a folded towel from the cabinet and place it at the edge of the tub. Everything that she'll need is in place.

I make my way toward the basement door with her robe. It's time to remind her of the other part of me. Not the one who hurts or punishes her, but the one who always puts her back together.

Pain, then care. Shame, then comfort. That's how she finds her way back to me.

6

MAREN

I don't know how long I've been here. My wrists burn from the cuffs, and my arms ache from being pinned above my head. The air is cold against my skin, and my thoughts are louder than the silence that surrounds me.

I try to move, but everything feels raw—my joints, my ribs, the back of my neck. Time doesn't pass here the way it's supposed to. It stretches and folds in on itself until I'm not sure if I've been here for hours or days.

Finally, the door opens, and light spills into the room. My eyes adjust to it slowly. By the time I see clearly, he's already right in front of me.

Adrian carries a robe, folded in his arms, thick and expensive looking. He kneels beside the mattress, but doesn't speak or explain. He unfastens the restraints one by one, as if removing them is routine.

My muscles scream when I lower my arms, but I don't make a sound. I won't give him the satisfaction of hearing my pain.

Once the last cuff is gone, he lifts the robe and drapes it over my shoulders. His hands brush down my arms, smoothing the fabric gently. When I feel the warmth of his touch, it only deepens the chill under my skin. It's not just fear—it's the confusion of being cared for by someone who also kidnapped you, hurt you. The contrast messes with my head. He touches me like I'm fragile, as if he didn't just break me open.

"I drew you a bath," he says. I stare at him. For a second, I think I misheard. He's offering steam, lavender, and a soft robe like this is some twisted honeymoon.

"You drew me a bath," I repeat, my voice flat.

I'd rather be screaming and clawing at the door.

He nods slowly. "I always do."

I laugh, sharp and cold. "You think I'm going to relax in your tub like none of this happened?"

I want to smack myself in the head. *Why did I just say that?* I don't want to be punished again, but suppressing who I am is a lot harder than I thought it would be.

Foster care taught me I had to stand up for myself and not take shit from anyone, regardless of if they were bigger or stronger than me. But this isn't foster care. And I need to adapt to this situation.

"You need to calm down. The bath is for you."

His voice is too calm. He thinks this is normal, that he's the reasonable one.

"I didn't ask for anything. Especially not this."

My voice shakes, but I won't let it sound weak. He needs to know I've forgiven nothing.

"You didn't have to ask. I know what you need."

His words sink in like poison. He steps back just enough to study me, eyes scanning for the woman he thinks I am.

That's the problem. He believes knowing me gives him the right to decide for me. But he doesn't know me. He's just trying to shape me into whatever version fits his twisted fantasy.

I can't tell if he's insane or just desperate. He's handsome; he can get any woman he wants without resorting to this. But is this a pattern? Kidnapping women who look like Eleanor, and then what? Kills them? Am I going to be killed? He doesn't seem like a murderer. But isn't that how murderers get away with it? By looking normal? I knew I should've said *fuck it* and left work early. None of this would've happened in the first place.

My hands curl into fists inside the robe sleeves. "No. You don't know me."

My chin stays up even as my throat tightens. I hate how confident he looks, how sure he is of this version of me that doesn't exist.

His voice softens. "I do, time away may have made you forget who you are, but I'll remind you."

I blink at him. That's what he thinks? That I've somehow lost myself? That I forgot my name, my memories, my entire life? Who forgets who they are unless they've had a head injury? And I didn't. There's no injury, no amnesia. Just him, talking in circles and trying to convince me I'm someone I'm not. As if saying it gently makes it sane.

He moves closer, and I flinch, forcing it down before he can see. I stay still. I won't give him the satisfaction. "I'm not your wife."

He doesn't flinch, but his expression changes just enough to show he's forcing himself to stay composed. He doesn't care what I say, because he's already decided who I am and won't let go of it. That's what scares me most.

He watches me closely, as if searching for a sign that I don't mean what I say. "You're angry, which means part of you still cares."

Heat rushes to my face. Not from fear, but from fury. "I didn't leave you. I didn't promise you anything."

"You did. You don't want to remember because it makes you feel guilty."

My chest tightens. I don't know how to reach someone this far gone.

"I'm not Eleanor. She left you. Not me."

He looks at me like I'm a problem to solve, not considering a single word.

"You left without a word. Not even a goodbye. Just a note that said, 'I can't do this anymore.' That's all I got from you. A single sentence after everything we built together."

"That wasn't me." The words come out too small, too quiet, but they're all I have left.

I grip the robe tighter, like it can hold in what he's trying to drag out. If I had a husband, I'd never leave with a note. I'd tell him to his face. But maybe she tried, and he wouldn't listen. Perhaps the note was the only safe way out. He's unhinged—that much is clear.

"What do you want from me?" I ask, my voice raw.

"I want you to admit how much you missed me."

"You think I enjoyed being punished? You tied me down, spanked me, and locked me in a room, then called it healing."

"You used to love pleasing me. And you *know* this pleases me. It helps us move on from things."

"I didn't. She did."

He doesn't answer. Nothing I say will change his mind. "I want out of this room, so fine. I'll take your bath."

He nods, as if we've reached some quiet agreement, already convinced this is progress. But he's wrong.

I stand. My legs are weak, but I steady myself. I don't look at him or speak again. When I walk past him, my shoulder brushes his arm, and the contact makes my stomach turn.

I climb the basement stairs, wrapped in a robe I never asked for, heading toward a bath I never wanted. He is punishing me for a goodbye I never gave. And when this ends, I'll be the one who walks away—and this time, he won't stop me.

7

MAREN

As we reach the stairs, his hand slides down my back, gripping my ass like he owns it. The robe barely covers me. I can feel his gaze pressing into me, hungry and hot, as if punishing me wasn't enough, and now he needs to claim what's left.

He leads me through the bedroom and into the bathroom, his hand never leaving me. The door swings open, and the vanilla scent hits me first. The lights are dim, and candles flicker along the edge of the tub. Flower petals float on the surface of the bubbles. It's romantic, and I hate it. While everything looks soft and inviting, none of it feels safe.

He bound and whipped me until I screamed, and now he believes all is forgiven because the water is warm and the room smells sweet. As the warmth of the room sinks into my skin, some small, pathetic part of me wants to let it mean something. Even though I know it doesn't, it should make resisting easier, but it doesn't.

He lifts me into the tub without asking. The water is hot against my skin, and I hiss as the sting from the earlier flares. Every part of me wants to pull away, but I don't. I can't deal with more of the basement. For a second, I think I'll be alone. Then the water splashes as he steps in behind me.

When he sits, his chest pressing against my back, I tense, but don't move. His cock, already hard, nudges against me under the water. I will never sleep with him again.

His hands find my shoulders and move gently, massaging the tension he put there. He reaches for the shampoo and works it into my hair. It's the same brand I use in my apartment. That detail shouldn't matter, but it does. Has he been watching me, or is this just a coincidence? His fingers caress my scalp, and I hate how good it feels. He's quiet as his fingers move gently, massaging in slow circles until I almost forget who he is.

Even though I want to be numb, my body keeps reacting anyway, tilting into his touch and relaxing before I can stop it. This version of him, the romantic one, makes it harder to remember the pain. I shouldn't relax into this or want any part of him near me. But it's easier to pretend I'm his wife than to fight.

"You needed this," he says softly, rinsing the suds away.

I nod. I've learned it's smarter not to argue with him. He wants obedience and compliance. And if that gives me even a sliver of space to breathe, to one day escape, I'll take it. But a part of me wants the illusion of being cared for, because the illusion is easier to deal with than the emptiness.

His hands glide down my arms, over my stomach, and then lower. His touch lingers on my thighs. He runs his palms over my breasts as he kisses my shoulder.

"You need me, and you're going to remember that."

I open my mouth, then close it. I don't want to test him right now.

"I know you're mad, but you'll forgive me. You always do."

"Why do you need to do this?" I ask.

He leans back a little. "Because it's how I've always been. It's pleasurable. But it's more than that; it keeps us balanced."

"Balanced?" I repeat, the word bitter in my mouth. "It just makes someone pretend to be someone they're not, to please you, because they're afraid."

He freezes. I see a flicker of confusion in his eyes for the first time. "You felt like you couldn't be yourself because you were afraid of punishment?"

"Yes, I did." I'll say whatever I have to in order to keep me safe. The truth doesn't matter here. Only the version he believes.

He goes quiet for a moment. His hands stay on my body, but they don't move. "I thought you left because I don't love you."

That makes me freeze. *He doesn't love his wife?* This is even more twisted than I thought, if that's even possible.

"You don't?" I ask, keeping my voice quiet despite my disbelief.

"You know I don't believe in it. I believe in devotion, not love."

It sounds like something a man says after being left too many times. It's an excuse not to feel anything real. But he dresses it up like wisdom.

"What's the difference?"

"Devotion is loyalty. It's honesty. It's respect."

To him, devotion means following the rules he made up to feel powerful. He kisses the back of my neck and pulls me tighter against him.

"I know we had our arguments about it, but we don't need love, Ellie. We need each other. But if you need me to say the words, then I'll do it. For you."

I sit still. He's not offering me anything real. Not that I want that. But if he says it, they'll be a lie I'll never unhear. I want him to get bored enough to let me go, but he keeps doubling down.

"Why say something you don't mean?" I ask.

He doesn't answer right away. His hand drifts beneath the

surface, fingers brushing along my thigh. "Because it matters to you. And you want something to make this feel real. If it gives you something to hold onto when you're unsure, I'll say it."

I stare at the faucet, trying to stay still.

"So you're lying."

He doesn't flinch. "I'm giving you what you need. I've given you everything else."

The worst part is, he believes it's generous.

"It's not about truth," he adds, quieter now. "It's about what works. I don't need the word. But if you do—then fine. I'll say it for you. If that keeps you from running again."

There it is. Everything he gives comes with an invisible leash.

I turn my head slightly and say, low but clear, "I don't need you to love me. I never had love, and I don't need it now—not from you or anyone."

His hand freezes. I was in foster care—no one loved me. My several foster parents didn't, never even heard the word said to me. They said those words for their own kids.

I expect him to argue, to press, to twist it into another reason I'm lying to myself. But for a second, he stares at me because the version of me in his head apparently wouldn't say that.

"I don't believe you," he says finally, his voice tight. "You used to say everyone needs love."

I shake my head. "No. They think they do. What people need is to survive. And I've done that without anyone's love."

His jaw tenses. Not in anger, but confusion. Maybe even disappointment. Because if I don't want love, or even believe in it, then what is he offering? What is he trying to earn?

He cups my jaw, thumb brushing under my cheekbone like he can change my answer with touch. "You've never let anyone in long enough to know what you need."

"I don't want to need anyone," I snap. "Especially not the man who chained me up and called it *care.*"

His gaze hardens, but he doesn't pull away. "You'll change your mind," he says, softly now. "When you stop pretending you don't remember what we were."

Obviously, she hated who she was with him, or she wouldn't have left. But there's no point in saying that.

He tilts my chin with two fingers. "Look at me when I'm talking to you."

As I meet his gaze, my stomach churns. This isn't love and never will be. Not that I care. He's not my husband. Still, he's trying so hard to sell it. Even though I know the truth, I almost believe him.

8

MAREN

Adrian rises from the water, grabs a towel, and lifts me out of the tub. Water trails down my body, dripping from my thighs onto his chest. His skin is hot and slick, and mine clings to him. His hands stay firm beneath me, one under my knees, the other cradling my back.

I don't resist or flinch. Resistance only blurs the line between pain and tenderness, and I'm too tired to define it again today.

He takes me to the bedroom, lowering me onto the edge of the bed, and I wince from the soreness caused by sitting. The cool air in the room cuts through the warmth. He drags the towel across my skin, brushing my hip and trailing down the inside of my thigh. I inhale sharply as he pulls it higher. It skims across my chest, against my nipples. Then he presses the fabric between my legs, and I tense from the heat still pulsing there.

He kneels in front of me and kisses the inside of my legs as he dries them. When his fingers touch a bruise on my thigh, he pauses like he knows what he left behind. But he looks at me like he already knows I've forgiven him.

"You're quiet," he says.

He slides the towel across my chest again.

"What do you want me to say?" I ask, not looking at him.

He ignores my comment.

"I need you," he says, running the towel down my arm, across my breasts, then over my thighs.

"That's not the same as wanting me," I say, softer this time. I'm not fighting. Just stating a fact.

He doesn't correct me. Because we both know I'm right. He kisses me slowly, his lips warm and patient. His hands frame my face, and his thumbs glide across my cheeks. I need to act, play along. I don't want to get punished again. It's easier this way.

"Open for me," he whispers.

My lips part, and his tongue slips past them. My breath catches, and my shoulders relax. My thighs press together, trying to contain the heat he draws from me.

The kiss deepens. Heat blooms inside me, low and slow. He drops the towel and steps between my legs. His skin burns against mine, and his thigh nudges mine apart. I feel his hard, hot cock against my hip. His hand grips my leg and pulls me closer.

He groans when he pushes inside me, causing my body to draw tight around him with each inch. I clutch the sheets, my breath catching. My thighs tremble and my head tips back as he thrusts.

"You're tighter when you're angry," he mutters. "You know that?"

My mind flashes to the prick of the needle and his hand over my mouth. The fear still lingers beneath the surface, but it slips away. Pressure builds inside me instead. He presses his forehead to mine, his green eyes staying locked on mine. But I close mine. I don't want to feel connected.

"Open your eyes," he says.

I do, because I know what happens when I don't.

"Don't look away. I want your eyes on mine when I fuck you."

His hips rock slowly. He pulls out, then thrusts back in. My fingers dig into his shoulders, and his muscles pull taut with each thrust. His breath hitches when I clench around him. He's holding back. I can tell by the way he moves. Each thrust shifts the mattress under us, and his hips grind down, driving me into the bed.

Leftover drops of bath water drip from his jaw onto my collarbone. Then he shifts his angle and thrusts harder. A moan escapes my throat, and I don't try to stop it. He groans in response. His hand presses into my stomach, holding me down.

"Louder," he growls. "I want to hear what I do to you."

Each stroke drives deeper. My legs wrap around his hips. I claw at his back, the heat and pressure tearing through me. My walls clench hard around him, pulling him deeper, drawing him closer to the edge.

"Fuck—you feel that?" he pants. "You're so fucking wet for me. Say it."

"I'm—*fuck*—I'm wet," I breathe out. "You make me like this."

His lips brush my neck. "Say how much you love this."

My voice breaks. "I love it."

I hate how easy it is to say that, and how much truth there might be in it.

"You like being fucked by the man who punished you?" he hisses. "You like that I still want you, even when you're disobedient?"

"I hate you," I whisper—because I do, and I don't. And I need him to hear both.

"You hate how much you want me," he shoots back, his voice ragged. "But you always fucking want me."

His hips slam into mine, faster now. His grip turns bruising.

The bed jerks beneath us. Each thrust hits harder. A tremor tears through me and strips away the last of my resistance. My body pulses around him, desperately and involuntarily.

Then he grabs my thigh and holds me open for him. His fingers dig in, and every thrust feels thicker, deeper, harder. I take all of it. I cry out as I come, even while my mind begs me to stay quiet, to not give in, to not give him the satisfaction. My thighs shake around his waist, and my toes curl against his back.

He growls into my neck. "You're not leaving me," he grits out. "Not again."

He's not talking to me. He's talking to who he needs me to be. But his body doesn't care.

His breath stutters near my cheek. "I love..." he starts, but the words break off into a guttural sound as he starts coming.

I freeze. He wouldn't. Not after everything he said. Not after saying love doesn't matter.

"I love coming inside you," he finishes, his hips jerking once, twice, then he groans loud against my throat as he empties into me with a shudder.

He stays deep, his hips rolling in shallow thrusts. One hand moves to the back of my neck, the other holds my thighs open, possessive and final.

"You think this makes it real?" I whisper. Even I don't know if I want an answer.

He breathes hard like he didn't hear me, or maybe he did and doesn't know what to say. He stays inside me, arms locked around me. One hand trails down my back and settles at my waist. The other keeps me close, like holding on might stop me from slipping through his fingers again. He stays quiet for a full minute, then brushes my hair aside like nothing happened.

"You know how to please me. That's all I need," he murmurs.

I say nothing. That's all I am to him. Just a body who lives inside this bed, inside these walls. I stare at the ceiling, searching for anything I can hold on to. I'm not the woman he sees. He's still chasing someone who isn't me. But I let him believe in the illusion. Pretending keeps me desired. Right now, that lie feels safer than whatever waits outside this room. If I'm convincing enough, I might find a crack in the armor he hides behind. So I let him kiss my shoulder and wrap his arms around me, letting him believe I'm his. Because right now, I want to be.

9

MAREN

When I wake up, Adrian sets out a long, silky, deep royal blue robe with simple embroidery on the sleeves. I slip it on and follow him, still sore where his touch left me tender.

Downstairs, the dining room is bright with morning light. The table is too long for two people, yet every seat is set. Silverware catches the sunlight, and the china is flawless. A breakfast spread stretches across the surface—eggs, pancakes, fruit, pastries—more food than we can eat. It looks like something meant to impress a crowd. He was with me the entire night, so he didn't do this. So, there is someone else here that can help me.

Adrian pulls out a chair for me. I hesitate, then sit. The robe pools around my legs as I lower myself into the chair, my eyes cast down.

He takes his place at the head of the table and eats, as if yesterday didn't happen, as if punishment followed by pancakes is just part of the routine. His routine.

"Greta made all your favorites," he says.

I glance at him. "Greta?"

He raises an eyebrow. "Our housekeeper. She's been with us for years."

If she's been here for years, then she would know I'm not his wife.

I nod, forcing a smile as I reach for my fork. My hands shake, but I steady them. I have to remember who I'm supposed to be in front of him.

An older woman in a maid's outfit with her hair pulled into a bun enters through the side door. *Can she help me get out of here?* I need to corner her when he's not around.

She moves quietly. "Good morning, Mrs. Montgomery," she says kindly. Her accent is soft and European.

I didn't know his last name until now. It sounds old and formal. Fancy in a way that doesn't feel earned, as if it came from money passed down instead of self-made.

"Please, call me Nora," I say.

I don't know where it came from. I don't want to be called by another woman's name, so I made one up. She pauses and glances at Adrian, waiting for his approval. He doesn't respond right away. He sets down his fork and watches me.

"Greta, can you give us a few minutes?" he asks.

"Of course, sir," she replies. Then she leaves without another word.

He tilts his head. "Nora? Where did that come from?"

"I want to be called something different. That's all."

"You can't just change your name."

"Why not?"

"Because Eleanor is elegant. It suits you."

Does he give the women he kidnaps the same name? What if Eleanor was his wife, but is now dead, and he can't let her go?

He sips his coffee and studies me since I've gone off script. Then he speaks again, completely changing the subject.

"That dive bar rubbed off on you. You used to know how to carry yourself."

It's not just criticism, but disappointment. He sees me as someone who's broken and needs to be fixed. That makes me feel like I'm not enough.

Although I've never been enough. Not enough to be adopted, not enough to be hired for a great job. No, he's trying to get into my head. I'm not broken, and I don't need to be fixed.

"I want people to call me Ellie, then," I say quietly.

He puts his glass down and stares at me.

"No. That's my name for you. No one else's."

I hold his gaze, but I don't argue. I go back to cutting my food, pretending I'm not unraveling inside, that this all makes sense. Pretending I belong here, at this table, in this robe, surrounded by a meal no one could finish and a man who only sees what he wants to see.

I take a bite, chewing and tasting nothing. I'm still chewing when he sets his fork down.

"Ellie, I want you to come over here."

I raise my eyes. "I'm right here."

He tilts his head slightly. His eyes have darkened, no longer soft but focused. "Come closer. I want a kiss."

My stomach tightens. I reach for the cloth napkin, dabbing at the corners of my mouth before pushing back my chair.

He doesn't move, but his arms open in silent invitation. I walk to him and stoop, offering a kiss—soft, brief, a whisper against his lips. But it's not enough for him.

His hand slides to the back of my head, and his fingers weave into my hair. He deepens the kiss slowly, pulling a breath from my lungs I didn't realize I was holding. His other hand settles on my hip, drawing me closer until my thighs press against his. I brace my palm against his chest, but he keeps lowering me until the hardwood bites into my knees and my robe pools around me. He lowers me, placing me exactly where he thinks I belong.

At his feet.

"Open your mouth. Show me who you belong to."

My lips part, but no sound comes out. He reclines and spreads his legs just enough.

"Go ahead," he murmurs.

I hesitate. My fingers hover near the tie of his robe. I've never done this before. He notices my pause, but he doesn't wait. He loosens the knot himself and lets the robe fall open.

His cock is already hard, thick and flushed where it rests against his thigh. He takes my hand and wraps it around him.

"I missed your mouth," he says, his voice taut with hunger.

His thumb brushes my cheek. The gesture steadies me, even though it shouldn't. He doesn't push. He waits.

So I lean forward and press my lips to the base of him. His breath catches as my lips drag slowly up his length before I ease him into my mouth. His fingers tighten in my hair. He groans, low and immediate. The sound sinks into me.

I move slowly at first, feeling his body tense beneath me; though my ass and thighs still burn from last night.

I keep going because that's what he expects, while in reality, I want to bite his dick off. It would distract him. Cause a commotion. But he would punish me severely for that. I focus on every twitch, every breath as I take him deeper, his thighs flexing when I push myself further.

I hate the heat between my legs—the slick, undeniable proof of it. I try to ignore the pressure building low in my body, but it coils anyway, slow and insistent. I hate that my thighs clench when he groans. I hate that the taste of him doesn't repulse me the way it should. There's a part of me that wants to make him fall apart like this—because it means I have power, too. Even if I'd rather crawl out of my own skin than admit it.

"That's it," he whispers. "Even now, you still know how to make me feel worshipped."

I don't speak. I can't. And I'm grateful for the silence. He shifts his hips and slides deeper into my mouth. I try to fight the heat rising between my legs, but it spreads anyway.

He groans again, louder now. His body shakes beneath my hands. This isn't about sex. He needs this to prove I'm still his. And I give him what he wants because I know what happens when I don't. Obedience keeps me safe, and a small, fractured part of me wants to be wanted, even like this. His grip tightens in my hair as his breath catches, and then the door opens. The creak of the door cuts through the moment like a blade. I freeze. Footsteps follow, and maybe a gasp. I don't know who it is. Greta? Someone else? My stomach turns, and I pull back.

"No, keep sucking," Adrian says. His voice is colder now. "I didn't tell you to stop."

I look up at him. My lips are still around him, and my eyes go wide.

He cups my cheek. "Let them watch. All they'll see is how good you are for me."

Humiliation burns through my chest. But I do what he says. I don't know who saw me, but I know what they saw. And worse, I know what they'll think. Not a prisoner. Not a wife. Just a woman on her knees with his dick in her mouth.

I close my eyes, I shut out the shame, and I keep going. The intrusion fuels him. He groans again and presses deeper into my mouth. "You know how to please me better than anyone ever has. That's why I married you."

I hate how my body listens. I hate that I keep going even though I feel exposed in the worst way. But I do. I match his rhythm, letting him guide me with his grip on my head. My mouth works over him exactly how he wants it, because that's the only way to keep him pleased. I feel the tension climb in his thighs. And then he groans, louder this time, and his thighs lock around me, hips jerking forward as his body seizes. He swears under his breath—like he's coming undone from the inside out. One hand fists the edge of the table while the other holds my head where he needs it, trembling as his climax rips through him. He gasps, and his release hits my tongue in thick, pulsing waves—hot, overwhelming, inescapable. His hand presses harder into the back of my head, keeping me there while he finishes. The sounds that come from his throat are rough and desperate.

"Good girl. Now swallow. All of it."

I do. Because I don't want to know what happens if I don't. He strokes my cheek again, softer now. His fingers linger. The ache between my legs doesn't disappear, but I feel sick about how my body responded. The lingering slickness between my thighs feels like betrayal.

"That's more like the wife I remember."

I sit back and wipe my mouth with the back of my hand. I don't look at him. He strokes my hair like I'm his lover. But all I feel is the taste of him drying on my tongue and the bruises on my knees.

He's still breathing hard. His robe is open. He watches me, gaze fixed and possessive. But mine are full of shame.

I don't move. I stay on the floor, my robe open at the thigh, my hair clinging to the back of my neck. The silence is louder than anything he's said to me all morning.

My eyes blur and I blink hard, but the tears still come. No sobbing, or even a sound. Just the sting and the slow collapse.

Adrian stiffens. He rises from his chair and comes to my side.

"What's wrong, Ellie?" he asks softly, crouching beside me.

He reaches for my hands and wraps them in his. His thumbs brush across my knuckles, slow and steady.

My voice breaks as it leaves me. "I'm miserable."

His brows draw together, confused. "Why?"

"Because you treat me like a whore."

He doesn't flinch. For a second, I regret saying it. Not because it's untrue—but because I know he'll never see it that way, and twist it into something else.

He only shakes his head and moves closer to reassure me. "You think I'd treat a whore like this?" he asks, brushing his fingers down my face. "You think I'd let just anyone this close?" he asks, his fingers tightening around mine.

"You say that," I mutter, wiping beneath my eyes, "but everything you do says otherwise."

He rests a hand against my cheek, wiping away a tear with his thumb.

"You think that's what this is? That I don't care about you?"

I lift my chin. My voice is shaky but sharp. "You don't care."

He keeps wiping away my tears. "You're my wife. I protect you."

My laugh is small and cracked. "Protect me? From what?"

"I have my reasons."

Who cares? I'm not married to him. But it feels like I am. The arguments and constant tension only fuel that feeling.

I rise to my feet. My robe slips farther off my shoulder. He stands, too, but doesn't stop me.

"Why did you marry me?"

He doesn't answer right away. He stares.

"I had my reasons," he says again.

"Reasons." The word curdles on my tongue. "What were they?"

He exhales. "Ellie, it doesn't matter. Drop it."

"No," I whisper. "It doesn't matter. Because I'm not your fucking wife."

I turn to walk away.

His voice hardens. "Eleanor. Don't walk away from me."

I stop in the doorway, but I don't look back. My hands curl into fists, nails digging into my palms.

"You don't want to let go," I say, my voice flat. "You won't admit the relationship failed. That she didn't want you anymore."

He says nothing. So I keep walking, and for now, he doesn't follow. I don't even know where I'm walking to, but every step feels like peeling myself out of someone else's skin.

10

ADRIAN

She walked out on me. No slammed doors, no shouting —just her back turned with the robe slipping from her shoulder like I wasn't worth another word. That cut deep, but it wasn't the worst of it. What gutted me was her saying the marriage was over, and that she didn't want me anymore.

She has too much power over me, because no one else could make me feel this furious, this desperate, this undone.

I almost followed, ready to drag her back. But I didn't. So I sit here instead, jaw tight, staring at the door, waiting for her to realize walking away only proves that I'll have to be harder, more relentless, until she stops fighting what she already is— my wife.

But I can't stop thinking about what led her there, how she tried to twist herself into someone else. Nora. She said it in front of Greta. Eleanor never called herself that, and Greta knows it, too. So why now? A test, a game, another push to see how far she can go before I snap. She knows I won't fall for it, won't believe for a second she isn't my wife. And still, after that, she dropped to her knees. Too fast for someone who wants me to believe she's resisting. She looked up at me with tears in her eyes and still kept going, her mouth trembling around me, and now she wants to pretend that meant nothing. I gave her comfort. I offered patience and warmth. I kissed her. I asked for her softness before I demanded anything else.

She could have stayed in that moment. She could have eaten her breakfast and leaned into me like she used to. I gave her every chance to surrender gently, but she chose to fight instead. Because admitting she feels safer here than anywhere else would destroy whatever lies she's holding onto. She'd rather call this a prison than admit she wants to stay. Rather call me insane than face the truth—that no one else will ever want her like this.

Not just her body—everything. The rage, the silence, the mess. I took every broken piece and made room for it. I built a life around her chaos and called it home.

She needs punishment when her mind won't stop screaming to pull away. I see it in her eyes when she finally gives in. It's not fear. It's relief. Afterwards, it quiets everything that tells her to run.

She can scream, lie, invent new names, and pretend she doesn't know who she is. But I remember. Every inch of her. Every sound she made when she gave in. Every time she cried and still begged me not to stop. She still loves being wanted by me. She just doesn't want to need me. That's why she's unraveling. The truth terrifies her more than I ever could. That's why I won't let go, because I already have her. She just hasn't admitted it yet.

That's why it burned when she said that I treat her like a whore. She doesn't understand the difference. A whore is disposable. Replaceable. What I give her isn't a transaction. I built an entire life around her.

The word *miserable* stung sharper than I expected. She should be grateful I married her at all. I wanted to shake her until she swallowed it back. I wanted to soothe her until she admitted she needed me. Both urges fight in me, and both dueling for dominance.

She pressed further, demanding why I married her. I told her I had my reasons. I couldn't give them to her now—she'd twist them, turn them into something ugly. But I remember the first time I saw her, at La Pierre, a restaurant in Chicago. She was gorgeous. I couldn't stop staring at her, and when she finally looked at me, it was like no one else existed that night. She wanted my attention, and she got it. From that moment, I knew she'd be perfect. Obedient. Devoted. Mine. Until she fucking left me. But I rectified that. She has nowhere else to go. There's no exit without me. So she'll surrender to me. They always do. I've been doing this for a long time.

I pull out my phone, the cameras lighting up with one touch. She's running the halls like she's lost, as if she didn't help me design it. That's what time away has done—made her forget her place. She can cry, run, curse me under her breath, but I'll see all of it. She can't hide from me in my house. I see every room.

Greta moves across the frame, head lowered, hands folded in front of her. Loyal as ever. I hired her years ago. I needed someone who wouldn't flinch at what I did. She came from Zurich, and never once asked questions. She's seen other women, their tears, the times I lost patience and bound them, and she never faltered. That's what's kept her here all this time. She's seen worse. Before Eleanor, privacy was optional. But it's different now. She's my wife. Privacy is hers, but only when I allow it, and I choose when her devotion is displayed.

Greta understands that. So when she walked in and saw Eleanor on her knees, I didn't care. Why should I? She won't question me. To her, it only proved that Mrs. Montgomery is exactly where she belongs. With me. And still, that name lingers. *Nora.* Wrong, foreign, an insult to everything we've built. She'll come back when she's done pretending. And when she does, I'll decide whether she earns my tenderness or my discipline.

11

MAREN

The hallway stays quiet. I don't know what I'm hoping to find, maybe an unlocked door he forgot to check. The floor grows colder the farther I walk, slick under my bare feet. Without the rush of running, everything is noticeable. The ceilings stretch too high, too formal for a house. The paint looks new. The walls are too smooth—too clean to be real. Nothing here feels used. Between the doors, paintings hang in perfect rows, each one framed in thick gold like they're trying to impress. I don't recognize a single piece, but they all look expensive enough to be locked away.

This isn't a home. Every inch of it is meant to be seen, not lived in.

One door opens into a library. Shelves fill the walls, floor to ceiling, and the books are arranged by size. The fireplace isn't lit, but the logs inside are stacked like decoration. Another room looks like a sitting area, but the furniture placement is too perfect. Velvet chairs are angled like a showroom. A glass table holds white flowers set in the exact center. The whole space feels like it was staged for a photo and never taken down.

The third door doesn't open. Near the end of the hallway,

something's off. A faint line cuts across the wall—barely there, but enough to make me stop. Like someone patched over something they didn't want found. I press against it, and the surface shifts under my hand. A hidden door. This one isn't locked.

Behind it, a narrow staircase winds upward. The carpet is thick beneath my feet, the kind that swallows sound. The wallpaper changes again—cream, patterned with faint flowers. The air smells faintly like flowers, like someone decided how the house should smell and made it happen.

At the top, the space narrows into another hallway. Two doors face each other as brass lights glow low along the walls. I reach for the door on the left.

The sitting room looks pale and picture-perfect. Pink and cream furniture rests untouched beneath white lace curtains that filter the sunlight like gauze. The air carries the scent of old perfume. Every detail feels intentional. Books line the shelves in symmetrical stacks. Cushions sit fluffed and centered on the sofa. It looks more like a movie set than a room someone uses, that someone lives in.

I step inside and spot a series of framed photos on a small table by the window. I freeze. There she is. Eleanor. She's real—and she looks like me.

In one photo, she laughs with Adrian on a beach, wind sweeping her hair across her face. In another, they pose together—his arm draped over her shoulder, her body leaning into his. Her brown eyes look soft, her lips parted slightly. These are wedding photos, vacation snapshots, and candid moments that seem curated, but still feel real, far too real. And the resemblance is undeniable. It's like staring at a version of myself I've never met. Her brown hair falls longer. Her body's slightly slimmer. But the eyes, the mouth, the shape of her face —those features could easily be mine.

I glance around the room. These are the only pictures I've seen of her in this house so far. They don't hang in the bedroom or line the halls. They only exist here, hidden in a room no one uses. A shrine he visits when no one's watching. I step back. I don't want to see more. I close the door quietly behind me and keep walking.

The next room radiates warmth before I even cross the threshold. The scent of paint hits fast. Sunlight pours in through a large window, flooding the space in gold. Beyond the glass, the coastline stretches wide. The beach rolls into soft dunes, and the ocean behind it rests calm and endless. The view almost looks peaceful.

The room is a mess of half-finished canvases, open tubes of paint, and stained rags draped over stools. The sunlight makes the colors look more vivid than they should. There are rows of canvases leaning against the wall, some blank, others alive with color and shadow. I don't know why I walk toward them, only that I do.

There are two bodies, bare and tangled together, on the first canvas. His hand grips her hair, and her thigh is wrapped around his hip, holding him close. Their mouths don't touch, but they hover—open, aching, inches apart. His body strains toward her. Her eyes are half-lidded, lips parted. She looks like she's giving in to something, and he seems like he's taking it.

In the next painting, he's behind her. There's one arm wrapped tightly across her chest and another at her throat. Her head tilts back into him, and her mouth hangs open. His face is pressed against her neck, their bodies flushed and slick. There's no question what they're doing. No space between them. No hesitation in how he holds her.

My thighs ache before I realize I've tensed them. The heat in my stomach hasn't gone away. It's worse now. In another painting, she's straddling him this time. Her arms are wrapped around his neck while his hands dig into her waist. Her back arches in motion, her head thrown back. He watches her like he doesn't need to look at anything else. Her mouth is open.

Her expression is unguarded—like she forgot where she was, or maybe wanted to be caught.

I feel dizzy. My skin feels tight. I'm not sure if I'm turned on or sick. Maybe both. Each painting is more intimate than the last. The positions and colors change, but the couple doesn't. It's always him and the woman. The woman looks exactly like me. A flicker hits—just a flash. My hand in paint. A moan in my throat. Fingers tightening in someone's hair. My breath catches, and the image is gone before I can hold on to it. I'm just imagining things. I've barely been here a couple days, and he's already making me lose my mind.

I press a hand to my chest. Behind me, the door creaks open. Adrian stands in the doorway, one arm resting against the frame. He doesn't speak. He watches me and doesn't say a word. Neither do I. He walks toward me slowly, like I'm skittish and he doesn't want to scare me off. His hand finds my waist, barely touching, waiting to see if I'll move. When I don't, he pulls me gently back against his chest.

I keep my eyes on the paintings.

"Are these models?" I ask. My voice comes out flat, tight in my throat.

He doesn't answer right away. His breath slows behind me.

Then he asks, "You don't recognize us?"

I blink. The word sinks. *Us.*

"You painted this?" I ask, but my voice isn't steady anymore.

He turns me to face him, his hands careful. "I didn't. I can't paint, but you can. You're talented. Best I've ever seen."

I glance over my shoulder at the woman in the painting—the way her body wraps around his, the way her mouth opens.

"Even if I could, I wouldn't paint something like this."

"But you did. We used to record ourselves. You'd watch the videos afterward. Then you'd paint, late at night. You said it helped you remember."

Remember what? I shake my head, not to argue, but because

I can't stand how certain he sounds. He steps beside me and nods toward the third canvas where she's straddling him, caught mid-movement, completely exposed.

"This one was your favorite," he murmurs. "You told me it was the closest we ever got to the truth. That no one else ever looked at you like that. Touched you like that."

I stare at it. At her. At the face I know too well.

"I still have the videos. You couldn't stop watching. Couldn't stop touching yourself after."

The words hit harder than I want them to. I try to avoid the painting, but it stays in my head, even when my eyes move.

"No, I'm not watching."

I won't watch him have sex with another woman. It's gross, and it makes me want to rip these paintings into pieces and throw them at him. He doesn't respond. Instead, he reaches down and tucks a strand of hair behind my ear. His fingers brush my cheek like he's done it a thousand times before. The touch isn't harsh. It's worse than that—it's becoming familiar. His gaze stays locked on mine, like he already knows how this ends. He doesn't argue. He doesn't have to. Because in his mind, I've already remembered. And I know he'll show me, whether I want to see it or not.

12

MAREN

I rush out of the painting studio as if the walls might close in if I stay a second longer. The paintings burned themselves on my mind: how she painted him, how I mimic her poses without realizing it, and the slow unraveling of it all. I feel like I'm being rewritten in real time. I need to breathe. I need a door that opens. *Am I losing it?* He follows me, but doesn't raise his voice or chase me because he's convinced I'll go exactly where he wants me to.

"Ellie," he says when I reach the landing, "that's enough for today."

I keep walking, refusing to look back.

"You should relax for a while, go to your sitting room. You should take some time to read. I'll have Greta bring you some tea."

I nod once, not trusting my voice. The door is already ajar, so I step inside. The sitting room is too pink. Cream armchairs and a rose-colored loveseat sit beneath lace curtains that mute the sunlight. The walls and pillows are pale blush, and even the rug has pink threaded through it. It's supposed to feel peaceful, but it doesn't. It feels artificial and overdone. It feels like I've stepped into someone else's version of calm.

I can't stop looking at the framed photos on the shelves. Eleanor appears in different outfits, smiling at everyone. Her flawless makeup and perfectly styled hair are visible in every shot. Each picture is lit and staged like a catalog spread. I stare at one too long, and it makes my skin crawl.

She belonged here. That's the whole point. But I don't belong here—I'm just the woman he inserted into her place. I move toward the bookshelf, not thinking. I need something to focus on. Anything that isn't her face in every frame, her voice echoing in my head through his.

Curated fiction lines the shelves. Classics. Modern hardcovers. Perfect, untouched spines. It's all for show. I scan the rows anyway, pretending I'm looking for something to read. Then I see it. Tucked between two novels is a book that doesn't match the others. It's leather-bound with no title, and its frayed edges show wear from use. I pull it free, and it's heavier than I expected.

I flip it open, and my breath catches. It's not a novel or a planner. It's a journal. And it's not just any journal—it's hers. My fingers tighten around the leather cover as I sit and open to the first entry. Eleanor's handwriting is neat, but there's pressure behind it. The pressure of her writing forced the ink deep into the page, as if she needed the words to stick. If this house contains anything real, that hasn't been staged by someone, it's this. And I'm going to read every word, because maybe it will give me answers and a way out.

I noticed Adrian the second I stepped out onto the floor. My feet ached, and I hadn't had a break since the dinner rush, but he caught my eye right away. Tall. Tousled, blonde hair. Green eyes that didn't

flinch when I looked back. He wore an expensive suit—nothing flashy, but perfectly tailored. He was the kind of man who didn't look at the menu because he already knew what he wanted. Broad shoulders, solid build. I could tell he was muscular under the suit.

When our eyes met, he looked at me like he already knew who I was. Like I'd walked into his space, not the other way around. He was seated at a prime table near the window. No one asked if he had a reservation. The host just walked him straight over. They knew better. When I reached his table, he didn't look away. His eyes dropped to my chest, then returned to my face without apology. I expected it to bother me. It didn't. Not really. Before I could even speak, he did.

"What's your name?" he asked.

"Eleanor."

"I'm Adrian."

He ordered a bourbon, neat, and a steak. Said it like he was giving me something to remember him by.

Then came the follow-ups. A second napkin. More ice. A new fork. It was always one thing, always spaced out. Just enough to keep me coming back. He knew exactly what he was doing. Never demanding, but completely intentional. Every time I returned to his table, I felt it—that slow pull. He looked at me like I was already halfway into his bed. He wasn't cocky, just confident. And he knew I felt it, too.

"Are you here every night?" he asked the fourth time I passed by.

"Most."

"How late do you stay?"

A strange question. Most customers didn't care about my schedule—or, at least, they shouldn't.

"Until close."

"Good. I was hoping I picked the right night."

That made me pause. Had he been watching me? And why would someone like him take an interest in someone like me? Unless he wanted to get laid. I wasn't easy. If that's what he was looking for, he should've talked to my friend Izzy. But even the thought of him being interested in someone else pissed me off, which made no sense. He was a stranger.

At the end of the night, I brought him the check. He leaned back in his chair and looked me over the same way he had all night— slow, unapologetic, assured. I swear he was staring at my lips.

"You've been coming over here all night. Why don't you come home with me instead?"

I froze. "Seriously?"

"We'll fuck. Nothing too complicated."

It caught me off guard. A man like that being so open about what he wanted—it should've made me uncomfortable. But it didn't. It turned me on. He wasn't subtle. He wasn't trying to charm his way around it. He just said it. And meant it. A man saying what he wanted without trying to manipulate me. That's rare.

I stared at him. "You think that works?"

"It's not a line. I want you. That's it."

He seriously thought that would work. I wasn't sleeping with a stranger. Never have, never will. Even though it'd been a while, I wasn't taking that risk—no matter how hot he was. I was sure he did this with every woman he was attracted to, and it probably worked on some of them. But not on me.

I laughed. "I'm not that kind of girl."

He tilted his head and smirked. "I figured. But you're still standing here."

He wasn't wrong. I was standing there. Because I was curious. But there was no way in hell I was saying yes.

"I have to check on my other tables."

I turned and went back to work. Not because I didn't want him, but because I knew better. Because saying yes meant risking being played. And I couldn't afford that.

Still, it wasn't the smartest move. Tips were how I survived, and I needed every dollar for rent, for my car, for everything. Dismissing a customer like that wasn't exactly strategic.

When I came back, his table was empty. The check was folded, and the tip was larger than what I'd made in my last three shifts combined. He didn't take my rejection personally. I appreciated that. At the bottom, in neat handwriting, was his phone number and a message:

Call me if you change your mind. Or don't. I'll still be thinking about you either way.

I shoved the note into my bag and tried not to look at it again. I told myself I'd throw it away when I got back. I didn't. I still haven't. What would've happened if I'd said yes? Because I haven't stopped thinking about him. Not since that night. Not even now.

I exhale slowly and tighten my grip on the journal. Eleanor had noticed him right away. She wanted him. Although she tried to say no, her writing made it clear. She wanted to say yes. But she's not me. I never would have fallen for that. It would be off-putting to me, how bold he was. I swallow and turn the page.

The next day, the staff met before dinner service for a mandatory meeting. I thought it would be the usual—schedules, upselling desserts, reminders to smile more. Instead, Adrian walked in. I didn't expect to see him again. Not like that. My manager introduced him as one of the restaurant's top investors. Adrian stood at the front of the room, nodding when he was supposed to, but his eyes weren't on him. They were on me.

Every time I shifted my stance, crossed my arms, glanced at the door—I felt him watching. Not glancing, watching. My pulse climbed, and I tried not to show it.

He could've had anyone. He had money, power, and a face that made people look twice. I was just another waitress. My hair was tied back, makeup light, uniform standard. Nothing about me stood out. But he didn't look away.

The manager wrapped up the usual talking points and handed the floor to Adrian.

He stepped forward like he'd done it a hundred times. Tall and confident.

"Service is the most important part of the dining experience. A great meal isn't enough. Guests should feel like they've had something they can't get anywhere else."

Then his green eyes locked onto mine. "That starts with the staff. Knowing how to read a table. How to engage. How to hold attention. That's what separates good from exceptional."

He wasn't talking about customer service. He was talking about me. Heat crawled up my neck. I uncrossed my arms and stood straighter. I didn't look away, but it was harder than I thought it'd be. When the meeting ended, the staff left. Adrian didn't. And neither did I.

He walked over like he had nowhere else to be, then stopped close enough that I had to tilt my head to look at him.

"Do you want to go out with me tonight?" he asked. "For drinks."

I shook my head. "I don't drink."

He smiled. "You don't have to. But we can still meet up."

I raised an eyebrow. "So it's a date?"

He tilted his head. "It can be whatever you want. As long as it ends with you in my bed."

I didn't flinch, but my grip on my notepad tightened.

"I expected better lines from you. You'll have to try harder than that."

He didn't miss a beat. "A pleasurable night doesn't come easy."

He leaned in just enough to make sure I heard it exactly how he meant it. His eyes dropped to my mouth. Stayed there. Then he pulled out his phone.

"Put your number in."

I hesitated. He was an investor. Someone with power over this place. If I kept saying no, what would that mean? Could he get me fired? Maybe it would be fun. I didn't have to sleep with him. It was just drinks. I could say I tried. Maybe he'd think I was boring, not worth the effort. I typed in my number, anyway.

He glanced at it, then said, "I'll text you my address. Come over tonight."

I blinked. I thought we were going out. To go to a stranger's house? That was risky. But he didn't give off dangerous vibes. Just confident and sexy.

So I nodded. Then he stepped back and walked away. He just left me standing there with my pulse shot to hell, still pretending I wasn't going to think about it all night. I hated how much I liked the chase.

I need to find out more, and maybe that will help me manage him until I can escape. Or, at least, give me context to the past if he insists I keep pretending. He'll be angry if I don't seem like I am trying to work things out with him. This is so messed up. Still, I can't stop turning the pages and reading more of her journal.

His penthouse was spotless—minimalist and modern, with sharp, black accents, polished floors, and ceiling-high windows that looked out over the city like it belonged to him. The view made it hard to focus on anything else. I stood in front of the glass, listening to the sound of his footsteps behind me.

I told him I didn't like wine, but I still took the glass when he poured it. I drank it slowly, letting it sit on my tongue longer than necessary. He never looked away.

He kissed me without warning. His lips were soft. His hand moved from my neck down to my lower back. I didn't stop him. When his fingers reached the zipper of my dress, I turned around and let him pull it down. The fabric slipped from my shoulders and fell to the floor.

He looked at me—really looked at me—then kissed my shoulder. No words. Just touch. I let him undress me because I was already wet, and he was right there.

He pushed me onto the couch gently. The cushions dipped beneath my weight. His hands skimmed my thighs, spreading them apart as he kneeled between them. He pushed my underwear aside like he'd done it a million times before, like this was a continuation instead of a beginning.

Then his mouth was on me. Warm. Sure. No hesitation. His tongue moved slowly at first, teasing, then faster, focused. I'd never had a man go down on me before. Never had anyone who cared if I came. But he did. He wanted it. I could feel it in the way he groaned against me, the way he sucked harder when I started to tremble.

I grabbed the edge of the cushion. My hips rocked. My legs shook. I whimpered when he didn't stop, moaned when I got close—then cursed when he pulled away too soon.

He stood, unbuttoning his shirt slowly, his eyes locked on mine. Each button undone with purpose, each piece of clothing peeled away.

He stepped out of his pants, climbed over me, and pushed my knees back. My breath caught at the sight of him, hard and ready. He kissed me hard, his breath shallow against my mouth as he rubbed himself against me—not sliding in yet, just letting me feel how ready he was. My thighs tightened around him, and I arched, trying to pull him closer.

He didn't rush. He dragged the head of his cock through my wetness, teasing me until I whimpered, before sliding in deep, all at once, groaning.

I gasped. He filled me perfectly. My nails dug into his back, the couch creaking beneath us. His grip on my thigh tightened and relaxed with each thrust. My skin was damp. His chest brushed mine, and his breath came fast against my shoulder.

I hated how much I needed it. Hated the heat curling low every time he groaned against my neck. I was soaked and completely at his mercy—and somehow, that made me wetter.

He kissed me and said, "You're so beautiful. I've been thinking about this since I first saw you."

My heart skipped. It was sweet. Honest. I hadn't expected that.

Everything was fast, loud, and overwhelming. He fucked me like I was a conquest, and part of me was saying you made it too easy.

But the other part...the darker part...liked how it felt to be taken. To be wanted this much.

"This pussy's mine. I already own you."

I should've slapped him for that. Instead, I moaned—and hated myself for it.

"Say my name," he said, still buried deep.

"Adrian," I gasped. "Fuck—Adrian."

His smiled against my skin. "That's my good fucking girl. No one's ever fucked you like this, have they?"

I said, "No. Never."

He laughed, then growled, "I'm not letting you leave. You'll come on my cock like a good girl, and then I'll fill you up."

And I came—loud, without shame. My body clenched around him as I came, and he followed right after, moaning, pressing his forehead to mine.

Then he whispered in my ear, "I'm going to fucking marry you, Ellie."

My whole body went still. He called me by another name. Was it someone else he was sleeping with? Or worse, someone he was dating?

"Did you just call me Ellie?"

He didn't flinch. "Yeah. It suits you."

I pulled back just enough to look at him. "You don't even know me."

"I know enough."

His voice was calm. Assured. In his head, this conversation was already over.

Then he added, "It was in the heat of the moment."

I nodded, even though I didn't agree. "Right."

I didn't stay to finish the wine or ask him to explain. I didn't even put my shoes on before heading for the door.

He called out behind me, "You don't have to leave."

I left and walked barefoot to the elevator, adrenaline still high, trying to process what had just happened. Everything about him was intense, seductive, overwhelming.

That night, everything changed, and I still didn't know if it had been my choice.

I had been so caught up in how he made me feel that I ignored the most important part of what he said. Not the name, but the promise buried in it.

I'm going to fucking marry you.

I should've questioned why he said it. Walked away before he made sure I never would.

But I didn't. I let him explain it away. And it felt dangerous.

The next night, he came back. Same table. Same seat. He asked for me by name.

I was carrying a tray when my manager called me over. "He requested you," they said, nodding toward him.

I walked over without rushing. His suit was darker than the night before, his collar open, no tie. A drink sat in front of him, already half-finished.

"Sit," he said.

"I'm working."

"Take a break."

I looked toward my manager, waiting for an excuse to escape it, but they nodded. I set the tray down behind the bar and pulled out the chair.

His eyes stayed on me the entire time.

"Are you done running?"

"I didn't run."

"No?"

"It was a one-night stand. That's all."

Even though I could still feel the weight of his body, the arch of my back, and the weakness in my legs after my orgasm. It was the best sex I'd ever had, and that wasn't something I could explain away. But good sex didn't mean he was good for me.

He let out a laugh, tipping his glass slightly in my direction. "You think that was a one-night stand?"

"Yes."

It didn't sound convincing. Not to him or me.

"I want more than one night, Eleanor."

"I'm not looking for anything."

"Neither am I. Doesn't mean I'm not going to take what I want."

I hated that my pulse jumped, how quickly my mind started filling in the blanks. His touch. That look he gave me just before he thrusted inside me. I knew better than to believe any of this could stay casual, but part of me still wanted to hear what he'd say next.

"Why did you say you're going to marry me?"

I tried to keep my voice steady, but my body was already giving me away. I needed to know why he said he was going to marry me. I was a complete stranger. It didn't make sense.

My legs felt warm, and my chest was too tight.

He smiled and his eyes lit up. "Because I am."

Was he just fucking with me? If so, that's so fucked up. But if he wasn't, I didn't know how I'd feel about that. He was obviously wealthy and good-looking. But husband material? I wasn't sure yet, and I didn't know if I wanted to find out.

"I'm not looking to get married to a stranger."

"I've been inside you. I'm not a stranger anymore."

My face burned as I glanced over my shoulder to make sure no one heard. I should have walked away, but I didn't. I stayed in the chair, still feeling him between my legs.

"Adrian, not here."

He leaned in. "Then come home with me."

"I have to work."

"Become my wife and you'll never have to work again."

It was tempting. Everything about him made it hard to think straight. He wasn't offering love, just himself. But I still said no. Not because I didn't want to say yes, but because the part of me that left his bed was louder than the one yearning to fall right back into it.

I stare at the wall for a second after reading that last entry. Eleanor didn't just want him. She let him in. Piece by piece. And maybe she thought she was still in control by pushing back, but he was already inside her head. She stayed when she should've walked away. Maybe that's why I'm still reading. Because part of me understands exactly why she stayed. Then there's a knock at the door, and I slam the journal shut.

13

MAREN

The door creaks open. Greta steps inside, carrying a silver tray with a porcelain teapot and one delicate cup. I don't even want to look at her. She saw me on my knees with Adrian's dick in my mouth. But despite my embarrassment, I'm relieved to see her because I need her help getting out of this prison. She's the only person I've seen in this house so far. She's my only hope of getting out of here. If she worked for them for years, she should know whether or not I'm her.

She walks slowly, eyes locked on the tray, and sets it on the table near the sofa, adjusting the napkin beside it even though it's already perfect.

"I brought tea, ma'am," she says.

I don't answer. She turns to leave, already halfway to the door before I speak.

"Wait."

She pauses, her hand resting on the knob.

"Yes, Mrs. Montgomery?"

My heart pounds, but my voice doesn't waver.

"I need your help. I have to get out of here."

She doesn't move. *Does she realize I'm not her?* We look the same, but that doesn't mean others don't see a difference because he refuses to.

"I'm not Eleanor. My name is Maren Bellamy. Adrian kidnapped me."

She still doesn't face me, but her shoulders are rigid. After a second, she turns slowly. Her eyes flick to the door, as if she's expecting someone to be listening, then she meets my gaze.

"Mrs. Montgomery..." Her voice is quieter now, the words slightly off. "I am sorry to hear...you are struggling."

My words snap out fast. "I'm not struggling. I'm telling the truth. I'm not her, and I never was."

Greta looks down, then up again. Her hands tremble around her waist.

"Mr. Montgomery...He missed you, yes?" she says quickly. "All of us, we did."

I don't give a shit about him missing me. Who else is here? I haven't seen them. But if she's useless, then maybe someone else will feel bad for me and call the police. I need to meet the other staff.

I step toward her. "I don't care. Please. Just help me get out."

Her mouth opens like she wants to say more, but she hesitates. Her accent thickens again, slipping further out of her usual polished tone.

"I cannot," she says finally. "I won't tell him, but please leave me out of it."

She turns and walks out, closing the door with quiet finality. The silence she leaves behind feels louder than her voice. For a second, I stand there, wondering why she won't help me. I know he signs her paychecks, but does that mean undying loyalty? I sure as hell was never that loyal to my employer. He must be holding something over her.

Regardless, Greta will say I imagined it. Whoever else he's paid to keep this house running will nod along. They'll say I was tired, overwhelmed, and didn't know what I was saying. Everyone will look at the expensive clothes, the porcelain teacup, and the mansion around me, and ask how bad it could be.

That's how he set this place up. No one questions it. Even I start to wonder if I'm overreacting. That thought alone is enough to scare me. No wonder Eleanor left. Even if she'd screamed, no one would've listened. They'd smile, pour tea, and pretend they didn't hear it. Now, it's happening to me. How much money and power does Adrian have?

I sink into my seat, my hands resting limply in my lap. The silence bears down on me, a heavy pressure urging me not to succumb to the lie that lurks just beneath the surface.

I force myself to breathe, but my chest stays tight. Then my eyes drift toward the corners of the ceiling. There are cameras in this house. I saw them in the hallway, but I don't know where else they are or when he's watching. That's what makes me spiral. He could be seeing this right now, already planning what comes next. I wasn't thinking when I talked to Greta. Now, the doubt clicks into place like a trap. *What if this room is monitored? What if this was the mistake he's been waiting for?*

I can't sit still. I tip the lamp. Nothing. I loosen the curtain rod. A screw falls and rolls across the floor. I open drawers. Check the shelves. Run my hands along the mirror's edge.

Nothing. No wires. No cameras.

If Greta tells him what I said, he won't come in shouting or asking questions. He'll wait and smile. Then he'll close the door behind him, and the mask will disappear. He'll say *I have to punish you,* and I'm trying to avoid that.

My ass stings even more just thinking about it. I should have stayed quiet. But I didn't. Now, I have to lie. I have to make him believe that I'm grateful. That I'm devoted. Because if he thinks I'm hiding something, he won't wait for proof. He'll act.

I don't know or care if Eleanor really loved him. But maybe

in her journal, she left breadcrumbs on how to escape for the next woman unlucky enough to end up in her place. Or worse —how to survive him until you break into pieces.

My fingers tremble as I reach for the journal, like they already know what I'm risking. I don't need comfort, I need information. Because if I don't figure something out soon, I won't make it out at all.

I need to hide it so he doesn't find it and take it. It's the only information I have. If I'm going to be here, I have to be able to fill in the blanks and be able to pretend to be her.

If I keep being the clueless person I truly am, he's going to get frustrated and punish me. I slide the journal under the couch cushion and press it flat. It's not a perfect hiding spot, but I don't have time to be perfect. Hopefully, he never comes in here.

I need to look like I belong here, like the thought of escape never crossed my mind. I wipe my hands on my robe and head for the bathroom. I need to fix my face before I see him. I splash cold water on my skin and dry it quickly. The sting helps me focus.

I move to the mirror. My lips lift, but the smile doesn't reach my eyes. In the reflection, I look like someone playing a part she never auditioned for. I pinch my cheeks until the color rises. I smooth my robe again, even though it's already straight. He can't see hesitation. He'll smell it like blood in water. Every move has to look natural. If he senses performance, I've already lost. The mask is ready, even if I'm not.

I open the door. Adrian is already there. He leans against the far wall, arms crossed, one foot kicked back. His posture is relaxed. Too relaxed. He looks like a lion ready to pounce.

Was he standing there the whole time, or did Greta warn him? His gaze lingers on my legs, bare beneath the robe. I cross my arms, but it's too late. He's already looked. And he's smiling because he likes what he sees.

"Everything alright?"

I meet his eyes. "I was just about to come find you."

His head tilts as he studies me. Then he steps forward and takes my hand, lifting it to his mouth. His eyes never leave mine as his lips brush my knuckles. I feel that pull again, the one I keep trying to ignore.

"I thought you might," he says. "But some people need time to see things clearly."

"I'm one of those people."

His smile widens. "I know."

He releases my hand and gestures toward the bedroom.

"Go rest. You've had a long day."

Long day is an understatement. We argued. I saw her erotic paintings of them. I read Eleanor's journals, trying to figure out how she got into this mess.

I need to get out of here. Because we are not the same person. I didn't forget. I would remember writing all those things down. These memories aren't mine. I wouldn't just forget my life and create a false identity to get away from my husband. But even if I did, that says more about him than it does about me.

14

MAREN

I wake up with Adrian's chest pressed to my back, his arms locked around my waist, and his cock hard against my ass. He hasn't moved, but I know he's awake. I feel it in the way his fingers tighten around my stomach, holding me like I belong here.

The sheets are warm, and his skin is hotter. I don't remember falling asleep like this, but it doesn't matter. He kisses the back of my neck, slow and open-mouthed, and I melt into it before I can think better of it.

"You're so beautiful in the morning," he murmurs, his voice thick and low.

His hand slides lower, dragging across my stomach before slipping between my thighs. His fingers find me already wet, and he strokes my clit in circles. I twitch beneath him, my body reacting before my mind can catch up.

"Always ready for me, even before you open your eyes."

I push into him, chasing more and grinding into his palm like I need it—and I do. I shouldn't, but I do.

He moves down between my legs and parts me with his fingers before pushing his tongue deep inside me. I've never done this before, but it feels so good. I've been missing out, clearly.

His thumb finds my clit again, this time with more pressure, and every motion is designed to take me apart. I gasp and reach down, grabbing his head because I need something to hold on to. I'm already trembling.

He looks up. "You taste so good," he says.

I moan loudly, wrecked and shameless, as my hips roll into his mouth, desperate and thoughtless. Every time he hits that spot that makes the world blink out, the room disappears —and the shame disappears with it. All I know is the drag of his tongue, the pressure of his lips, and the ache between my legs.

God, I hate how much I need this, but I don't pull away. I pull his head tighter against me, grinding harder.

He fucks me slowly with his mouth, and his thumb punishes my clit until my legs shake. When I'm right at the edge, he stops, and the emptiness makes me whimper.

It feels like punishment.

Then he grabs my thigh and pulls it over his, opening me wider. The head of his cock slides through my folds, and the stretch knocks the air out of me. I flinch, but the ache slides into heat, and I grind against him like I want more of it. I feel every inch of him as he sinks deep, thick and pulsing, until I'm completely full. I feel so pathetic; I went from looking for an escape to laying on my back, distracted.

"Fuck," he groans into my neck. "You are made for me."

He starts slowly, and each stroke brushes my clit, building tension I can't escape. I arch into him, and he grabs my hips harder. His fingers dig in like he's trying to stay in control, but I know he's losing it, too.

"You always take my cock like this. So greedy for it."

I reach up, grabbing his neck and pulling him closer. He holds my hand, deepening our connection as his powerful thrusts cause my body to tighten, pushing me toward my climax again.

The stretch burns, and the pressure builds fast. Each time he slams into me, my clit throbs, begging for him. I attempt to breathe, but my breath hitches, then escapes in a shaky moan.

"Don't stop," I whisper.

He laughs under his breath. "I wasn't planning to."

He grabs my hips and drives into me again and again, harder each time, until the headboard knocks into the wall and my moans break apart.

He grabs my breast and rolls my nipple between his fingers, and I cry out as everything clenches tight. The second he thrusts again, I shatter—legs shaking, muscles locking, vision going white around the edges. I lose myself in it. No thoughts, no boundaries—just sensation and the sound of us.

He keeps going, rough and wild.

"Shit," he gasps. "I'm gonna come. Fuck."

He slams into me one last time and groans into my neck as his cock throbs once, then again. I feel him pulse deep inside me, hot and thick.

I don't move, and neither does he. We're stuck together, slick and breathless. His hand stays between my legs, palm pressed over my pussy. He kisses my shoulder, then lower, then stops. A few seconds later, he pulls out slowly, and the emptiness aches more than I want to admit. Then the door clicks shut behind him.

I stay frozen. I'm still warm from him. Everything smells like him and feels like him. The slick between my thighs still aches in the best way, and that's what makes my stomach turn. My body doesn't know better, but I do. The pleasure doesn't last —guilt never lets it.

I sit up slowly and stare at the mess between my legs. The more times we have sex, the more chances I'm fucking stuck here for life with a baby. I don't even want to think about that becoming my reality. I tried to have a conversation, but he brushed me off, accusing me of starting a fight—which makes no sense. Unless he wants me to get pregnant. What if that's been the plan from the beginning? It would be a permanent tie, a leash, a trap he can watch grow.

I was supposed to be smart, careful, one step ahead. Instead, I'm here—still aching, still full of him, still pretending I'm in control.

I press my palm to my stomach like I can stop something from happening just by holding it still, but it's too late.

I don't get long to spiral.

His voice cuts through the door, casual and commanding. "You coming?"

I blink. "Where?"

"The shower," he says. "I'm not done with you yet."

My heart jumps. Panic presses hard against my ribs, but I bury it with a breath. I won't let him see it.

So, I fake smile and let it reach my voice.

"Coming."

I walk toward the bathroom like I always meant to, like nothing matters. He doesn't have to say anything else. I already know I'm being watched.

15

ADRIAN

Eleanor walks toward the bathroom like always, calm and quiet, with no protest or pause. She even smiles. I stay behind the door longer than I have to.

The water starts, first a hiss, then a rush. She's in there now, and I picture it perfectly. She steps under the stream too early, letting it hit her full in the chest before it's warm. I don't walk in right away. I wait. I listen.

Steam slips beneath the door and fills the room, slow and thick. I close my eyes and imagine the way it wraps around her skin. I picture her hair damp and heavy, dripping at the ends. I imagine the trail of water sliding down the arch of her back, over the perfect curve of her ass, then lower. I'm hard before I even open the door.

The last time she let me see her like this, she looked over her shoulder with hesitation. That's gone now. She doesn't tell me to stay out. She doesn't pull the curtain. She walks in like she expects me to follow.

So, I do.

She's already under the water, facing away. Her hands are on the wall, her head tilted forward. Her spine glistens, pink from the heat, and the water traces every line of her body like it knows exactly where to go.

I stop and look. Really look.

The water clings to her, not just dripping off, but dragging down between her thighs. It makes me ache. Her legs are slightly parted, and her back arches just enough to make it worse. The roundness of her ass is a fucking masterpiece. It's obscene how good she looks like this.

My cock twitches, hard against my thigh. I clench my jaw and take a breath, but it doesn't help. Nothing does when she's like this.

She moves slightly, adjusting her stance. The muscles in her thighs shift, and water slips down the inside of her leg. I want to follow it with my mouth. My hands. My cock. I want her to feel me everywhere that water touches.

I press my palm to the fogged glass door and watch the mark bloom under my hand.

Then I slide it open and step inside.

She doesn't turn around, but she knows I'm here. She doesn't need to see me to know what I want.

I move behind her slowly. I could make a sound, say something, warn her, but I don't.

I want to see what she does when I touch her.

I press my chest to her back, and she exhales.

She doesn't stiffen. Doesn't flinch. Just lets out a slow breath like she's been waiting for it. Her arms relax against the tile. Her head dips slightly to the side.

Good girl.

I slide one hand to her waist, then lower, gripping her hip hard—enough to make her feel it later. My cock presses against her ass, and I don't hide it. I rock into her once, then again, just to hear her inhale. Still no resistance.

I bring my mouth to her neck, open-mouthed and wet, letting my breath drag across her skin. She tilts her head further, exposing her throat. I kiss her there, then just below her ear. My hand slides up to her breast, under the spray. I roll her nipple gently, then pinch, just enough to make her gasp.

She's quiet, but I feel her body shift. I feel her thighs clench, the tiniest grind of her hips against me. She's not thinking or resisting. She's letting me take her.

"You look so fucking good like this," I murmur, my voice low and rough.

I slide my other hand between her legs, slow and steady. My palm brushes her inner thigh. She parts for me without needing to be told. And when I reach her center, she's already soaked—and not just from the water.

My cock throbs painfully, and I curse under my breath. I knew she'd come back to me. Her body tells me what her words won't. She doesn't say she missed me, but she's not stopping me. She's not even trying. She's taking everything I give her, and that's all I need.

I press a kiss to her shoulder. My hand strokes between her legs, slow and possessive, just enough to keep her trembling.

"I missed this," I say.

She doesn't answer. Doesn't need to.

Her silence says more than her voice ever could. She's letting me touch her like I never stopped. That's all I need to know.

She's mine again.

My hand stays between her legs, stroking slowly, spreading warmth across her folds. She tilts her hips into my touch. It's the kind of subtle movement that tells me everything. She's letting me lead, but she's not passive.

Not anymore.

I kiss her shoulder again, lower this time. My mouth traces the line of her spine as she leans forward, palms flat against the wall. Her skin is so soft under the water, and I can't stop touching her.

I bend her over, lift her leg, and almost slide inside, but then she moves. She turns under the water and drops to her knees.

She doesn't look up at me right away. She just reaches for me, wraps her hand around my cock, and strokes once. Then again. Her grip is firm, like she remembers every inch of me, and when she finally looks up, her eyes are steady.

Then she takes me into her mouth, and I don't breathe again for a full minute.

"Fuck," I breathe. "Just like that."

Her mouth is hot, wet, and eager to please. There's no hesitation. When she takes me deeper, it nearly steals my breath.

It used to be like this. Back in Chicago before we got married and she was still just a waitress, she'd look at me with wide eyes, like I'd handed her the world just by wanting her. She swore she wasn't materialistic, didn't care about money, said all she needed was me. And I believed her, because in those early days, I liked spoiling her. I wanted her to feel chosen, to see that being with me meant her life would never be ordinary again.

But her requests started to grow—first jewelry, then artwork, then a car. I indulged her, always. I thought I was keeping her happy and secure. But with each yes, her eyes stopped lighting up and the gratitude's grew fewer. It stopped feeling like she wanted me, and started to feel like she only wanted what I could give.

Eventually, I gave her a black card so she wouldn't have to wait on me, so she could take what she wanted without asking. I thought it would make things easier for both of us. Instead, it took the spark out of it. No more surprise. No more gratitude. She was pulling further away from me.

And now—it doesn't feel like that. She isn't asking or bargaining. She's on her knees, swallowing me down like she missed this as much as I did. Her mouth is hot around me, her throat tight as she takes me deeper, and there's no request waiting behind it. Just her giving.

But I can't ignore the thought. I've seen her use seduction to get what she wanted before. Maybe she thinks this will buy her forgiveness or more freedom.

Either way, it doesn't matter. She's here, on her knees, and I'm the only one she'll ever give herself to like this.

I brace my hand against the tile above her head. My other hand slides into her hair, gripping the back of her head, not to guide her yet, but to feel her devotion.

Her lips glide down my length with slow, even pressure, and I groan when she swallows around me.

"You missed this, too, didn't you?" I ask, watching her take me deeper.

She moans around me, and the vibration shoots through my spine. I tighten my grip in her hair.

"You remember how to ruin me."

She sucks harder, deeper, using her tongue to tease the underside of my cock with an almost cruel rhythm. She doesn't flinch when I curse. She doesn't stop when I twitch.

She's giving me everything again. Because she remembers how good we are together. I thrust gently into her mouth, still letting her set the pace. Her hands grip my thighs as her lips stretch wider. Her throat flexes, and I lose it. Then she grabs my ass and holds me there.

"You want it?" I whisper. "You want every fucking drop?"

Her answer is a confident hum. I come hard, my cock pulsing against her tongue, and she swallows like she used to. She pulls back slowly, licking her lips. Her eyes meet mine.

She stands. No shame, just water sliding over her skin. She still needs me, and I'll never let her go again. But just before she turns away, she looks at me. And I swear, for half a second, she looks like she hates me. Just like she did right before she left.

16

MAREN

Adrian didn't say anything after I gave him a blowjob in the shower. No praise or demands. Just a clean towel handed to me and a soft, dismissive order. I didn't want to have sex—the less we have sex, the less likely I'll get knocked up. So, I got on my knees and gave him a blowjob. That was good enough for him, and I feel relieved.

"I've got work to do. You should relax. Read something. Or paint."

Paint.

I don't flinch, but my stomach knots anyway. He says it like it's harmless, like he doesn't remember what I saw in that studio. Or maybe he does, and this is his way of testing me, seeing if I'll go back in there and stare at the woman who looks too much like me—the poses, the mouths, the hands. The one I didn't even know I was mimicking.

I won't go near that room again. Not yet. When I step out of the bathroom, there's a dress laid out at the foot of the bed. Soft cotton. Pale blue. Thin enough to show everything. It isn't the kind of thing you wear to relax. It isn't meant for comfort; it's meant to be seen in.

I glance at him. He's still standing by the window, shirtless and silent. He looks up, lets his eyes drag over my chest beneath the towel, then turns and leaves without a word. I don't put the dress on. I fold it once, drape it over my arm, and walk down the hall barefoot.

My skin is still damp, and my body is still sore. I don't look back. The house is quiet, but not lifeless. Every surface shines. The floors are smooth and spotless. The air smells faintly of flowers. The art on the walls is real, and the lighting is soft and perfect, as if someone designed the mood for every hour of the day. It's effortless—the kind of wealth that doesn't have to prove anything.

And I hate how beautiful it all is. How easy it is to admire the architecture, the curved staircase, the velvet furniture that never seems to wrinkle. Even now, part of me wants to run my hands over everything, just to know what a life like this feels like. It isn't home, but it is perfect. And I can't pretend it doesn't impress me. I pass Greta in the hall. She doesn't ask where I've been. She doesn't even meet my eyes.

I stop her and ask, "Who else works here?"

"The chef comes in everyday, so does the gardener."

I haven't seen the chef, so maybe I should go into the kitchen. And I know Adrian won't let me outside, so talking to the gardener isn't happening. I wonder if she won't help me because she's afraid of Adrian making it impossible for her to find work elsewhere. The rich wouldn't want their house-keepers talking about what goes on in their homes, let alone interfere.

I nod, and she keeps going.

The sitting room is empty when I get there, the way it always is. Neutral tones. Soft lighting. A curated escape from reality. I close the door gently behind me and sit on the edge of the sofa.

For a second, I just stare at the floor. My legs are still damp, and my hair sticks to my neck. I should dry off, but I don't. The chill makes me feel sharper, like if I move too quickly, I might snap. I reach under the cushion, and my fingers close around the journal. Still hidden and safe.

I pull it out slowly and set it in my lap, staring at the cover without opening it yet. My skin feels too thin. Anything on the next page could cut through me if I'm not careful.

I didn't come here to remember Eleanor. I came to figure out how she got out. I want to know if she left a map, a clue, a mistake he made—something I can use.

But I don't flip to the end. I start where I left off. If I'm going to find a way out, I need to know what kind of man I'm really dealing with. And maybe, if I read carefully, I'll find out his weaknesses.

I sit back on the couch, the journal open on my lap. I'm not reading for comfort anymore. I'm not even reading for truth. I'm looking for leverage. I need to understand how she went from a waitress to his wife. If I can find the moment he started controlling her—then maybe I can stop myself from going through it, too.

So, I keep reading.

∾

I didn't expect another date. But Adrian didn't ask this time. He called the restaurant and asked my manager to pass along a message.

"Tell Eleanor to send me her address, and I'll pick her up at eight."

I was furious. There was no question in it. He was also involving my manager and using my workplace to arrange dates with me. They'd look at me as just another waitress fucking a rich man, hoping for more while the man wasn't. I'd seen it happen more times than I can count.

Still, at 7:45, I was standing in front of my closet, staring at the few nice things I owned. I chose a long-sleeved, black dress. Fitted.

Simple. Not too much skin. I didn't want to look like I was trying, even though I was.

At 8:00 sharp, his car was waiting outside. The driver opened the door without saying a word. Adrian was already inside, wearing a navy suit and no tie. He didn't say hello. He just reached into the seat beside him and handed me a small black box.

"What's this?"

"Open it."

Inside was a bracelet. A thin gold chain with a diamond at the center, small enough to look modest, expensive enough not to be.

"Adrian...I can't accept this."

He didn't respond. Didn't take it back. Just sat there, watching me like he was waiting me out.

"It's too much. We barely know each other."

Still nothing. His decision had already been made. After a few more seconds of silence, I put it on. He watched my fingers at the clasp. Didn't smile. Didn't say a word. He didn't need to.

The restaurant was one of those places where the staff knew your name before you walked in. Rooftop. Soft lighting. Food so pretty you felt guilty touching it. He ordered for me, which I didn't mind—I could barely think, and there were so many options that I didn't know if I could choose. Wine appeared without request. He poured for me. I drank it this time without hesitation, even though I don't like wine. The food is delicious. The salmon melted in your mouth. This was even better than the restaurant where I worked.

"You look nervous," *he said.*

He was making me nervous. He talked about marriage and gave me expensive gifts. I didn't know how I felt about him yet. Did I even want to be with him? Did he truly want to be with me, or was he just messing with my head? Before I could answer, he reached across the table and took my hand in his. His grip was warm and steady, his thumb brushing across my knuckles.

"No need to be nervous. I've already fucked you on my couch."

I froze. My eyes darted around the room, half expecting someone to have heard him.

He let out a soft laugh. "You're cute. But prudish."

I didn't know if that was a compliment or an insult. He said it like it was both. I pulled my hand back slowly, not to reject him, but to breathe. He didn't push. Just kept eating his steak like nothing happened.

I asked nothing about the restaurant. I didn't ask how he knew the staff, how often he came here, or how many women he'd brought. I really didn't want to know that.

Instead, I asked, "Why are you doing this?"

"Dinner?"

"This whole thing."

He cut a piece of steak and paused, his eyes still on the plate. "Because I like you."

"You don't know me."

He looked up and smiled. "I don't need to."

"That's not how this works."

He gave nothing away. I couldn't get a good read on him and his true intentions.

"It's how I work."

I didn't respond. I wasn't sure what I would've said. The plates were cleared, and dessert followed without a word. I didn't eat it right away. I just looked at it. Too beautiful to touch. Too expensive to waste. He didn't rush me. Just leaned back in his chair, watching. So, I picked up the fork and continued to eat.

Once dinner ended, he stood and offered his hand again. Outside, the night had cooled, and he walked me to the car in silence. When I slid inside, he stood outside for just a second longer than he needed to. Then he leaned in.

His hand grabbed my jaw, then his lips crashed into mine. His tongue slid into my mouth without waiting. His other hand moved straight to my thigh, gripping it tight.

I kissed him back, open-mouthed and greedy. I pushed into him, and his thumb dragged across my cheek as he leaned deeper into the kiss. My chest rose hard. My thighs clenched. His mouth moved over mine again before he pulled back.

My lips were slick. My body was already aching. I didn't speak. I didn't need to.

He got in beside me.

I said, "I have work in the morning." I had the day off, but I wasn't about to invite him back to my studio apartment. Not after that kind of dinner.

He turned his head toward me. "You don't want me to come inside?"

"It's late."

He looked at the driver. "Take us home."

The car started moving.

"Home?" I asked.

"My home," he said, placing his hand on my thigh again. Firm. Familiar. "We'll spend the night together."

It wasn't a request. It was already happening.

"I couldn't wait to get you alone," he said, undressing me.

"Do you only want me for sex?" I asked.

He chuckled. "If I only wanted sex, I wouldn't take you out."

He was charming, but I wasn't convinced this wasn't all about sex and would go beyond it. I thought the whole wanting to marry me thing was a ploy to keep me close. He didn't mention it at dinner, and I was grateful. That's what I was really nervous about because I was so tired of struggling, I didn't know if I could keep refusing.

After a night of passionate sex, I woke up in his bed. The sheets were cold on my side; Adrian was already gone. For a moment, I thought I'd dreamed the entire night. Then I saw the bracelet on the nightstand and felt the faint ache between my legs.

He'd left a note on the pillow beside me:

Help yourself to breakfast. Don't leave before I get back.

His assumptions that I didn't have anything else to do was frustrating. Why did he want me to stay? But I was curious, so I got up *and wandered barefoot into the kitchen. It was already set: fresh bread, cut fruit, coffee still warm in the pot. I ate in silence, glancing toward the door every few minutes, waiting to hear his key.*

He didn't come back for hours. When he did, he kissed me like we were something real. His hands were on my hips, his mouth rough, then softer. I asked where he'd been. He said work. Then told me to shower—we had somewhere to be.

I asked where.

"You'll see," he said.

That night, he took me to a private lounge. Everyone seemed to know him. They shook his hand, nodded at me, and asked nothing. I didn't know what the place was for—just that the women looked polished, the men confident, and I wasn't either.

When we sat down, Adrian handed me another small box. Earrings. Diamond studs.

"Why did you buy this? You just gave me a bracelet," I said.

"Because I want to spoil you."

I started to protest, but he was already watching the room again. I put them on because it was easier than arguing. After dessert, I asked if he brought all the women he was sleeping with to places like this.

He looked me in the eye and said, "I'm only sleeping with you, and I intend for it to stay that way."

I should've been more suspicious, but I didn't want to be. I wanted to believe I was the only woman he was with right now. Even though it was too good to be true.

Eleanor wanted him—that much is obvious. Maybe she wanted him for the power, or the money, or the idea of a life that looked easier than hers. And maybe she thought she could handle what came with it.

But Adrian wasn't romantic with her. At least, not at first. He was cold. Blunt. He gave her expensive things and made decisions for both of them. He didn't try to make her feel seen, at least at first. He just moved forward and expected her to keep up. I'm assuming that didn't change because she left.

With me, he's still cold, but he has moments of tenderness. But if this wasn't how he was before she left, that's scary. Changing for someone means you aren't letting them go anytime soon. You only change for people you love. I don't care what lies he tells himself. It's obvious he's in love with her—or worse, me.

17

ADRIAN

She's quiet again. Not withdrawn or tired—just quiet in that particular way that means she's thinking. Plotting. Slipping into that calm headspace I've seen before.

I cycle through the surveillance feeds: kitchen, hallway, entryway. Nothing unusual. But that only sharpens the edge in my chest, because she's been in the few places I can't see—the sitting room or the art studio.

There are no cameras in there. That was intentional. I told myself she needed one space that felt personal. A room she could claim as hers. I thought giving her a sliver of freedom might keep her compliant, might convince her she still had a choice. I left the bedrooms and bathrooms alone for the same reason. Boundaries breed trust. Or at least, that's what I told myself.

Now it feels like a mistake. She's been spending more time in that room. Long stretches of silence. No questions. No pushback. That's exactly how she was before she left.

She doesn't lash out or break things when she's unraveling. She watches. She calculates. And when she moves, you don't see it coming.

She has no phone. No access to the outside world. Greta knows better than to get too close or do anything to interfere in my personal life. There's no one to talk to. I've ordered all staff to not be seen or heard. There's nowhere to go, but still—I don't like how quiet she's gotten. She needs to have something to do.

I press the intercom. "Greta."

"Yes, Mr. Montgomery?"

"Call Margo. I want her here next week. Eleanor's wardrobe needs new clothes, full fitting. Make it a priority."

I hired Margo as her personal stylist, because she does exactly what I say. She knows my preferences, knows how to make Eleanor into what I want, and she has an entire team to handle it—clothes, hair, makeup, the works. I made her sign an NDA, so if Eleanor ever starts running her mouth, she won't repeat it or act on it. She relies on me. I'm even an investor in her clothing boutique.

"Of course."

"And plan a dinner. Keep it small. Five or six guests. Nothing over the top, just enough to get her re-engaged. I'll let you know the guest list."

I already know who should be there. Familiar faces she can't reject without exposing herself. My sister and her husband are family, so their opinions don't matter. Diane—her best friend—and Peter, her husband who's a long-time business partner. And two more bodies, someone who doesn't matter, just to make it feel casual.

"I'll take care of it." She hesitates, then adds more softly, "Sir...may I speak with you?"

"Yes, come in."

That phrasing puts me on alert. Greta is careful, always deferential, never one to push. If she's asking for a private word, it isn't trivial.

The door opens a moment later. She steps in, smoothing her apron, her eyes lowered.

I study her. "What did you want to speak to me about?" Her hands knot together at her waist. She hesitates, gaze fixed on the floor. "Mrs. Montgomery."

I don't answer until she finally lifts her eyes.

"What about her?"

"I brought tea this afternoon." Her voice catches, quiet but steady. "Sir...I think she should see a doctor."

I keep my expression flat. "Why?"

Greta swallows, her fingers tightening against her apron. "Her memory. She seems...confused. Forgetful. I thought it best to tell you."

I sit back, eyes on her. As if I don't already know that. But she won't hold my gaze for long, and that tells me enough. She's holding something back.

Greta knows her place, knows who pays her, yet here she is, pushing past the line. If she starts second-guessing me, or worse, talking to others, it becomes a problem. And I don't need her whispering doubts in the wrong ears. One careless word, and this house stops running the way I built it.

A flicker of irritation cuts through me, but I remind myself —Greta is loyal. So is her husband, the gardener. Their daughter is our chef. I employ her entire family, and that was by design. They're dependent on me. I even had them relocate here because I know where their loyalties lie. And the thought makes me smile to myself. All of them tied to me, their livelihoods, their families, their futures—built on my money, my decisions.

I don't just keep this house running, I own every piece of it. If they don't fall in line, they'll be blackballed and won't work for any prominent family here again. So as long as they're what I need them to be, they'll be paid generously for it.

"Thank you," I say evenly.

She dips her head quickly, grateful for the dismissal, and slips out the door.

Part of me thinks Ellie is pretending so that she can be the victim and take no accountability for her actions in the past. But another part thinks she truly has memory loss. Sometimes she looks at me like I'm a complete stranger, and hesitates around me in a way she wasn't before.

I'll take her to a doctor to confirm there isn't anything medically wrong with her since Greta also seems to notice and is worried. There is no reason for Ellie to pretend to have memory loss in front of her. It is my job as her husband to make sure she's healthy. But if she is, then I want the dinner party to be a test, to know how she acts in front of others. If she fails, then she'll earn the punishment I'm way too excited to give her.

18

MAREN

After Greta told me about the other staff, I'm taking my chances on the chef. I got up early this morning to slip in the chef's kitchen, which is separate from ours. It's stupid to have two kitchens. It's obvious the rich want to separate themselves from what they see as their servants. It makes me sick.

When I walk in the kitchen, it's warm, thick with the smell of garlic and herbs. Pots simmer on the stove, knives hit a cutting board in quick rhythm. The chef—a woman with dark hair pinned back, apron already stained—moves with fast, practiced motions, too focused to notice me at first. Asking Greta for help was useless, but maybe the chef won't be.

I linger near the doorway until she finally glances up. Her eyes flick to mine, then back to her work.

"Breakfast will be ready soon, Mrs. Montgomery."

"Do you remember me from before?" I ask.

She has to see I'm not the same woman, I'm different.

She stops chopping. Her expression doesn't change, but she pauses. Then the knife moves again, steady. "Of course."

"Then can't you tell I'm not the same woman?"

That makes her falter. She looks confused, her brows pulling in.

I take a step closer. "I was kidnapped by Adrian. I'm not his wife, I'm just a lookalike. Please—can you help me? I need to get back home."

Her knuckles whiten around the knife handle, the blade hovering over the board. For a second, I think she might listen. But she shakes her head hard, like the thought itself is dangerous.

"I can't."

Why is everyone so fucking scared of him that they throw morals out the window? It's obvious he's rich, but he can't be that powerful. That going against him is career ending. Or is the pay just that good that money matters more than anything else?

"Why not?"

"I don't have time," she says quickly, almost too quickly, turning back to the vegetables. Her hands move faster, knife striking wood with a clipped, nervous rhythm.

My eyes shift past her to the back door—staff entrance, narrow window, no lock turned. My pulse spikes. If I can make it there before she calls out...I take a step. Then another. My hand closes around the cool metal of the knob.

"Don't." Her voice cuts through the clatter, low and tight. I glance back. The knife is still in her hand, her eyes on me now, dark and serious. "There's no point."

My grip falters. "Why not?"

"At the front there's an iron gate, twenty feet high, and it never opens without a code. No one gets through without him knowing. Even if you did and made it to the main road, you'd still be several miles from town. And you'd have to walk. No one comes this way unless they're coming here. Even if you reached town, you'd need to get to the ferry or airport to get off the island. He'd catch you before you ever got that far. There's no way out. So there's no point."

The words are like hot water, numbing more than burning. My hand slips from the knob, and I force myself to step back, my face hot with shame even though she never raised her voice. She only turns back to the board, her blade moving fast and precise, already finished with me.

I stand there a second longer, useless, caught between wanting to scream and not daring to make a sound. My chest is tight, my throat raw. I begged her. I fucking begged, and she didn't even flinch.

"Why is everyone afraid of him?"

She sighs. "Sometimes the person you fear the most pays your bills."

She might as well have said I offer her nothing. How many people rely on him to pay their bills? Will I ever get out of here?

Then the oven beeps, and she pulls out a tray and asks, "Would you like a croissant, Mrs. Montgomery?"

I shake my head. It's like the conversation never happened, and I realized it's all for the cameras. I leave the kitchen, each step dragging, the air in the hall colder than before, like the house itself heard me try and fail. Cameras in the corners, code at the gate, ocean cutting off every other escape. The walls press in until I can barely breathe.

By the time I shut myself inside the dining room, my hands are trembling so badly I can't unclench them. I sink into a chair and fold forward, pressing my palms over my face. A sob breaks out, sharp and unwanted, gone almost as quickly as it came. I choke it back down, forcing the sound into silence, dragging in air until I can steady myself.

She said there's no way out, and for a moment, I believe her. The thought hollows me, but I know I'll keep looking. Because if I stop—even for a second—he's already won.

The door creaks behind me. Adrian walks in with his phone

in his hand. He sets it face-down on the table with a soft tap that makes me jolt.

"Get ready. We have somewhere to be," he says.

I look up at him, throat dry. "Where?"

"Appointment." He drains his coffee, eyes fixed on me the whole time.

"What kind of appointment?"

"You'll see when we get there."

He takes me through the garage. Rows of cars gleam under the lights, silent and waiting. Any of them could take me away from here, but I slide into the passenger seat because I don't have the keys, and because I don't have a choice.

The car ride is silent. I keep my eyes on the road, watching the stretch of forest swallow everything. No houses, no shops, no signs of life. Just trees closing in on both sides, endless and empty. Even if I slipped out and ran, he'd find me before long. Unless I hid in the woods—and then I'd probably never make it out. I'd get lost, starve, disappear in the very place I thought would save me.

The faint, red glow of the child lock taunts me from the door panel. He's thought of everything.

His voice cuts through the quiet. "You don't speak unless I tell you to, or you're asked a question directly. If you do, you'll be punished."

I keep my eyes forward, hands pressed together in my lap.

"I'll leave you in the basement until I decide you're ready to come out," he adds, calm, like he's talking about the weather.

The word *basement* crawls under my skin. Cold floor, dark walls, the silence pressing until I can't think. I can still feel the sting of the belt if I let myself remember too long. The thought of being locked down there again makes my stomach twist.

As we get through the desolate forest, the town is quaint. You can see the water in the distance. The town looks like any other. We aren't completely isolated like I thought, but we are secluded. When we stop, he comes around to my side. He opens the door like it's courtesy, but his hand closes around my arm before I can move. To anyone watching, it would look tender, protective. To me, it's a leash. His grip stays until I'm standing where he wants me, walking beside him into the building. "Come on, Ellie."

I follow him out, the heat rising off the pavement, every step toward those glass doors pushing the hope I had further away. I realize we are at a doctor's office, because the walls inside are the kind of beige that makes you nervous. The receptionist doesn't hand me any paperwork, so I can't slip a note. He's orchestrated everything.

Adrian sits next to me, his arm draped along the back of my chair, an unspoken reminder that I'm not here alone.

The doctor introduces himself, polite but distant, the kind of voice that makes you feel studied instead of spoken to. He starts with the easy questions about headaches, dizziness, vision problems, accidents, and head injuries. And all my answers are no.

There isn't anything wrong with me. I was kidnapped from my life. But if I say that, I'm fucked. If I could just have a second alone with the doctor, then maybe I can tell him the truth.

He leans forward. "So you can cook, clean, drive, do basic tasks—but your actual memories are lost?"

I haven't done any of those things since I've been kidnapped. But I did it all before I was.

"Yes." My hands twist together. "I don't remember getting married or anything that he says..." My throat catches.

Adrian interjects smoothly, his voice calm. "She went on vacation, and then went missing for months. When I found her, she didn't recognize me. She was living under another name, with memories of a life that didn't exist."

That's the story he's going with? I went on vacation, got lost, and forgot who I was? That makes me sound crazy, when he's the one who's actually insane.

The doctor frowns, jotting something down. "Interesting. Let's do a brief cognitive test."

Adrian's hand squeezes my shoulder lightly, a signal to cooperate. The questions come quick, my mind blanking when I need it most. He slides a paper across, tells me to copy a shape, and my hand shakes enough to skew the lines. He tells me to remember three words, and I forget one of the three words he gave me. The scratch of his pen feels louder than his voice. Adrian doesn't say anything, but his silence beside me is worse than correction.

The doctor closes the folder. "We'll run imaging and run some bloodwork to see what we may be dealing with."

They take blood from me and send me to imaging. The MRI swallows me whole, the machine clanging like a factory. Adrian watches from the door, hands in his pockets, calm as I lie still. I try to hold on to my memories of the Rusty Nail, and every sticky, nasty detail.

By the time we leave, I'm buzzing with nerves. Adrian opens the car door, his hand brushing my back.

"You did well in there," he says on the road.

It sounds like praise, but I can't tell if it is.

"Was that the point? To see if I'd behave?"

He smiles faintly. "It was about getting answers. I promised you I'd always take care of you. This proves it."

Proves what? That I'm Eleanor? That I can be shaped into her? Or that if a doctor stamps me as healthy but crazy, then I'll never get out?

Back at the house, the silence feels suffocating. He loosens his tie and studies me.

"You're quiet."

"Just tired."

He comes close and rubs my cheek. "Are you alright?"

He sounds like a concerned husband, but I'm not buying this act.

The truth slips out. "I'm terrified."

He cups my face and kisses me. "We'll get through this together. I'm here. Always."

I nod, because that's what I'm supposed to do. But I don't believe him. Not for a second.

Every day I sit in the room, staring out the window at the ocean until the light fades. I can't even bring myself to open the journal. I don't want to think about that woman, especially not her thoughts. Adrian leaves me alone during the day, while I assume he buries himself in work. At night he makes me come, even when my mind wants nothing to do with him.

A week later, we're back at the doctor. Adrian looks relaxed, ankle crossed over his knee, while I sit like I'm waiting for a verdict for my prison sentence.

The doctor clicks through images, then freezes one on the screen. "Everything looks completely normal. No brain damage or signs of disease."

Normal. The word strips me bare even though I knew nothing was wrong with me.

"So what does that mean?" I ask.

"We look at psychological explanations. Mental illness. Trauma. Stress-related dissociation. That could explain the memory loss."

The word rings in my ears like an alarm. I don't have memory or psychological problems.

Adrian leans forward with a smug smile I want to wipe off his face. "So she should see a psychiatrist?"

This is exactly the story Adrian wants written down. The perfect excuse to keep me here for good.

"Yes. I think that's the next best step."

I nod, numb. But inside, panic builds. This is how it happens. Once they put on file that Eleanor Montgomery is delusional, no one will listen. No one will ever believe the truth. I'll never leave this house, this island, this life. I'll be his forever.

Adrian stays calm, but I sit there, staring at my own brain on the screen. I've just been handed the paperwork for my erasure.

The drive home is quiet. Adrian keeps one hand on the wheel and the other wrapped around mine, his grip constant the whole way. I lean against the window, the glass cool against my temple, pretending to be absorbed by the blur of trees and water flashing past.

Freedom keeps circling my mind in pieces I can't shake. If I'd had even a few minutes alone with the doctor, I could've told the truth. I could've said I wasn't his wife, that I'd been taken. But Adrian never left my side. He wouldn't risk it. This was my chance, and it's already gone.

The scans showing normal activity don't mean relief, because Adrian will twist that into whatever suits him. If I push too far, if I refuse to let this go, he'll probably have me taken to a hospital. Lock me up, medicate me, erase me for good.

By the time we pull into the garage, my chest aches from holding it in. He doesn't let go of my hand as we walk inside.

Later, I slip into the bathroom alone. The mirror over the sink throws back a version of me I barely recognize. My hair, my eyes, my skin—it all belongs to someone I don't know how to be. I run the faucet and let the water pour too long, just for the sound, just to pretend I'm somewhere else.

But when I step back into the bedroom, he's already waiting.

That night, I lie on my side of the bed, facing the wall, pretending sleep might shield me. I've barely looked at him since we got home, every excuse to move away from him used up, until now there's nowhere left to go.

The mattress dips as he shifts closer. His hand finds my hip under the blanket, warm and steady, and I freeze.

"You've been quiet since we left the doctor's office," he says. His voice is soft, but it feels like pressure in the dark.

"I'm just tired."

He doesn't buy it. "You've been avoiding me."

My throat tightens. "Are you going to take me to the psychiatrist?"

"No. That appointment was enough. If there had been damage, I would've gotten you treatment. But you're fine."

My stomach twists. "So that's it? You're not worried at all about what he said?"

"That's it." His thumb brushes the curve of my hip, and he sounds almost patient. "You don't need anyone else trying to interfere. If you need reminders, I'll give them to you. If we're in front of others, I'll prompt you. And if anyone asks questions, we'll tell them you had an accident and it caused memory loss. That's all anyone needs to know."

The neatness of it makes me cold. He's already built the cover story, decided what the world will see. It erases me before I even open my mouth.

I turn toward him, blinking back tears. "But I'm telling you —I don't remember marrying you. I don't remember this house, this life, any of it. Doesn't that matter to you at all?"

His eyes catch mine in the dark. There's no hesitation. "It matters to me that you say it. But it doesn't make it true." His hand presses firmer against my hip, holding me still. "The scans proved you're healthy. This is you holding on to a story that doesn't exist."

My breath stumbles. "Why would I do that?"

His mouth curves, faint but sharp. "Because you've always had a way of avoiding things when life gets too much. But that stops here. You are my wife. And no amount of pretending changes that. Do you understand me?"

The word *pretending* hits harder than anything else tonight. To him, it's not confusion or trauma. It's me choosing to deny him.

I swallow the words I want to say, because if I push, he'll punish me. If I stay quiet, maybe he'll believe silence means agreement. But inside, the panic won't stop. If he thinks I'm just pretending, then nothing I say will ever matter. He'll twist it until I'm the liar, the one making things up, the one who's broken.

And that means there's no way out.

I force the words out before I can stop myself. "So you don't care if I have some kind of mental illness?"

The word *illness* makes me cringe the second it's out. I don't want to hand him an excuse to brand me as *crazy* when I know I'm not.

He doesn't even pause. "No. Because you don't."

I twist the blanket between my hands. "You just don't want me to talk to anyone about how I feel."

His hand tightens on my hip, firm enough to warn me. "You're right, I don't. I'm not letting someone drive a wedge between us by entertaining these ideas. You're mine, Ellie. And I won't let anyone convince you otherwise."

The word *wedge* clings to me. If my truth is treated as a wedge, then saying it out loud is already a betrayal. There's no way to win.

His voice hardens. "And I don't want you to talk about this again, and definitely not with anyone else. If you bring it up, people will start asking questions. That won't end well for you."

"I won't," I whisper, because it's safer than silence.

But even as the words leave me, I know they mean nothing. Even if I had the chance, what would I say? *Help me, I'm not his wife?* He'd twist it before the words left my mouth. He'd make me the liar, the unstable one, and I'd be the one punished for it.

No one would believe me, not with the way he speaks so confidently.

His hand stays there. "Everything will be okay, Ellie. If you have questions about the past, I'll answer them for you."

If he thinks nothing is wrong, why would I be asking questions about the past, and why would he be so willing to answer them if he's convinced I remember?

Unless that means he has doubts about either my mental health or even my identity. Maybe I have a fighting chance if I can convince him. Or he chalks it up as I'm delusional, but I don't know what he'd do about that, nor do I want to know. The words only raise more questions I can't ask, and every one of them closes a door.

19

MAREN

The next morning, Adrian leads me down the hall with a hand on my back, guiding me as if I might change direction if he lets go. We stop outside a door as he reaches for the handle, then glances at me. His face is a blank mask, showing nothing, and it stays that way as he leans closer, his voice low and firm.

"You do what you're told. Don't speak unless spoken to. They're not here to chat, and you don't mention your health issues. Understand?"

I almost laugh. Health issues. There's nothing wrong with me. Nothing except him.

I nod anyway, my throat tight.

Then he opens the door.

The change is instant. His hardness falls away, replaced by a smile so smooth it feels real, his green eyes soft, warm, husbandly. The shift is so sudden it jars me, and I realize it isn't meant for me at all. It's for whoever's waiting. He doesn't even do this in front of the staff.

"Eleanor, you remember Margo, right?" he asks casually. I

start to answer, but a tall woman with a sharp jawline and even sharper heels steps into view. She has short, black hair and brown eyes. She's dressed like a magazine spread. Leopard-print pants, a black, silk blouse tucked neatly at the waist, and stilettos that make her taller than Adrian. A Louis Vuitton bag hangs from her wrist like it's part of her ensemble.

"Eleanor," she says with a wide smile. "It's been too long. How have you been?"

I force a nod. "Yeah...of course. Hi," I lie, because I have no idea who she is, but I know I'm supposed to.

She kisses the air near my cheek, leaving a light trace of her floral perfume in her wake.

Adrian doesn't wait. "I'll leave you two to it."

I want to call after him and ask what's happening, but he's already gone. Margo's heels click against the floor as she turns and gestures for me to follow. "Come on, let's get you looking like yourself again."

That makes me pause, but I move anyway, trailing behind her down the hall, upstairs to a door next to our bedroom. No, not ours. *His* bedroom. She walks like she owns the house, like she's done this dozens of times.

The room she opens is huge. It resembles a designer boutique more than a closet. Adrian has picked out my clothes so I haven't been in it, nor did I care to. Racks of clothes are organized by color, while custom shelves are filled with shoes. Jewelry sparkles under the lights like it's on display for an auction. I spot pastels, creams, pale blues, and soft yellow clothes for brunches and country club patios. It all makes my stomach turn. This is a transformation chamber.

Margo picks up a measuring tape from the counter. "Let's take a look at what we're working with."

She doesn't ask for permission before she starts wrapping the tape around me.

She hums softly while checking numbers. "Your bust is bigger," she says, half to herself. "And your waist, too. You're curvier now."

I clench my jaw. My stomach turns so sharply I'm afraid I might throw up.

"I suppose that happens when you trade fine dining for fried food."

I smile like I didn't hear her, even though I think she's a bitch. If I weren't in this situation, I'd tell her to fuck off, but that's not how I'm supposed to act.

That's not how Eleanor is supposed to act.

She lays a few dresses across the chair. Pastels. Lace. High society brunch chic. I imagine myself in them, sitting between women with tight smiles and manicured claws, all of them asking about their skincare routine while sipping mimosas. That sounds awful. I am a t-shirt and sweatpants kind of girl.

The only time I wore dresses on a regular basis was when one of my foster families dragged me to church every Sunday. It was my first time being exposed to religion. I almost believed in it because they were the kindest family I ever had. I prayed they would adopt me since they couldn't have a child of their own. Then one day my foster mother said their prayers had been answered, and she was pregnant. But mine weren't. But maybe I should start again, this time asking for my own miracle of escape.

I shake my head and push the memory away. I study Margo as she glides through the room, pulling out accessories and pairing shoes. She doesn't question anything. She looks at me and sees Eleanor without a second thought.

Whatever differences there are between us, they don't matter. People see what they want to see. Two women arrive. One heads straight to a bathroom door that has a shampoo station. The other starts unpacking a case of nail polish on the vanity. I sit where they tell me, my legs stiff, my hands resting on the chair's arms.

Margo runs her fingers through my hair. "You need a trim."

"I want a cut," I say.

I can't keep looking like Eleanor. She had long, luscious hair, and mine pales in comparison.

She pauses. "Mr. Montgomery prefers it long."

Fuck what Adrian thinks. I bet he sat down with her and told him exactly what he likes, because my preference doesn't matter in this life.

I look at her through the mirror. "And I want it short. I trust you to make it look good."

Her mouth opens, but no sound comes out. There's a flicker of nervousness in her eyes.

But then she forces a smile and nods. "Of course. It's up to you."

It takes hours. I stay silent through it, letting them move me like a mannequin. If I speak, I'll break character. So I don't.

Soon, my long, wavy locks are gone. The new cut is a chin-length bob, slightly angled, with longer pieces at the front that frame my face. It shows off my jaw and neck. I look less like her and more like me, and it's freeing. I barely recognize the woman in the mirror.

Margo dresses me in a soft beige pastel dress with matching tan heels. The fabric is soft and expensive, made to be admired, not worn. The heels hurt my feet. I only wore tennis shoes or boots before.

When I leave the room, Adrian is waiting at the bottom of the stairs. His gaze flickers as I step into view. It moves from my heels to my hips, then lingers on my face. There's a shift in his expression, first surprise, then cold restraint. But underneath it, I can still see the desire in the way his jaw tenses.

"You look..." His jaw tightens, but he recovers quickly. "Stunning."

It doesn't sound like a compliment, but a correction. As if he was prepared to criticize, but remembered just in time that even husbands who control everything don't tell their wives they hate their haircut. Not if they're smart. And while Adrian is many things, stupid isn't one of them. And if he hates it, I don't care. It doesn't hurt my feelings.

He offers his arm like I didn't cut off everything he thinks I should be. I take it because there's no choice. We're being watched. The heels click softly against the marble floor as we walk together down the hall.

Dinner is just as elaborate as always. The lighting is dim and warm, candles flickering along the center of the table beside a fresh bouquet. There's roasted meat and vegetables drizzled in a glaze.

I sit where he pulls out a chair for me, smoothing my dress and folding my hands in my lap.

"How did your day go?" he asks, his tone casual.

I pause. Most of my day was spent being measured, styled, and dressed like a mannequin. It wasn't difficult, but it wasn't fulfilling, either. I didn't do anything that mattered. It was superficial, and that's never been a word to describe me.

"Good," I say, keeping my voice even. "I tried on a lot of clothes."

His smile is brief. He nods, cutting into his food. "That's good. You deserve to be taken care of."

"What about you? How was your day?"

"Great," he says easily. "Closed a deal on some property I've been watching for a while."

I blink, caught off guard. "What do you do again?"

He pauses, his fork hovering above the plate. He looks at me like I just asked him how to spell his name. "I own a business that designs luxury homes, hotels, and lounges. Business is booming on Creswell. People are flocking here."

I know it's not appropriate to ask, but I need to know how

rich this guy is. He must have millions for people to be intimidated by him.

"How much money do you have?"

He raises an eyebrow. "At this point, billions."

My mouth drops. *No fucking way*. He's full of shit.

"How? Designing homes can't make you that much money."

He leans back slightly, gauging my expression. "It was founded by my father, but I was able to expand around the world. The money I made allowed me to invest in real estate and other industries, which helped grow my wealth. That's how I can give you anything you want."

I never had anything I wanted in material things. Growing up in foster care, I had nothing of my own. Only a bag full of clothes and my birth certificate, just in case I was randomly moved to another home. Compared to mine, his life sounds polished and perfectly curated, just like this room.

I nod slowly and return to my plate, chewing carefully. His answer tells me more than he realizes. Not just about his money. But about what he thinks I should want.

"We're having people over for dinner this weekend," Adrian says, checking his watch.

I turn toward him. "Dinner?"

I almost cheer. I haven't seen people in forever. Hopefully some of them have morals and can help me get out of here. But another thought comes—what if I just sound crazy? Will they believe him or me if I say I'm not his wife? Who am I kidding, they will think I'm insane.

He nods. "Small gathering."

"How many people?"

"Six," he says. "Diane and Peter. Chance and Sasha. Josie and Frank."

I have no idea who these people are. All couples, and that alone tells me what this is. He's showing me off. I wonder if he's testing me, seeing if I can fool people into thinking I'm Eleanor. But if I fail, I'm not sure I'll be allowed to leave the table. But could one of them be willing to help me? Will they see that I'm not his wife? If I could get one of them alone, it could be my escape or aid in my destruction.

20

MAREN

I have been on edge the last few days thinking about this dinner. Adrian of course picks out what he wants me to wear, an elegant, short, pink dress, and it makes me want to vomit. He also hands me a wedding ring, and it's a huge, gaudy diamond. It's so big it's weighing my finger down.

When the doorbell rings, Adrian adjusts the cuff of his shirt, smooths his jacket, and walks toward the foyer without looking at me. I follow, forcing my face into something neutral as I fix my dress and tuck my hair behind my ears.

He opens the door before Greta can reach it.

"Diane, Peter," he says warmly. "Come in."

The first couple steps inside. The woman has long, dark hair, a thin face with sharp cheekbones, and red lipstick. She wears a green, silk, wrap dress and black heels. Her nails are painted the same color as her lips. She looks like the type who's on the board of some charity. Her husband follows, clean-shaven with graying hair and a navy suit. His shoes are polished. Probably a lawyer or old money. Maybe both.

"Eleanor," Diane says with a smile. "It's been too long."

She leans in to kiss both cheeks. I copy her. Her perfume

hits me instantly, strong and floral, probably expensive. I hate it even though I'm sure the same scent is in my own collection.

"It's good to see you again."

"How's your mom doing?" she asks.

Adrian didn't tell me what he told these people. I never thought about Eleanor's parents. Could they help me?

"She's doing great."

"Glad to hear her health is improving."

Peter, I assume, gives me a quick hug. His cologne is sharp and fresh. He probably just applied it in the car. "You look lovely as always."

"Thank you," I say. He smiles too easily, like he doesn't notice anything out of place.

The doorbell chimes again. Adrian opens it without a word, but this time with a subtle grin.

"Chance, Sasha," he says, stepping aside. "Right on time."

The next couple walks in. The man is tall and tan, with short, dark hair slicked back like he spends too much time in front of a mirror. He wears a gray suit with the top buttons undone and no tie. Probably thinks that makes him edgy. The woman next to him has long, blonde hair in a low ponytail and green eyes. Her silver dress hugs her hips and stops just below the knees.

Her heels are sharp and white. She walks like she expects people to get out of her way.

We go through the same motions. More cheek kisses. More practiced smiles. But her smile isn't genuine at all.

She looks at me, my shoes, dress, and my face, and her eyes stay too long. "Still using Margo, I'm assuming," she says. There's no warmth in her voice. She isn't just looking for flaws, she's out for blood.

I pause before answering. "Margo is amazing. This dress is a one-of-a-kind."

She tilts her head like she's trying to find the flaw. "Hmm. I don't know if it is."

I hold her stare. "It fits like it is."

She says nothing else. Her mouth tightens, and she turns away. She clearly doesn't like me. That makes two of us.

The next couple arrives last. The bell rings again, and Adrian's already moving.

"Josie, Frank," he says, his voice still smooth. "Glad you made it."

They're older. The woman wears a beige dress with matching earrings. Her dark brown hair is streaked with gray and curled at the ends. Her lipstick is light pink. The man beside her is heavier, with a round face and a dark suit that strains across his stomach. His tie is crooked.

They greet me warmly, as if nothing has changed. There's no hesitation or second glances, and that's what gets to me. I can't believe the absurdity of it all. My name is Maren Bellamy, but why is it starting to feel like a lie? They don't question anything—not my tone, nor the way I stand, nor how I answer. They see the dress, the hair, and they see Eleanor. It doesn't matter that I'm not her; that's all they want to see. I stand in a room full of strangers, deceiving every one of them. And they all believe me.

The dining room is already set. The table is long and narrow, with white linen napkins folded over gold-rimmed plates. There are two sets of wineglasses at each place, one for red and one for white. A floral centerpiece runs the length of the table. White roses, eucalyptus, and long-stemmed greens are arranged beautifully.

Adrian pulls out a chair for me on his right. I sit without hesitation, because hesitating would make them look twice. He sits at the head. Everyone else finds their seats like this is normal, like this is just another Saturday night in someone's perfect life.

Greta enters with the first course. Small bowls of creamy soup sprinkled with herbs. I can't tell what kind. Everything smells unfamiliar.

The conversation begins like a script. Peter launches into a story about his latest golf trip. His voice is too loud, like he needs everyone to know he's important, it reaching a crescendo while he brags about his hole-in-one. Chance interrupts to name-drop a place in the Caribbean he went to. Sasha laughs too hard. It's fake, but she knows how to work a table. Josie and Frank stay quiet. They're more observers than participants. Diane scans the room like she's tracking wrinkles and weight gain in real time.

I eat slowly and keep my back straight. I match their pacing, their tone. I smile when they smile. I nod when the topic shifts. I act like I've sat at this table a hundred times. But I haven't. And every second I do this, I feel like I'm one question away from slipping.

"Eleanor," Diane says suddenly, her eyes sharp and her tone light. "Are you still painting?"

My hand tightens around the spoon. She could've asked anything, and she picked that.

Adrian doesn't flinch. He looks at me like he's waiting for the performance to continue.

I set the spoon down. "Not as much as I used to," I say.

She tilts her head, smiling like she knows something I don't. "That's surprising. You're so talented. Didn't you have a piece in that gallery in Chicago?"

I nod. "A few years ago."

I have no idea which gallery Eleanor showed in, if she even did. I'm guessing. I don't have room to hesitate.

"She took a break since she hasn't had much time once her mom got sick. It was hard on her taking care of her full-time," Adrian adds, cutting in smoothly. "We've been keeping her paintings more private since."

He calls it a break, like Eleanor went on sabbatical and didn't disappear from his life on purpose. I wonder what they'd think of Eleanor's erotic paintings. Adrian wouldn't want them out in public, but could they be worth a lot. If I could sell them, that could be my ticket out of here.

Sasha picks up her wineglass and turns her body slightly toward me. Her green eyes are sharper than before. "You really haven't painted at all? That seems unlike you."

I keep my tone level. "I've been focusing on other things."

Inside, I'm frozen. She's baiting me, testing for cracks. She doesn't entirely believe my performance.

She glances at Adrian, then back at me, but this time her smile tightens at the corners, too sharp to be polite. "I suppose there's no need when you have a house like this."

"Or a husband like him," Chance says. He grins like he's charming, but he's not.

But what he's saying is true. Adrian calls the shots in this marriage.

Adrian laughs softly, like it's the compliment he was waiting for.

I want to throw the wine in his face. Instead, I smile. "It's nice to have options."

Greta returns to clear the soup and replace it with plates of roasted duck and vegetables. Everything smells like a five-star chef cooked it.

Frank speaks for the first time. "Adrian, did I hear right? You bought that property by the cliffs?"

Adrian nods. "Closed on it last week."

"That's prime land," Peter says. "Any plans?"

Adrian pauses just long enough for everyone to wait. "I'll hold it for now. The right use will show itself. Maybe a retreat, maybe something bigger. I don't rush decisions."

Chance leans back. "Always the mystery. One day you'll let us in before the walls go up."

Adrian smiles, just a curve at the corner of his mouth. "Where's the fun in that?"

The line lands, drawing laughter, but I see how they look at him—half amused, half wary. He likes that balance. I think about how he said he had billions. That probably means he's planning to build something big.

Then Josie speaks. "Are you two thinking about expanding the family?"

Something cold sinks into my gut. I don't know if it shows, but I feel it pressing against my skin, curling like a secret I can't afford.

Adrian looks amused. "We've talked about it."

No, we haven't. Not once. Not even indirectly. I don't even want to think about it. We've been having unprotected sex, and the thought of being pregnant scares me. Because I would be stuck with him forever.

I force a soft laugh. "In the very distant future."

Hopefully I'll be gone in the near future.

Diane turns to me with a serious face. "Eleanor, you used to talk about children all the time."

I don't even know what Eleanor dreamed of, but they expect me to remember it.

I glance at Adrian. He gives Diane a look. It lasts barely a second, but it's enough. She quiets, but *why?*

Sasha tilts her glass toward me. "Why wait? With a house this size, and Adrian..." Her tone trails like it's an invitation for me to stumble.

Adrian turns his smile on her, polite but edged. "Timing matters. We'd rather enjoy each other a little longer."

His non-committal answer is relieving, because children isn't on his mind for now.

The table hums again, laughter filling the pause. He makes it seem easy.

Conversation picks up. Adrian plays host perfectly, never

dominating but always present, each time the table revolves around him. He listens, answers when asked, and adds just enough wit to keep the spotlight on him.

I pick up my water and slowly sip so I don't have to answer. I can feel Sasha's eyes on me again, watching every move.

The conversation continues, but I don't hear most of it. I sit there, chewing food I can't taste, answering questions with the voice of someone I'm not. I keep my hands still. My posture is perfect, and my expression is easy. I don't slip. I can't. But every question is a trap, and every smile is a mask. Every second I sit at this table, I pretend to be a woman who stopped existing when she walked away from Adrian Montgomery.

We're halfway through the main course when Sasha decides to strike. She lifts her wineglass, swirling the deep, red liquid as she watches me. Her tone sounds casual, but I know she chose her moment deliberately.

"So, Eleanor, really where have you been these last several months?" she asks.

My fork pauses halfway to my mouth, but she keeps smiling and leans closer. "We've wanted to see the house for ages, but Adrian said you were also volunteering." Her head tilts a little. "Where did you go? And for which charities?"

My mind blanks completely. I can't think of a single charity. Not one. I could name luxury brands faster than I could name a place that helps people. I've never had a life where giving money away was an option. I've always been the one needing help. I'm sure I benefited from a few growing up, but I have no idea which ones.

I glance at Adrian, but he doesn't say a word. He lifts his glass and takes a slow sip of wine, his face staying unreadable. His silence says enough—I'm on my own. He's letting me fumble, watching me dig myself deeper. This is a setup so he can punish me later. But I won't flinch.

I take a steady breath. "I left the country. Spent time in

South America helping families in remote areas. The sick. Mostly people who needed basic medical supplies. I love helping people."

That sounds like a damn good answer for off the fly, but everyone is staring, wanting more.

I pause and nod faintly. "I also taught art classes while I was there. Most of the kids didn't have access to education, let alone art supplies."

That sounds believable, she's an artist helping kids make art.

Sasha raises her brows, her smile tightening. "How admirable. So...you left Adrian to help kids with crayons?"

When you phrase it like that, it does sound really fucking stupid. But I'm not backing down.

I stare her down. "Yes. I did."

She doesn't believe me. It is written all over her face. Her smile is too sharp, her eyes cutting through me. She's been waiting for me to trip. But why does she care so much about what I was doing? There is something I'm missing here. But I don't know what.

Adrian sets down his glass. "Sasha, education should be available to anyone. Education looks different for different people," he says, smooth but firm. Finally, he says something, but the damage is done.

Her voice softens to sweet. "Of course, Adrian. I was just curious."

She glances back at me. "Tell me the name of the charity. We'll donate. I'd love to support it."

I swallow. "Adrian can text it to you."

He quickly looks at me. He's the idiot who made up the charity lie. I don't have a phone, so he can tell her the name of one.

She tilts her head. "Why can't you? Do you still have my number?"

"I don't have a phone." The words slip out before I can stop them.

Adrian's head snaps toward me. His face doesn't change, but the energy in the room shifts. The table falls quiet for a second too long.

"I just...don't anymore," I say quickly, trying to brush it off. "I haven't needed one."

Sasha's smile widens, and she gestures at the house. "Strange. You've got all this." She pauses. "But no phone?"

She glances at Adrian. "Get your wife a new phone. She deserves it. Don't you think?"

Adrian nods once. "She has one, she just doesn't like to use it."

It's a lie, but no one questions it. The conversation picks back up. Laughter spills again as glasses clink. But I feel it. The slip. The damage. And Adrian won't forget.

After dessert, Diane folds her napkin and looks at me. "Eleanor, would you mind giving us a tour? I'd love to see the house."

Adrian's voice cuts in from across the table. "Start with the lounge."

I rise, smiling like it was my idea. "Of course. I'd love to."

They follow me from the dining room. My heels click against the marble as we move down the hall. The house feels even bigger tonight with wide halls, vaulted ceilings, and soft light from the chandeliers.

Peter and Chance drift closer to Adrian. They murmur about construction details.

"Peter's company built it," Adrian says. "We've worked together on several properties."

So they're business partners. That explains their easy rapport. I wonder if Peter knows what Adrian's really like or if he only sees the polished version.

We stop in a sitting room by the staircase. Cream couches

line the walls around a single glass coffee table. A chandelier glows overhead and spills a sterile light across the polished floor. It is an impressive house.

"This is one of my favorite spaces," I say, glancing around. "It's where I relax. I like sitting here with friends, drinking tea, reading."

Sasha's voice calls from behind me. "The friends who also don't have phones?"

I freeze. Though my smile holds, my stomach flips. I feel Adrian's gaze from across the room. When I glance his way, his jaw is tight. His hands are buried in his pockets. I know that look. He's angry, but I don't know if it's at her or at me. He won't say anything here, but he will later.

"I've enjoyed disconnecting," I say, smoothing my voice. "It's been nice. Not always being reachable."

Nobody responds. I move forward like nothing shifted. "And this room."

As I open the next door, Adrian's voice follows softly from behind. "Show them the view."

We step into the back living room. A long sectional wraps around a marble fireplace. Floor-to-ceiling windows overlook the garden.

"This one's more casual," I say. "Adrian and I usually sit here in the mornings. Sometimes we read the paper together."

Peter runs his hand along the back of the couch. "Beautiful fabric. Imported?"

"Yes," I answer quickly.

Frank lets out a low whistle. "You've got the best view on the island."

Sasha edges closer to the glass. "Some people would kill for a view like this. Not everyone deserves this."

I stiffen, but she doesn't look at me when she says it. She gazes out into the garden, her reflection sharp in the glass.

Adrian steps up beside her, his voice smooth. "We enjoy it."

Josie moves closer to the painting above the fireplace. "This one's interesting. Did you pick it out?"

"Yes." I nod. "It reminded me of a trip to the coast."

Adrian steps beside me, his voice sliding in smoothly. "Barcelona. It was raining that day."

I nod again, covering the stumble. "Yes. Barcelona."

Frank studies the frame quietly while I lead them through more rooms. A guest room with blue walls.

A study I call "Adrian's retreat," though I've never seen him inside it. A gallery hall lined with abstract paintings I couldn't explain if I tried.

Diane stays close to me, her smile feeling softer now, more cautious, like she senses how hard I'm trying to hold it together.

I narrate the house like I belong, but I'm fumbling. I forgot which room I described earlier. I call a lounge a library. I correct myself when no books are in sight.

I point to a chair and say I journal there even though I haven't written a word since I've been here. I'm walking through a life that doesn't belong to me. I'm reading a script I don't know. And Sasha. She catches every slip. She crosses her arms, trailing me in perfect rhythm. Her eyes tracking everything.

As the tour winds down, Adrian's voice floats over. His tone is quiet but final. "End with the gallery."

I lead them toward the gallery hall, feeling every step.

Diane steps closer and lowers her voice. "Would you show me the bathroom?"

"Of course." I nod and guide her down the hall, stopping near a door.

Before I can open it, she grabs my wrist and pulls the door open herself. She steps inside, tugging me in with her as the door shuts behind us.

The light is already on. The marble sink gleams as towels hang neatly on the rack.

She turns to face me, her smile now gone. "What the fuck are you doing back here?"

My throat tightens. I try to speak, but nothing comes.

"I don't know what you're talking about."

Her stare sharpens. "Don't play dumb."

I freeze.

"I helped you get out of Chicago." Her voice drops lower. "And now you're back like none of it happened."

She helped Eleanor leave. Could she help me? I want to tell her she's wrong. I want to beg. But if I say I'm not Eleanor, she'll think I'm crazy. Worse, she'll tell Adrian. And Adrian will punish me.

I force a shallow breath. "I don't know what you mean."

She studies me for a moment. "You used to be smarter than this."

She opens the door and walks out, her heels clicking down the hall like nothing happened. I didn't even get a chance to speak, let alone ask for help. I stay in the bathroom, staring at my reflection. My pulse pounds in my ears. I don't know what scares me more—what she knows or what she'll do with it.

As the last goodbyes are said and the door finally closes, I let out a slow breath. The hallway is quiet now, too quiet. My thoughts are a mess—circling, crashing, all tangled together.

Tonight was a shit show. I fumbled. I lied badly. And if I think it was bad, then Adrian definitely does. That's how it works with him. Every misstep echoes back louder. But he should've fucking helped me. I would've done better if he just threw me a life raft instead of letting me drown.

He holds onto the doorknob for a few seconds too long, jaw tight, then turns toward me. His eyes land on mine, and I already know what's coming.

"You're rusty, Eleanor," he says flatly, no emotion. That's worse than anger.

"I didn't realize how much your social skills had suffered

since you left me," he continues. "But when you spend your time working at a dive bar, using your tits for tips, this is what happens."

The words hit hard, sending my blood spiking. "I'm a damn good bartender," I snap. "Give me a bar and I'll make the best damn drink you've ever had."

He chuckles, because he knows he got to me. "Okay, Ellie."

I feel it like a slap. "Don't call me fucking Ellie."

His expression shifts to anger. "I'll call you whatever I want."

Something in me snaps. "Well fuck you, Adrian. This was a setup, the entire night. Some test, right? You wanted me to look unprepared and stupid."

He doesn't deny it. "I needed to see where you're at," he says calmly. "Before we host anything more important. Bigger events. Higher stakes. People who matter."

I laugh bitterly. "And what? I failed?"

He steps closer, slow and steady. "You did."

My fists clench at my sides. I want to scream, or cry, or punch something. Instead, I stand there in the expensive dress he chose, with my fresh haircut and aching feet, swallowing the truth that this night was never about me succeeding. It was about him knowing exactly where my weaknesses are.

This was proof I'm a poor substitute to his beautiful, polished, submissive wife. If he can't see it and they can't, then I have no chance on getting out of this hell.

21

ADRIAN

Tonight was a fucking disaster. I stand by the door a moment longer, staring at the space where Sasha and Chance were standing.

Right now, I'm beyond angry. I'm disappointed, and I don't like being disappointed. She humiliated herself—and by extension, me. But if I helped her too much, then I couldn't gauge what she needs to improve on, at events I can't be by her side the entire time.

The good thing is it wasn't board members, investors, potential clients, or anyone whose opinion actually matters. That would have been catastrophic.

I turn to look at her. She's standing in the hallway, trying to look composed. But I can see the panic under her skin. The stiffness in her shoulders. The way her hands are balled at her sides. She has completely lost everything we worked so hard to build together.

The way she spoke tonight was flat, uncertain, grasping at half-truths. It wasn't just embarrassing. It was infuriating. She couldn't carry on a conversation.

She couldn't name a single charity. She used to be able to

talk about charity all day, she's volunteered for many. And then she had the nerve to claim she'd been helping kids with art in South America.

I grit my teeth. That was the worst lie I've ever heard. Sasha didn't believe her for a second. I wouldn't have, either. That story wouldn't pass a ten-second Google search. It wouldn't hold up in a room full of people who sit on boards, write checks with six zeroes, and talk about causes as a form of social currency. I don't know what to do with her now.

Etiquette courses might help. She needs them. Even though she was a waitress, she worked at a very classy establishment and knew how to carry herself. She needs to relearn posture, language, and timing. But that won't fix the root of the problem.

She doesn't know how to exist in my world anymore. She's forgotten how to speak it, how to move through it, how to control it. I cannot afford a liability. But I can't get rid of her, either. Being married helps me get new clients, investors, impress board members because in my world, a wife helps foster those relationships by being a great hostess.

I don't have time to start from scratch. And replacing her means I'll have to get divorced. But that's not an option. We don't have a prenup. She was offended when I first brought it up. She was very convincing on her belief that marriage was for life, and thought we shouldn't be planning for a divorce. Plus, I was convinced she'd never leave me. But she did, and a divorce would be messy, public, and take years.

But she's back, and now she's mine to deal with. Mine to correct and manage, whether she's ready for that or not. I'll fix it. I always do.

Next time, there won't be room for mistakes. There is nothing medically wrong with her. Unless…she's suffering from memory loss or delusions. It's not the first time it's crossed my mind, but I've pushed it aside again and again. I refused to believe it. I told myself it was a deflection. She was manipulating, stalling, and avoiding consequences.

But what if it's not any of that? What if she's confused and disoriented from some trauma I don't know about that she suffered when she left? What if something is genuinely wrong and she's suffering from a mental illness? If she's been struggling all this time, and I've been treating her like she's lying? Then I haven't just failed to manage her—I've been punishing someone who needed help.

That makes me the one who failed. But I don't want to take her to a psychiatrist and have them dissect our lives. But I also can't fail her. I'll figure something out, even if I have to resort to unconventional ways. I look at her again, and she hasn't moved. Her arms are stiff at her sides. Her dress is perfect. Her hair is in place. But her eyes are the only honest thing left on her face. She looks lost and scared.

When I step toward her, she doesn't move. I wrap my arms around her and pull her close. She tenses at first, then softens —just barely—against my chest.

"It's alright," I murmur into her hair. "I'll fix you."

Because that's what I do. I fix things. And I care about her more than I should, more than I ever planned to. And for a moment, I almost believe it. Until the next thought comes—I didn't break anything. She did by leaving me.

But comfort alone won't correct her. She won't learn from being held, from empty reassurances. If I let this go, she'll make another scene, next time in front of people who matter. She needs structure, consequences, something she'll remember the next time she opens her mouth.

I smooth a hand down her back, steady, almost tender, while my mind is already made up. She needs to be reminded of her place. Reminded that with me, mistakes have a cost.

I press a final kiss to her temple, then draw back just

enough to meet her eyes. "Let's go to the basement," I say quietly.

Her eyes search mine, wary, the panic she's trying to swallow showing anyway. "Adrian, it was one mistake," she says quietly, but firm enough that it grates.

One mistake. She still thinks in excuses. She still thinks this can be smoothed over with words. She doesn't understand—every slip cuts deeper than she realizes.

My gaze hardens. "It wasn't one. It was enough."

Her lips part, turning cautious, pleading. "You don't have to—"

"I always have to," I cut her off, each word clipped. My hand closes around her and I steer her toward the basement. "Move."

I keep my grip on her arm as I take her downstairs. She digs in her heels, dragging against the steps, but she's coming with me whether she wants to or not. Her pulse is racing under my fingers. I can feel it. She knows what's waiting down the stairs.

The bench sits where it always does, bare and waiting. Built for discipline, not comfort. I had laid the paddle out hours ago, lined up on the table where she couldn't miss it if she looked. Because I knew she'd mess up, and I won't let it slide. So when I grab it now, it is not an afterthought. It is planned.

I lift it and hold it in her line of sight, turning the oak so the low light catches on its broad face. Heavy, solid, wide enough to spread pain deep through muscle and bone. My hand fits around the thick handle, familiar, already itching to swing.

Her eyes widen and mouth parts. She finally looks scared, and that fear in her expression hardens my cock immediately. I want her to see it coming, to dread it, to know I chose this for her.

"You know the drill. Strip," I tell her.

She stays on her feet, her chest rising, eyes sharp. "You don't have to do this. I did my best."

I meet her stare. She embarrassed me tonight, and that does not go unanswered. "No. You weren't even trying."

I pull the cuffs free from the side of the bench, the metal clinking.

She mutters under her breath, shaking her head, "This is insane."

I raise the paddle just enough so she sees I'm not waiting. It makes my cock throb before it even lands. She thought my collection was for show. Foolish. Every piece has its place, and this one is for nights like this.

"Don't stall. Kneel."

Her knees hit the floor, skin to cold concrete. I take her wrists, lock the cuffs around them, and drag her chest to the padded edge. Her ass lifts high, her legs spreading just enough that I know she cannot close them. That is how I want her, pinned open, nowhere to run.

I press my hand to the back of her neck, steady, keeping her down. "Tonight you'll remember not to embarrass me. So after every strike, you will say the words, 'I will not fail you again, master.'"

Her jaw locks. "I won't—"

The first strike cuts her off. The paddle lands flat and hard against her ass, the impact jolting through the wood into my palm. The sound fills the room, a sharp crack that makes her gasp. Her body jerks forward, but the cuffs hold her where I want her. Heat rises under the skin already.

"Say it."

She grinds her teeth. "No. You gave me no time to prepare," she breathes, still catching her voice. "You set me up."

A smirk curves my mouth. "You should always be prepared."

She's right, I did want this. I wanted the night to end with her exactly here—bound, punished, mine.

I bring it down again, sharper this time. The oak bites

deeper, spreading heat under her skin, raising the welt I will trace later. Her whole body jerks, and the sight of her bound and swinging makes my hips tense with the urge to thrust into her right now. I hold back. The control is as good as the fuck.

"Say it."

Her voice burns with refusal. "You're pathetic. This is nothing compared to a belt."

Pathetic. That one cuts through the calm. Most of her curses I let slide, because they keep her fighting, but this one digs deeper. She thinks she can strip me down with one word.

I tighten my grip on the paddle and slam it across the tops of her thighs. The flat wood cracks against muscle and bone, and she screams loud, raw, the kind of sound I want. The noise claws through me. This is why I do it. This is why I can't stop.

"You think you're strong," I murmur, close enough for my words to curl against her ear. "You're not."

"Stronger than you think," she whispers back, and it only makes me harder.

"Say it," I tell her. My voice doesn't rise. The paddle makes the point louder.

She twists under me, hair in her face, and snarls her response, "Fuck you."

Good. The fight is better than silence. Every curse, every refusal makes me harder. I don't want a quiet wife, bent over the bench taking her punishment without a sound. I want this one rowdy, vulgar, and giving me reasons to go further than I have ever gone before.

I swing low, cracking the paddle against the backs of her legs. She screams again, her voice broken, the sound bouncing off the walls.

I lean close, my mouth brushing her ear. "Do you still think this is nothing?"

She does not answer, but her body does. Her legs tremble, her shoulders sag forward, and I know it hurts the way I intended. Upstairs, I smooth her, reassure her she is more than enough. Down here, I do the opposite. Because it works. I see the flinch, the humiliation, and it gets me harder.

Words strip her faster than wood. And the mix of tears and curses they pull out of her makes me want to spill inside her too soon. I grit my teeth and hold back. I want to drag it out.

Each blow lands heavier, lower, building heat across her thighs and ass. She writhes, trying to fight it, but the bench keeps her in place. The sounds she makes are no longer controlled. Sobs, cries, and sharp gasps fill the air.

"Say it," I demand, steady. "Or I won't stop."

Her tears spill, and the words claw out of her throat, ragged. "I won't fail you again, master."

I smooth my palm over the bruises, slow, savoring the heat under her skin. "Better."

Words are stronger than cuffs. If I make her repeat them enough, they will settle into her bones, and the belief will live there. That is what keeps me hard through every strike.

The paddle comes down again. Each strike drags the phrase out of her lips, first defiant, then weaker. By ten, she sobs it into the pad. By fifteen, her whole body jerks forward with the impact, her voice cracking as she chokes out the words.

By twenty, her sobs echo, her voice thin as she repeats it over and over. I keep her pressed down, my hand firm on her neck, not letting her slip an inch.

"Now say 'I'll do better, master,'" I tell her when her voice falters. The paddle cracks across the backs of her thighs, brutal and exact. She jerks forward, nearly collapsing on her knees, and screams it out.

"I'll do better, master."

The sound cuts sharply through the room. I let it sink in before I strike again. The paddle has done its job. Her skin is hot, welted and red, every inch marked by me. The fight has been carved into her body, and that is what I want, obedience.

The last blow falls, heavy and final. She sobs the words one more time, broken and gasping. "I'll do better, master."

Her chest heaves against the bench, her wrists straining in the cuffs, her face wet with tears. I keep my hand on her neck, reminding her that no matter how much she fights, she is still mine.

"You will remember this. The next time you open your mouth in front of others, you will think of this floor, these bruises, and how quickly you can be brought back here."

Her tears streak down her cheeks, burning hot, and I know the words will stay with her longer than the marks. That's why I use them. Bruises fade, but words scar.

I drop the paddle onto the bench, and drag her to the edge, pinning her with my weight. I'm ready to fuck so I take out my cock and drag it across the curve of her ass, sliding lower until I feel the slick proof of how much she needs me, no matter what comes out of her mouth.

"Look at you," I murmur, savoring the sight. "Bent over for me and so fucking wet."

I don't push inside, not yet. I tease her, grinding against her entrance, making her feel every second of what I'm holding back.

"You don't even know how much you need this," I mutter, my voice rough in her ear. "But your body does."

Her voice cracks on my name, breathless. "Adrian."

The sound makes me groan, my control fraying. "Not yet. Not until you beg."

I feel her try to push back against me, but my grip tightens on her hips, pinning her where I want her.

"Beg me."

The word tears out of her, raw, too desperate to be faked. "No."

That defiant single syllable undoes me. I'm too horny to

keep waiting. So I enter her inch by inch, my cock pulsing inside her.

"I'm going to fuck the defiance out of you," I growl, my hands clamped tight on her hips.

Her pussy grips me so tight I groan. I dig my nails into her hip, fighting the urge to come too soon.

I smirk. "Maybe you are my whore."

She forces the words out, shaking. "I'm not your whore."

I slam my hand down on her ass, over and over, until her sobs spill into moans she can't stop. "Yes, you are. You are when I tell you. You are when I take you."

Her thighs tremble, her body clenches tighter around me, slicker with every thrust. She hates it, but she can't stop responding. That is why I push. That is why I use words like blades. They cut deeper than the wood ever could.

"You are in denial, whore," I snarl, my pace breaking as I drive harder. "Here you are, greedy for more."

She shakes her head against the pad, but her body tightens. "Don't call me that."

I spank her raw ass with my free hand, and she jolts against the cuffs.

"You fight me because you want more," I groan. "But you'll never admit it."

I feel her orgasm rising, violent and fast, and I don't let up. She lets out filthy, desperate moans I couldn't get from her any other way.

"I hate—" she says, but her climax rips through her, pulsing around me, muffled screams spilling into the bench. I hold her down and fuck her through it, every moan proving I'm right.

"Fuck, I'm going to fill you up," I growl, slamming deep until I'm spilling hard inside her. The pleasure tears through me, raw and shaking, my chest pressed to her back, sweat slick between us.

I don't let her go. My hand slides into her damp hair,

stroking slowly, steadying her. My breath comes rough against her ear. "You'll break for me one day," I tell her, low and certain.

She trembles under me, tears streaking her face. I gently pet her hair.

"What can I do to stop this? I can't keep doing this," she says, her voice shaking.

She always does this. She's gets conflicted and tries to pull away. She won't admit she loves this just as much as I do.

I tilt her face just enough to catch her brown eyes. "I need you to strive for perfection. As long as you can do that, we don't have to do this."

Her voice cracks, raw. "No one is perfect. That is unrealistic."

I pause, meeting her eyes. I know she'll never be perfect. That was never the point. Punishment was always the point. The excuses are what keep me clean. Without them, I'd have to admit the truth—that this is what I crave. But there's no point in pretending. She knows the truth. She called me out on it earlier.

My mouth brushes her ear, and I laugh. "But I like having excuses. Otherwise, I'd just be considered sadistic."

She doesn't see it yet, but every fight, every curse, every refusal only feeds me. I'll always find reasons to go harder, because reasons let me take everything I want.

Her breathing stays ragged under me, face damp with sweat and tears, the marks I left still glowing red across her skin. I pull out and unlock the cuffs one by one.

She lays against the bench like her body has nothing left to give. She's strong. I'm not worried, she'll be okay.

I crouch beside her, and for a moment I just take her in, the wreckage of her body, the imprint of my paddle stamped into her skin, the words I forced past her lips still echoing in the air. This is what keeps her mine.

Then she whispers it, her voice cracked and raw. "Why do you hate me?"

The words punch straight through the high still burning in me. My jaw locks. *Hate?* How could she think punishment is hate?

I grip her chin, lifting her face so she has to look at me. Her brown eyes are glassy, wet, but defiant enough to still cut. "I could never hate you." My voice is steady, but it grinds out of me harder than I mean to.

"I think you do," she whispers. "Because I abandoned you."

Abandoned. The word digs deeper than the paddle ever could.

My mouth tightens. "I was upset, but we moved past that. Don't ever say it again."

Her lips tremble, and she nods fast, fear tightening her face. "Okay."

I linger, studying her. The look she gave me when she said it, the idea that she believes it, sits in my chest heavier than the paddle in my hand. I force it down, lock it away, the same way I always do.

I stroke her hair once, grounding her, grounding myself. "Collect yourself. Then come upstairs."

I stand and leave her there on the bench, bruised and shaken, because if I stay another second, I'll hear that line again. *Why do you hate me?* And the truth is, I don't. Hate would mean letting her go. What I feel is the opposite, and that's what terrifies me.

22

ADRIAN

The bath water runs smoothly as I set the temperature the way she likes. Not too hot—she used to say it made her skin feel raw. That was back when she would tell me her small preferences instead of silence.

Tonight I've stripped her bare and claimed every inch, but this part's for recovery and stability. That's how we keep the rhythm intact. But her recklessness with her words soured everything, even this.

I should still be riding the high. She called me master for the first time since she came home. It should've satisfied me. But then she asked why I hated her, and the fun drained out of it the second those words left her mouth. They keep circling back.

She said it like it was truth. My actions should've been proof I don't and never could. I forgave her for leaving because I wanted to start over. But maybe she's still holding on to whatever made her run. My jaw grinds at the thought.

I grab a towel harder than I mean to, the sound snapping in the quiet. She doesn't come up. She used to retreat after punishment—first with slammed doors, then with silence. But even then, she never looked at me like I'd abandoned her. She definitely never believed I hated her. At least I hope she didn't.

Unless she hates me and thinks it's mutual. No—she could never. Not now. We've grown closer than ever since she came back. So this must be a test. If I wait long enough, she'll settle, recalibrate, and come find me.

So I wait. Five minutes. Then five more. Nothing.

The house is too quiet as I step into the hall. The basement door stands wide open. She's not on the floor. Not curled near the bench. The restraints sit exactly where I left them.

She's gone.

A cold jolt shoots down my spine. My vision narrows. My fists clench before I even realize it. She can't leave. Not unless I forgot to lock down the house.

The front door is bolted. I cut through the kitchen. The slider's open just enough. *Why was the back door unlocked, but the front door wasn't?* I don't have time to dwell on it, I need to find Ellie.

Outside, the salt clings to the damp, cold air, the grass bending under my steps.

Then I see her. She's on the dock, legs swinging above the water, robe clinging in the breeze, hair moving in the wind. Her feet make quiet ripples that spread into the dark.

I walk. Then I run.

"You can't swim," I snap, grabbing her wrist before she can slip.

She turns her head slowly. "How do you know that?"

"You told me. You almost drowned at a lake as a kid."

Her face doesn't change. She looks back at the water. "I wasn't going to jump."

I never said anything about jumping. Was she thinking about it? Leaving me forever by her own hand? I can't imagine she'd put me through that. She knows how suicide wrecks the ones left behind. She wouldn't do that to me.

"You shouldn't be out here," I say, lowering my voice.

"I needed air."

"No. You need to be inside," I tell her, gentler this time. "You aren't supposed to leave without me knowing."

She doesn't argue. She just sits there, too quiet. If she'd slipped, it would've been fast. Silent. No scream, no cry for help. I wouldn't have made it in time. They might never have found her. I'd be left with her absence, and my cold heart would be broken.

When I pull her to her feet, she doesn't resist. Her skin's cold. Her silence is heavier than anger. That's what gets to me —not what she says, but what she doesn't. It's like she's already gone, and I'm the only one who doesn't know it yet.

But her voice echoes in my head. *Why do you hate me?* I've never hated her. I never could. But if she keeps saying it, I can't allow it. I'll prove her wrong until she understands. And I'll never stop until she does.

We walk back in silence. I close the door, lock it, and flip the panel open. The green light blinks.

Locked down.

She's not leaving again. Not slipping through cracks. Not disappearing into the water.

Back in the bedroom, she climbs in first, lying on her side with her back to me. She's not tense. She's just still.

I strip down and slide in beside her. She's here, in my bed, in my house. But it doesn't feel like victory.

I stare at the ceiling, listening to her breathing. I don't know if she's asleep. I don't ask. If I reached for her, it'd be comfort, and comfort unravels discipline. And if I gave her that, I wouldn't stop.

23

MAREN

I don't sleep. I lie still, but nothing inside me is quiet. My mind spins through everything that happened, how I moaned his name, how my body betrayed me. How afterward he left me alone in a room with nothing but pain in my body and silence in my throat. Sometime in the night, he got up and left the bed. He left me.

No word or touch on my shoulder. No whisper. No goodnight. Just gone. When I finally open my eyes, the light through the curtains is bright and soft. My skin aches from too much contact and not enough care.

Then I see it. The phone. It's sitting on the nightstand with a piece of paper folded beneath it. I sit up slowly. My muscles are tight and tender. My fingers tremble as I unfold the note.

Use wisely.

That's it. My stomach sinks.

Last night, Sasha asked why I didn't have a phone. Her tone was sharp. Her eyes were smug. She knew exactly what she was doing. Now Adrian's making sure it doesn't happen again. This isn't about me needing connection. It's about him making sure no one looks too closely at us.

Still, I reach for it. No passcode. Of course not. He wants me to know he's watching. He wants me to see this as a reward. For falling apart under his touch.

I set it down slowly. I didn't go to the dock last night because I needed air. I went to the kitchen to get water, and I saw the door to outside was ajar. So I went to see if there was a boat. Something I could use to get off this goddamn island. I've never driven a boat or know how to start one. But desperation doesn't need directions. It just needs a maybe. Part of me wonders if it was an accident or if Greta left it unlocked on purpose.

I stared at the black water and thought about all the fake people at that stupid dinner. The fake smiles. The champagne. Sasha's judgmental little comments about my dress. About my lies.

I think about Adrian and how he couldn't kiss me after what we did.

What kind of man strips you bare, fucks you like he owns you, punishes you like it's his right, and then walks away like it meant nothing?

Deep down, I wanted something. A touch. A word. Anything to tell me I hadn't just lost the last piece of myself. But I didn't get it. That's all the proof I need to confirm he despises me. But what do I expect? He kidnapped, humiliated, and punished me. And he thinks he's going to come out of this clean.

No. He doesn't get to break me and walk away whole. Not while I still have breath left and there's a phone sitting in front of me.

This life he's trying to wrap me in, with the perfect clothes, the fake friends, the curated routines, isn't mine. But if he's handing me tools, I'll use them. Not wisely. Not obediently. I'll use them my way.

I go to the sitting room to read the real Eleanor's journal. I don't ease into it. I flip past the early entries. Past the ones I've already read. I search for a fresh date. Something closer to now, after things started shifting, and they stopped pretending.

Then I see it. A November 4th entry. I settle into the couch, curling my legs underneath me. I flip through the pages, searching for something. Then I see her handwriting again, steady and sharp, spilling another confession onto the page.

I keep thinking I've proven myself. Then something like last night happens, and I realize I haven't even scratched the surface.

Adrian says it's not about perfection. He says I need to be comfortable in my own skin.

But that's a lie.

He wants a woman who walks into a room and knows exactly what to say. To the right people. In the right tone. With the right smile.

I didn't do that last night.

I tried. I made jokes. I followed conversations. I remembered names.

But I still fucked it up.

Sasha asked about a designer I'd never heard of. She mentioned a property Adrian just acquired. He hadn't even told me, or maybe he did, and I forgot. I saw his expression shift. Just barely. But I saw it.

Afterward, he said he was leaving for a few days. Business out of town.

He kissed my cheek and told me not to stress.

But it's been four days.

No calls. No messages. Nothing.

I keep checking my phone like a lunatic, waiting for it to light up with something.

Anything. Something that tells me I didn't ruin everything. That he's not calling it off. Because if he does, I don't know what will happen to me. Not after everything I've given up to be here with him.

And the longer I wait, the more I realize I've never met a colder man in my life, and I'm supposed to marry him. He doesn't flirt or tease. He doesn't do any of the things I thought a man getting married would do. He won't even say I look nice when I dress up for him. No emotion. No softness. Just approval.

He won't bring me flowers unless it's Valentine's Day. Unless someone's watching. A bouquet left out where the housekeeper can see it. But random? Thoughtful? No. Never.

I feel like I'm marrying a machine. A charming, well-dressed, emotionally vacant machine.

Adrian doesn't talk about his past. He barely mentions his parents. His mother? I don't even know where she lives. I'm not sure he does, either.

I met his father when we went to dinner at his house. He's a cold man. The kind of cold that explains everything. Everything Adrian said was picked apart. If he spoke about work, his father called it shortsighted. If he tried to share something lighter, his father dismissed it as a waste of time. He found fault in tone, in timing, even in the way Adrian told a story. He's lived with that coldness his whole life. He doesn't chase perfection because he wants to—he does it because he has to.

When Sasha's name came up again, he stiffened. He said she was family. He changed the subject. I should have realized before, but it only clicked today—Sasha is his sister. Maybe I didn't want to because that means I have to deal with her. The way she looks at me, it's not just judgment. It's personal. She's cold and distant because she thinks I'm after his money. A gold digger in designer heels. And the truth is, sometimes I wonder if she's right. Or maybe it's worse than that. Maybe she already knows I want to run.

~

I stop breathing. Sasha is Adrian's sister. My pulse kicks up. My stomach turns. Everything I thought I understood about last night reshapes in a split second. That fake smile. That smug tone. The way she eyed me like I was trash in designer clothes. She wasn't just judging me. She was protecting him, or trying to. That's why she didn't believe the charity's lie. Because in her mind, I'm the girl who abandoned her brother. Or worse. I'm the one who'll do it again. I stare down at the handwriting, willing it to tell me something I don't already know. Something that will help me. But all it's done is remind me I'm exactly where she used to be. But she escaped, and I need to figure out how.

24

ADRIAN

I walk into the bedroom with my jaw tight and my fists clenched at my sides. I haven't seen her all day, and every second of it, I've thought about her sitting on that goddamn dock, dangling over the water like she didn't care about the danger. If she had fallen, and if I hadn't gotten there in time, I wouldn't have forgiven her or myself. Now I have to be stricter, to make sure she never gets the chance to pull something like that again. I expect a cold shoulder when I step inside. But I don't expect sadness.

She's sitting at the edge of the bed, small and still, with her head down and her hands twisted together in her lap. The sight of it punches something hard and ugly into my chest. I shut the door harder than necessary, but she doesn't even flinch. I cross the room and stop in front of her.

"Ellie. What's wrong?"

She doesn't look up, and her voice is barely a whisper. "Nothing."

I stand there, watching her shoulders tighten. I don't believe her, but if she won't talk, I won't force her. Not yet.

After a long moment, she lifts her head slightly, and her

eyes are glassy with unshed tears. "Why didn't you kiss me last night? You just left me in the basement."

I stare at her. "You were supposed to come to me. I ran you a bath, but you never showed up. Instead, you went to the dock and sat on the edge when you can't even swim." My voice hardens. "You're not supposed to leave the house without my permission. So no, I wasn't going to reward you with affection after you disobeyed me."

She flinches. It's subtle, but I catch it, and her arms pull tighter around herself like she's trying to hold something in.

"You're so cold, like a machine," she whispers.

A machine. Does she really think I feel nothing? She doesn't understand what it's taken to keep her safe, and myself. If I let her see how much she matters, she'll test every line until there's nothing left, and I can't afford that, not after what she pulled last night.

Her lips tremble, and her shoulders shake as tears spill over. I tense, and every muscle locks. I hate crying. It's weak, manipulative, and it makes everything inside me turn hard. She never used to cry this much before she left. She would give me the silent treatment, but not this. She knows how I feel about it, and still she sits there crying, like she's peeling me open on purpose.

I crouch down in front of her and grab her hands, forcing her to meet my eyes.

"Ellie. Stop crying. You know I hate it."

She cries harder, and the sound rips out of her, raw and helpless. I wipe her tears roughly with my thumb, trying to erase them, but they keep falling.

"Stop," I mutter, the words catching low in my throat. "Tell me what you want."

She doesn't answer. Instead she stares at me, glassy and distant, like she's already slipping away. I pull her into a hug, locking my arms around her tightly so she can't move.

Her body stays stiff, but I hold her close.

"You don't care," she says against my chest, her voice soft enough I almost miss it.

She's wrong. I care. I cared when I saw her on that dock and every worst-case scenario ran through my head—with her gone and me standing here with nothing left.

I cared when she gave herself to me. I felt it in the way she held on to me. I heard it in the way she said my name. I saw it in the way she broke under my hands, not from fear but from need. Even if she's pretending otherwise now, I know the truth. So no, I'm not letting her go. Not now. Not ever.

"That's not true," I answer, sharper than I mean to.

Her head tips up, eyes wet. "Then say it. Tell me you care."

The words stick in my throat. "I show it in my actions."

She laughs, bitter and broken. "Your actions say you hate me. They say you feel stuck with me."

I freeze. She doesn't believe me. I've been so focused on keeping her here, I haven't thought enough about how to make her want to stay. So I'll show her the only way I know how.

"How can you believe I don't care?" I murmur low, almost not for her at all.

I strip off my clothes slowly, never taking my eyes off her. She watches me through wet lashes, her breath trembling, and when I move toward her, she shivers faintly. My hands slide down to her waist, my fingers slipping under her shirt as I drag it up slowly, making sure she feels every inch of the pull. Her breath catches, her belly tightens, and goosebumps rise under my touch. I peel the fabric higher, strip it off completely, and pause to take her in.

She's beautiful. Her brown eyes are sharp, her nipples press against thin lace, flushed and sensitive, and she looks at me like she's already half-undone as I take off her bra. Her chest lifts with a shaky breath, and I roll one nipple between my fingers, watching it harden instantly under my touch. I lean in and close my mouth over it, sucking slow and deep, flicking my tongue until she shivers hard.

When I pull back, I kiss lower, down her ribs and across her stomach, teasing her skin until she squirms and soft, uneven sounds slip free. Reaching her panties, I hook my fingers in the waistband, dragging them down slowly, savoring how the fabric clings from the dampness between her thighs.

I kneel between her legs, spreading her wide as I drink in the sight of her flushed and slick. I run two fingers through her folds, feeling the way her hips twitch, the way her breath hitches sharp when I stroke her just right.

"Let me take care of you," I whisper against her.

I kiss the inside of her thigh, then higher, brushing my mouth against her clit. She gasps, a startled, shaky sound, her fists tightening in the sheets.

"Don't hold back."

I suck her clit into my mouth, pulling soft, then harder, flicking until a whimper breaks from her throat. Her thighs clench tight around my shoulders. I push two fingers inside, curling deep, feeling her squeeze around me stroke after stroke, until her hips lift and a broken moan cracks from her lips. She thinks she's strong, but I know better. I know how she needs me no matter what she says.

Pulling back, I drag the thick head of my cock through her slick folds, slow and steady. Each pass grazes her clit just enough to make her gasp, her hips twitching and her thighs trembling.

I press against her entrance, letting her feel me right where she wants it, but I don't give in yet.

Her breath shudders, the word barely making it out. "I...I need—"

I thrust forward slowly, filling her inch by inch, stretching her tight around me as I watch her eyes widen, glassy and full, and shaky gasp tremble past her lips.

"That's it," I groan, sinking deep and locking us together.

She gasps again, her back arching sharply as her nails bite into my shoulders. I pull out slowly, dragging against every nerve, then slam back in and grind deep.

Her moan tears free, raw and unguarded, as she clutches at me, her thighs shaking. Her hips lift, her breath hitching louder with every thrust.

Her body trembles harder, her hands gripping me like she's afraid she'll come apart. I press her wrists above her head and lean in close, my forehead pressed to hers, and I kiss her hard.

Her lashes flutter wildly, her lips parting on a helpless, shuddering moan, and I thrust deeper, grinding until a sharp, breathless cry spills into my mouth.

My mouth brushes her temple, my voice rough. "I'm devoted to you. I just want you to stay."

Her lashes flutter, wet and uncertain. She doesn't believe me. Not yet. But I'll prove it.

Her body grips me tighter, desperate. When she breaks, crying out, I follow, grinding deep, spilling inside her with a groan that rips through me.

I stay inside her, kissing her lips and her temple, stroking her damp hair back, pressing the words into her skin.

"I'll never let you go."

"Don't." That word could mean anything. I don't care which because it's a promise I intend to keep. But even with her wrapped around me, trembling and wet, I feel the distance. I've locked every door, sealed every crack, but I still don't know if I've given her a reason to stay.

25

MAREN

After a few seconds, he shifts, rolling onto his back and pulling free, leaving me beside him, staring at the ceiling. That's all. He lies there, chest rising and falling, silent and still, like everything between us is magically fixed.

My body aches in ways I can't sort through. I stare up, trying to breathe around the knot twisting tighter with every second he doesn't move toward me.

Then I hear it, low and rough, like he almost doesn't want me to catch it.

"You're special to me, Ellie," he whispers. "I hope you know that now."

"I know," I say as I squeeze my eyes shut. He thinks sex and whispering sweet words is enough to fix what he refuses to see. He acts like letting me stay beside him proves we're whole again. This is his version of saying I love you, I don't even care to ever hear the words from him.

He seems to think I need him, but I feel ashamed for saying all those things he told me to say in the basement. He gets to hear what he wants, so why can't I?

If I'm stuck in this life, if this is what forever feels like, then the least I want, the bare minimum, is to feel loved. I don't even know what love's supposed to feel like, but I know it's not this hollow ache in my chest while he lies next to me, already half gone.

I lie there for what feels like forever, trying not to suffocate under the silence, until I can't stand it anymore. Slowly, carefully, I sit at the edge of the bed.

I feel his eyes on me. He doesn't reach for me or speak. He watches from a distance. It feels like a wall I'll never climb.

I pull the sheet around my body and hold it close against my chest. For a second, I sit there, staring at the floor, breathing through the hollow ache scraping through my ribs.

I stand up slowly. My knees shake. My skin still bears every mark of him. The floor's cold beneath my feet. I hear the bed creak as he shifts again, but he doesn't follow.

I walk to the bathroom without looking back, and close the door quietly behind me.

The soft click sounds louder than it should.

For a second, I lean my forehead against the wood and clutch the sheet tighter around my body like it can hold the rest of me together. I could cry. I want to cry. But I don't. I've already lost too much of myself. I can't lose this, too.

I straighten slowly and force my legs to stay steady as I move to the sink. I grip the edge of the counter with white knuckles and study my reflection.

The woman staring back at me looks nothing like the girl who used to dream about being loved. Her mouth's swollen. Her eyes are too glassy. Her skin's blotchy where his hands and mouth left their marks. She looks empty. Hollow.

But somewhere deep under the exhaustion and hurt, there's still something burning. A flicker. I'm still here. I'm still me. Even if he never sees it.

I towel off my hair and try to quiet the noise in my head when I hear his footsteps behind me.

The door creaks open.

I brace for something. A command. A demand. Another cold silence.

"Our anniversary's coming up," Adrian says instead.

I freeze.

Slowly, I turn to face him, clutching the towel tighter around my body. My heart pounds so hard it hurts. I have no idea what he's talking about. I don't even know when it is.

He smiles faintly. "You didn't think I'd forget again, did you?"

How do you forget your anniversary when you've got a phone, a calendar, and a dozen reminders? How do you forget something like that unless it never mattered in the first place?

And now he stands here, like remembering fixes everything. Like remembering proves something. Like it erases every other way he's failed.

I press my lips together and force myself to meet his gaze. "No."

His smile deepens. "Good."

He steps closer. "Three years, Ellie. We've been through a lot. But you always come back to me."

My stomach twists hard. Three years. His wife left him after less than three years of marriage. He thinks we've built something real.

But I'm still angry. Angry he forgot something that was never mine. Enraged that he talks like it belongs to me, too. And somehow I'm standing here, feeling smaller for it.

When I step out of the bathroom, he's sitting at the edge of the bed, holding a small black box.

I stop in the doorway, pulling the towel tighter around my body.

He lifts the box slightly. "I got something for you. Consider it an early anniversary gift."

I stay still, watching him watch me. His smile is faint, expectant, waiting for me to ask. But I don't. I already know what happens if I question too much.

"Open it," he says.

I walk closer and take the box from his hand. It's heavier than I expected. I hesitate, then flip the lid open.

Inside is a delicate diamond bracelet, catching the light. But it's not a bracelet.

"It's an anklet," he says, answering before I can ask.

An anklet. I frown, tilting the box. "I've never worn one before."

"You will now." His voice is quiet. He pats the bed. "Sit."

I lower myself onto the mattress, still holding the box. He takes it gently from my hands and sets it aside. Then he kneels in front of me and lifts my leg into his lap.

I watch as he fastens the anklet around my ankle. The metal's cool against my skin, snug but not tight. Then he does something I don't expect.

He slips his wedding ring off his finger and leans in. There's a tiny groove in the clasp, barely visible. He presses the ring into it, fitting it like a key.

A soft click follows, quiet but final.

What the fuck.

My pulse slams in my throat. His wedding ring is the key.

A cold jolt shoots up my spine, winding through my chest until it squeezes so tight I can barely pull a breath. He didn't just put jewelry on me. He locked it, and only he can take it off.

The weight of it on my ankle feels heavier by the second, sinking into my skin, like it's already part of me whether I want it or not.

He lifts the ring into view between his fingers, then slides it back onto his hand.

I glance down. The anklet stays locked. I brush my fingers over the clasp, searching for a catch or release, but it doesn't budge.

I press my lips together as my ribs lock up. "What did you do?"

He looks up at me. "You can't take it off. Not without this." He holds up the ring again before lowering his hand.

I stare at the anklet, heat crawling under the metal. "Why?" I whisper, even though I already know.

He rests his hand on my knee. "You can take the ring off. You won't be able to take this off, though."

The ring. The one he told me to wear at the dinner party. I wore it, quiet and obedient, letting the diamond flash beneath the lights. And the moment the guests left, I slipped it off without a word. He never said anything, but of course, he noticed. Now he's made sure I can't undo this one.

I run my fingers along the anklet again, testing for any give. It stays locked. He traces his fingers lightly over the metal, his touch soft but certain, like he's checking a finished piece.

"Perfect," he murmurs.

I can't speak. I can barely breathe. I stare down at the anklet. It's locked, and so am I.

26

MAREN

I wait until his footsteps fade down the hall, staying on the edge of the bed, staring at the anklet locked around my ankle, still feeling his hands even though he's gone. I walk to the closet, ignoring the dresses he's lined up for me, and pull on black leggings and an old t-shirt. Nothing fancy or beautiful, but it's mine. It feels childish, maybe even petty, but the flicker of defiance curling through the ache tells me I need this. Adrian's going to be pissed when he sees me dressed for bed, but at least this is still mine to choose. At least I can still decide what goes on my own skin.

I slip down the hall toward my sitting room, the only place that still feels even a little mine. The journal is still stacked neatly under the side table. I sink onto the couch and pull the top one into my lap. I need to find it. I need to know when our anniversary is.

I flip through the pages, scanning dates and ink, until I see it. A date circled in the corner. The night of their engagement party. My stomach knots. I press my lips together, fingers tightening on the page as I start to read.

We got back from the engagement party after midnight. My feet ached from the heels, my head buzzed from too much champagne, but Adrian never let go of my hand. I thought we'd just fall into bed, drunk and laughing, like engaged couples are supposed to.

Instead, he squeezed my fingers. He told me he needed to show me something.

I laughed a little, thinking it was some surprise. I asked him what it was.

"A space you and I will spend a lot of time in."

He said it as if it was something special.

He led me down a hallway I'd never seen before. No lights, no sound, just the steady echo of our footsteps on polished floors until he unlocked a door like it was something he'd done a hundred times.

I expected candles. Maybe a private room he'd decorated just for me. Instead, the door swung open, and the air turned cold.

A thin mattress was shoved into one corner. A steel pole rose from the floor to the ceiling. Chains hung from heavy hooks. Belts and whips lined the wall like trophies.

I stopped breathing. "Is this some kind of joke?"

Adrian's face didn't change. "No. I need you to see who I am before we get married."

I couldn't move. I could only stand there, staring at something that had no place in the future we were supposed to be making.

"I like being in control," he said, like it was as normal as liking red wine or black coffee.

"This is something else."

"You're submissive," he said calmly, like it was already settled in his head.

I let out a shaky laugh. "I'm not submissive."

He smiled. "Then why do you do everything I ask?"

"Because we're getting married."

His smile widens. "No, you love to please me. You always have."

"Adrian, I can't have you chaining me up and whipping me. That's not who I am."

"You can and will."

The words hit harder than the sight of the room. He meant it. He wasn't asking. He was stating what would happen.

"I can't do this." My voice cracked. This is insanity. Why didn't he tell me this before we got engaged? I would never allow myself to be treated this way. I'm in so deep, but there is time to call it off. Maybe I should give him an ultimatum. If he expects this, we won't get married.

He narrowed his eyes. "Do what?"

"Marry you if this is what you expect."

He sighed, annoyed, acting like I was the problem. "Don't be ridiculous, Eleanor."

"I need time." The words rushed out. "I need space."

I walk towards the bedroom and lock the door. I start grabbing clothes and putting them in a suitcase. I move quickly and then head towards the front door.

Adrian raises an eyebrow. "Eleanor, where are you going?"

"I just need space."

He didn't reach for me or argue. He just stood there, watching me with that same look that told me nothing I said would change anything.

"You'll be back," he said.

I went to my old apartment and I looked around, realizing I can't go back to this. That night he texted me asking me when I'll be back, and I ignored it. He didn't try to call or text after that. Deep down I was hoping he'd chase me, but he's not that kind of man.

I came back a week later. I can't end our engagement over this. What would I do? I can't give up this life he's given me, it's too good. This past week showed me that.

I knocked on the door, standing in the entryway, still holding the bag I'd walked out with, unsure if I should drop it or turn around again. My heart pounded so hard it hurt.

I remember Adrian stepping into the room, hugging me. He's not the most affectionate man, but he smiled, calm as always, pretending nothing had happened.

"I have the room ready for you," he said.

I thought he meant the bedroom. But I realized he meant the other room.

I needed to understand more. I needed to hear it from him directly, not just feel it in his touch or the way he leads every part of my life.

He sat across from me, confident and calm, fingers loose on the armrest, mouth relaxed, gaze softer than usual. Finally, he was trying to let me in.

"I want you to submit to me," he said. "Not just in bed. Everywhere."

I stared at him, chest tight. "What does that even mean?"

He leaned forward slightly, his hand reaching for mine, his fingers brushing lightly against my knuckles. He'd been uncharacteristically gentle and affectionate, as if he knew how close I was to pulling away and was trying to pull me closer.

"It means I have complete control over you. I make the decisions. You follow what I say without question."

My mouth parted in shock. I sat there, struggling for words, then shook my head hard. That's not marriage. Marriage is about making decisions together, compromise. If I agree to this, than I won't have a say in our marriage. It's archaic.

"I can't let you do that."

His thumb traced the edge of my hand. His gentle, green eyes watched me carefully before turning cold.

"For you, since you're new to this, we'll take it slow. Just little things at first. But once we're married, I expect you to obey me. Submit to me. You'll find life with me easier this way."

He said it so matter of fact. This isn't a negotiation. Of course, life will be easier that way for him. He'll be getting everything he wants.

I asked, "And if I don't obey?"

A slight smirk touched the corner of his mouth. He'd been waiting for the question.

"You'll be punished. But you'll come to enjoy it, maybe even look forward to it."

He's so confident I almost believe it. But I'm not. He'd only ever spanked me with his hand during sex, and I liked it, but to find out he's into this, is shocking. I don't want to be punished for upsetting or disagreeing with him. I would always be on edge. I won't be happy.

I shook my head. "Adrian, I'm not cut out for this. I mean, you're a great guy, and you can find any woman who'd want this."

His fingers tightened just slightly around mine, the smallest squeeze, his mouth softening.

"I only want you. You're my fiancée now, and that means something. You're in too deep now."

Am I? No, I'm not. But would he be upset enough to destroy my art career before it even started? He already introduced me to people in the art world. One phone call could end that, but he doesn't control the world. I can move, find another job, put this behind me.

That's when his voice lowered, his gaze hardening. "I don't want chaos, Ellie. I don't want games. I want certainty. I want to know you're mine, fully. When you submit, when you let me lead, I can take care of you, give you the life you deserve. No fear or doubt. Just peace. But only if you let me have this."

That hit deeper. He was talking about peace, and now I have it, but I can't do whatever he says to keep it. My life has been chaotic since I moved to Chicago. I maxed out my credit cards, nearly got evicted, almost got my car repossessed. I was at my wits end until I met him. He gave me stability, paid off my debts, bought me a car. I could easily go back into that situation. I need the stability he's given me. Then he added, "If you're my wife, it'll open doors for your art. I'll even build an art studio for you."

He's handing me everything I thought I wanted. I want my art to not just be in my house, but I want to be featured in museums, have art shows, sell my art and have it talked about. I want my legacy to be one of the best, not just his wife.

As I started shaking, he leaned closer, kissing my cheek.

"Ellie, you'll be happy with me." His hand stayed warm over mine. "You'll want for nothing. Anything you want, I'll get for you."

He was showing affection again, and it felt so easy. The connection pulled tight without effort. Still, I couldn't move. I sat frozen. He made it sound as though I should be grateful. That no one else would ever give me more, given where I came from.

What choice do I even have? I can't go back to waitressing after all this. He's spoiled me, taken me to the best places, dressed me in things I never could've touched on my own, and introduced me to people I never would've met. I'm only twenty-one. He's thirty-four. Mature, powerful, sure of what he wants. I don't think I'll ever find this again. Should I marry for comfort, not love? Just stability, safety, peace, and everything Adrian's promised me.

I slam the journal shut, my fingers shaking. This is what he expects. It was always implied. In the locked doors, in how he says I belong to him, in the punishments. But reading it laid out, hearing his exact words in her handwriting, makes my stomach turn. She was never fooled. She wanted to be his wife. She walked into this with her eyes open. All this time, I thought he misled her, that she was tricked or pushed or blinded by charm. But no. She stood there in the wedding, wearing the dress he chose, at the venue he arranged, smiling for the photos he wanted. She walked down that aisle and said the vows. And now I'm forced into her place, shoved into a mold I never asked for. And still, he expects me to submit the same way he expected it from her. She married him, lived in his world, enjoyed the money, the gifts, the attention, and she still hated it enough to run. I didn't even get the choice.

I was taken. Dragged into a life I didn't agree to, forced to play a part I never wanted. My hands press hard against the journal cover, nails digging into the edges. My chest tightens so hard it's painful. If she couldn't survive it, what chance do I have? If she ran, how am I supposed to stand a chance when I never walked into this willingly?

I sit on the edge of the couch, the journal open in my lap, Eleanor's words pressing into me.

I drag a hand over my face, my breath shaking. I press a hand to my ribs, trying to steady the ache crawling under my skin. I need a way out, because if I don't, I'm not sure how much of me will still be here.

Then I see it. A wall calendar above the bookshelf, with a charity logo printed in the corner and neat squares marking the days. I cross the room before I even think. My fingers skim over the dates as I count backward, faster and faster, until the numbers start to blur. I haven't been gone for just a day or two —I've been gone for weeks. The realization lands sharp and cold in my chest. *Did anyone notice? Did anyone at the Rusty Nail ask where I went? File a missing person's report? Did the old lady across the hall knock on my door? Did anyone wonder why I never came home? Was I even missed?* I press both hands to the wall, but the cold doesn't help. It only makes the truth harder to ignore.

Then an even worse thought comes. I missed my period. It's not something I can blame on stress, or fear, or the constant thrum of survival. I need a pregnancy test. The thought slams through me so fast it knocks the breath from my lungs. Maybe I could ask Greta. I could pretend I'm sick, slip it into conversation if she's planning to go into town, and make it sound casual or normal.

But no. That's reckless. Even thinking it feels dangerous. Greta would tell Adrian, maybe not on purpose. Maybe she wouldn't even realize what she was doing. But it would still get back to him. I shut the thought down before it can take root.

I start pacing. The floor is cold under my feet, and my thoughts are racing faster than my body ever could. I can't ask or even hint. I have to find one on my own. Somewhere in this house, there has to be something. Did Eleanor leave anything? I think of the guest bathrooms, the spare closets, and Greta's storage room.

I slip quietly out of the sitting room and shut the door gently behind me. My breath stays tight in my chest. I need to focus. I need to move.

I head down the hall toward the guest wing. The bathrooms there are barely used, maybe even forgotten. If anything's hidden, it'll be in a place like this. I check the first bathroom, opening the cabinets, drawers, and shelves. Everything is clean and orderly, with neatly stacked towels, a few old bottles of shampoo, but nothing that could help me.

I move to the next one. My heart beats harder in my chest. Did Eleanor ever worry she might be pregnant? Did she ever think about having kids at all? Did she ever let herself wonder, or was she too buried in everything else he forced on her? The thought twists through me. Adrian never mentioned wanting children. If anything, his focus has always been on control, perfection, and image. Not unpredictability. Not risk.

I pull open a drawer with shaky fingers. Inside, I find hotel soap, a sewing kit, and a hairbrush still wrapped in plastic. None of it helps.

I curse under my breath and move to the next bathroom, farther down the hall. The house is so big and so quiet that it swallows every sound I make.

I reach the last guest bathroom and step inside. I ease the door closed behind me and go straight for the cabinet handles. If she ever questioned it, if she ever feared it, would she have hidden something here? A tight ache twists beneath my ribs.

I move faster now. I open every drawer, shift every box, and scan every shelf. I find a spare toothbrush, a half-used bottle of Aspirin, and a crumpled packet of tissues. I press both palms to the counter. My chest rises and falls too fast, my breath catching.

I need to find out before he does. Because if Adrian knows first...It's not just over. It's locked in. I glance at the clock. It's later than I thought. Dinner time. How did that happen? I look down at myself. I'm still in the black leggings and old t-shirt I pulled on earlier. I could change into the clothes he set out for me this morning that I ignored. But I don't. I stay like this.

If he expects me to be in a dress tonight, I don't care. I grab a sweater and throw it over my shoulders before heading downstairs.

Adrian's already seated at the dining table, a glass of wine in his hand. His eyes lift as I walk in. They skim over the leggings, the t-shirt, the sweater. His mouth tightens just enough to show he notices, but he doesn't say anything. Just a quiet frown, quickly erased.

Dinner stretches out in silence. The only sound is the quiet scrape of silverware. His fork moves through his food. I barely touch mine. I can feel his gaze even when he's not looking at me directly, like he's waiting for something.

Then he sets his fork down. "What do you want for our anniversary?"

I lift my head slowly. "Wasn't the anklet my present?"

A low chuckle escapes him as he leans back. "That was one of your presents. You need to tell me what you want and where you want to go."

I stare at my plate. What do I want? To leave. Where do I want to go? I want to go anywhere where I can escape, but if escape isn't possible, I'd rather not do anything. It's not my anniversary. I want the anklet off. I want to stand on the dock and tear it loose. I want a boat tied up at the end of the pier, waiting. I want to leave. But I can't say that. But he's so desperate for my devotion, so if I'm offering that then maybe he will consider getting one.

I look up. "A boat."

His eyebrows rise. "A boat?"

"Unless we already have one."

He nods, and his smile widens. "We have one. But we can upgrade to a yacht. We could take it anywhere you want to go."

"How about one I can learn how to drive?"

He pauses, head tilting slightly. "Drive a boat?"

"You don't think I can?"

His expression is suspicious. "You don't know how to drive one."

"Do you?"

"Yes." He plasters on a smile.

"Then you can teach me. It's a great way for us to spend time together."

His fingers tap slowly against the table, thoughtful. A low dread coils in my ribs as I wait. If I'm pregnant, I need a way out. Something with an engine. Something I can control.

Finally, he lowers his hand. "I'll think about it."

I swallow hard, forcing myself to nod like it's enough. But it's not. It's never enough. Every answer from him feels like a gate swinging shut. Every promise feels like another chain tightening. *Think faster, Adrian, because I'm running out of time.* I nod, but inside, my pulse hammers.

I blurt out, "I want to go to the mountains in Colorado."

I'll be back on mainland and can easily escape. *But what if he takes us to a remote cabin and there is no escape?* I didn't think that through.

He smiles. "I can make that happen. But let's go in the winter."

Fuck, it's only spring. He must not trust me enough to go there. But why even ask if we won't go anytime soon? Everything with him is a fucking test.

He sets his napkin down and pushes back from the table. "Come on," he says.

I tense. "Where?"

"I want to show you something."

Every muscle in me stiffens. I follow him slowly, watching the way he moves through the house. My chest tightens as we reach a hallway I've never walked down before. Then he stops at a door.

I swallow hard. A basement door. My mind spins. Fuck. This is punishment, isn't it? For the leggings. For the t-shirt. For showing up to dinner looking like I didn't belong here. He didn't have to say it. Maybe it was just understood that I'm supposed to.

He unlocks the door and takes my hand, leading me down the stairs. Every step down feels heavier. My breath sticks. I keep waiting for the cold, the chain, the pole. But when he flips the lights on, I stop. It's warm. There's a couch that looks comfortable. A big flatscreen TV mounted on the wall, speakers tucked neatly around it. A popcorn machine sits on a side table, next to a stack of DVDs.

Photos of him and Eleanor line the wall. Not the posed, perfect ones from upstairs with the magazine-ready smiles. These are candid with laughter. Real smiles. Messy hair. This doesn't seem real. They're less staged than the ones I've seen before. I look closer and he looks genuinely happy. I didn't even know he was capable of real emotion. I don't care what he says, he must've loved her because he wouldn't have gone through the trouble of kidnapping someone who looks like her. But she didn't love him because if she did, she wouldn't have left and he can't accept that.

He looks at me. "I never got a chance to show you this room."

I stare around me, speechless.

"I know you said you wanted a space just for us in the last house," he continues. "So I made it happen here."

He gestures around with quiet pride. "I wanted this to be our sanctuary. Somewhere nothing could touch us."

Sanctuaries aren't locked. They're chosen. This one is hidden behind a door only he holds the key to.

I blink. "Why is it hidden?"

His lips twitch faintly. "Because designing homes is my job. My clients don't want a house that looks like this."

I glance at the photos again. The popcorn machine. "That's cold."

He shrugs. "It's the truth."

My chest pulls tight. "You did this for me?"

He steps closer. "I envisioned us down here. Watching movies. Eating popcorn. Just like you always wanted."

I stare at him, my heart knocking hard in my chest. It's sweet, but it's not for me. It's for her.

He runs a hand through his hair and smiles at me. "I can be what you need."

This isn't punishment, it's not the pole or the chains. It's something closer to human. It's the first real glimpse of the man behind all the power plays. But it's still him. And that's the part that scares me most. For a second, I don't know what to say. Maybe those photos are real because he's looking at me that way. How does he do it? Flip a switch and become a different person.

I don't even realize he's sat down until I hear his voice, calm and expectant.

"Aren't you going to sit?"

I blink, startled. I walk over and lower myself onto the couch, keeping a gap between us.

He watches me quietly. "Come closer."

I shift an inch, maybe two, but his eyes narrow as the tension sharpens.

"I said come here."

His hand closes around my arm, firm but gentle. He pulls me against him until my body settles into his side. His arm wraps around me, locking me in place. Then he leans down and kisses me.

I lean into his chest. Not because I trust him, but because I'm tired. It's easier this way. A small, quiet part of me wants this to mean something.

Maybe he can be gentle. Maybe there's a version of him who doesn't chain me to walls or track my every move. But I know better. Even as I let him touch me, even as my body starts to respond, I know better.

"I want you to be happy here," he says.

Here. Not happy everywhere. Not even happy with him. Just here.

Something about that difference makes my stomach twist.

He grabs the remote and flips on the TV. "This is your favorite," he adds.

I frown as the opening credits roll. A romantic comedy. I've never told him I liked this movie, so how did he know? Unless Eleanor had liked it, too. He laughs at one of the jokes. A real laugh. One that sounds like it belongs to a different man, and for a second, he seems normal. Not the cold businessman. Not the man who used his ring to lock an anklet onto my ankle. Just a man watching a movie with his wife.

But I'm not fooled. Not for a second. He's doing this because he thinks it will make me stay, or at least stop thinking about running. Because he thinks if he wraps me in warmth, feeds me softness, holds me close enough sometimes, I'll forget the feel of the chains.

I lean into him because there's nowhere else to go. But inside, every part of me stays sharp. Awake. Counting every breath. Because no matter how soft he makes this room, it's still a cage.

When the movie ends, he stretches, glancing at me like he's waiting for something.

"If you want," he says lightly, "we can sleep down here tonight."

Sleep down here? He stands and crosses the room, pushing open another door.

Inside is a bedroom. A real bedroom. Smaller than the one upstairs. Cozier. Not staged, or cold, or sterile. The bedding looks soft. The lamps are warm. The shelves are filled with old books and framed photos, not the curated, black-and-white prints that hang everywhere else.

I step closer, staring at it. Is this a secret space where we play pretend? A tucked-away stage where we cosplay as a normal couple, just for a few hours, so he can say he's giving me what I want? Because that's what it feels like. He built a place to mimic normalcy. A place where the walls don't feel so high. Where the decor doesn't scream perfection, but it doesn't touch me. Because it's not genuine, it's a performance.

He thinks this will make me happy. That softness layered over steel will trick me into staying. But it doesn't. It can't. Because even if the sheets are warmer, even if the pillows are softer, the door still locks from the inside. And I'll never forget that. But sometimes I wish I could.

I wish I could believe the softness means something, that the quiet in this room isn't manufactured. That the way he looks at me, like I matter, comes from something real. And maybe that's the worst part. A small, traitorous part of me wants this to be enough. Wants him to be enough. So that I can stop fighting and start living.

I don't even realize he's undressing me until I see my clothes on the floor. His hands are already sliding down my sides, warm and firm, mapping every curve like he already owns it. He doesn't rush. He doesn't fumble. He strips me down like he's done it before, like I'm already his.

He leans in and kisses my neck. His mouth drags down my skin, finding the dip of my collarbone, the curve of my breast. He lingers there, his lips brushing over my nipple before his tongue flicks across it, teasing once, then again. I gasp, my back arching without thinking. He presses his mouth harder, sucking until I feel the heat pull straight between my legs.

He moves lower, trailing kisses down my stomach. His lips stay warm and soft against my skin. Then he looks up at me, quiet, steady, his hands wrapping around my hips as he guides me onto the bed.

He stretches over me, his chest against mine, his cock thick and hard against my thigh. His hand slides down between my legs, his fingers stroking once, making me shiver.

"I'll never leave you," he murmurs.

He kisses me again, deeper, his tongue pushing into my mouth as his hand parts me.

His fingers slide through the wetness before he pulls them away, lining himself up.

"Let me in."

I nod because saying no would be a waste. His hips push forward, and he slides inside me, filling me inch by inch until I feel stretched around him. My mouth falls open, a low moan breaking free.

"Fuck," he groans, his hand sliding up to cradle the back of my head as he rocks forward again. "You feel amazing."

He moves deeper and harder with every thrust. His chest brushes mine. His lips find my jaw, kissing, biting softly, then sucking until I know he's leaving a mark.

"You're perfect for me," he says against my skin.

"Until I'm not."

"That day will never come," he says.

The words slam through me harder than his thrusts. I clutch his back as he drives into me again, my hips rising to meet him. Each push makes me gasp and whimper. He grips my thigh, pulling me closer, angling me to take him deeper.

"I want you to be happy with me," he murmurs. His thrusts are slow, deep and heavy, grinding against me exactly where I need it.

"I don't know if I can be."

He doesn't hesitate. "You already are."

I want to believe, to let his words fill a void in me. But I know better—nothing good lasts, not with him, and sure as hell not with me.

I moan louder, my body tightening under him, chasing that edge as he holds me still.

"Now come and show me how happy you are," he orders, his hand slipping between us, his thumb finding my clit, rubbing hard and fast until my whole body clenches around him.

I cry out, shaking beneath him, every nerve snapping tight as he thrusts through my orgasm. He groans again, his rhythm breaking, his hips jerking forward until he pushes deep and stills, spilling inside me with a rough growl. He lifts his thumb to my cheek, wiping a tear I hadn't noticed.

"You deserve my love," he whispers.

I open my mouth, but nothing comes out.

"I just can't give it to you," he adds, softer.

"Then why say anything at all?" The words scrape out of me, sharp and trembling. His body goes rigid. For a moment I think he might answer, but he doesn't. His jaw tightens, and instead he pulls me closer, crushing me against his chest, not letting me move as he kisses my forehead.

The story of my life is that no one has ever loved me. Even

though I'm not his wife, it still hurts when someone tells you to your face that they don't love you, knowing you deserve it, yet they're willing to remind you of that without trying to change it. Then he kisses my forehead again, lingering there, his lips warm and steady, leaving behind a promise I never asked for, but one I know he'll keep.

27

ADRIAN

Ellie's in my arms. She's soft and warm against me, quiet, still. I know she's been distant lately. Pulling away, overthinking. That's not what we need right now. Not with everything ahead. I have big plans for us. She needs to get back out into society. I think that will help her. She thrived in throwing parties and hosting others. She's missing that right now.

I brush my hand down her back, slow and steady, feeling every inch of her spine beneath my palm. She exhales against my chest, a small sound she probably doesn't even realize she's making. I press my lips to her temple, holding her closer. She needs this. She needs me. She won't admit it, but I know.

Tonight, she disobeyed me. She didn't dress for dinner like she should've. Showed up in leggings and an old t-shirt, like she was testing me, waiting to see what I'd do.

I let it slide. I could've punished her. I didn't. Because I saw what it really was. She wanted my attention. Good or bad, she craves it. So I gave it to her.

I showed her the room I built for her. Even when she was

gone, when she left without a word, leaving me waiting. I kept building, even when she was gone. I needed to believe she'd come back. And she did.

The moment she stepped inside, I watched her shoulders relax. Her eyes lingered on the couch, the photos, the little details she didn't expect. She looked at the popcorn machine like it was a gift. I've handed her a piece of the life she forgot she wanted. She loved it. She won't say it, but I saw it.

But this space? This isn't an everyday thing. This is a reward. A gift. A reminder of what I can give her when she's mine the way I need her to be.

I tighten my arms around her, stroking her hair. She shifts closer, curling into me. I kiss her forehead softly.

"You're safe with me," I murmur. "You always will be."

She exhales, barely audible. "If you say so."

I tilt her chin up with my hand. "Don't question me."

She doesn't pull away. I feel her settle against me. I keep my hand moving down her back, tracing the curve of her waist. I cup her hip, pulling her tighter until her body flushes with mine. Doubt is poison, and I won't let it take root. The sooner she accepts that, the safer she'll feel and will be.

Tomorrow, I'll take her out on the water. Let her feel the breeze. And when she asks to steer the boat, I'll say yes, because a leash doesn't have to look like a leash.

I lower my mouth to her jaw, kissing it, then lower, letting my lips graze her throat.

"I know you," I tell her quietly. "Better than anyone ever could."

She tilts her head, giving me more access. She doesn't even notice. I kiss her neck again, slower, keeping my mouth there, tasting her skin, refusing to let doubt sink into her.

"I made this for you. For us."

I press another kiss below her ear and pull her tighter. Her breathing slows, and she sinks against me, starting to believe. I hold her there, exactly where I want her. Force won't get me what I want. This will. And she's already giving in.

28

MAREN

I wake up disoriented, blinking at the unfamiliar ceiling. For a second, I don't know where I am. Then it comes back—the hidden room, the couch, the warmth of his arms, the way he held me like it meant something.

I turn my head. Adrian's still beside me, but he's not touching me. His arm's pulled away, his back half-turned.

It feels...wrong. Like something's missing.

I lie still, watching him breathe, trying to make sense of last night. He'd been different. Softer. Gentler. He'd shown me a side of him I didn't know existed. For a few hours, I almost believed it. I almost believed him.

But now, in the daylight, with his body turned away from me, it feels like a story I imagined.

He stirs. His eyes open slowly, those cold, green eyes settling on me without a hint of warmth.

He sits up, swinging his legs over the side of the bed. He doesn't speak. Doesn't kiss me or even smile. He stands, stretching once before glancing over his shoulder. His voice is flat.

"Breakfast is in an hour. Get ready. Dress properly."

That's it.

He walks out without another word. I stay frozen under the blanket, staring at the space where he'd been. *Was it all a lie?*

My chest tightens, heat crawling up my neck as the truth sinks in. He gave me exactly what I wanted last night. Just enough warmth to pull me closer. Just enough tenderness to make me lower my guard. And I fell for it.

I squeeze my eyes shut, furious at myself for believing him. Angry at him for knowing exactly how to play me.

I throw the blanket off and sit up, my legs shaky as my feet touch the floor.

His hand stroking my back. The way he kissed my forehead like he meant it. I wanted to believe it, but it was never going to last. I need to remember that.

No matter how good it felt in the moment, or how gentle his hands were, or how soft his kisses were, it wasn't real.

And it never will be.

I glance down at my ankle.

The anklet glints under the soft light, snug around my skin. I reach for it, my fingers fumbling with the clasp. I try to pry it open, search for a catch, anything. But it doesn't budge.

My nails scrape uselessly against the metal.

"Come on," I whisper. "Come on."

It won't come off.

I press my thumb against the edge until it hurts, biting down the rising wave of panic.

I want it off. I want it off so badly I could scream.

But it's locked.

I let my hands fall into my lap, my chest heaving, my heart hammering hard enough to hurt.

I stare at it for a long moment, the reality settling deep in my gut. He showed me tenderness last night, but what it means is that I'll never be free unless he lets me.

And he never will.

I stand, pulling the blanket tighter around me.

He wants me dressed properly. Fine.

But he doesn't get to decide everything.

Not how I think. Not how I fight.

Not how I get out.

Not forever.

He didn't lay out an outfit for me this morning, so I choose a white blouse and pastel skirt from the closet. I've slowly learned his preferences based off what he picked out for me. He seems to prefer me in pink.

At breakfast, Adrian leans back in his chair, fingers tapping the table as he says, "I want you to throw a masquerade party."

I frown. "For what?"

"A charity event for a new children's hospital. My company is hosting it here, in the ballroom."

We have a ballroom? What is this, a castle?

Almost as if he hears the doubt in my silence, his tone shifts. "You won't do it alone. I got a party planner to handle every detail. But I want you to show your face again. This is how you step back into your place, Ellie."

My pulse skips. He's serious. This isn't just another dinner, this is an event. A stage. Every eye will be on me, waiting to see if I stumble, if I remember which fork to pick up or how to smile in the right way. He wants me polished, perfect, proof that I belong here. If I falter, it won't just embarrass me, it'll embarrass him. And I know how that ends. His gaze flicks to me. "I expect it to be better than the ones you've done before."

Of course, it has to be better. Nothing is ever enough. Not even me.

He studies me for a moment, then adds, "I need you to show off our house to anyone who wants to see it."

I fold my arms. "You mean parade guests around like they're potential clients?"

"If that's what they want." His voice stays smooth and

completely unbothered. "You'll give them the perfect experience."

He says it like it's simple. Smile, host, and pretend I'm proud to be part of this.

"I need you to be the perfect—"

"Trophy wife," I cut in, my voice flat.

His expression shifts, his jaw tightening and his eyes darkening. "What did you just say?"

I stare at him. "Trophy wife."

A muscle jumps in his cheek. "You're not one."

I scoff. "Then what am I, Adrian? The perfect hostess? The perfect showpiece? The woman who makes you look good while you network with other men who probably treat their wives the exact same way?"

"You're smart," he says, his voice harder. "You know how to carry a room, and you do it well."

He didn't think that after the failed dinner party. But I have a feeling this is another test, and if I fail, I don't even know what to think about what the punishment will be for this failure.

I let out a humorless laugh. "Right. And that's why you need me to smile, nod, and pretend I don't see what this really is."

He exhales slowly. "I need you to do your part."

I tilt my head. "And what part is that? Planning parties? Playing gracious host while you make business deals? Standing there, looking pretty while you talk about things I have no say in?"

His stare sharpens. "You're my wife."

I lean forward. "Then treat me like one."

The air turns heavy, neither of us breaking the silence. I wait for him to prove me wrong, to say something real.

Adrian watches me for a long moment, then stands. "You'll do it. Because you know what's expected of you."

I swallow the tightness in my throat. The room feels smaller than it did a second ago.

I know what's expected of me, but for the first time, I'm not sure I can do it. I've never thrown a party before, and it's expected to be better than the last. I don't even know what that one was like.

"And if I don't?" I ask.

His expression hardens. "If I want you to fuck me, you fuck me. If I want you to plan a party, then plan the damn party."

The words hit harder than they should. Maybe because I know they're true. They've just never been said that bluntly before.

Heat builds in my chest, and pressure rises in my throat. "And what the fuck do I get out of this?"

I think of the silence. Of meals eaten with no conversation. Of days blending together in a house I didn't choose. Of the man who watches everything, but sees nothing. He has always treated me that way.

His eyes narrow. "What?"

I step closer. "What the fuck do I get out of this? A painting studio when I don't paint? A sitting room with no access to the outside world? No friends. No money to buy anything. I don't even have a car." My voice rises. "So tell me, Adrian, what do I get besides selfish sex?" The moment the words leave my mouth, I see it. The crack. The part of him that still believes I won't talk back, fractured.

His mouth parts, slightly caught off guard. "Selfish sex?" he repeats, his tone sharp, like I've slapped him. That's the part that breaks through. Not the isolation or the control. Just that. He doesn't hear the word selfish the way I mean it—emotional, one-sided, empty. But it still cuts. I let out a cold laugh. "That's the only thing you care about." His nostrils flare. He still doesn't speak, because he knows I'm not wrong.

I shake my head. "You have an answer for everything. Every argument, every complaint, you twist it. So tell me. What do I get? What's my reward for being your wife?"

His jaw tightens. "You have a closet full of designer clothes. A beautiful home I designed for you."

I scoff. "So clothes that I can't wear anywhere because I'm stuck in this prison?"

It's beautiful, sure. But it's still a prison. I can't even open a window without him noticing. I can't breathe without permission. He exhales through his nose. The vein in his temple starts to pulse.

I lean in closer. "You always have an answer. So answer this. What do I get?"

His lips part, but nothing comes out. His brows pull together for half a second before his face resets. He wants to defend himself. I can see it. But there's nothing he can say that doesn't prove me right. So the silence drags while he says nothing. The truth is, I get nothing, and no answer makes this okay.

Then I turn to walk away. "That's what I thought."

His voice drops low. "Eleanor. Sit back down."

I keep moving. If I stop now, I'll fold, and he'll win again.

"Eleanor."

Still, I don't stop.

"Eleanor, calm down."

"Fuck off, Adrian."

Consequences be damned. I shut the door behind me, my chest tight and breath unsteady. My sitting room is the only thing he thinks he's given me. One room in a mansion. A place to sit and look pretty. A cage with nice furniture. Even with the door closed, I can still feel him watching.

I sit on the sofa, lean forward, and press my hands to my face. I tell myself not to cry, but it doesn't work. I'm not even sure what I'm crying for. What I've lost, or what I never had.

A knock hits the door.

I inhale and wipe my face. "Go away, Adrian."

Then a voice, quiet and soft, sounds behind the door. "Ma'am, I brought you food."

I pause, then open the door. Greta stands there, holding a tray. She must hear it in my voice, what's left of it. But she doesn't ask if I'm okay. No one ever does. She's avoided me ever since my plea for her help. No eye contact. No small talk. Just distance.

"Come in," I say, stepping aside.

She sets the tray down by the window without a word. The sandwiches are cut into neat triangles with the crusts gone, exactly how I like them. My chest tightens. *How does she know that?* Maybe she's seen me peel the edges off before. Or maybe Adrian told her. Either way, it means they're watching me closer than I ever realized.

I stare at the plate, my stomach twisting. He hasn't spoken to me since the fight. He just sent food, as if that would fix it. As if that would make me forget I get nothing.

As she leaves, she says, "After lunch, Mr. Montgomery wants you ready by the dock."

I blurt out before I can stop myself, "Is the money worth never leaving this place?"

She freezes. "I made my choices just like you did," she says flatly, then shakes her head and hurries out without looking back.

Her words stung. *Choices.* As if staying here is the same as whatever bargain she made. I didn't pick this life. But then my chest clenches, because part of me knows that's not the whole truth. I chose what hurt less—food over hunger, silence over punishment, anything over nothing. Maybe that's what she meant. Maybe survival looks like choice from the outside.

After lunch I walk down the path toward the dock, my heart thudding harder with every step. Adrian's already there, standing beside the boat, his hands resting on the railing like he's been waiting.

He turns when he hears me. And he smiles. Not the tight, cold smile he wears in meetings, and the coldness in his eyes is gone. He kisses my cheek. I guess he'll let my outburst earlier slide this time.

I step closer, taking it in. It's smaller than I imagined. A sleek, modest speedboat, glossy white with navy trim. The leather seats gleam in the sun, clean and new. There's a small console with controls I don't understand yet, a steering wheel that looks almost like a car's, and a folded canopy overhead. The water laps gently against the sides.

"I'm going to teach you how to drive it," he says.

My breath catches. "Really?"

He nods. "You said you wanted to learn. I told you I'd think about it."

I nod quickly, trying not to let the excitement show too much. "I'd love that."

He smiles again, broader this time, clearly pleased. "Good."

He helps me climb in. The boat rocks underfoot, but his grip steadies me. I settle into the seat beside him, pulling the life jacket straps snug as he hands me a pair of his sunglasses to wear.

He starts explaining things. The safety features, the radio, what to do if we capsize, and how to throw an anchor. His voice is patient, and it feels like a lesson, not a performance.

I watch his hands as he demonstrates the controls, the way he flips switches and turns knobs. He explains how the throttle works, where the emergency cut-off cord is, how to check the gauges.

He leans closer, showing me how to adjust the steering wheel height.

"This is serious," he says, giving me a quick look. "You're not just playing with a toy. This is real responsibility."

"I understand," I say, keeping my voice soft, respectful. "Thank you for trusting me."

That does it. His chest lifts with pride, his jaw relaxing as he looks out at the water.

"You'll do fine."

He starts the engine and pulls us away from the dock. The boat hums beneath us, smooth and powerful as it glides over the water. The wind lifts my hair, cool and clean against my face. Sunlight bounces off the waves, bright enough to make me squint even behind the glasses.

Adrian looks relaxed at the wheel, one hand resting lightly on the throttle, the other draped over the wheel. His sunglasses hide his eyes, but I can see his mouth soften, his shoulders lose their usual stiffness.

I wonder what he's thinking. But I don't ask.

Instead, I lean closer, resting my hand lightly on his thigh. "I'm glad you brought me out here," I say quietly. "I've like spending time with you."

The lie makes me feel sick. He glances at me, pleased. I see it in the slight uptick of his mouth, the way his fingers flex against the wheel.

That's what he wants. Adoration. Devotion. I give it to him because it's what keeps him calm, and gets me what I want. But inside, I'm already memorizing every control, every dial, every emergency procedure he showed me. I'm calculating the distance from the dock, watching the shoreline fade. This boat is my ticket out. If he ever lets me take it alone, even once...

He slows the engine after a while, coasting us deeper into open water. Then he kills the motor entirely and drops anchor. Silence folds around us, broken only by the soft slap of waves against the hull.

Adrian leans back in his seat, pulling off his sunglasses. His green eyes shine in the sun, sharper now, though still calm.

Then he shifts, turning toward me.

"I want you to do something for me."

I tilt my head. "What?"

His mouth lifts at one corner.

"Blow me."

My lips part. I stare at him, caught between disbelief and frustration. Of course, this wasn't just about teaching me.

His smile widens as he watches my face. "Come on, Ellie."

I close my eyes for a second, then look back at him, forcing a smile.

"Anything for you."

But inside, I'm screaming. Because even here, even now, there's no freedom. Only the illusion of it. He knows it, and I know it. But neither of us is going to say it out loud.

I guess I don't move fast enough because he pulls himself out, his hand wrapping around mine and guiding it to him. His skin's hot and hard under my palm, and when I close my fingers around him, he lets out a quiet groan.

"Feel that?" he murmurs, watching me. "That's all for you."

I swallow hard, unable to stop the heat curling low in my stomach. I shouldn't want him. Not like this. Not when I know what he's doing. But my body doesn't listen.

I drop to my knees beside him. He leans back in the seat, his mouth curving into a pleased smile.

When I take him into my mouth, his head tips back with a groan. His hand finds my hair, gripping tighter as I sink lower, taking more of him.

"You're a good student," he says, his voice rough, his breath catching.

I pull back, looking up at him. "You're a good teacher."

That makes him grin. "Keep going."

He tightens his hold on my hair, urging me forward. I feel his hips shift, his body moving with me, pushing deeper. His breath turns ragged, and I feel the tension building under my hands as his muscles flex.

When I slow, he grips my hair harder and starts thrusting into my mouth, controlling the rhythm. His jaw clenches as he watches me, eyes dark and hungry.

"Fuck," he mutters, his chest heaving. "Take off your clothes."

I pull back just enough to strip off my shirt, then my bra, sliding them off as quickly as I can. His gaze never leaves me, and he strokes his cock as I shimmy out of my pants and underwear.

"Keep going," he orders, his voice low and tight.

I lean forward again, wrapping my lips around him. He runs his hand down my chest, his palm warm as it grazes my breast, his thumb circling my nipple until it tightens beneath his touch.

It's hard not to feel aroused. Hard not to respond to the way he's touching me, even though I hate that I'm giving him exactly what he wants.

He groans louder as I move faster, sliding my tongue along the underside of him, hollowing my cheeks to pull him deeper. His hips jerk forward, his breath turning harsh.

"Fuck, your mouth's so wet, so hot," he says, his voice breaking. "You're going to make me..."

I swirl my tongue around him, pressing closer, and he doesn't finish the sentence before his body stiffens and he groans, tilting his head back. His hand holds my head steady as he spills into my mouth.

"Swallow all of it," he commands, and I do with no hesitation. I enjoy making him lose control, even if it's just for a few minutes.

When he finally lets go, his chest rises and falls. Sweat beads at his temple. He looks down at me with a satisfied gleam in his eyes.

"You're everything I've ever wanted," he says, tucking himself back into his pants.

And in that moment, I don't know if I've won or lost. Maybe both.

After I pull my clothes back on, he zips up and glances over at me, a faint smile still lingering on his lips. "You want to try?" he asks, nodding toward the controls.

I blink, surprised. "I can?"

He pats his lap. "Come here."

I climb onto his lap, settling between his legs as he places his hands over mine on the wheel. His chest presses against my back.

"Go ahead," he murmurs. "Steer."

I grip the wheel tighter, guiding it gently as he lets me turn it. The boat shifts beneath us, cutting through the water, and for a brief moment, I feel a flicker of excitement. I glance back at him, but he's relaxed. Sunglasses still shield his eyes.

"How am I doing?" I ask.

"You're doing fine," he says.

I look forward again, keeping my hands steady on the wheel. "When can I start driving it by myself?"

He pauses. "Once you get your boating license," he says.

I turn my head, frowning. "I need a license to drive it?"

He smiles faintly, almost indulgently. "Of course. You can't take it out alone without one."

I chew the inside of my cheek. "Okay...when can I get it?"

His hand squeezes my hip gently. "When I'm confident you know what you're doing."

I stare at the water ahead, the waves breaking in soft ripples. "And how long will that take?"

He doesn't answer right away. His hand slides higher, brushing under my shirt, stroking my side. "It'll take as long as it takes."

I wait. He doesn't offer a timeline or date. Not even a vague promise. That's when it clicks. It won't happen. He'll always say I need more practice, more supervision, more time. Even if I memorize every control and every rule, he'll find another reason to delay. He'll never be confident. I know what I'm doing. Because confidence would mean freedom, and freedom isn't part of the offer.

I keep my hands steady on the wheel, biting back the frustration bubbling under my ribs. I force a small smile, leaning back against his chest.

"Well, I'd better make sure I'm the best student you've ever had."

He chuckles low in my ear while kissing my neck. "You already are."

But I know the truth. I'll never be more than a passenger. He taught me how to steer.

But he'll never let me drive.

29

ADRIAN

Ellie seems disappointed she can't drive it herself. I catch it in the way her smile fades, the way her gaze lingered on the water a little too long, like she was imagining riding without me. But why would she need that? We're doing this together. This isn't about her going off alone. I thought she wanted to spend time with me, not drift away or picture herself leaving me behind. She doesn't need that. She shouldn't even want that.

It's not safe, anyway, because she doesn't even know how to swim, which only proves she's not ready. I lean back in my seat while I watch her grip the wheel tighter, her brows pulling together in frustration she thinks I can't see. Maybe she feels like I'm holding her back or she thinks I'm the reason she isn't steering alone. But she's wrong, because she's not ready, and the truth is she doesn't need to be. This boat is meant for us to enjoy together.

Yet the way she keeps staring out at the water makes me wonder if she's imagining leaving. I watch her closely as a tightness creeps into my chest. Is she thinking about taking it? Does she really believe she could go? I don't want her to want that. I want her to want me, to stay devoted to me.

It stings more than I expected. The way she looks past me instead of at me. But that's just proof she needs more time. More structure. More of me.

She thinks she wants space. But what she really needs is to feel secure, even if she doesn't realize it yet. That's why I'm here. I'm here to protect her, to keep her close. If she's a good girl, I'll take her out and make her feel special. She'll thank me for it one day. And if she doesn't, then she won't get a choice but to. I rest my hand over hers on the wheel, steadying it. "You're doing fine, Ellie. Just don't forget, I'll always be right here with you."

30

MAREN

We pull up to the dock, the boat slowing until it bumps gently against the edge. Adrian ties it off, glancing back at me with a rare smile.

"You did well out there, Ellie," he says.

I nod. "Thanks."

"You're welcome." His mouth curves a little more, pleased with himself.

We step off the boat, and he walks beside me up the path toward the house.

I open my mouth to say something, but he keeps going. "Oh —and I almost forgot. Sasha wants to do brunch later this week."

Sasha, who looks at me like I'm gum stuck to the bottom of her shoe. The woman who smiles at me like she knows every secret I don't. So why the hell does she want to waste her time eating brunch with me? Unless she's figured out that I'm not the real Eleanor, and this is a test or an interrogation.

"She...does?" I ask carefully.

He nods. "Yeah. You two used to go every month back in

Chicago. Now that she's moved here, she wants to keep it up. Spend more time with you."

After that dinner party, I have no desire to spend time with her, and he's lying to himself if he thinks she wants to spend time with me.

I swallow the tightness rising in my throat. "When?"

"I'll let you know," Adrian says, already pulling out his phone as we reach the steps. "Probably the end of the week. She's excited."

I wonder if he hears how hollow that sounds or if he cares. I linger by him, watching him scroll through his phone, his back already half-turned. I've been dismissed. But something pushes me forward. Diane looked at me differently. She noticed things. Things no one else dared to say out loud. I need that again, even if it's only for a few minutes.

"I want to spend time with Diane," I say. "Catch up. Since... we had them over for dinner."

He stops typing. His shoulders stiffen, just a flicker, but enough. He looks back at me, his face carefully neutral.

"Diane?" he repeats.

"Yeah." I try to sound casual. "I haven't seen her in a while. It'd be nice."

Diane is different. At dinner, she watched me like she was cataloging differences. Not cruel—curious. That pause before she smiled. The way she asked gentle, specific questions Eleanor would've answered in her sleep. Then she cornered me at dinner in the bathroom, wondering what I was doing back. She knew her before I ever stepped onto this island. If anyone could notice I'm not her, or at least slip me a phone, a window to run, it's Diane.

He studies me a second longer. Something shifts behind his eyes, a tightness he tries to mask with a smile.

"That's a good idea," he says, his voice light but a little too smooth. "It might be good for you. Socializing again. Getting back into society."

He nods once, almost to himself, then taps something into his phone. "I'll see when it fits into your schedule."

I blink. I didn't realize I had a schedule. "My schedule?"

"I hired you an etiquette teacher."

I blink. "Etiquette teacher?"

"Yeah," he says, like it's obvious. "Pauline is great. You'll like her." He throws me a sideways glance. "It'll be good for you and help prepare you for the party."

He glances at me. "So you got your training sessions starting up. Brunch with Sasha. The masquerade to plan. It's filling up fast."

He steps closer, brushing a hand down my arm, his tone gentle. "Don't worry, I'll make sure it's balanced this time. You'll have time with Diane. I'll handle it."

I force a smile, even as something cold seeps under my skin. He'll handle it like I'm just another event to arrange. Then he starts walking away, leaving me standing on the porch, still smelling the water, still tasting the salt on my lips.

I glance down at the anklet locked around my ankle. Diane is my only shot. If I can get five minutes alone, I might get a way out.

And that means I have one job. Make those five minutes happen.

After the afternoon on the boat, I curl up on the couch in the sitting room, one leg tucked beneath me, the other shaking. The journal's already in my lap. I hadn't planned to open it tonight, but I couldn't stop myself.

I flip to a bookmarked page and stop. This entry is about their wedding day.

∿

While I was getting ready for the wedding, my mother, with her brown hair in an updo and her long blue dress, stepped into the room. She asked everyone to leave. We hadn't talked in years, but I felt compelled to call her when I got engaged. She's the only family I have, and it's not a good look if the bride's mother isn't there even though she's alive. Even Adrian invited his mother. Also, being the only child, I know my mother wouldn't want to miss it either. She said, "I want a few minutes with you."

She sat beside me, smoothing her hands over her dress. "Marriage is a commitment. It's hard work. Are you sure you're ready for this? Because if you aren't, now's the time to end it."

I stared at her. I was already dressed, about to go out there, and now she was asking me? Why not last night, or the night before? This is horrible timing, but I'm also grateful she asked that shows me she does care about my happiness.

She gave me a small smile. "My mother did the same thing. And I want you to know, I'll support whatever you choose to do." Then she added, "Even though it will embarrass our family, I'll still support you."

There was the catch. For a second, I almost gave her credit for doing something selfless. But no, I was wrong. She isn't selfless, she just cares about appearances. She only asked because she thought that's what's what a mother is supposed to do.

I lifted my chin. "I'm marrying Adrian today. Nothing's going to stop that."

She nodded. "Very well. I'll see you out there."

When I walked down the aisle, I took everything in at once. The venue was perfect. The rows of white chairs. The soft candlelight flickering along the sides. The tall, vaulted ceiling with chandeliers glittering high above. It was elegant, polished, expensive, beautiful.

And then there was Adrian.

He stood at the front, tall and composed, dressed in a sharp grey suit tailored perfectly to his broad frame. His blonde hair was styled neatly, his face clean-shaven, his green eyes locked right on me. He looked like a man who belonged here, confident, poised, powerful. He watched me like I was the prize he'd already claimed, and his faint smile only deepened the closer I came.

I felt my hands shake slightly even as I smiled.

This was happening.

When we got to the vows, the priest asked, "Eleanor, do you promise to love, honor, and obey your husband, for as long as you both shall live?"

I know I heard my mother gasp softly at the word obey, *and I almost gasped, too. But I smiled, pushing the hesitation down, telling myself this was the life I'd chosen.*

When I said the words, I saw Adrian's smile widen, like the final piece had clicked into place. I told myself I could live with this. I told myself I'd be fine, but I wasn't.

I close the book, pressing the cover shut harder than I meant to. The word *obey* keeps echoing in my head. Her mother gasped. She almost did, too. But she said it. Smiling.

I rise from the couch, suddenly too hot, too aware of the anklet around my ankle and the empty bedroom waiting down the hall.

I'm not Eleanor. But if I keep pretending long enough, maybe I will be. And that is fucking scary. That I've been a captive for so long I start believing the lies I'm being told. I still want to escape, but some days I'm content. Because I'm not struggling to pay rent or worried about eviction. Or stuck working at the Rusty Nail. I'm living in luxury, and it's almost hard to think about life before. But these thoughts just prove I've fucking lost it and need to get the hell out of here. Could I find her? Eleanor's mother? Would she know? Would she look at me, hear my voice, the way I talk, and realize I am not her daughter? Or would she not notice?

I run a hand through my hair, pacing the room. I can't go to the police, Adrian has made sure of that and will make it seem like I'm the crazy one. I can't go to anyone here because they all see me as Eleanor. But her mother might be different. If I can reach her, maybe she will help me. Maybe she would be the one person who could look Adrian in the eye and say, "This is not my daughter."

I chew my lip, my chest tightening as the possibilities fill my head. Would Adrian let me contact her? Would he monitor my calls? Would she even believe me? I have no idea. But if I could slip one message through, just one, maybe there would finally be a crack in all of this.

I sink onto the couch, heart pounding, fingers gripping the edge of the cushion. I am not Eleanor. I have never been Eleanor. And maybe her mother is the only one left who could prove it.

I stop at Adrian's office door, gripping the handle tight. My heart beats faster, but I push it open and step inside.

He looks up from a folder, eyes sharp, his focus snapping right to me. "Ellie?"

"I want to contact my mother," I say, forcing my voice to stay even.

His brow pulls slightly, suspicion flickering across his face. "You haven't spoken to your mother in years. Why now?"

I swallow hard. He wants to keep me cut off. He wants me tied to him, no outside voices, no escape routes.

"There's no better time than the present," I answer, lifting my chin.

Adrian leans back in his chair, watching me carefully. His fingers rest against the desk. "Why the sudden interest?"

"Life is too short, all I need is her number," I press. This might be my only way out, my only chance to reach someone who could break this illusion, someone who'd know I'm not Eleanor.

He lets out a slow breath, tapping his fingers once against the wood. "I'll think about it."

I clench my fists. "What's there to think about?"

His expression hardens slightly. "She upsets you more than she helps you."

"That's my choice," I shoot back. "If you want to talk to your family, you do. But don't stop me from talking to mine."

His jaw flexes, and for a long second, he watches me. I hold my breath, refusing to look away.

Without another word, he opens a drawer, pulls out a piece of paper, and writes quickly. He slides it across the desk.

"Don't come crying to me when things fall apart with her," he mutters.

I snatch the paper, the corners crumpling under my fingers, and turn sharply.

As I leave, my heart pounds hard in my chest, my fingers tightening around the slip of paper. I can't waste this. But as I step into the hall, a new thought strikes, cold and sharp.

Why did he know the number by heart?

I stare at the number for too long. It's just ink on paper. But it feels heavier. It feels like it could collapse everything if I dial it. I don't even know her name. Eleanor never wrote it down. Just referred to her as *my mother*. I sit on the edge of the couch, my thumb hovering over the screen. I don't know what I'm expecting. That she'll pick up and say, "Oh, thank God, I knew something was wrong." That she'll hear my voice and know.

That she'll become the kind of mother I've never had, that's the part that really messes with my head. I've seen foster moms pull their kids into their arms, kiss their heads, wipe their tears. Love that isn't earned or conditional. Love that doesn't expire when you're inconvenient.

I never had that. I've been the extra mouth to feed. The afterthought. The girl who aged out without anyone calling me daughter. I don't think about my egg and sperm donor. I don't know if I was given up or taken away, but either way, they didn't want me.

But maybe Eleanor's mother is different. Maybe if I speak calmly, if I tell her I'm not who she thinks—I'm not her daughter—she'll believe me. She'll help me. She has to. I punch in the number before I can change my mind. The second she picks up, I don't hesitate.

"Who's this?" she asks.

"Hi, Mom."

That feels so unnatural.

"You're calling me mom now? Not Betty?"

I hadn't expected that. I didn't even know Eleanor called her by her first name.

"I need help. I'm trying to get away from Adrian. He monitors everything. I can't leave."

"I told you to back out before the wedding. I knew this would happen."

"Then help me now."

She can't be that cold, she should care about her daughter.

"I can't."

"Why not?"

"Because he paid off my home. He checks in. More than you ever did."

My fingers tighten around the phone. He has control over her, too? Another pawn on his payroll. What else has he taken?

"When did that start?"

"After the wedding. He believes in taking care of family. And honestly, I do, too."

"He's not family. He's controlling you, too."

"He's not as bad as I thought."

"You think that because you're benefiting from him."

"Calm down. You haven't called me in years, and now you expect me to help you? After how ungrateful and disrespectful you've been?"

So that's it. She's no different. Just another part of his world. Maybe Eleanor never stood a chance.

"You're my mother. Aren't you supposed to help me?"

"No."

She hangs up.

I lower the phone and stare at the blank screen. What a fucking bitch. There's no lifeline. No one to say, *You're not Eleanor.* No one to pull me out of this. I thought mothers were supposed to love their biological daughters. Even my fake mom doesn't want me. That fucking hurts. Why does no one ever want me?

I never had one. Growing up, I told myself it didn't matter, that I was better off not knowing them. Foster homes taught me to keep my expectations low—no one's coming for you, no one's staying. But part of me still wondered what it might feel like, to hear someone call me theirs and mean it. For a second, I thought maybe pretending could trick the ache into quiet. I thought maybe even a lie could fill the hole.

But even Eleanor's mother chose him. I feel rejected, and she's not even mine. That part hits harder than I expected. I thought I was calling for help. Maybe what I really wanted was to belong to someone, just once, even if it wasn't real. But even that was too much to ask.

Later that night, I don't say much at dinner. The silence between us stretches long, broken only by the occasional clink of his glass when he sets it down.

Adrian leans back in his chair, his gaze lingering. "Did you call your mother?"

I nod once. "Yeah."

"How did it go?"

He doesn't need to know about my call for help, and hopefully she doesn't tell him about it.

"It went as expected."

I don't look at him. He was right; she does upset more than help.

He doesn't say anything. He just watches. I wipe under my eyes, but the tears are already falling.

Adrian rises and crosses the room. He lowers himself beside my chair, rests one hand behind my back, the other on my arm, and pulls me forward until I'm against him. His hand moves slowly along my spine, fingers spreading and drawing close again with each pass. I rest my cheek against his chest. I almost feel guilty. The whole purpose of that phone call was to get away from him, and now he's comforting me on my failed attempt he doesn't know about.

"Aren't you going to say I told you so?" I murmur.

His hand pauses, then keeps moving. "No."

"Why not?"

If the roles were reversed, I would.

He draws in a breath. "I don't talk to my mother, either."

I lift my head slightly. His eyes are steady. He doesn't explain further. The journal did mention he wasn't close with his mother.

"What about my father? I want to contact him."

His body stills. His hand, warm against my back, goes motionless.

"Ellie..." His voice drops, almost gentle. "Your father died. Years ago."

My chest tightens. Damn it. I didn't know that. How would I? Eleanor never mentioned him, not once in the journal. But now it makes sense. Panic crawls up my throat. No parents. No one left to save me from him.

"How?" I whisper.

He doesn't answer right away. His jaw tenses, eyes narrowing like he wants to protect me from it. Or maybe from himself.

"Tell me," I press.

His gaze locks on mine, unflinching. "He killed himself when you were a teenager."

The bluntness punches through me. I don't even know this man, but grief rips through anyway. Maybe because it's the only family I thought I could cling to, even in this twisted role. Even a lie feels like a loss.

"You don't remember?" he asks quietly.

I had no idea, but the truth doesn't matter here.

I nod, slow and small. "I do. I just wanted to believe someone could help me."

The second the words leave my mouth, I want them back. Stupid. That's going to sound like more than it is. Like I've been looking for a way out.

His hand stills against me, subtly. Then starts stroking my back again, comforting me. But I know he heard me.

He brushes a piece of hair behind my ear, his fingers lingering. "You don't need anyone else. You have me. That's all that matters."

"You don't talk about your family."

He exhales slowly, warm against my neck. He doesn't want this conversation. But instead he says, "What do you want to know?"

"Why don't you talk to your mom?"

He looks away. "She abandoned our family when I was a kid. She'd only come around for holidays or when she wanted to show us off. She was focused on finding rich men to take care of her."

So he has mommy issues.

"Didn't you come from a wealthy family?"

"Yeah." He shrugs slightly. "But I guess it wasn't enough. My father isn't an emotional man. He'd throw money at us growing up, he wasn't interested until I was older."

And he has daddy issues.

"Who raised you then?"

"Nannies. I looked after my sister. She always got in trouble, but I was the golden kid. My father wanted a son. He didn't know what to do with a daughter."

His voice stays even, but his eyes shift away, closing the door on more questions.

"Is your father still alive?"

"Yes. Still in Chicago. We don't talk. After he retired, he gave me the reins on our family business."

"You never wanted to try with him?"

His mouth pulls in something that isn't quite a smile. "He's not a man you try with. You take what he offers, or you get nothing. And I wasn't going to get nothing."

There's an edge in his voice now, sharp enough that I feel the change. He probably doesn't even realize when he slips like that, the same way he can go from soft to demanding in a single breath.

"So the only family you have is your sister."

"And you," he says without hesitation. His arm tightens around me just enough to make it clear the conversation is over. But it isn't for me. Not yet.

"Is that why you want control over people? Because you were abandoned growing up?"

His eyes hold mine. "It's not that. I like making good decisions for you, ones that make you happy."

I study him, the way he says it like it's harmless. But happiness isn't always the same thing as agreement, and I'm not sure he sees the difference.

I don't answer. His hand curves along my cheek, thumb steady under my eye. He looks at me for a long moment, then leans in and kisses me. I kiss him back, my hands sliding around his waist, pulling him in until his body presses into mine. His hand tightens at my waist, his grip firm through my shirt. I tilt my head and let him take more, my fingers curling into his back.

When he finally pulls back, his hand lingers on my face before falling away. His eyes stay on mine. "Let's go to bed."

My arms are still around him, but I let go quickly as he turns and walks off like nothing happened. I stand there, feeling stupid for thinking it meant anything. He doesn't do tender. He never has. Just sex. Rough, raw, nothing more.

I follow him down the hall without a word. The rejection still clings to me—the call, the father I never had, the reminder that no one's coming. Even in someone else's life, I can't hold on to family. The only arms left are his, but they don't feel like home. They feel like the trap I keep falling into. And I hate that some part of me still wants to call it love.

31

ADRIAN

She follows me down the hall without a word, quiet in a way that unsettles me more than her resistance ever has. I can still feel the weight of her words pressing at me, the way she said she wanted to believe someone could help her. She tried to swallow it back, but I heard it. She gave herself away.

In bed, she lies stiff beside me until her breathing evens. I don't sleep. I watch every small movement feeding the question I can't shake. Is she really struggling to remember, or is she refusing? There's a difference. But she never used to falter like this. When she left, she knew who she was. When I brought her home, she should have known it still. Instead, she stumbles over the simplest things—names, places, pieces of her past. Each time, she looks at me like she's waiting to be corrected. Or rescued. I think about the way her eyes watered when I told her about her father. That wasn't fake. She felt that loss.

I already humored Greta once, sat Ellie in a sterile room while a doctor searched for answers. They found nothing physically and had suggested it was psychological. It's possible, but I won't tell her that because she doesn't need them. She needs me, and I won't let her think otherwise.

If it's trauma, then time and structure will soften her. The memories are in her, buried, bleeding through. Whether she can't or doesn't want to face them is up for debate, but if it's choice—if she's burying pieces of herself, or hiding them from me—then that's defiance. And defiance won't be tolerated.

Her voice comes back. *Is that why you want control over people? Because you were abandoned growing up?*

I didn't expect it to cut the way it did. She's asked me questions before, but not like that. Not about who I am underneath, not about why I am the way I am. She thinks control is a scar. She thinks it's proof of damage.

She doesn't understand.

Control isn't about abandonment. It's about making sure no one walks away without consequences. That isn't weakness. That's strength. That's love.

It has never been about cruelty. It's about order. People lie, betray, leave—but when I hold the reins, I know where they stand.

And the truth is, things between us used to stay on the surface. She pleased me, gave me what I wanted, never asked for more. I didn't want her to dig, and she never did. Now she is. She's reaching into places I keep buried, and I don't know if it's to understand me or to test how much I'll give. That is what unsettles me.

Because my grip isn't punishment, it's protection. When I tell her what to do, it's because I want her safe. She resists, but she always comes back. And every time she does, I feel the pull no one else has ever given me.

I love her most when she's vulnerable like tonight, when the walls crack just enough for me to see what she hides. The tears, the ache, the raw truth makes me want to hold her tighter, keep her closer. She'll never admit it, but she needs that. She needs me. And I need her to need me.

She's too raw tonight. Pushing now would make her shut down. Better to wait. Better to test her when she doesn't expect it.

32

MAREN

Today, I stand in front of the mirror, smoothing my hands down the soft pastel fabric. The dress fits perfectly, hugging my waist, flaring just enough at the hips. The pearls feel heavy against my collarbone. I tuck a stray hair beneath the brim of the wide hat, tilting it just so. I look like I'm going to high-society brunch. Like I belong somewhere I've never truly felt welcome.

Adrian steps behind me, his reflection filling the mirror. His eyes sweep over me, lingering with approval. "You look gorgeous," he says.

I turn to face him. "Are you dropping me off?" Some pathetic part of me wishes he'd let me drive there myself. He has several cars.

He shakes his head. "No. I've arranged a driver, David. He'll take you anywhere you need to go." He pauses, his smile sharpening just a fraction. "After you get my permission."

I nod. He watches me a beat longer, then holds out a small wallet. "Here."

I open it. My ID—no, Eleanor's—stares back at me. We have the same birthday, February 29th, and we are both twenty-four. My breath catches. He had my wallet when he took me. He could've copied every detail, swapped the name, printed a new card with my birthdate to force me into her life. The cash, the black card, the other credit cards don't matter. All I see is proof he'll do anything to make me fit into her life.

He places his hand at the small of my back, guiding me through the house and out to the driveway. A sleek, black SUV waits at the curb. A man stands beside it, polished and professional in a dark suit.

"David," Adrian says. "This is Eleanor."

David nods once, professional, distant. "Ma'am."

Adrian opens the door for me himself. "David's your chauffeur. He'll get you there safely and take you anywhere else you need to go."

I slide into the seat, the leather cool under my legs. Adrian leans down, his hand braced against the doorframe, his smile turns gentler. "Have fun."

I glance at him, swallowing the knot in my throat. "Thanks."

The door shuts, cutting off his voice. David starts the engine, pulling smoothly away from the house. I glance back once, watching Adrian stand in the driveway, his hands in his pockets, his figure growing smaller as we drive away.

The pearls feel tighter around my neck. I stare down at the wallet in my lap. At the ID that isn't mine. At the cards that aren't freedom.

I guess I'm not allowed to drive. Not really. Not yet. David doesn't say a word the entire ride. Instead, he lifts the privacy screen once we pull away from the house, sealing me into silence.

I sit back, staring out the tinted window, my hands resting in my lap. I didn't realize how strange it would feel to leave the house. Like stepping out of a bubble. Like the world kept turning without me while I stayed locked inside those walls.

I watch the city rush past—the sidewalks are busy, storefronts are shining, and people are going about their day. It hits me harder than I expected. Adrian never takes me anywhere. Never lets me see this life beyond the gates. But maybe today changes that.

David pulls the SUV to a smooth stop outside the restaurant. I glance out the window. It's upscale, sleek, with a terrace overlooking the street. Waiters move between white-linen tables, glasses gleaming under the sun.

David lowers the privacy screen and looks at me in the mirror. "Ma'am, call me if you need anything. I'll be parked right here," he says.

I meet his gaze in the mirror. "Thanks, David."

He nods, calm and professional. "Just doing my job."

I watch him a little closer as I step out of the car. A driver could be a powerful ally. Someone who knows the streets. Someone who can take me places Adrian doesn't approve of when he's too busy to notice. I glance down at the phone in my hand. He doesn't need a tracker in the car when I'm carrying one in my pocket.

A bitter taste rises in my throat. Still, I slip the phone back into my purse and walk toward the restaurant. I don't have a choice.

I force a smile as the hostess leads me toward the terrace, my stomach twisting tighter with every step. I'm dreading this brunch. I already know Sasha will look at me the same way she always does, like she's waiting for me to fail. But I'll smile. I'll sip the champagne. I'll play the part. At least for now.

I walk up to the hostess stand, trying to keep my shoulders straight even though my stomach's twisted into knots.

The hostess glances up with a bright, polished smile. "Mrs. Montgomery? Mrs. Taylor is waiting for you on the terrace."

Mrs. Taylor. How formal and unassuming.

I nod. "Thank you."

She leads me through the restaurant, weaving between

tables until we step outside onto the terrace. Sunlight glints off polished glass, and I spot Sasha immediately.

She stands as I approach, her sunglasses pushed onto her head, her smile sharp around the edges. She leans in, pressing an air kiss against each of my cheeks. "You look lovely," she says, her tone flat, "for once."

I keep my face still. I can't give her the reaction she wants. That's half the game with Sasha, bait and watch.

"Likewise."

She doesn't bother replying. Instead, she gestures to the empty chair across from her.

"Sit."

I slide into the seat, smoothing my skirt over my thighs. I'm already counting down the minutes until this is over.

"This is one of my favorite places on the island," she says, lifting her glass of white wine. "Once Adrian moved out here, we visited and fell in love with it. So we moved here, too." She takes a sip, her eyes flicking over the terrace like she owns it. "So many people moved here after you left. The island's growing fast."

I nod, my fingers curling around the napkin in my lap. "I didn't realize."

She hums, setting her glass down. "Adrian's been busy. Building homes. Selling estates. Expanding his reputation. He's done quite well." Her gaze cuts back to me, sharper now. "Even in your absence. Almost makes me wonder...if he does better without you."

I meet her eyes without blinking. "Maybe he does."

The second it's out, I see her blink. That wasn't the response she expected.

Her smile falters and eyes narrow. "So, Eleanor...where were you really these last several months? Because we both know that story about teaching art to underprivileged kids is complete bullshit."

I lift my glass, letting the cold press against my lips before I speak. "Does it matter?"

"Yes," she says, her voice flat, smile tightening. "It matters. Because you're back. And I missed these brunches." She tips her head, studying me like I'm an insect under glass. "I like to remind you where you came from. Before my brother married you. A waitress. A nothing."

The words cut deeper than I want them to. Not because they're true, but because she wants them to be. Because she still can't believe Adrian chose me, and she thinks this life was wasted on someone like me. But I never was a fucking waitress, I'm a bartender. I had plans to one day own a bar before I was plucked up and made to be some rags to riches story, trophy wife edition.

Her smile sharpens further. "He ended his engagement with my lifelong friend because he fell for you. And then you left him. After he gave you the perfect life." She shakes her head, eyes gleaming. "You're so ungrateful."

He ended an engagement for Eleanor? That doesn't seem like something he would do. If that's not love, I don't know what it is.

I'm tired of the digs. I'm about to fucking snap.

I set my glass down slowly. "And you're a fucking bitch."

Sasha's smile freezes, a small crack showing before she lets out a light laugh. "Ah. There's the Eleanor I remember."

I lean back, my heart thudding in my chest, refusing to give her more. But inside, it stings.

She lifts her glass again, toasting the air between us. "This is going to be fun."

I grip my napkin tighter beneath the table. Fun for her because every word out of her mouth today is going to be a knife aimed straight at my throat.

I stare at her across the table, barely tasting the wine sliding down my throat. "If I'm not good enough for your brother, then help me leave him."

She laughs quietly, swirling her glass. "I'd do no such thing."

I narrow my eyes. "Why?"

"I won't get involved in your marriage."

I mutter under my breath, "Too late."

Her smile sharpens. "Adrian loves you. Why, I will never know." She sets her glass down, her fingers tapping the stem. "But I know you had an affair."

My throat tightens. "I never had an affair."

I didn't—but that doesn't mean Eleanor didn't.

Her lips curl as she reaches into her handbag and pulls out an envelope. She slides it across the table. "Tell me that after you look at these."

I hesitate, then pull out the photos. My stomach sinks.

One photo shows Eleanor wrapped in a man's arms, her face buried in his shoulder, crying. Another shows her stepping into an apartment building, the man holding the door open for her. Another shows them walking side by side, too close, too familiar.

It's not me, but it's her and her life before I took her place. But from the outside? It looks like me. Unless I did forget and there's something I'm not remembering. No, that's not me. I would've remembered this. Wouldn't I? No, I didn't do this. I'm starting to doubt my fucking sanity because of him. But if Adrian sees this? He won't care what's real. He'll only care what it looks like.

I'm so fucked. I can imagine the punishment now. Severe. Unimaginable. I can picture it now, being tied in that basement for months, making me apologize every day for it. And that won't be enough, he'll make my life hell because of this blow to his ego.

"This doesn't mean anything," I say, trying to keep my voice steady.

"It doesn't look innocent."

My hand curls around the photos. "You had me followed?"

She lifts her shoulders lightly. "You kept canceling brunch. I thought it was strange."

I swallow hard.

She leans forward, her gaze locked on mine. "But when I talked to Adrian, he asked me how our brunches had been. I lied. I covered for you." Her voice lowers. "I didn't want to break his heart. So I hired someone to follow you."

I didn't realize Adrian had a heart to break. The only thing that would hurt is his ego.

She picks up her wine again, sipping slowly. "Turns out you were fucking a chef. Of all people."

I feel the heat crawl up my neck. "I wasn't—"

She holds up a hand. "Don't bother denying it. You're sloppy, Eleanor. You've always been sloppy. Adrian doesn't deserve this."

My throat tightens because I know what she's really saying. She wants me gone, and she's giving me just enough rope to hang myself. But if she knew Adrian, she would know he'd never divorce me.

I stare down at the photos again, bile rising in my throat. If Adrian sees these, I'm done for. He'll never believe the truth. And even if he does, it won't matter. He'll use this as an excuse to tighten the leash to make sure I never leave.

I glance back up at her, forcing my face to appear unfazed. "Why are you showing me this?"

She smiles. "Because I'm giving you a chance to fix it. Before he finds out."

I tighten my grip on the photos, shoving them back into the envelope. "This proves nothing," I snap. "He was a friend.

That's all. If your brother weren't such a tyrant, maybe I wouldn't have been looking for friends in the first place."

Her smile widens, slow and cold. "Really? A tyrant?" She tilts her head, giving me a pitying look that feels like a slap. "Adrian is the sweetest, most generous man I know. And is very good to you."

I almost laugh at that. She's just as delusional as he is. It must run in the family.

She leans forward, resting her elbows on the table. "And you have the nerve to call him a tyrant? The man who took care of you? Who saved you from the gutter?"

The words hit like stones. She's rewriting the whole story, painting me as a nothing before him. Maybe that's how they all see me. A stray he cleaned up. A charity case dressed in designer clothes, but I'm not her. I'd never marry a man for money. I had goals and pride, but I'm reduced to this in these people's eyes.

Her smile sharpens, teeth bared beneath the gloss. "Admit what you did, Eleanor. Tell me the truth."

I shake my head, refusing to give her what she wants.

She lowers her voice, the threat coming out quietly. "Admit it first, or I'll tell him. And you know Adrian. You know he'd rather hear it from you."

My pulse pounds in my ears. She's right. He'd rather hear it from me. But he won't listen. He won't believe it wasn't what it looks like. He'll see those photos and decide I betrayed him. And once he decides? There's no undoing it.

I lift my chin. "There's nothing to admit."

Her smile doesn't fade. "Then I guess we'll see how long that holds up. You have two days before I tell him."

She picks up her wine again, sipping slowly and smugly while I sit frozen across from her, counting the walls closing in. I have two days to come up with an explanation for something I didn't do.

I stand, grabbing my bag. "I'm leaving."

Sasha smirks, swirling the last of her wine. "Take the photos. I've got copies."

I snatch the envelope from the table, shoving it into my purse. "Be careful, Sasha," I say, forcing my voice flat. "Adrian's told me a lot about you."

Her smile falters. "Like what?"

"Things you wouldn't want your friends to know."

She narrows her eyes. "What things?"

I lean closer. "Don't throw stones when you live in a glass house."

She stiffens. "What do you know?"

I let a slow smile curl my lips. "Your husband isn't so innocent, is he? Maybe you should have him followed—or maybe he should have you followed instead."

Her mouth opens, startled. *Got her.* Even though I'm bluffing, it's plausible Adrian told me things about her she wouldn't want to get out. I don't wait for her comeback. I turn and walk out, heat pounding under my skin, my pulse racing.

As I push through the doors, sunlight slams into my face. David stands by the SUV, already holding the door open.

"Everything alright, ma'am?"

I slide into the back seat, gripping my purse tight. "Perfect."

I glance back once as we pull away, watching Sasha still sitting there, her gaze pinned on me.

"Drive, David."

I stare out the window as David drives, the road blurring into color and motion I can't process.

Jesus.

What the hell am I standing in the middle of?

Adrian ended an engagement to be with Eleanor. He left another woman behind for her. I squeeze my eyes shut, my body twisting tighter. If Sasha tells him her suspicions, I have something to throw back at him. I can use this. I can hit back.

I press my hand to my chest, feeling the way my heart kicks hard against my ribs.

I glance down at the photos in my purse, tucked inside the envelope Sasha gave me.

My reflection stares back at me in the dark glass of the SUV window. How much more don't I know? I stare at the photos again, at a version of a person I never knew. A version of me I can't explain. But how much longer can I pretend I'm still her?

I shut the sitting room door behind me. I pull the envelope from my purse, sit on the edge of the couch, and slide the photos out. My hands stay steady only because I force them to.

One by one, I lay them out across the floor. Same face. Same hair. Same pearl necklace. But the expression isn't mine. The body language isn't mine. The memory behind it belongs to someone else.

In one photo, she's pressed against a man's chest, her arms wrapped tightly around him. Her face is buried in his shoulder. In another, he's holding a door open as she steps inside beside him. Their bodies are close, her posture relaxed. In the third, her hand rests gently on his arm.

It's not overt, but it's intimate. Enough to raise suspicion. Enough to look like a betrayal.

I stare at the man's face. He looks young and clean-cut, with sharp features and ordinary clothes. I don't recognize him or know his name. I don't know what he meant to her or what Adrian will see when he looks at this.

I whisper to myself, "Who are you?"

I study the background. There's a brick building, a parking meter, and part of a sign behind the man's shoulder. I lean closer. The name is only partially visible, but I can still make it out.

Drake and Co.

I pick up my phone and type it into the search bar. The result loads quickly. A bakery in downtown Chicago. So the place is real. The photos are real. The man is real. But the memory doesn't exist for me. I wasn't there. I didn't live it. I didn't touch him. I didn't cry in his arms or walk into that building. I have no idea what she was feeling in that moment. I don't know what she said. I don't know what came before or after.

But Adrian will expect an answer. He'll expect a reaction. I flip through the photos again. Each one twists tighter in my chest. I have nothing to defend myself with. No version of the truth. No way to be sure of what happened.

I walk to the mirror and hold the top photo beside my face. The angle is slightly off, but it doesn't matter. It looks like me. To Adrian, it'll be me.

I speak softly, practicing what I might say.

"It wasn't what it looked like."

I stare at my reflection. The words sound flat.

I try again. "I was upset. I left after a fight. He was just a friend."

Still wrong. It sounds rehearsed.

I lower my voice. "I needed comfort. He was the only person who offered."

That sounds really bad. Adrian will lose it, thinking I went to another man for comfort.

I lower the photo and gather the stack again. I slide them back into the envelope, then place them in my purse. It's not the safest place, but it'll have to do.

I sit down and unlock my phone. My thumb hovers over Diane's name.

She might know who the man is. She might remember something. A detail. A conversation. Something that could help me.

I could lie. I could tell her I saw an old photo, and it brought back a half-formed memory. I could fish for context.

But Diane's too sharp. She'd hear the wrong pause. The wrong tone. She'd ask questions I can't answer.

I lock the phone and set it aside. This is the danger of living someone else's life. Even the truth becomes dangerous when it's not yours.

I sit still and take a deep breath. If Sasha's planning to use this, I need to be ready. I need to figure out who that man is. I need to understand the story behind the photos before someone else tells it for me.

Because if I guess wrong or say something Eleanor would never say, Adrian will know.

And if he knows, I won't get another chance.

33

ADRIAN

My phone buzzes across the desk. Sasha.

I roll my eyes. *What the fuck does she want now?* Probably to complain about Ellie. She's hated her since day one because I didn't marry her best friend. That ruined their friendship. Why I almost married that girl, I'll never understand.

I just needed to get married. People kept asking when I'd settle down. People don't want to do business with a man who looks unsettled, especially when I design homes. They want to see a wife standing beside me, showing off the life I build. And she was convenient. Well-bred, always had a crush on me, pretty enough, and familiar. But she told Sasha everything I did wrong, and Sasha meddled.

I answer anyway. "What?"

"Adrian," Sasha snaps, sharp through the line, "Eleanor lost it on me."

I sit back. "What?"

"She caused a scene. Called me a fucking bitch, loudly, in public. I can't show my face there again."

I pinch the bridge of my nose. That's not Ellie. She's

reserved in public, always aware of her image. For her to lose it in public isn't like her. But Sasha wouldn't make this up—she's too bothered. That fucking bar rubbed off on her, made her more volatile. Too much time around drunk mouths and short tempers.

"There's something up with her," Sasha says. "I think you should talk to her."

"I will."

This isn't good if even Sasha notices she's different. But there's nothing medically wrong with her. Maybe she does need a psychiatrist, but I don't want to risk it. But I also don't want to risk everyone thinking there's something wrong with her. I don't know what to believe at this point.

When I think she's about to hang up, her voice climbs again. "And why the hell did you tell her about my DUI?"

My brows knit. "I never told her about it."

"She said you told her things about me."

How the fuck did Ellie know about that? I never told her. She must have overheard or been snooping. I don't want that getting out. If she's running her mouth in public, I'll have a long talk with her.

"I don't talk about you. Not ever." My tone hardens. "But dealing with your shit? I'd rather not."

That shuts her up. I'm pacing my office now, anger rising. I invite her to things because she's family, because it makes people overlook how dysfunctional we are. Not because I want to.

I've been covering for her my whole life, and even now. Birth order put me in charge, but I hate it. Since she was a teenager, she had a drinking problem. My father even sent her to rehab. So after that, she started calling me for help to get her out of trouble caused by her drunken shenanigans.

My voice cuts through the line. "You think I want her

knowing how much I have to cover for you? You should be thanking me," I grind out. "Not accusing me."

"Adrian, I didn't mean to offend you. You know I appreciate everything you do."

She stays quiet. The memory of Sasha's DUI night claws back. Sasha hit a guard rail while drunk. I covered it up using my influence, donated a fat check to the Creswell Police Department, and even paid for the damages because she didn't want her husband to know.

She's trying to save face because she needs me. But I don't need her. At this point, I can't have my sister looking like a danger to society. Not when I'm building one here. She's lucky she didn't die that night. That would've been her legacy—another drunk driver.

After I hang up the phone, I find Ellie in her sitting room, back straight, legs crossed, a book open on her lap that she isn't reading. She doesn't look up when I step inside.

"Sasha called me," I say, watching her carefully.

Her fingers tighten on the edge of the page. "And?"

"She was hurt."

Her eyes flick up. "About what?"

"About what you said to her. Calling her a fucking bitch in public."

Eleanor shrugs, calm and unbothered. "Because it's true. I'm not taking shit from anyone. Whether they're your family or not."

I exhale slowly and move further in. "You know I don't have much family."

"Yeah, and I have none," she snaps. "And somehow I'm the one who always has to absorb the damage because of it."

"She's just like that. You shouldn't take it personally."

Her voice sharpens. "You never defend me."

That catches me. "What?"

"I'm your wife," she says, louder now. "You should take my

side. You should shut her down when she disrespects me. Not act like I'm overreacting. Don't let anyone make me feel less than—especially not her."

My jaw tightens. She doesn't understand. I do defend her, in my way. Not in front of Sasha, because I won't make a scene. But always after. Always reminding her Ellie belongs to me, that I don't believe or care about Sasha's bullshit. That I married Ellie because she's mine, because she pleases me.

"I'm trying to keep the peace," I say.

"You mean you let your sister say whatever she wants, and then come home and expect me to pretend it didn't happen?"

"I let her vent," I answer tightly. "And then I comfort you. That's always how it works."

Her laugh is short and bitter. "That's not defending me. That's damage control."

I stay silent, because deep down, I know she's right.

She stands now, facing me fully. "Defend me. Or I'll defend myself."

"Do not act out in public again," I warn, my voice low. "Do not embarrass yourself or my family."

"I'm not doing brunch with her again," she fires back. "I don't care how you feel about it. I'm not going. And you can't make me."

"I sure can if I have to."

Her eyes flash, but she doesn't move. For a moment I picture dragging her out, forcing her into the car, reminding her exactly how much control I have. She forgets too easily.

I force my tone softer. "Or maybe I'll go with you. Be a buffer."

"No," she says, folding her arms. "Because the solution isn't for me to have a babysitter. It's for her to stop being cruel, and for you to actually take my side. But that's not going to happen, is it?"

I don't answer.

Instead, she reaches into her purse and tosses an envelope onto the table. Photos spill across the surface. My chest tightens.

"Do you know she had me followed?" Eleanor asks, her voice low, shaking with disbelief.

My head jerks slightly. "What?"

"She hired someone to follow me. Went as far as showing me doctored photos of me and another man. Then she black-mailed me. Told me to confess before she brought them to you."

I pick up the stack, eyes narrowing as I scan each one. It looks like she is a cheater. But she told me herself. That doesn't sound like a cheater. She isn't nervous or hiding.

"She's making me look like a cheater," Eleanor says, her breath catching in her throat. "When I've never done anything to betray you."

I keep staring. If Sasha really had these, why didn't she tell me before? She was just whining on the phone about Eleanor knowing about her DUI, acting offended, playing the victim. Why not drop this then—unless she wasn't planning to? Unless this is her trying to fuck with Eleanor, trying to push her until she snapped.

Eleanor steps closer and jabs a finger at the one on top. "Look at this. That doesn't even look like me. The face is off. You can't even see the man's face. And she thinks this proves something?"

Why hire someone to stalk her if it's fake? Why pay for this? I look again. Eleanor wouldn't cheat on me. I know she loves me. She doesn't say it anymore, but I see it when she looks at me, feel it when she's under me.

Her voice cracks. "Why would I be crying on another man's shoulder, when I cry on yours?"

That hits. She does cry on my shoulder. Rarely, but always with me.

"When would I even have the time?" she demands. "I'm always here. Painting, reading, tending to you. When have I had five minutes to myself, let alone a chance to have an affair?"

Still, the thought gnaws. Did she leave me for another man in Chicago? Is that why she didn't want to move? I worked too much. I wouldn't have noticed. Another man touching my wife. Another man seeing her cry.

"She went this far," she whispers, "and you're standing there like you might actually believe it."

I look down at the photos again, rage twisting tighter. If Sasha doctored them, she's dead to me. Family or not, she's finished. But if Eleanor really did this—if she lied to me, gave herself to another man—I'll put her in the basement and keep her there. She'll never share my bed again. Never enjoy what I built. I'll never divorce her. We don't have a prenup.

I crush the photos in my fist, fury burning through me. I tower over her, brushing her cheek with my fingers, deceptively gentle.

"I'll handle this," I tell her, my voice low, dangerous.

Then I lean in, mouth grazing her ear. "But if I find out it's true, if you lied to me—you'll regret ever touching another man."

Then a chuckle slips out. "And I'll leave you in the basement for months, maybe years."

34

MAREN

I feel the threat settle into my spine. His hand lingers on my face, soft again as if he didn't just threaten to lock me underground for months, or worse, years. He caressed my face while promising me hell.

The second the door clicks shut, my legs give out. I sink onto the edge of the couch, gripping the cushions, trying to steady my breathing.

I think he bought it. The way he crushed the photos and said he'd handle it. His voice dropped, almost tender, like he still believed I belonged to him and only him. But I know the truth.

Those photos might be fake. They might be real. I don't know anymore. My stomach twists as I replay them in my head. The angle. The lighting. The way the woman—me, or not me—is half-turned away. The man's face is never visible. That helps. That keeps it murky. But if Sasha has more? If she pulls out something clearer, more definitive, I'm fucked.

I grab at my hair, pulling hard at the roots, like I can squeeze a plan out of the pain. I don't even know who the man in the photo is. I never had an affair. Not as Eleanor. Not as me.

But Sasha doesn't care about what's true. She cares about the story she can make stick. And Adrian?

He won't divorce Eleanor. He doesn't believe in it. He sees it as a weakness. He'd rather keep her—keep me—trapped and punished. He won't let go. He'll punish me. Not just with rules or silence. But severely. The basement. The kind of isolation that strips you bare until you forget how to speak.

What do I do? I press my hands to my face, breathing harder now. My mind races.

How do I get around this? How do I destroy proof I can't see?

And underneath it all, the question I hate most—how long until Adrian starts wondering again? How long until he stops pretending he believes me? Because when he does, I'll pay for it. And he already promised how.

I can't let this linger. If Adrian starts digging, if he asks the wrong question or lets Sasha get too close, it's over. I need to reroute his focus. Fast. Adrian feels the most connected during sex. So I'm going to use the oldest trick in the book and seduce him. I will ride him so good that he won't dare look any further into it.

I go to the closet and go through the drawers of lingerie. I've never worn any for him, but I know he'll love it. So I put on the red lingerie. The one tucked in the back of the drawer with the tags still attached.

I've never initiated anything like this before. He's always the one who takes. But now, I have to make him believe me. Not just with words. With obedience. With devotion. With something he won't want to question.

I walk down the hall and into his office without knocking. He's on the phone, speaker on. His voice is low as he reviews something, financials, logistics, I don't care. He doesn't see me at first. Then he looks up and freezes.

I walk toward him slowly, hips swaying, my gaze locked on his. I lower my voice, sultry and soft. "Do you have a minute?"

He hits the mute button quickly. "Yeah."

I climb onto his lap without hesitation, straddling him in the leather chair, my arms sliding around his shoulders. He doesn't stop me.

I press my mouth to his. I kiss his neck. I feel his cock harden beneath me, trapped behind his slacks. That's good. That's what I need. His body is listening, even if his mind is still calculating.

I lean into his ear. "Are you going to end your call?"

He murmurs, "No."

My lips graze his neck. "That's so hot."

He smirks faintly. "You have to be quiet."

"I can do that," I whisper.

I slide my panties down and kick them off behind me. I unbuckle his belt, unzip his pants, pull him free. My fingers wrap around him, his warm and thick cock.

I sink to the floor between his legs, watching his eyes darken as my mouth wraps around him.

He leans back in the chair, eyes fluttering shut for a second, mouth slightly open.

Then he unmutes the call.

"Yes," he says calmly, his voice composed as if I don't have my mouth on him. "That timeline works. Send the revised agreement to Claire. I'll look it over tomorrow."

He grabs a fistful of my hair and moves me faster. I hollow my cheeks, taking him deeper, ignoring the ache in my jaw and the tears already forming at the corners of my eyes. This has to work. He can't doubt me.

He mutes the call again, groans low in his throat, his hips jerking slightly. "I needed this."

I lift my head, breathless, tears slipping down my cheeks. "I'd never betray you. Ever."

His hand slides into my hair again, fingers gentler now. "I know."

"You mean everything to me."

His smile widens. "You're so good to me."

I'm lying through my teeth. I lower my head and take him back into my mouth just as someone on the call asks him a question. He clears his throat, voice strained. "Let me... follow up on that later."

I swirl my tongue around the tip, slowly, and he gasps on the call.

He mutes again, eyes snapping to mine. "Go faster."

I do.

His hands tighten. He's close. I feel it in the way his body tenses beneath me, the way his breath shortens. But just before he loses it, he growls, "Get on top of me."

I climb onto his lap and straddle him again, my knees pressed into the leather cushions, the hem of the red lace brushing against his shirt. His cock is thick and ready beneath me, slick from my mouth, hard from the power I'm pretending to give him.

I guide him to my entrance and sink slowly, letting out a shaky breath as he stretches me open.

His head drops back for a moment, his fingers digging into my thighs. I start to move, slow, steady, tight around him, rocking my hips.

He watches me like he's trying to figure out where this came from. I've never been the one to initiate. Never ridden him like this, never looked him straight in the eye while doing it.

But I do now.

I place my hands on his shoulders and grind down harder, forcing a groan out of his chest. His hands slide up my waist, grabbing the sides of my ass, guiding me, making me move faster.

The chair creaks beneath us. The muted phone call on the

desk still blinks, forgotten. I bounce on his lap, tightening around him, using every part of my body to make him forget the conversation, forget the questions, forget the photos crumpled on the desk. My thighs burn. My breath is ragged. But I don't stop.

I moan just loud enough for him to hear. His hands slide under the lace of my bra, fingers squeezing my breasts, and I grind down harder, letting him feel how wet I am for him.

This isn't real; it's a performance worthy of an Oscar.

His mouth finds mine again, desperate, bruising. "Fuck," he murmurs against my lips. "Just like that."

I ride him faster, slamming my hips down until I feel him start to unravel. His grip tightens. His breath catches.

"I need you," he groans again, his voice low and raw.

I lean close, panting into his ear, "Then keep me."

His whole body shudders under mine, and I feel him lose it, his hands gripping me like he's never letting go. I follow a second later, crying out, burying my face in his neck.

He holds me tighter and rubs my back slowly. And I stay on his lap, heart pounding, sweat cooling on my back, hoping to God I just bought myself time.

He had a satisfied grin on his face when I stood to leave. Smug. Possessive. Like he had just conquered something, even though I am the one who orchestrated every second of it.

Then he smacked my ass before I made it to the door. I didn't fully turn around, just smiled over my shoulder, soft and easy, then slipped out of the office.

The second the door shut behind me, I let out the breath I had been holding. He bought it. Completely.

I felt the shift in him. His suspicion crumbled the moment pleasure took over. That deep, possessive part of him wants to believe I am loyal. He needs to accept it. So he clings to the version of me that would never lie, never stray, never kneel between his legs with a plan hiding behind her eyes.

Now that I have given him this version, he won't dig too hard. He won't want to risk shattering the image I just handed him. I was open. Seductive. A little desperate. Everything I've never been with him before.

Oddly, I am starting to feel more comfortable sexually with him. I've figured out the power I have over him because of it. The sex is fantastic. That part is real. The way he touches me, holds me, fills me, it is enough to make my body forget what my mind still fears. I didn't expect that. I didn't imagine I would feel so much pleasure in pleasing him. But I do. Or maybe I've just learned how to bend without breaking. Either way, tonight I survived. And he isn't going to ask again. At least not yet.

I walk back to my room, legs still shaky, heart still racing, skin flushed from more than just the sex. I close the door behind me and lean against it, staring into the dimly lit space.

It's quiet making my thoughts echo louder than they should.

I move to the mirror, still in the red lingerie, and stare at myself. My hair is messy, my lips swollen, and my makeup smeared. I look like a woman who knows exactly what she's doing and enjoys what she's become. But I don't recognize her.

I touch the edge of the mirror, then press my palm against the glass, as if it could remind me of who I was.

I told myself I was doing it to survive, that it was manipulation. Strategy. A means to an end. But it doesn't feel like just survival. I enjoyed the way he looked at me when I took the lead. That scares me more than anything because the line is supposed to be clear. Me. Right. Him. Wrong. But now?

I don't know where the performance ends and I begin. I don't know if the pleasure was fake or if part of me really wanted it. If part of me really wanted *him*. I used to have boundaries. Rules I swore I'd never bend for anyone. Not even him.

Now I bend every time he looks at me like I belong to him. And worse, sometimes I want to.

That's what terrifies me. Not that he'll hurt me. Not that he'll punish me. But that I might start choosing it. That I might already be choosing it. I sink onto the edge of the bed, hands in my lap, staring at the wall without seeing it.

What am I becoming? How much more of myself will I lose before this ends? My eyes drag to the nightstand. The wallet waits there, the license on top. The date stares back. February 29th. Mine. Hers. Proof he'll forge anything, even my birthday, until I can't tell if the life I remember was ever real.

35

ADRIAN

W*here the fuck did that come from?* One minute I'm on a call about a multi-million dollar deal, the next she's taking me into her mouth like she's never wanted anything more.

She's been distant for weeks. Careful with her words. Stiff when I touched her. But now? Now she walks into my office in red lingerie, climbs on top of me, and fucks me like it's her goddamn mission. While I'm on a live call. And the craziest part? I sat there with her mouth on me, answering questions, trying to stay composed while she broke me open under the desk. And then when I told her to get on top of me? She didn't hesitate. She owned the moment.

I sit alone in my office, still catching my breath, her scent lingering on my skin. She's never done that before. It was bold and perfect. Every moan, every grind of her hips, and even the tears in her eyes when she said she'd never betray me because she's mine. Maybe she's right that the photos are bullshit, and I've been too ready to believe the worst. Because she quickly dropped to her knees to prove she's mine and wants it to stay that way. That doesn't sound like a cheater. And I loved every fucking minute of it.

Ellie told me I don't defend her. That I let Sasha talk down to her. That I let things slide. That I stand in the middle and call it peace, when all I'm doing is keeping my hands clean. She's right. And that's going to change.

Whatever Sasha believes she's doing, whatever she thinks she can get away with, ends now. I don't care that we share blood. She crossed a line. She made my wife feel cornered. Hunted. That's something I won't ignore. Not anymore.

Later that day, I pull into her driveway, tires crunching against perfect gravel. Her house looks the same as always— white stone, black shutters, manicured lawn trimmed within an inch of its life. Perfect. Lifeless. Even the flowers along the path look arranged, not grown.

She opens the door, blinking in surprise when she sees me. A robe is pulled tight, wineglass in hand.

"Adrian?" she asks. "I wasn't expecting you."

I walk straight past her. Inside, the air smells faintly of wine and lavender polish. Clean. Cold. Nothing lived in. She follows me as I move through the house without asking, without slowing down. I don't sit. I don't greet her. I don't pretend.

"Don't ever have my wife followed again."

I'm furious at the thought of a stranger tailing her, snapping pictures like she's prey.

Her brow arches. "Excuse me?"

I turn to face her, eyes burning. "And don't try to blackmail her."

Sasha lets out a sharp, forced laugh. "Blackmail? You're overreacting."

"You think I don't know what you did? She told me. The photos. The threats. You call that helping?"

"I was trying to protect you," she snaps.

Protect me? She exposed Eleanor to strangers with cameras. That isn't protection. That's sabotage.

"You walked away from everything," Sasha keeps going. "Your engagement. Your future. For a waitress who disappears for months and walks back in pretending nothing happened."

"The photos don't prove anything. They don't show the man's face. Half of them barely show hers."

"They show enough. You don't want to believe it because it shatters whatever fantasy you're clinging to. But something's off about her, and you know it, too."

Heat spreads through my chest. "You really thought hiring someone to follow her was a good idea?"

"She needed to be watched."

"You need to be fucking watched," I snap, stepping closer, my voice rising before I can stop it. "You're an alcoholic. You can't go a night without a bottle in your hand. You sit in this mausoleum of a house, drunk and bitter, and call it concern."

Her face hardens, color rising in her cheeks. "Don't you dare—"

"Don't *I* dare?" I cut her off. "You hired a stranger to stalk my wife. You put her at risk so you could feel self-righteous. Meanwhile, you can't even keep your own life from circling the drain."

The wineglass trembles in her hand before she slams it down on the coffee table, liquid sloshing over the edge. "At least I see her for what she is."

"No. You invited drama into our life. One leak and the story goes public. Headlines. Scandal. You would burn both of us just to prove a point."

Her chin lifts. "I kept it contained."

"You didn't contain anything. You gambled with my reputation. All because you've never wanted her around."

"She's changed you."

I take a step forward, voice low. "No. She didn't change me.

She reminded me who I am. And that's a man who protects his wife."

Her lip curls. "Don't act like you're some saint who can judge me. You smother every woman you've ever been with until they can't fucking stand you. Maybe she didn't cheat. Maybe she just finally saw you for what you are. A tyrant."

The word slams into me, cold and hot at once. *Tyrant.* For a second, I feel it stick, daring me to deny it, daring me to admit she might be right. My hands clench. My jaw locks. She has no idea what the fuck she's talking about.

"Careful, Sasha," I say, my voice low, controlled rage threading through every syllable. "You don't get to call me that. Not when you've spent your whole life needing me."

Her smile twists, sharp and cruel. "Those words didn't come from me. They came from her."

I don't show it, but my stomach drops. Did Eleanor really say that? Did she call me a tyrant to Sasha, of all people? Did she run from me because she believed it? There's no way she'd be so desperate to get away from me that she'd go to Sasha for help. Sasha would be the last person to help her. At least she better be.

I see Ellie's face in my mind, the way she cries on my shoulder, the way her voice shakes when she swears she hasn't betrayed me. That doesn't sound like a woman who hates me. That sounds like my wife. But if she did say it—if she spoke those words—then she's fighting me. And I can't let that be true.

I shut it down, bury it, lock it under the rage that steadies me. Sasha's lying. She has to be. She wants me doubting Eleanor because doubt is the only weapon she has left.

Sasha steps closer, eyes gleaming. "You think it is just her? Katie. Natalia. Rachel. They all left you the same way. One disappeared without a word. One moved across the country.

One threatened a restraining order. They weren't women leaving a man, Adrian. They were women escaping a tyrant."

The words scrape at me, threatening to stick. But I crush it before it takes root. Sasha is exaggerating. Using scraps of the past to poison what I have now.

My exes have nothing to do with my wife. That was years ago, and she wanted me to marry her friend—so I can't be the terrible man she's making me out to be if she was pushing for that.

"You're exaggerating. You wanted me to marry your friend."

She smirks. "Because she made you normal. You didn't obsesses over her. It was a healthy relationship, but you chase women who don't want you."

That's far from the truth. They all wanted me. Especially Ellie. She loves me even if she doesn't say it, I feel it. Maybe I need to get her saying the words again.

I lean forward, lowering my voice. "Say whatever you want about me. But if you ever interfere in our lives again, you'll regret it."

Sasha blinks, taken aback. She thought she'd landed the blow. She thought she'd won.

I head for the door, hand already on the knob. "I mean it."

Then I walk out and don't look back.

36

MAREN

Adrian walks in the sitting room. His expression is calmer than I expected, but there's something in the way he walks—surer of himself, almost satisfied.

"I handled Sasha," he says. "She won't have you followed again."

I nod, forcing the right amount of relief into my expression. "Good."

Thank God. My plan worked. He bought it. He won't dig deeper.

I step toward him and press a kiss to his cheek, soft and slow, then look him in the eyes. "Thank you for believing in me."

"You're my wife. I should've defended you more. But I will. From now on."

The way he says it, firm and final, almost makes me believe it, too.

I wrap my arms around him in a tight hug, laying my head against his chest. "Thank you," I say, sweet and grateful.

He exhales, steady and content. I feel the tension drain from his body, replaced by pride. His arm wraps around my back, his fingers stroking my hair like he just saved me from something cruel.

He thinks he did a good deed, and that I'm happy now. He looks down at me with that self-satisfied gleam in his eye, the one he gets when he believes he's done exactly what a husband should.

I should ride him more.

His hand moves to my waist, pulling me against him. "I won't let anyone hurt you." His voice is low, protective, possessive.

I smile against his chest and whisper, "I know."

But inside, I'm still surviving. Because the second he doubts it, I'm done. And I'm not ready to lose yet.

37

MAREN

The morning starts the way it always does. Adrian is already dressed—dark gray slacks, crisp white shirt, sleeves rolled once at the forearm. His watch catches the light when he lifts his coffee. I watch him from across the kitchen island, still in my robe, hair unbrushed, feeling more like the help than the woman he married.

Then I see the vase on the counter. Roses, deep red, their scent heavy in the air.

Adrian looks up from his phone. "You're awake."

I glance at the flowers, unsure if I'm supposed to touch them. "What's this?"

He steps closer, slips a hand under my chin, and presses his mouth to mine. The kiss is warm, lingering, more intimate than routine. "Happy anniversary, Ellie."

My throat tightens. I should have remembered. I should have been the one to say it first. Instead I stand frozen, caught off guard by something that sounds so simple.

My stomach knots. Of course. Our anniversary. I force a smile, leaning into the kiss like I expected it. "Happy anniversary," I whisper back, pretending I'd remembered all along.

I can't let him see that I forgot. One slip and he'll read it as something else, another crack to pry open.

No one's ever given me flowers before. And I don't know if I'm supposed to feel grateful or trapped.

I never took him as the flower-buying kind. It feels performative, or maybe he just wants me to think he's a romantic. Either way, it doesn't feel like it's for me. Even flowers feel like a display meant to remind me how easily he can play the role of the husband everyone thinks he is.

"I'm glad you're back for us to celebrate," he says quietly. "I never wanted to spend it alone."

For a second I almost believe him, but it doesn't feel directed at me. It feels meant for her.

He sets his phone down. "We have dinner plans tonight."

I blink. "With whom?"

"With each other," he says.

That shouldn't feel strange, but it does. "Why?"

Adrian takes another sip, his tone even. "Do I need a reason to take my wife out for our anniversary?"

I don't answer. He sets the mug down and looks at me. "Wear something nice."

"Define nice."

His mouth curves slightly. "Margo will be over this afternoon."

Of course. He walks past me and brushes a kiss against my cheek, like we're some polished couple from a lifestyle ad, but I don't move.

"I'll have the car pick you up at seven," he adds. "Don't be late."

That afternoon Margo comes by, sweeping through the closet until she's pulled a pastel dress two sizes too tight. By seven, the car is waiting.

The rooftop restaurant is beautiful, sure, but I barely register the view.

Adrian leans forward, the city lights catching in his hair. A few strands fall across his forehead, that perfectly careless look he somehow pulls off without trying. His green eyes lock on mine, sharp and steady, and I can't look away.

He's devastating in that suit. The collar open, sleeves rolled, his watch gleaming. It's not just the way he looks, it's the way he looks at *me*. His fingers brush the base of his wineglass before disappearing under the table, and I stiffen when they find my thigh—cool at first, then warm as his palm settles, stroking slow, once, twice.

"Relax," he murmurs. His voice is low and smooth, sliding down my spine.

I glance around. The server's across the terrace, distracted. Still, my pulse spikes as his hand moves higher. He hooks a finger under the lace edge of my panties, pushing them aside like it's nothing. Heat flares low in my belly as his fingers tease between my thighs, already finding me wet for him, and a helpless breath escapes before I can catch it.

His mouth curves. "I knew you'd be ready for me." His fingers move slowly, circling, building pressure until my spine arches slightly, my thighs clenching on instinct. I fight to stay still, but my hips shift anyway, desperate for more.

Adrian watches with calm, hungry eyes. "You love this, don't you?" He leans in. "Even here, you'd let me do anything. Wouldn't you?"

My heartbeat is all I hear. Then he slides two fingers inside me. My lips part on a shaky exhale as I grip the table, breath catching, heat climbing, and Adrian says, "Keep your eyes on me," his voice low and commanding.

I meet his gaze. His eyes never leave mine as he works me deeper, slower, harder.

The buildup is sharp, unbearable, my thighs trembling with every subtle stroke. I can't think. Can't breathe.

"Come for me, Ellie," he says, and the words pull the climax straight from me.

I tense and gasp, my whole body shuddering with release, flushed and raw, my eyes squeezing shut as a broken sound escapes. He strokes me through it, slow and possessive, like he's claiming every last tremble.

Then he pulls his hand back, wipes his fingers with a napkin, and lifts his wineglass like nothing happened. "Good girl."

My hands shake slightly as I lift mine. I'm flushed and light-headed, my body still ringing from the aftershocks of my orgasm. The city sparkles around us, glittering in the dark.

But it doesn't feel real. All I can feel is him.

The server walks away, and Adrian's hand lingers higher.

His voice drops. "Do you remember the first night we met?"

I read Eleanor's journal about their first meeting, so I need to recite those details.

My stomach knots. I keep my tone even. "You spent half the night staring at my chest more than at me."

Was that in the journal or my memory of meeting him at the Rusty Nail?

His mouth curves, no apology in it. "You noticed."

"Hard not to," I say quickly, forcing a small shrug. "And then you went straight to the point. You told me you wanted to fuck me. No charm. No pretense. Just that."

I almost feel like he used the same script with me when we first met at Rusty Nail. Asking me to go back to his hotel room and if I was up for the challenge after barely having a conversation. Was he trying to recreate that first meeting of Eleanor with me?

Adrian leans in, elbows on the table, calm and sure. "And you didn't walk away."

Heat creeps up my throat. I lift my glass, taking a slow sip instead of answering.

He studies me, eyes steady. "You liked it. You liked that I said it plainly. No games. No lies."

I thought he was an asshole for coming onto me like that, but I was intrigued, too. His confidence was impossible to ignore. I could see how those lines could work.

I set the glass down a little too hard. "I wanted a big tip."

That's true. I needed money for my rent.

His eyes don't leave mine. "That's not why."

I was drawn to him, but he unsettled me, too.

The waiter comes by with the drink menu. I wave it off.

"Just bourbon," I say, without looking.

The waiter pauses. "Neat?"

"Yeah. And two shots of tequila."

He nods and disappears.

Adrian's eyebrows lift slightly. "Not in the mood for wine tonight?"

I lean back in my chair, tugging the hem of my tight pastel dress down. It doesn't help. My breasts are practically spilling out of the bodice, and I've already caught two men across the terrace sneaking glances. I don't blame them. I look like a doll that got squeezed into the wrong box.

"Wine's for people pretending they're relaxed," I mutter. "Bourbon's for people who know they're not."

Adrian watches me, his eyes flicking to my chest before he speaks. "You look incredible tonight."

"Don't thank me, thank Margo," I say, squeezing the sides of my dress under my ribs. "She's the one who picked this lovely number. I'm pretty sure it's a size too small. Or two."

He leans forward, intrigued now. "You never said anything before."

I smirk. "You mean never complained? Guess I'm not supposed to. Wouldn't want to disturb your aesthetic vision." I mimic a stiff voice, twirling my fingers like I'm conjuring magic.

"Pastels only. Tight waists. Plunging neckline." The server drops the two shots of tequila off at the table first.

Adrian's mouth lifts faintly. "Didn't realize you had thoughts about your wardrobe."

"I have thoughts about everything," I shoot back, taking one of the tequila shots and downing it fast. It burns down, but it wakes me up.

He watches me with a strange stillness. "Then why not say something?"

I shrug. "Because it's easier to let Margo dress me than have another argument about whether I should wear this or not." I tip back the second shot. My throat's on fire now, but I don't stop.

The bourbon arrives next. I wrap my fingers around the glass like its something solid I can hold on to. He doesn't stop me. That's what surprises me most. No correction. No soft command to slow down. He just watches.

And for a moment, I think he sees me—not Eleanor, not his perfect wife. Just me, raw and slightly flushed, sitting across from him with sarcasm dripping from my tongue.

I tilt my head, challenging. "What? You don't like your wife drunk in public?"

Adrian leans back in his chair, folding his arms, eyes steady. "I like that you're not pretending tonight."

I swirl the bourbon in my glass, then take another sip.

"I'm not drunk," I mutter, setting it down. "I can handle my alcohol."

Adrian raises an eyebrow. "You've had two shots and a bourbon in ten minutes."

"Yeah, and every one of them sucked," I shot back.

He chuckles. "It's a five-star restaurant."

"And a one-star drink menu. It's watered down, pretentious, and they can't even make a shot right."

I take the last sip anyway and glare at the empty glass like it personally offended me.

"Give me a bar and I'll make you the best damn drink you've ever had," I say, my voice sharper now. "Something that doesn't taste like it came out of a spa menu."

Adrian leans back in his chair, eyes gleaming. "I don't doubt that. You're great at everything you do."

He's not talking about me, he's talking about her, but I want to get into his head.

I set the glass down. "Why are you so uptight?"

Adrian blinks. "Uptight? I just fingered you in public."

"Yeah. You kind of are." I shrug. "I don't know what's going on in your head. What makes you tick? What makes you laugh? You're...blank most of the time."

His jaw shifts, but he doesn't look away. "I'm not blank. I show how I feel in the bedroom."

I roll my eyes. He keeps deflecting to sex.

"You don't show anything outside of it. You sit there in your perfect suit, drinking your perfect wine, saying everything like it was rehearsed. You ever actually relax?"

He leans in slightly, his expression unreadable but not cold. "I feel the same way about you."

I raise an eyebrow. "Excuse me?"

"I don't know what goes on in that pretty little head of yours. But I'd like to find out."

That should sound like a line. Maybe it is. But something about the way he says it makes my stomach tighten. He's looking at me like I'm not a replica or a problem to solve. Just something he's trying to understand. And for once, I can't tell if that's more terrifying or disarming.

I look away first because I'm not sure I want him to figure me out. Not yet. Not ever.

I glance back at him, my voice quieter now but still firm.

"I'm real, Adrian. I don't want to pretend to be some elegant, polished wife. I want to be me."

He doesn't flinch. Doesn't blink.

"Who said you can't be yourself?" he asks, like it's obvious. Like I imagined all the pressure and expectation.

I stare at him, not sure if I want to laugh or scream. "You don't have to say it. The rules and high expectations. The way everyone acts like I'm supposed to be someone else. That's not me."

He tilts his head slightly. "I never asked you to pretend."

I huff out a breath, sitting back. "No. But you made it very clear who I'm supposed to be."

His gaze sharpens. "I made it clear who I thought you were."

I swallow hard. That's not the same thing. And we both know it.

I look at him, my voice low. "And what was that, exactly? What did you want in a wife?"

He leans in, gaze steady. "A woman who made me restless until I had her. Who reminded me that settling down didn't have to mean settling."

The bluntness knocks the breath out of me. I laugh, but it's thin, shaky. "So I was just a challenge, then."

His mouth lifts faintly, but his tone softens as he leans closer. "Not a challenge. Mine."

The words hit harder than they should. And worse, there's something in the way he says it that makes my stomach flip. Not because I want it. But part of me can't decide whether to fight him or give in. I glance away before he can see too much in my face.

Because even if I never wanted to be anyone's possession...I sure as hell wasn't supposed to enjoy the attention that comes with it.

38

ADRIAN

I'm looking at a different woman tonight. She's blunt, funny. All while not even trying to be. There's fire in her voice, and I don't know what flipped the switch, but I'm not about to put it out.

She doesn't realize how magnetic she is when she stops pretending. She thinks it's the bourbon talking, but it's her. It's always been her.

She keeps tugging at the top of her dress as if it's strangling her, and I don't understand it. The dress fits her body perfectly. Her curves are exactly where they should be, impossible to ignore. She should see that. She should own it.

But I'm not going to tell her any of that. Not tonight. Not when she's finally giving me something real, even if it's soaked in sarcasm and alcohol.

I watch her tip back another shot. Bourbon, tequila, downed without hesitation. That isn't her. She never enjoyed bourbon. She used to sip wine, order cocktails, hold her glass as though she wanted to make it last. This fast burn is new. Too fast, too reckless.

Still, the recklessness pulls at me and makes me wonder if it will carry into the bedroom, if that rowdiness will make her wild under me. Angry, hot, unrestrained. The thought makes me hard, and I don't bother hiding it.

She leans back in her chair, arms crossed, defiant and flushed with frustration. She says she wants to be real. Says she doesn't want to play the part.

This is the Ellie I want. The one who bites back so I can tame her again. The one who burns hot so I can decide when the fire goes out.

But she needs to remember the setting. I don't care if strangers are close enough to see me touch her, but I won't risk them seeing her turn on me. The bourbon gives her teeth, and if she bares them too far, it will be in front of the wrong audience. That I cannot allow.

She's raw right now. If I say the wrong thing, she'll shut down. She'll lock me out, and I'll never get back in.

So I hold my tongue. Not yet.

I pick up my glass and keep my eyes on her. I'll let her talk tonight because I would rather have her angry and open than quiet and gone. And if it means swallowing my pride for a few more hours to keep her close, I'll do it.

She believes this dinner is about our anniversary. What she doesn't know is that I moved it up a few days, just enough to see if she would notice.

Her reaction to the flowers this morning still sits in the back of my mind. The way she looked at them, confused, as though she couldn't understand why they were there. She knows I don't give flowers often. Only anniversaries and Valentine's Day. I'm not the type to buy them on impulse. Jewelry is what I give her. It's lasting and shows what she is to me.

So if she hesitated, what did that mean? Did she not remember the date?

The last time I forgot, she punished me for it. She didn't speak to me for days. She left for almost a week. That was when she started shutting me out completely. I told myself I was too busy to notice, but the truth was I was furious when she left. I pulled her back the only way I knew how, taking her on a two-week vacation, giving her all of my attention, smoothing over every edge until she softened again. I blamed my forgetting on jet lag. She believed it, or at least she wanted to.

And once she did, that became the truth. The fight didn't matter anymore. What mattered was the trip, the way I pulled her back, the way I proved she was mine. The past only matters if I let it.

So why doesn't she question me now?

It was risky to pretend it was today, but I needed to know. If she had called me out, I would have told her I was worried, that I needed to see how bad her memory really was. She would have believed me.

Her memory has been troubling me. She forgot her father was gone. She asked me for her mother's number, when she should have known it. Those are slips I can't ignore. I can't keep ignoring or denying it. Maybe it's memory loss, or worse, she's delusional.

So this morning I set the stage. Roses in the kitchen. A kiss. The words she would expect me to say. If she faltered, if she questioned it, I would know there's nothing wrong with her.

But she didn't. She kissed me back, smiled, and said the right thing. She even gave me details about the night we met.

And yet it didn't sound like memory. It sounded like a story, practiced instead of recalled.

That's the part I can't shake. Did she recall it herself, or did she only give it back to me because she knows how much I need to hear it?

If it's delusion, I'll have to ground her. If it's memory loss,

I'll have to manage it. Either way, it leaves me with the same truth.

She needs me.

Forever.

39

MAREN

I passed out when I got home last night after all the drinks. As soon as I wake up, Adrian debriefs me before the etiquette coach—or whatever the hell that is—is brought in to mold me into the version he wants on display. Like I'm another light fixture in his house.

"You will show her respect. She's worked with high-profile families. Don't embarrass me."

"So what exactly does she help with?"

"Posture, presence, public speaking, hosting. It's like polishing a diamond. You'll need it before the masquerade."

I set the glass down. "I didn't realize I was up for auction."

His mouth twitches into a smile that never reaches his eyes. "Don't be dramatic. You're my wife. I want people to see what I see when you walk into a room."

"I thought they already did."

"This helps."

Pauline arrives at ten sharp. I watch her step into the foyer with perfect posture, cream blouse tucked neatly into tailored trousers, beige heels tapping a rhythm on the marble. Her perfume reaches me before she does, faint and expensive, and suddenly I feel like the guest in my own house.

"Mrs. Montgomery," she says with a polished smile. "It's a pleasure."

"It's El—" I start to say.

Adrian steps in behind me, his hand firm on my back. "Eleanor," he says without hesitation. His tone is soft, but leaves no space for argument. "She prefers Eleanor."

The correction burns, but I swallow it. "Right. Eleanor."

She opens her portfolio on the dining table, sliding out neatly tabbed pages. Within minutes, she's correcting the way I sit, the way I cross my ankles, the slope of my shoulders.

"Back straight, but don't strain," she says, pressing two fingers between my shoulder blades. "We want elegance, not stiffness. Poised, not rigid. When you walk into the room, people should see confidence, not nerves."

I adjust, the muscles in my back already protesting. "You know I already know how to sit, right?"

"I'm sure you do," she replies, unbothered. "This adds refinement. Presentation is everything."

Adrian leans against the doorway, arms crossed, watching with satisfaction that makes me feel less like a student and more like an object being assessed.

"She's a natural, isn't she?"

"Absolutely," Pauline says. "She just needs direction."

Adrian's phone buzzes. He glances at it, then at me. "I'll leave you to it." He leaves with a final look that feels more like a warning before he disappears down the hall.

By the afternoon, I'm rehearsing introductions tailored for the masquerade, practicing how to steer conversations toward compliments about Adrian's work, and learning to become approachable without ever being real. Pauline's binder is full of notes—posture, diction, and refined femininity. Whatever the fuck that means. I'm an independent woman. So ending up in this situation, being corrected on how to sit, how to speak, how to breathe, makes my blood boil.

"You seem tense," she says.

"I don't want to be here." The words come out before I can stop them.

Her lips curve, faint but smug. "Then we'll work on that. The masquerade is no place for tension."

"You can't fix something that's not broken."

Her brows lift, but her tone stays calm. "I'm not here to fix you. I'm here to refine you."

"Same thing."

"That's one way to see it." She flips through her notes without looking at me. "I would suggest another."

"I'm sure you would," I mutter.

She glances up, her smile just a little sharper. "Adrian said you were cooperative."

My jaw tightens. "Adrian says a lot of things."

"Then perhaps we should prove him right."

I nod and smile when I have to. I repeat her drills while she watches me like I'm some broken doll in need of polishing. My spine's too stiff, my hands too restless, my tone too blunt. There's always something wrong with me. Always something that needs smoothing.

Later, Pauline circles back. "You want people to feel drawn to you. That comes from voice, eye contact, presence. You're not just yourself. You're the face of his world."

My throat feels raw, but I force the words out. "So I'm part of his brand now."

"Legacy," she corrects smoothly.

"And if I don't want to be part of a legacy?"

Pauline doesn't blink. "Then you're wasting your potential."

The words make my stomach clench. "Maybe I liked myself before all this."

Her smile is perfect, brittle, rehearsed. "Then let's make sure everyone else does, too. Starting with the masquerade."

By the time she leaves, my face aches from holding pleasant expressions, my spine from being forced straight, my throat from repeating lines that don't sound like mine.

Adrian walks her out, thanks her with a warmth I don't recognize, then comes back to find me still sitting exactly as she taught me.

He kneels beside me, brushing his thumb along my jaw. "I know today was a lot," he says. "But you handled it perfectly."

I keep my expression still.

He kisses me softly. "I just want the world to see you the way I do."

A laugh almost breaks through, but I trap it behind my teeth. "I don't know if I see me anymore."

His smile sharpens. "You're becoming the best you can be. And it's beautiful."

He thinks he's winning, that I'll play along if I have to, smile when they tell me, sit the way they want, let them believe they're remaking me—but the whole time, I'll be waiting for the perfect chance to fuck it all up. At the masquerade. When masks are meant to slip, and everyone will be watching.

40

MAREN

A few weeks before the masquerade party, Adrian brings in a planner. Her name is Lola; tall, blonde hair with blue eyes, wearing a blazer and pants, and sure of herself. She walks into the living room like she owns it and drops a leather portfolio on the coffee table, flipping it open without even glancing at me.

"We'll need a focal point in the ballroom," she says, already flipping through swatches. "I'm thinking velvet draping, suspended lighting, and a three-tier floral arrangement behind the string quartet."

She's not asking. She's telling. And she's talking to Adrian.

He nods from the armchair beside me. "Sounds good."

Lola keeps going. "We've locked in a guest list of one hundred and twelve—investors, donors, a few from the press. The catering team arrives on the morning of the event. We're doing a plated dinner with passed hors d'oeuvres during the first hour. I've already scheduled two tasting menus."

She finally turns to me, smiling like she's doing me a favor. "You'll handle the personal touches—greeting guests, working the room. There's a short program you'll open with. Just a few minutes of welcome remarks. Don't worry, I've already drafted the speech."

"Perfect," I say. "Let me know when I'm allowed to rehearse being decorative."

She hesitates, like she's not sure if I'm joking. Adrian doesn't say a word at first.

Then he looks at me, calm as ever.

"Lola's one of the best," he says. "This should take some of the burden off of you."

Burden? He thinks he's doing me a favor by bringing in a party planner? A *favor* would be not making me do it at all.

I'm not a social butterfly. I don't have the mannerisms or the charm of Eleanor; he keeps speaking about her as if she were royalty. I'm a poor bartender with no elegance—just down-to-Earth and not used to being around wealth. I don't glide across a room. I don't know how to smile like I'm part of this world. I'm just going to fake it until I make it.

Lola flips to a page labeled DRINKS and taps it with her nail. "Servers will pass signature cocktails during the welcome hour. We're calling them 'The Montgomery' and 'The Masquerade.' Bourbon and vodka-based. Classics. Nothing too playful."

Of course not. God forbid anything is fun. Even the drink names sound lame. Drinks made for photos, not for people.

If it were up to me, I'd bartend the whole thing myself. At least then I'd have a reason to be there. She moves on to floor plans, lighting, vendor arrivals, and valet protocol. I nod in the right places, but don't say much. She knows every detail. She has every answer. By the time she leaves, the entire night is planned—and I haven't made a single decision. He had already planned out with her, she was just here to inform me of what was happening.

When I go to the sitting room, I don't know what I'm hoping

to find anymore. An escape plan before this damn party? Something she figured out before I got here?

I flip open the journal and let the pages fall where they want. Every entry makes it harder to lie to myself. She doesn't exaggerate. She writes things down because no one else is listening.

The deeper I go, the more it stops sounding like her life—and starts sounding like mine.

Adrian told me this morning that I need to start planning the next party. He said it over coffee. Same place as always—at the kitchen island while I stood across from him, still in my robe.

"You should start on the guest list today," he said. "We'll need something impressive this time. New investors. Potential clients."

I rubbed my temples. "I just finished the last one."

He didn't look up. Just scrolled through emails.

"Don't let stress ruin your energy."

"I'm not stressed. I'm tired."

He set down his cup. "That's not the same thing."

I didn't answer. There wasn't a point.

He smiled like nothing was wrong. The polite kind. The one he gives clients. That signals the end of the conversation.

It's always the same. I say I'm tired, and he calls it something else. He doesn't hear me. Or he does and spins it into something easier to deal with.

I don't remember when these conversations stopped being about planning and started feeling like instructions. But they don't sound like questions anymore.

"Can we take a break from the events?"

Just a few months. No heels. No fake smiles. No pretending to care about people I'd never see again.

He didn't even pause.

"There's always something coming up," he said. "A new deal. A new client. The house has to look perfect. So do you."

My head was pounding. I couldn't keep food down. Standing too long made the room tilt. The goalpost for perfection keeps moving. I'll never get there, and was naïve to think I could.

"I can't do it, Adrian. I need to cancel this one."

He clenched his jaw and let out a long breath, as if I was wasting his time.

"It's not a big deal," he said. "Just a few hours. Power through."

"I can barely stand."

"Then sit between speeches."

I stepped back from the counter. "I'm serious. I feel like I'm going to pass out."

"You're being dramatic."

"I'm sick."

"You're inconveniencing me."

That was it. He grabbed his keys and walked out without looking at me. No offer to help. No change in tone. Just the door slamming behind him like it was supposed to be the last word. I married a man who doesn't care about my health and wellbeing.

I'm still waiting for my results to see if I'm at risk for breast cancer since it runs in my family. I can't imagine what would happen with us if I got it. I might get the best treatment money can buy. But he'd see me as a problem, and not a sick person.

He came back later. I don't know how much later. He didn't say anything. Just dropped a bouquet of roses and a bottle of Tylenol on the nightstand, and stood there watching me. He should know by now I'm allergic to Tylenol and hate roses.

"Take this," he said. "You'll feel better in the morning."

That was the fix. No apology, flowers I hate, and medicine I can't take.

I thought I was choosing stability when I married him. I didn't care about love at the time, I thought it would come eventually. Now I know what that costs. I'm empty inside. And I can't live like this *much longer. He doesn't see me as a wife—or even a person. Just a doll that has to look perfect. I can't stay here waiting for the day he decides that's not enough.*

After that entry, there are pages ripped out and the rest are empty. There are no entries about her escape. So I close the book and press my palms to my face. The air feels thinner than it did a minute ago. He did the same things to her. The same parties. The same commands. He didn't break her all at once. He wore her down slowly. Until there was nothing left. If I'm not careful, I'll vanish the same way. I reach for the edge of the desk, grounding myself. I don't feel strong. I feel real. And that's enough for now.

41

MAREN

Margo arrives in the early afternoon, right on time, carrying a garment bag and a shoebox.

"This is the final look," she says, breezing in like she owns the place.

She unzips the bag and holds up a black dress—tight, floor-length, and low-cut. The neckline dips far more than I'm comfortable with, and the slit up the side is high enough that I'll have to think about how I move. She lays it out next to a pair of black stilettos and a gold mask shaped with swirls and cutouts. Pretty, but dramatic. The kind of thing meant to draw eyes.

"Mr. Montgomery requested this exact dress," Margo says as if it's a compliment.

Of course he did. I can't even choose my fucking clothes.

I stare at it for a second too long. "Why would he want his wife paraded around like this in front of all his investors and clients?"

Margo shrugs, all nonchalance. "It's elegant. It makes an entrance."

Right. Is that what this is about? Another kink? God, I hope not. But knowing him, I wouldn't be shocked.

I strip down and step into the dress. Margo zips me up and lays the shoes at my feet.

"You're going to need hair and makeup," she adds before I can say anything. "Sit.

They'll take care of you."

Two women appear like clockwork and take over the sitting room. One handles my hair, pulling, curling, and spraying until I lose track of what it's even supposed to look like. The other works on my face, layer after layer, until I barely recognize myself. It takes forever.

I sit still through the whole thing, too annoyed to speak, too tired to fight it. By the time they finish, I look like the perfect trophy wife.

Margo nods in approval. "Perfect. He's waiting for you downstairs."

I walk toward the stairs, heels clicking on the floor. When I round the landing, Adrian is standing at the bottom, eyes already on me.

He doesn't say anything right away. He looks—slowly, from my legs to my waist to the deep dip of the neckline. There's nothing polite about it. Nothing formal.

It's the kind of look that lands heavy. The kind you feel in your skin.

"You look beautiful," he says.

I don't thank him. I don't smile. I keep walking.

The planner intercepts me near the ballroom and hands me a notecard with my lines. I already know them. I've been rehearsing them all day. Two sentences. A smile. A handoff to the charity rep.

That's my role tonight.

The doors open and the guests start arriving. Music hums

under the chatter. The lighting makes everything shimmer. I take my place near the entrance and do what I'm supposed to.

"Welcome," I say with a practiced smile. "We're so glad you could make it."

"Oh, you look stunning," a woman gushes, reaching for my hands. "I haven't seen you since the summer event in Boston!"

I blink once. Smile tighter. "That was such a lovely night. It's good to see you again."

Another man steps up beside her. "You probably don't remember me, but we sat near each other at the fundraising dinner in the city."

I nod like I do. "Of course I remember. You were the one who brought the wine, right?"

He laughs and pats my back. "Exactly."

I wasn't there, so how did I know that?

I keep smiling. Keep greeting. Keep pretending I'm the person they think I am.

And I can't stop thinking about this dress. About how he picked it. About how all of this was planned without me, but somehow still revolves around me. I'm not here to enjoy the party. I'm here to decorate it.

The ballroom buzzes with conversation. Music drifts through the air as more guests filter in. Glasses clink, and polished shoes move across the marble like choreography. I move through the space, smiling at strangers, pretending I've met them before, acting like I belong here.

But I see it. One bartender is missing. The other scrambles, barely keeping up. Three people are already waiting, and the line keeps growing. One of the staff members leans in, whispering that someone's looking for a replacement.

I hadn't planned to step behind the bar. But once I hear that, I stop pretending. Adrian wants the perfect hostess. I'll serve the drinks myself.

I walk straight behind the bar. The bartender looks up, wide-eyed.

"Ma'am, I don't think—"

"I'm not asking. You're understaffed, and I know what I'm doing."

The younger one hovers near the bar. "Mr. Montgomery didn't say—"

"I'm Mrs. Montgomery," I cut in. "And I'm going to serve my guests drinks. Do you have a problem with that?"

They don't answer. One of them steps aside, watching me like I might catch fire.

I grab the bourbon, drop a single cube into the glass, and pour.

"Old fashioned?" I ask the man waiting at the bar.

He watches me stir. "Didn't expect the lady of the house to be behind the bar."

Of course, they don't think I can do shit but look pretty. I want to tell him to fuck off, but I slide the drink across to him. "I like being useful, and I have a background in mixology."

I slip one of Adrian's business cards that was by the bar under the base of the glass. He raises an eyebrow before he picks it up.

I move on. Another drink. Another hand. Another guest I don't recognize is pretending we're old friends. I keep smiling. I keep handing out cards. The bartenders don't stop me again. They move around me now, adjusting to my rhythm.

I know this pace. I know how to manage a room with alcohol and charm better than I ever could with small talk and fake compliments.

The second I stepped behind the bar, I stopped pretending because this feels real. This feels like mine.

But then I see him. Adrian stands at the edge of the crowd, his posture stiff, jaw locked. His fingers tighten around the glass, green eyes fixed on me, unmoving even when someone brushes past him.

I've done what he hates most. I made sure he wasn't the center of attention. He doesn't want the world to see the bartender, but the pretty hostess who gives speeches and greets people by his side.

The instant his hand wraps around my wrist, I know I'm in trouble. He doesn't drag me. He's too careful about that. But his grip is firm as he leads me away from the bar, through the murmuring crowd. His expression stays composed, but I feel the storm behind it.

The music shifts to a slow waltz. He stops at the center of the dance floor, presses his hand to the small of my back, and pulls me close.

"Smile," he murmurs through clenched teeth. "Everyone's watching."

I rest my hand on his shoulder, barely touching the crisp fabric of his tuxedo. My heart races. I don't know how to dance, but I force a smile and let him lead, just enough to play along.

His fingers tighten around mine. "You just can't help yourself, can you?"

"I was helping," I whisper, keeping my expression calm.

"You were making a fucking spectacle," he snaps. "My wife, slinging drinks, like some desperate—"

"Some desperate what? I'm a woman with a skill."

Adrian exhales hard through his nose, spinning me in time with the music. From a distance, we look poised. Effortless. The perfect couple. But his fury is sharp enough to cut.

"Do you have any idea what you looked like?"

"I looked capable. Besides, people loved the drinks."

Before he can respond, a man in a tailored navy suit steps into our path and claps him on Adrian's shoulder. "Adrian, hell of a party."

His wife beams at me. "And the cocktails were amazing."

Adrian stiffens. But I smile wide.

The man chuckles. "You've got a hell of a woman, Montgomery. Didn't take her for a bartender, but damn, those were the best drinks I've had all year."

I want to roll my eyes. He's talking about me like I'm not here and it's shocking what I can do.

Adrian's grip tightens. He forces a smile. "She has many talents."

The man nods and moves on.

I glance up at him, enjoying the way his composure cracks. "See? They loved the drinks."

He says nothing. Instead, he spins me again.

"Dance with me," he says.

"We are dancing."

His hand slides lower, pressing firmly against my waist. He leans in, lips close to my ear.

"Not like this. Dance with me properly, like a pretty little trophy wife."

He's making digs, but I looked anything but that tonight. I proved to him and to everyone I'm not some useless statute next to him. But I exhale, and let him take the lead. I let him press me against him, our steps in sync, our bodies aligned. We move together, silent, rehearsed. I hate how good it looks and how natural it feels.

The last of the guests leave, their voices fading, the ballroom falling quiet. But the tension doesn't disappear.

Later that night, we didn't make it to the bedroom. As soon as the doors close, Adrian grabs me. He pulls me against him, spins me around, and pushes me toward the heavy table.

My palms hit the wood. My breath catches as he presses into me from behind.

"You love disobeying me," he murmurs. His fingers trail up the back of my thigh.

I don't answer. Heat builds in my chest, sharp and steady,

pushing against my ribs. My skin tingles, and when his hand slides higher, parting the slit of my dress, I don't stop him.

His other hand grabs my hair, pulling my head back so his lips graze my ear. "Say it."

I grind my teeth, refusing.

He chuckles. He isn't in a rush.

His grip on my hip tightens as he pulls me back and thrusts into me. I gasp and grip the edge of the table, barely steady as he drives deeper. He doesn't give me space. He doesn't let me move.

His pace is brutal. Each thrust pushes me forward. Each one is a claim.

"Tell me you love me."

My stomach turns. That word again. The one he doesn't even believe in.

"Why?" I snap. "You don't believe in love."

"I don't," he says calmly. "But I believe in loyalty and honesty. And if you won't say it, it means you still think you can leave."

I shake my head, biting my lip hard enough to taste blood.

Adrian growls, low and rough. One hand slides to my throat, not squeezing. The other moves between my legs, his fingers working in time with his thrusts, pushing me toward the edge.

"Say it," he commands.

A whimper slips out, but I keep my mouth shut. He pulls my hair again, forcing my body to arch. His mouth brushes my neck, his voice drops.

"Tell me how much you fucking love me," he growls. "Or I'll take you to the basement, chain you down, and make you say it."

I hate the way my stomach tightens. The way heat coils low in my spine. I should be scared. I am scared. But my body doesn't know the difference between punishment and pleasure anymore. That's what he's done to me.

"I love you," I whisper. It's a lie, I'm only doing what he asks.

He groans, his grip tightening. His thrusts get harder, sharper, each one hitting deeper as he pushes toward release.

"I knew you didn't stop. You just needed reminding," he growls against my ear.

He keeps me there, buried deep, his body jerking once as he comes. His lips brush my shoulder. And I realize I'm not sure if I said what I meant. Or if he made me believe I did.

42

ADRIAN

She said it. I haven't heard the words since she's been back. Not once. I told her I knew she still did, but I didn't force out the words. But tonight I wanted to hear them again. I had to fuck it out of her, but that doesn't matter. She said it. I didn't need it to sound sweet or perfect. I just needed it out of her mouth. I know her. When she lies, she hesitates. She shifts her weight, drops her eyes. She didn't do any of that. It came out low and wrecked, like it hurt to admit. But it was honest. Or close enough.

She said it before she left—real soft, sometimes when she was pressed up against me, sometimes when she thought it would fix something. Begging for affection. Desperate for attention. When she was trying to pull me back toward her instead of letting me drag her where I wanted her to be, that's how I always knew it was real. It wasn't casual for her. She never needed to say it then, not really. I already knew. And last night, it sounded the same.

Now she's asleep on my chest like she used to. Curled up without thinking, like some part of her still remembers this is where she's happy, where she belongs. Her leg is draped over mine, her hand against my ribs. I haven't moved in an hour, I won't risk waking her. Because this? This is how I know I still have her.

She didn't pull away. Didn't turn her back. She let me hold her, and now she's here, breathing slowly like she's not afraid of me anymore. You don't fall asleep like this unless you want to stay. She was beautiful and magnetic last night despite her role-playing as a bartender. But I saw what she was doing; she was trying to prove to me she can show off her talents while still being the perfect hostess. I had guests come up to me to say how great of a party it was. So she fulfilled her role. I couldn't take my eyes off her all night, but she was giving away smiles that she never gives me. It made me angrier as I stood staring at her and she didn't notice me. So she needs to let this bartending dream go, it's distracting her. If she wants to make a drink for the two of us alone at home, that's fine, but she won't bartend at our parties. She belongs by my side.

I was tempted to punish her, but I needed to take her first and those frustrations went away when I had her, when she was shaking and gasping and mine again—she said it. *I love you.*

I don't care how they got there. They're in her mouth now. That means they're in her and they'll come easier next time. And maybe, eventually, I won't have to ask. She'll say it on her own.

43

MAREN

When were in bed this morning, Adrian asked if I'd go to an art show with him tonight. I said sure before I even think about it—because really, what else can I say?

He smiled, kissed my temple, and told me, "I think you'll enjoy it," like it's something I asked for, like this was a favor to me.

Now I'm halfway through curling my hair when he steps into the room this evening, holding a small velvet box. I freeze, curling iron still in my hand.

"I got you another wedding ring," he says casually, like it's normal to replace a symbol of eternal devotion without a second thought. "Something more your style."

Inside is a round diamond. It's huge, but not gaudy; subtle enough to pretend it's modest if you squint. Elegant, tasteful, expensive. Just like everything he picks out for me.

"It's beautiful," I whisper, slipping it on.

He looks pleased, like he just made the right bet. I kiss him on the mouth and say, "Thank you. I love it."

His smile deepens as he nods toward the closet. "Go get dressed. We can't be late."

He smacks my ass and walks out like this is just another night out.

The gallery is massive, echoing with soft music and murmured conversation. Patrons in designer gowns and tailored suits drift between canvases, holding champagne flutes like they were born with them.

I follow Adrian through the crowd, keeping pace with his long strides. Every stare slides over the black dress he chose for me. Tight, low-cut, impossible to ignore. I feel like a prop. A very shiny, very expensive prop.

Adrian stops to greet a couple near a sculpture I can't even describe. The woman's jewelry could pay my rent for a year. I stand quietly, smiling when they look at me, nodding when they speak.

I hate this. I hate how I never know what to say. That's why I worked late shifts at the Rusty Nail. So I didn't have to be social.

Adrian hands me a glass of champagne. I take it without thinking and down half in a single sip.

"Slow down," he says under his breath, not unkind, but firm.

"I just need something to take the edge off," I mutter, adjusting my grip on the glass.

He watches me for a second longer, then nods. "Fine. But slow down."

We move again. More introductions. More names I won't remember. Everyone here looks perfect, sculpted, completely at home in a world that was never meant for someone like me.

Eventually, someone turns to me and asks, "And what do you do?"

"I bartend," I answer without thinking.

The woman blinks, her brows lifting slightly.

I force a quick laugh. "I mean, for fun. I'm an artist."

Her eyes sharpen with new interest. "Oh? Do you have work in the show?"

My mouth goes dry. I blink. "I..."

Adrian cuts in smoothly. "Yes. There are a few of her pieces here tonight."

I turn sharply, trying to read his face, but he's already guiding me toward one of the abstract canvases near the back wall. I had no idea.

It's a chaotic mix of red, black, and pale streaks of white. It looks like paint got pissed off and threw itself against the canvas.

He gestures toward it. "Tell them about your inspiration."

I stare at it, heart racing. I've never seen this painting before. Maybe it's mine. Maybe it's Eleanor's. Maybe he paid someone to slap my name on it. I don't know anymore.

"It's based on chaos," I say, the lie sliding off my tongue like wet glass. "There was a time my life felt chaotic, but now I have peace."

They nod slowly, like it means something.

"How much?" someone asks.

My brain scrambles. "Five thousand," I say, grabbing the number out of nowhere.

Adrian's jaw tightens just slightly. "They're part of the gallery. Not for sale." He says it with a smile, but his eyes are sharp.

Message received. I shouldn't have spoken.

I sip my champagne and let the silence settle around us as the crowd drifts away. Adrian leans in close, brushing his hand along the small of my back. "You're doing fine," he murmurs in my ear. "Just follow my lead."

I smile, lips tight, and nod. Because that's what I do now, I follow.

During the night, I let Adrian lead, and he leans in, brushing his lips against my cheek.

"You're doing great," he whispers.

The kiss catches me off guard. He's never affectionate in public. He keeps his voice low, intimate. "I did this for you. I wanted you to know I can make your dreams come true, like you've made mine. I haven't been a perfect husband, but I will always be what you need. Don't forget that."

I nod, the champagne turning sour in my stomach.

Then I see her.

Diane.

She's standing near a sculpture, tall and elegant in navy silk.

I plaster on a smile and approach. "Hi," I say, leaning in for air kisses.

"Eleanor. Adrian." Her tone is pleasant, but her smile is muted. "Glad to see you here tonight."

"I was planning to reach out. We should do lunch, catch up."

"That sounds nice," she replies, but her voice is flat. She doesn't mean it. *Damn. I misread her.*

Adrian slips his arm around my waist, his smile perfectly smooth. "I think it would be great for you two to catch up."

Good. I got his permission.

Diane adjusts the clasp on her purse. "Do you want to go to the powder room with me? I need to reapply my lipstick."

I nod and follow her through the gallery. The bathroom isn't some cramped public stall. It's warm and softly lit, with velvet chairs and fresh flowers by the sink. A space designed for quiet conversations and carefully hidden breakdowns.

Diane turns toward me as she pulls a tube of lipstick from her bag. "I'm surprised you hadn't called."

"I've been busy."

She lifts an eyebrow. "Reuniting with your husband. The one you desperately wanted to leave."

"I still want to leave," I say, keeping my voice low. "He dragged me back."

Her reflection meets mine in the mirror. "How did he find you?"

"I don't know. I was in Chicago."

"You went back to Chicago?" Her eyes narrow. "Why?"

"Because I didn't think he'd look close to home."

She turns slowly, her lipstick untouched. "I can't believe I helped you. I risked a lot. And you just came back, pretending like none of it happened."

"I'm not pretending."

Why does everyone think I'm pretending? How can these people not see I have no idea what they're talking about?

"You're smiling. Attached to his hip. Wearing his ring again. I thought you'd divorce him so you could meet someone who could have kids."

Adrian can't have kids? Even though I've been having my period regularly again, I'm so relieved. I can't get pregnant ever. Because he can't have them. I pretend like I know that.

I take a breath. My throat feels tight. "It's all a lie. He's horrible."

She waits. Wants more. But I don't say the word *basement*. I don't describe the mattress or the chains. I don't tell her about the punishments or the way he watches me like he's waiting for me to fall into line again.

I could say it. But I don't. Part of me wants to protect him. Why, I don't know. But I have to.

Diane caps her lipstick and gives me a long look. "I've known him a long time. Just admit it. He lured you back in."

I stay quiet, eyes locked on the mirror.

"It wasn't like that."

"He's charming," she says, soft but pointed. "He knows how to make you feel special. Even when he's neglecting you. Even when you're miserable." Her voice tightens. "And he kept you—"

"Controlled," I finish, the word slipping out before I can stop it.

She goes still for half a second. Her gaze sharpens.

"Close," she corrects, but there's a flicker in her expression. "You didn't get to pursue your dreams, but I guess he's making that happen now. Since you're being featured."

I blink. "Featured?" My voice is flat.

She tilts her head. "Isn't this whole thing for you?"

I raise an eyebrow. "You think this is all for me?"

She doesn't answer.

I straighten up, forcing my tone lighter. "Let's catch up at lunch. I really should get back to Adrian."

She watches me a beat longer, eyes narrowing just slightly, but she nods. I push open the door before I say something I'll regret. I need to stop talking before I give too much away. Because I'm slipping, and Diane knows it. The second I'm out of the bathroom, I head outside for a breather. The night air hits me hard, cool against my skin and sharp in my lungs.

I can't breathe inside that gallery. Not with Diane's voice echoing in my head. Not with strangers praising art I didn't make.

I'm being featured when I can't fucking paint. My whole life is a fucking lie. I pace along the side of the building, heels digging into the gravel, fingers pressed to my temples like I can squeeze the noise out. I probably look insane, wandering back and forth in this designer dress like a madwoman. But I don't care.

The door clicks open behind me. Adrian's voice cuts through the dark. "I've been looking everywhere for you."

I stop walking, but don't turn around.

"You were supposed to come back to me," he says, stepping closer.

"I needed air."

"You always need air," he mutters, softer now. "What's wrong?"

I spin to face him. "I'm overwhelmed. That's what's wrong." I pause. "Why didn't you tell me I was being featured tonight?"

His expression doesn't change. "I thought you knew. You didn't recognize your own work?"

"I have memory problems," I snap. "I don't remember."

He raises his eyebrows slightly. "Clearly."

He steps forward, voice low. "I just want you to feel like yourself again. That's all I want."

I take a shaky breath. Maybe he believes that. Maybe he thinks this is care. But all I feel is trapped.

"I'm not going back in there," I say, my arms crossed tight over my chest.

Adrian laughs. "Don't be ridiculous. You're going back in there, and you're going to smile and nod like a good girl." His hand lands on my ass, a firm squeeze that makes my whole body tense. "And I'll reward you when we get home," he adds, his voice low and smug.

I flinch from the way he says *reward* like I'm a pet he's training. I don't want to be rewarded. I want to be respected.

I stare at him, but he's already turned back toward the door, expecting me to follow. My legs won't move. My chest's still tight, heart hammering. I could walk away. I could disappear into the street and never come back. But I don't. I stand there frozen, his words crawling under my skin like heat I can't shake off.

He doesn't even notice. Because in his mind, this is done. I'll follow. I always do. But I don't move. Not yet.

"Can I get a few moments?" I ask, my voice quieter now, almost calm. "I'll come back inside."

Adrian narrows his eyes, studying my face. "Fine. But for a few minutes. That's it."

"Okay."

He stares for a second longer, then finally turns and walks back toward the gallery doors.

I wait until he disappears inside.

Then I start walking.

Then I start running.

This is my only chance, and I'm going to take it.

I don't know where I'm going. I don't care. My heels are loud against the sidewalk, sharp with every step, but I don't stop. I clutch my purse tight and just run. The streetlights blur past. A few heads turn, but no one stops me. My lungs burn, my legs ache, but I keep going. Because if I stop, I'll freeze. If I freeze, I'll turn around. And if I turn around, he wins.

I don't even know how far I've gone until I finally look up. The gallery is nowhere in sight. My dress is clinging to my skin, my throat is dry, and I have nothing but the clothes on my back, and a clutch purse with a dead phone and a lipstick I'll never use.

Adrian is going to be livid. But I don't care. I can't keep doing this shit. I can't keep smiling, and nodding, and pretending this is a life I chose. I need to breathe. I need to think. I need to feel like a person again.

44

ADRIAN

Where the fuck is Eleanor? I said a few minutes. Not several. Not twenty. Not long enough for people to start asking where the hell the featured artist went. I scan the room again. Smiles. Champagne. Polite conversations. But no Eleanor. People want to see her. They want to meet the woman behind the work I curated for her. This night was for her. For us.

I walk back toward the bathroom. Diane's standing near the powder room doors, talking to someone in a black cocktail dress.

I step closer. "Can you check if she's in there?"

Diane gives me a strange look. "She's not. She left a while ago."

I clench my jaw, forcing my expression neutral. "Thanks."

I nod once and walk away. *Keep it together. Don't draw attention.* Back through the gallery. Past the art. Past the guests. Through the doors.

She's not outside. She's nowhere. Did she run again? Right under my nose? At an event for her? She wouldn't embarrass both of us like this. Not tonight. But she did.

I go to the car. Empty. No sign of her. Not in the back seat. Not across the lot. I even check the sidewalk.

Fuck. She ran again. She got overwhelmed and ran. She chases chaos. That's what she does best. But what she doesn't understand or never understood, is that she needs stability. She needs structure. A place to come back to.

That's why we're meant for each other. She runs. I chase. She falls apart. I rebuild her. I pull out my phone and open the tracking app. No signal. She either turned it off or the battery's dead. Doesn't matter. She's gone off course again.

I need my wife to come back. I start walking the perimeter of the lot, scanning every corner, every moving figure. The panic hits hard. I remember what it felt like when she was gone, waking up to an empty bed, going weeks without a word, months without touching her. I stayed faithful. I didn't want anyone else. Even when I had no idea where she was or who she was with, I waited. Now she's taken off again. She saw a window, and used it. I should've known she wasn't ready. I saw it in her smile, the way she played along too easily. I tried to give her a night that showed I see her, that I respect her. That I'll do whatever it takes to make her stay.

She said she loved me. That wasn't fake. I heard it in her voice. She meant it. I felt it. Then I see her walking back on the sidewalk toward the gallery, and I feel a mix of instant relief and anger. She's flushed and sweaty, her hair sticking to her neck, the fabric of her dress clinging to her skin. She looks like she's been running from something, or someone. From me.

"Where the fuck have you been?" I ask, stepping in front of her.

"I took a walk."

"A walk?" I look her up and down. "You look like a mess, and you have a speech."

"A speech?" Her voice spikes. "Who is this for? Me or you?"

"For the both of us," I snap. "This night is ours."

"I can't do a speech."

"You can," I say, lowering my voice. "Go up, thank everyone for coming, talk about your art. It can be brief."

She shakes her head, eyes darting like she's looking for a way out.

"Go to the bathroom," I continue. "Clean up. We'll tell them you were in there the whole time."

She still doesn't move.

My voice softens, but the command stays beneath it. "You can do this, Ellie. You need to pull yourself together for five minutes. Then we go home."

Her mouth tightens. She looks away, because I'm right, she needs this. She doesn't know it yet.

45

MAREN

I stare at myself in the mirror. My face flushed, my hair a mess, my chest still rising and falling like I ran a marathon. I grab paper towels and run cold water, pressing them to my neck, to my forehead, anywhere that might cool me down. My mascara's smudged. My lipstick is gone. I look like a woman barely holding it together. And I am. But I fixed it. I do what he expects. I clean myself up. I reapply the lipstick. I smooth my hair, tug at my dress, and square my shoulders.

I wanted to run, but I realized it was a bad idea. He can track my phone. He's given me a credit card, but I won't be able to use it without him knowing where I am. I wouldn't have made it far, so I turned around. Plus, what do I even have to go back to? Nothing. I have nothing, all because of him.

I whisper, "Just a few minutes."

Then I step out. Adrian is already moving through the room, gathering people. His hand gestures are smooth and polished, that perfect host mask slipping back into place.

People start turning toward us, flutes of champagne still in hand, eyes expectant.

He gives me a slight nod. My cue.

I step forward.

"Hi," I say, my voice thin. "Thank you all for coming tonight. To see my art. And all the other beautiful work in the gallery."

A few people smile. A polite chuckle from someone near the back.

"I've been an artist for many years now," I go on, my throat dry. "And I've always wanted to share it with people."

I glance at Adrian. He's watching me carefully.

"And...thanks to my *husband*, he made that happen for me."

The word husband catches in my mouth.

I stutter. I swallow. I keep going.

"That's it," I say quickly. "That's all."

There's a soft ripple of claps. Short. Awkward. Adrian's expression tightens, just enough for me to see it. He's embarrassed. And now, I feel it, too. But deep down, I feel in control.

46

ADRIAN

When I said brief, I didn't mean two sentences. That wasn't a speech. That was a disaster. I thought she was ready. I felt with the right dress, the right setting, the right push, she'd fall back into place. She loves art, and she could talk about it for hours.

At the masquerade party, she gave a wonderful speech, the etiquette courses were helping, too. She's been doing them weekly. I thought doing this would remind her of her true passion and spark that drive again so she stops dreaming about being a bartender.

I've seen her talk about her work like she believed in it. But she's not ready for non-scripted speeches. She's a mess. Even with the etiquette consultant I spent a fortune on. Now she stutters through a handful of words, thanks me like she's unsure if she means it, and ends it all with "that's it."

No presence. No polish. Just awkward silence and a few forced claps. She embarrassed herself. And me. I watch the crowd disperse, polite smiles fading as they turn back to their drinks. She's already retreating to the side, like she wants to disappear into the wall. This can't happen again. Because I can't keep bringing her into my world if she can't carry herself properly in it, but she will. Because I won't let her become a liability. I'll do anything I can to prevent that from happening. She needs to remember actions have consequences, and she will face them tonight.

47

MAREN

The car ride is silent. His jaw is locked. He doesn't say a word, but I can feel it rolling off him in waves—anger, disappointment, disgust. He's furious I managed to fuck this up.

I stare out the window, my body stiff from sitting so still, but my mind won't stop spinning. He thinks I embarrassed him, that I fell apart in front of his precious circle. Maybe I did. But I've done worse.

So what? He scolds me. Call me a mess. I can live with that. I've lived through worse. I grew up in foster homes where screaming was background noise and kindness was a transaction. I worked at the Rusty Nail dealing with mean, nasty drunks. He has no idea what kind of mess I can survive. Still, I don't say a word, either. Not until we walk through the front door.

Then he turns to me, his voice low. "Let's go to the basement."

I freeze in the hallway. "For what?"

He doesn't blink. "For running from me."

"I wasn't running," I say quickly. "I needed time to prepare. I was trying to get my head together."

He scoffs. "You were preparing for a disaster." He steps closer. "I did this for you. Everything tonight. And you manage to fuck it up like you do everything else since you've been back."

The words hit harder than they should. I don't flinch, but my breath stutters.

A tear slips from the corner of my eye before I can stop it. I blink fast, but another one follows. Then another. He called me a fuck-up. And that's not just cruel. It's new.

Not even the people who tossed me around from home to home said it like that. Not with that finality. That disgust. Not like it was a fact, something I couldn't ever un-be. My chest tightens. My vision blurs. I hate that I'm crying in front of him, but I can't stop it.

Because for once, it's not fear.

It's something worse.

Failure.

Tears start falling before I can stop them—fast and hot, streaking down my cheeks. I don't wipe them away. I just stand there, crying, not looking at him.

He watches me for a moment, then says, "Let's go to the basement. We need to get back on track."

I shake my head. "No. You'll have to drag me down there."

I don't yell. I don't move. I just keep standing still, my hands at my sides, jaw locked tight.

He doesn't step forward. He watches me like he's waiting for me to calm down. Waiting for me to fall back into place.

Then he says it, soft but pointed. "You're disappointed because you wanted to please me."

I look at him dead-on. "I don't care to please you."

Something shifts in his expression. I don't stop.

"I don't care about you."

His jaw clenches. "If you didn't, then why are you crying?"

"Because you called me a fuck-up," I snap. "Which is cruel and low, even for you. And I don't think highly of you."

The words hit like bullets. I want them to. I want him to feel it the way I do when he told me I ruin everything.

"I wanted to leave because I want nothing to do with you. You think controlling me is love? You think locking me in a basement makes you a good husband?"

My voice rises. I'm yelling now, venom in every syllable.

"You're a fucking joke. Those people at the gallery don't give a shit about you. They were there for me. My name. My art. Not for you. And if I give a shitty speech? Oh fucking well. I don't care."

He just stands there, breathing hard. For once, I don't shrink under it. I don't apologize. I don't retreat. Because I mean every word. And for the first time since he brought me back here, I feel powerful. Even if it only lasts a second.

"Watch yourself, Eleanor," he says through his teeth, "Don't forget who you belong to."

I step closer, eyes locked on his. "And what are you going to fucking do about it?"

"You know what. Stop stalling."

I laugh, sharp and cold. "Why do you have a dungeon? Tell me."

"It's a kink," he says. "You know that."

"One I'm not into."

"Yes, you are." He steps forward, voice dropping. "You come after every punishment."

"I fake it."

"Bullshit." His tone hardens. "You're into it. You fight me, push me, beg for more, then come so hard you forget your own name."

My mouth twists, stomach turning, but he keeps going.

"You want it rough. You want the punishment. You want to

feel it, every lash. You want to earn the way I look at you when it's over. Don't lie to me."

I shake my head, trembling now.

"You want to fight me so you can get more. That's what this is. That's what it's always been."

"I don't want it. You've trained me like an animal to endure it. You're a shitty husband."

For a second, something flickers in his eyes. Wounded. Human. But then it hardens, like it always does. Like the part of him that feels gets swallowed whole by the part that dominates.

"Eleanor," he says, his voice cold. "You want to leave? Fine. You leave with what you came in with. Nothing. Because that's what you are. Nothing but a waitress I took out of the trash."

"Fuck you. I'm a bartender," I snap. "Get your facts straight."

He straightens slowly, his face unreadable.

"Get out," he growls.

I stare him down, breath tight in my chest. "Make me."

That's all it takes. He grabs my arm and yanks me toward the door. I stumble, but keep my feet under me, trying to twist out of his grip, but he's too strong. He throws the front door open, shoves me through it without hesitation, and slams it behind me.

The sound of the lock clicks into place.

I'm outside.

Alone.

The night air hits me, sharp and cold. My bare feet touch stone. My hands tremble. I look at the house. Still. Silent.

He really did it. He actually threw me out. Like I'm a disposable toy. Like I didn't sleep in that bed, bleed in that basement, fake smiles for his gallery full of strangers.

I walk by the gate and push on it, and it's unlocked. Adrian must've forgot to lock it from his phone when we got inside, too distracted by arguing with me. It's freezing cold, I have nothing.

My best bet is going to town and begging someone to call the police.

But he could probably convince them I'm crazy. He has a lot of power and influence on this island. Maybe someone will pity me and give me money for a ferry, but then I'd need money to get back to Chicago. I'm sure my stuff is gone because I'd be evicted by now. Maybe someone from the Rusty Nail would take me in, at least for a while. They'd believe me if I said I was kidnapped. Getting home will be a nightmare, but I'd rather take my chances than stay here another second.

I rip off the necklace, then the earrings and bracelet. They're the only bargaining chips I have. Pawn them, trade them, whatever it takes to buy my way off this island. He dressed me up like his prize, but he just handed me my ticket out.

I wrap my arms around myself, blinking at the dark windows, the perfect exterior hiding everything I just survived. He wanted me to feel powerless. But all I feel is free.

48

ADRIAN

She wants to leave, so she's sleeping outside tonight. That's her punishment. By morning, she'll come crawling back. I check the cameras, flipping through every feed—the front drive, side lawn, and rear perimeter—but find nothing. She's not there. She's probably crouched in a blind spot somewhere, curled up in the dark like a child throwing a tantrum. I don't care. Let her sulk.

I should have dragged her to the basement and reminded her who made her what she is for disrespecting me in my own house like she won.

For now, she can sleep somewhere else and remember exactly who holds the key.

I go to bed. The house feels cold, quiet, and lonelier than usual without her beside me, but I don't care. Let her stew. Let her sit in the dark and think about what she did. Let the night strip away her anger and replace it with regret. That's what silence does. It humbles people.

She thinks she won something tonight. But I'll sleep just fine because I have the ultimate power.

She's still here, still on my property, and still under my

watch. I could go get her anytime I want, pull her back in, and set the rules straight. Or I could leave her out there longer and let her feel what it means to defy me. In the morning, maybe I'll let her in. Maybe I won't. Either way, she'll come back to me. They always do.

When the sun rises, everything feels wrong. I wake up and grab my phone before I even sit up. I expect to see her curled by the front door, shivering and ashamed, or pacing the porch, worn down from a night of stewing in her own defiance. Maybe she pounded on the door or cried, which would have been satisfying.

But there's nothing. I scrub through the footage, checking every angle and timestamp, but she never came back to the door, never knocked, and never begged. She's gone.

She didn't leave the property. The gate is locked and she literally has nothing. No money, and that's the only way she can get anywhere. So she'd have to walk miles before getting into town. But she didn't crawl back like I expected. There's no apology, no desperation, just silence. She's more prideful than I gave her credit for, willing to freeze before surrendering and suffering rather than ask me for anything. She wasn't always this prideful. I stripped that out of her a long time ago, but time away made her dig deep into that again.

That's fine. Let her be prideful. It just means I haven't broken her yet. And I will. I'll chip away at that pride until there's nothing left. I'll strip her down until she's exactly what she was always meant to be. Mine. Obedient. Soft. Dependent.

She can scream, curse me, and fight until her voice cracks. But in the end, she'll come back. She always does. Because deep down, she needs me. And if she doesn't yet, I'll make sure she learns.

She's still not on any screen. I go through every angle again —the front, back, and perimeter—but the result is the same. I throw on shoes and step outside, walking the grounds myself. I walk the garden paths, and look behind the hedges, the garage, and the back of the guest house. Maybe she's hiding. Maybe she fell asleep or curled up behind the shed, sulking like always.

But the second I reach the gate and see it wide open, I know she's completely gone. I forgot to lock it. I didn't even think about it. No way she would leave, barefoot, without money, and not without begging first.

When she left before, she had planned it well. She took all her jewelry with her, I'm assuming to sell it for money. She did it when I was out of the country, knowing I would be busy. But the money ran out, and she was stuck bartending to make ends meet. I don't think she'd ever want to go back to that after being back here for months in luxury with me. But she did. She really left.

At first, I tell myself it's a stunt, just a message. She wants to rattle me, prove something, show she still has some kind of power left. So I wait. I make coffee. I sit by the window. I check the cameras again. The confidence I felt last night begins to rot in my chest. She's not coming back. She's out there with nothing. No money, no phone, no coat, and no plan. And it's cold. She could be hurt. Or worse.

What the hell was I thinking?

The fight last night got out of control, but I thought shutting the door would fix it. I thought pushing her out would teach her something. I thought she would come crawling back, say sorry, tell me she loved me, and fold like she always does. But now all I see is her face. The pain in her eyes. Her bare feet. The way she didn't even look scared.

She wasn't afraid anymore, and I kicked her out while she looked like that, dressed like that, with nothing.

Now I don't know where she is, and I can't sit here any longer.

I get in the car and start driving. I don't have a destination, I just have her face burned into my mind. The dress. The bare feet. The tears. That last look she gave me before I slammed the door.

Where could she have gone? She didn't have a phone, which was either dead or abandoned on purpose. She had no money, not a single dime. Just that tight, black dress.

I check the roads near the house. Nothing. No trace of her. I head toward the main strip, slowing as I pass gas stations and quiet side streets. Every woman walking alone makes my chest tighten, but none of them are her. She's out here somewhere, alone and vulnerable. And then it hits me all at once.

She's not just angry. She's not bluffing. She would rather risk freezing or getting picked up by a stranger than come back to me.

I grip the wheel harder, my knuckles pale. This isn't how it was supposed to go. I was supposed to punish her, not lose her. I thought I could control her. But now I'm circling intersections like a maniac, searching for the woman who walked away from me. And if something happens to her, that's on me.

49

MAREN

Headlights flash across the gravel as another car barrels past me, the wind kicking up dust and whipping strands of hair across my face. I hold out my hand again, trying not to cry, even though my throat is tight and my chest already aches with frustration. But nothing happens. No car slows down, and no one bothers to stop.

I'm barefoot, stranded in the middle of nowhere, wearing a black designer dress and Adrian's diamonds. I look less like a person and more like the aftermath of a mugging and a breakdown. My body trembles, not only from the cold, but from the rage coursing through me and from the sick, humiliating realization that I probably look like an invitation. I don't know this island as well as I thought, but that's Adrian's fault, keeping me imprisoned. I decided not to walk down the main road so Adrian wouldn't find me.

So I thought I could take a side street, and now I'm lost. I've been walking around all night. This island is still developing, so there is not as many people as I thought. And the ones that are drive past me in their luxury cars. They probably think I'm a hooker.

Adrian is the fucking reason I'm out here standing on the shoulder of an unlit road, silently praying that the next car doesn't slow down for the wrong reason.

Should I go back? Should I crawl to the door like he expects me to and give him what he wants? Should I let him win just because I have no better option?

No, I can't. He needs to feel what I've felt for too long. He needs to be afraid, even if just for once, and he needs to experience the same kind of panic I carry every single day.

Another light appears in the distance, but this time it approaches more slowly. My heart leaps into my throat as I take a cautious step back. The car coasts to a stop just in front of me, its headlights blinding and its engine humming low. I squint against the glare and raise a hand to shield my face.

That's when I see it's Adrian in his silver Aston Martin.

The door flies open and Adrian storms toward me. His sleeves are rolled up, his hair is disheveled, and he's breathing heavily like he's been running this whole way instead of driving.

He grabs my arm with a grip that's too tight. "What the fuck are you doing out here?"

"Let go of me."

"Are you trying to get yourself killed?"

"You're the one who threw me out!" I shout, jerking my arm free with a burst of fury.

"What exactly did you think was going to happen? You idiot!"

He stares at me, eyes wide with disbelief, as if he genuinely doesn't recognize me anymore. It's like I've become something he can't control or contain. But I've always been that way now. Now I'm not playing nice anymore.

"My phone's dead," I snap. "I don't have any money, I don't have any shoes or a coat."

He doesn't say a word. He just keeps breathing harder, his

jaw clenched and his eyes flicking across me from my scraped feet and bare legs to the diamond earrings and necklace he clasped around my neck before the gallery. I could've been robbed. Or worse.

"Get in the fucking car," he growls, yanking the passenger door open.

I stay frozen. I don't have to, I could keep walking, but he'll just follow me and get angrier. I can't win this battle, but I won't lose the war.

"I said now. Or you're going to regret it."

With no real choice, I slide into the passenger seat, my heart pounding so hard I can feel it in my throat. He slams the door behind me, marches around the hood, and throws himself into the driver's seat. The moment he starts the car, it lurches forward, the tires spinning against loose gravel before catching. The silence that follows is thick and brutal, stretching between us like a held breath. Eventually, he speaks.

"You're in so much fucking trouble," he mutters without looking at me.

I keep my eyes on the window and my voice low. "Good."

"You could've been kidnapped or killed," he says, louder this time.

"You would've deserved it. At least I would've been away from you," I say, not bothering to hide the venom in my words.

He slams the brakes without warning, and the car skids slightly before jerking to a stop. When he turns to face me, his eyes are dark and his voice is tight with something dangerously close to fear.

"Don't ever say that again."

I stare straight ahead for a moment, then turn to look at him without a single flinch.

Because for the first time since this all began, I can see it clearly. He's scared. And I want him to be.

50

MAREN

During the drive, Adrian doesn't look at me when he says it. His eyes stay locked on the road, and his jaw tightens as though he's bracing for impact.

"We're going straight to the basement after you clean yourself up."

I let out a sharp, bitter laugh. "I'm not cleaning myself up. I'll get your precious basement dirty for all I care."

His fingers tighten around the steering wheel, and I see the tension ripple through his arms.

"Because that's what I am to you, right? Trash. Isn't that what you called me?"

He flinches slightly. "I shouldn't have said that."

"But you did," I snap. The words come out hard and fast. "And don't pretend it slipped out. That wasn't a mistake. It's what you've always thought. You just let your bitch of a sister say it first."

"I resolved that."

"No, I did," I shoot back. "I'm the one who called her out. You sat there and let it happen, just like you always do. You never defended me."

"We moved past that."

"No, you moved past it. I didn't."

His nostrils flare, and his voice lowers, controlled. "Then let's focus on moving past this."

I whip my head toward him, rage bubbling to the surface. "I will never forgive you for throwing me out of the house in the freezing cold. I was barefoot on the side of the road. And you think that's something I can just get over?"

He finally turns his head and meets my eyes. "I didn't think you'd actually leave. You were supposed to beg to come back inside and then go to the basement."

That is when it breaks. I don't hold anything back.

"You think everything can be fixed in your fucking basement?" I spit as my voice rises. "You think dragging me down there resets me like I'm some broken machine you can reprogram? You left me to freeze because I didn't say the speech right. Because I embarrassed you for five fucking minutes. And now you expect me to follow your rules like nothing happened?"

He doesn't respond.

"You don't even realize what you did. That's the worst part. You think I ran to punish you, but I didn't. I ran because I wanted to live. Because for the first time, I saw exactly what my life would look like if I didn't get out."

His voice is quieter when it finally breaks the silence. "Then why did you get in the car?"

Then I say it, clear and steady. "Because I didn't want to die out there. But that doesn't mean I'm choosing you."

When we get to the house, I march to the bathroom and get in the shower. The water is too hot, scalding my skin, but I don't move. I sit down hard on the tile floor with my legs folded and my arms wrapped tightly around my knees. The spray beats down on my shoulders like it's trying to wash the night off me, like it can erase what just happened, like it can reach deep enough to scrub out the part of me that let it happen.

But it can't. I cry. Not the quiet kind. Not the cinematic single-tear version people like to romanticize. This is ugly. It is messy, raw, and real.

And I can't stop it. Because he threw me out. He called me trash. A fuck-up. Maybe he meant it. Maybe he didn't. But it doesn't matter, because that word is still echoing in my head. It curls around everything I've ever tried to outrun.

I was born into nothing. Passed around like a problem no one wanted to deal with. Foster home to foster home. I poured drinks for men who stared too long and paid too little. I've survived things he couldn't imagine.

But Adrian? He was handed everything.

The world rolled out a red carpet for him the day he was born. He got wealth, power, and prestige without ever having to fight for any of it. He talks about discipline as if he's invented it, but he's never had to earn a living the way I have. And now he thinks he owns me.

He thinks he can slap diamonds on my neck, lock me in a house, and call it love. He thinks he can throw me onto the street and then drag me back inside like I'm his dog.

I choke on another sob and bury my face in my knees. My throat aches from holding it in too long. My chest burns. My whole body feels wrung out. But somewhere underneath the pain, deep in the part of me he hasn't touched, something shifts.

He thinks he's in control. But he's not. He thinks I'm weak because I cried. Because I ran. Because I came back. But I am done being shaped by him. I will act the part. I will take the punishment. I will cry and break and say what he wants to hear. Until I get the fuck out of here. And when I do, he won't see me coming.

There is a knock on the bathroom door. My whole body tenses.

"Go away," I croak. My voice is shredded from crying. "I'm not done."

But the door opens anyway. Adrian steps inside, calm as ever, like the night hasn't shattered anything. He doesn't speak right away. He just walks straight to the faucet and turns off the water without saying a word.

I blink up at him. I'm soaked, mascara smeared, my skin burning from the heat and shame.

"I wasn't finished," I say. My voice is low.

"You are now."

He doesn't give me time to argue. His arms slide beneath me and he lifts me like I weigh nothing. Like I'm not shaking. Like I didn't run from him hours ago and cry myself raw in the shower.

I don't struggle. What's the point?

Fighting gets me nowhere. Screaming only feeds him. So I let him carry me. I keep my eyes on the wall and go limp in his arms. I am not weak—I am detached. If I pretend I'm somewhere else, maybe I'll start to believe it.

51

MAREN

He doesn't speak as we move downstairs. The basement stairs creak beneath us. The scent hits me first—clean leather and faint antiseptic. I want to stall, beg, anything to slow him down, but it's pointless. I've been here before. I know what's coming.

When he sets me down, I see the restraints already hanging from the ceiling. Thick cuffs, chains bolted into the beam above. I know how this goes. He says this makes us stronger. The truth is, it makes me stronger. Because I endure it.

One day, I'll tell the world what I survived in this house. In this basement. I'll tell them what he did to me in the name of love, in the name of loyalty, in the name of dominance.

And when I do, he'll finally understand. He didn't break me. He made me unbreakable.

On the table sits a cane. My breath catches. He's never used one before—my skin crawls. The sight alone is different from the paddle's blunt force; this is narrow, sharp, built to split skin. I already hear the sound it'll make—a whistle first, then fire that lingers. He picks it up slowly, dragging it through his fingers like it belongs there.

"Fifty," he says.

"Fifty? You'll kill me if you do that. Is that what you want?"

His eyes narrow. "I want you obedient. You can and will take every one."

"I can't handle that."

"You can and will."

"You can't—"

"I will."

He steps behind me, and the restraints rattle as he fastens my wrists, pulling my arms high above my head. Then he locks my ankles, spreading my legs wide, making my feet barely touch the floor. I test the chains anyway, wrists twisting hard. No give. My ankles are forced wide enough that I can't even close my thighs. My shoulders ache instantly, my calves straining to hold steady. I'm spread-eagle in the air, on full display with no place to hide.

The cold from the concrete seeps into my toes, into my spine. But I can already feel the heat radiating from the lashes he's about to deliver.

"You've been a bad, bad girl," he says, almost amused. His hand trails down my back, the touch pretending to be intimate when we're about to go to war. "The worst you've ever been. Fifty will get you back on track."

He drags the cane over my ass slowly, letting it brush my skin like a tease. I feel the weight of it before the pain even begins.

Then he steps back. I hear it whistle through the air. I flinch—my body jerking on instinct before it lands—but feel nothing. He lets out a laugh, a mental game meant to rattle me.

Then it hits. The crack lands hard across my ass, fire ripping through me so fast my lungs forget how to work. *One.* If I can mark each one in my head, I can outlast him.

"Say you're sorry for leaving."

I shake my head, chest heaving, throat burning. I can't give him that.

The second strike lands, hotter, deeper. My body swings forward on the chains, the cuffs cutting into my wrists.

"Say it."

I bite down hard, shaking. "No."

The third lands lower, snapping across the tops of my thighs. I cry out, legs buckling, but the cuffs keep me upright.

"Say it," he repeats, steady as stone. He waits, patient, savoring the pause. The longer it takes, the sweeter it'll sound when I finally give in. My defiance excites him, but my surrender is what keeps him hard.

Tears sting as they spill over. The words scrape up, bitter. "I'm not sorry."

His hand slides over the welt, slow, savoring. "You will be."

The cane rises again, falls again. My body jerks with each crack, the count in my head slipping even as I try to hold it. He moves methodically, giving me just enough time to recover, to anticipate what's coming, but being powerless to stop it.

By ten, my voice shakes. The cane feels endless, every stripe still burning as the next one lands. By twenty, I'm sobbing, sagging in the restraints, legs trembling so badly I can't keep balance.

"You think this will keep me here?" I gasp. "It won't."

He strikes again, sharper, harder. "It will. You'll never walk away from me again."

This isn't breaking me, it's proof I can take more than he thinks.

The numbers blur into pain as I'm dangling, drenched in sweat. But I'm not just going to sit here and take it, I might not be able to move, but I can hurt him with my words.

I twist against the chains, spitting the words out like venom. "Every woman leaves you. Even your mommy left you. Your daddy didn't want you. And I'll leave you, too."

The words slice deeper than the cane ever could. He squeezes the handle so hard his knuckles pale. His green eyes flash, glassy with fury he can't hide.

"Shut up," he growls, his voice low, fraying.

"Did I hit a nerve?"

His hand rakes through his hair, yanking hard at the roots as he paces behind me, the cane trembling in his other fist. His chest heaves, trying to chew down the words he wants to say, but his control is slipping.

I sob through it, but my voice twists into a laugh sharp enough to cut. "That's why you chain me here. Because you know it's only a matter of time before I jump off that dock to get away from you."

He turns on me, eyes blazing. "Shut up, you fucking bitch!"

The next strike crashes down wild and brutal, the cane snapping against flesh with a crack that rattles through my bones.

He doesn't stop at one. The cane lashes across my ass, my thighs, again and again, each blow torn out of him with ragged curses. "Don't ever—ever—say those things to me!"

Pain bursts sharp. My scream tears loose, and I know I've gone too far. For the first time, I think he's going to kill me. And maybe he wants to.

"Stop!" My throat tears on the word, useless against the next crack. "Please—"

He doesn't stop. Another blow slams across my ass, fire racing under my skin. Then my thighs, the cut so sharp it steals my breath. The impact jolts me so violently I bite my tongue and taste iron. Each lash is ragged, fury shredding the rhythm into chaos.

I barely whisper. "Adrian, please—"

And then—he laughs. Low, guttural, the sound crawling down my spine. It's not amusement. It's madness. Right now he's not the man who's calm and composed upstairs, but one who wants to destroy me.

"You think you can run from me?" he snarls, his voice raw. The cane slams across the backs of my legs, the shock radiating up through my hips until I nearly collapse. "You'll never make it. You won't walk when I'm done with you."

Another strike, crueler, faster. My throat rips with a scream I can't swallow back. I'm either going to be killed or disabled by him.

"You'll have to crawl," he spits, his breath ragged, voice breaking with fury.

The last blow falls, savage enough to take my legs out. My wrists cut deep into the cuffs. My vision bursts white, then black at the edges as I sag in the restraints, limp and useless. He's going to break me until there's nothing left but the proof I stayed.

He yanks my head back by the hair, forcing my face up. His eyes are wild, unhinged. "You're mine," he hisses, the sound shaking with rage. "And you'll never leave me, alive."

When he lets go, my head slumps forward. I wanted to run. Now I know I never will. I'd be lucky if I can even walk again.

"Ellie?"

"Ellie?" His voice rises.

"Eleanor!"

There's panic now—real panic. I hear movement. Then his hands are on me, fumbling the restraints, unbuckling, catching me as I collapse into him.

"Oh, shit—no. No, no, no—Ellie, come on," he mutters, his voice cracking. "Ellie, look at me. Are you okay?"

My lips part. A whisper escapes, soft and frayed. "No... can't...can't take it..."

The floor tilts sideways, his voice fades, and then nothing. Everything goes dark.

52

ADRIAN

Ellie's in my arms, limp. Barely breathing. I don't even realize I'm shaking until I look down and see my hands trembling against her skin. Her head rests against my chest, her body damp with sweat, with tears, and I don't know which of them are hers or mine anymore.

What the fuck have I done? She pushed me there when she said she'd jump off the dock to get away from me. That was the moment everything snapped. I've been called too controlling, too jealous, too much, and the women before her always left. They slipped out without looking back. My devotion was a burden they couldn't carry. But Ellie was supposed to be different. She was supposed to stay.

Instead, she gutted me. She threw the parts of me I bury deepest right in my face. I trusted her not to go there, and she did. The damage she left behind might not ever fade. And I answered it with the cane.

I broke past the limit. Past fifty. Past reason. I didn't stop. I lost control because the words cut deeper than the cane ever could. And now? She's not moving.

Her lashes don't flicker. Her lips don't part. Her body doesn't flinch the way it usually does after punishment—no tremble, no tension, no aftershock whimper. No shallow breath or sleepy protest—just stillness, pure and terrifying.

"Ellie..." I whisper, cradling her tighter against me, rubbing strands of damp hair out of her face with shaking fingers. "You'll be okay. You're just exhausted. I'll get you some pain meds. I'll fix this. You'll be good as new."

But even I don't believe this is fixable. She doesn't stir, groan, or twitch. My stomach turns to ice. "Ellie," I say again, louder this time. "Come on. Open your eyes."

Still nothing. What if she doesn't wake up? What if I finally crossed the line I can't undo, and she doesn't come back?

I press my forehead to hers, eyes closed, breath ragged. "Please wake up," I whisper. "Please."

Because if she doesn't, then I've lost everything.

I carry her upstairs like I'm hauling a body. Because right now, that's what it feels like. Her limbs hang slack in my arms. Her skin's still hot, flushed in places, welted in others. The red stripes carved across her body make my stomach twist—but it's the silence that guts me.

I lay her gently on the bed, brushing the hair from her face again. Her lips are parted, her brow faintly drawn, but she doesn't wake. Panic claws at me, sharp and fast.

Should I take her to the hospital?

No. God, no.

They'd take one look at her and see the bruises, the welts I left, and they'd ask questions. They'd assume it was all violence and that I'd tried to kill her. I didn't mean to seriously hurt her. It was a line we've danced before. It got out of hand, it was never supposed to go this far. They'd never believe it was something we enjoy doing together, that there were rules I broke, that it was supposed to stop at fifty. Not when she's unconscious and looks like this. And even if they did? I'd lose her. She'd wake up in a sterile room, surrounded by judgment, and I wouldn't be allowed near her again.

So no hospital. But I'm not stupid. I knew, deep down, that one day I might push too far. That someone might break in my hands. That's why I planned for this. I pull out my phone, thumb shaking as I dial.

It rings once. Twice. Then—*click.*

"Montgomery," the voice says on the other end.

"It's me. I need you. Come quickly."

There's a pause. He hears something in my voice.

"How bad?"

"She passed out and is not responding." My voice cracks, just once. "Just hurry."

"I'm on my way."

I hang up and toss the phone to the side, sinking down beside her. I reach for her hand and hold it against my chest.

She might hate me for what I did and never forgive me for losing control, but she won't walk away. Not like the others. I won't let her.

I kiss her forehead, soft, desperate. "I'll take care of you, Ellie. You'll see how much I love you."

And I sit there, holding her, waiting for the man who might be the only one who can help me undo what I just did.

The knock comes twenty minutes later. My pulse hammers as I let him in. The doctor is carrying a black case.

"She's upstairs," I mutter, keeping my voice flat.

"What happened?" he asks finally, his tone even but suspicious.

"She fainted," I say too quickly. "Exhaustion."

That's all he needs to know.

He follows me to the bedroom. His eyes flick over her as soon as he sees her on the bed—her skin welted, striped, damp with sweat. I see the question form in his jaw, but he doesn't ask. He only sets the case on the nightstand and snaps it open.

"Pulse is weak," he says after two fingers press against her wrist. Then he listens to her heart. "Heartbeat's irregular, but present."

Fuck, this isn't good at all.

He pulls an IV bag from the case, the clear line snaking down into her arm and my chest loosens slightly when the drip starts.

"If this stabilizes her, she'll come around. If not—" His gaze flicks to mine. "She needs to go to a hospital."

My throat closes. "That's not an option."

"Then pray this works." His eyes linger on me a second longer, sharp enough to cut. Suspicion, or judgment, I can't tell. Then he packs the case halfway, leaving the IV running.

I never pray. I haven't been to church since I was a kid. But I sit beside her, gripping her hand harder than I should and think of one. Because if he's wrong, and she doesn't wake up, they'll take her from me. She'll tell them what I did, and they'll believe her without hearing my side.

I shake my head, pressing my lips to her temple. "You're mine, Ellie. You can't leave me."

But the truth gnaws in the back of my mind, louder than the drip of the IV. If she wakes up and turns against me, I'll lose everything.

53

MAREN

I wake up slowly. Too slowly. My body feels heavy, like I'm buried under something thick and warm. My eyelids drag open, and light burns my eyes. The ceiling above me is unfamiliar for a moment, too bright, too quiet. Then I realize I'm in bed. My body aches. My mouth is dry. My skull pounds. There's a strange tug at my arm.

I glance down. An IV. *What the fuck?*

Panic prickles up my spine, sharp and fast. I shift, trying to sit, but everything inside me protests. Bruised muscles, aching wrists, the raw sting of welts on my back, legs, and thighs.

Then it hits me. The basement. The restraints. The cane. His voice. My screams. The blackness.

Adrian really did it. He lost control and fucking broke me. I should've never said what I did. It was impulsive, an explosion of all the anger I've been holding back. It wasn't worth it. But no words I could ever say should result in this.

When I begged for him to stop, the strikes came harder, faster, like he wanted to prove he could break my mind, body, soul. And I'll never forgive or forget. He's going to pay for this. I just need to figure out how.

Then I hear voices, low, murmured. A man's voice I don't recognize, calm and professional. Then Adrian's. He's speaking softly, quieter than I've ever heard him. His tone sounds worried. Something I've never heard from him before.

I try to turn my head, and that's when he notices. He steps into view fast, crouching beside the bed. His green eyes are soft, unmasked, scared.

It's almost funny, how he can look at me like this now— gentle, worried—when the last time I saw those same eyes, they were wild, unhinged, promising I'd crawl if I ever tried to leave him.

"Ellie, you're awake," he says gently.

I try to sit up, but he rests a hand on my shoulder, gentle and warm. "You passed out. Dehydration and low blood sugar."

I blink, trying to speak, but my throat is so dry it feels like sandpaper.

"I called a doctor. He gave you fluids. Said you'll be okay. You were just...pushed too far." He pauses. "I pushed too far."

I swallow, and it burns. He tucks a damp strand of hair behind my ear, and his touch is cautious, afraid I'll flinch.

"But no need to worry. I'll take care of you, just like always."

I don't reply. Because I'm speechless at his delusion. I don't know if he means what he's saying or if he's putting on a mask for the doctor because of how bad this looks for his image.

He leans in slightly. "I'll run you a bath. Like I always do." His tone is so gentle I almost don't recognize him.

"I don't want your fucking bath," I snap. I'm not putting on a front for the doctor. Maybe they'll help me after seeing this.

His eyes flicker, a crack in the calm he's trying to hold. "Ellie, I'm just trying to help."

A bitter laugh breaks out of me. "Help? You did this to me."

He freezes. For a second he just stares, and then his gaze cuts to the doctor still standing in the doorway.

When he speaks again, his voice is pleading. "You know that wasn't intentional."

I shake my head, my throat raw but my words sharp. "Yeah, it was."

I turn my face toward the doctor, eyes locking on his. I don't even have to say it, but I do anyway, my voice cracking. "Get me out of this hell hole."

The doctor doesn't move. His jaw tightens, his eyes flicking between us. Suspicion lingers there, maybe pity, but no rescue. Just another pawn on his payroll.

Adrian shifts closer, his presence a wall between me and the door. "You're staying right here," he says, quiet but firm, as if my plea never left my mouth.

His tone is so gentle and his hands are shaking that I almost don't recognize him. And in that moment, I know he's more afraid of losing me than his image.

But I remember the cane. I remember my screams. I remember the way he lost control and told me I was his. And now I'm lying here, broken and bandaged, while he's trying to rewind time, and pretend the last twenty-four hours didn't happen. But they did, and he'll regret it.

I take a slow, shallow breath. My lips crack as I part them.

"I'm not..." My voice scrapes out, so hoarse I almost don't recognize it. "I'm not your fucking wife."

For a second, he doesn't react. Just blinks at me, as if he didn't hear. Then his face pales and all the softness drains out of him at once. His mouth opens like he's about to argue, but no words come out.

I keep going, because now that I've started, I can't stop. My voice shakes, but it doesn't break.

"I'm not her. I never was. You can say whatever you want. You can do whatever you want. But that doesn't make me her."

He stares at me like I just struck him, like every part of his carefully built world has started to slide out of place.

"Ellie," he says, but it's not a protest, it's a plea.

I shake my head. My vision blurs, but I don't look away.

"You heard me. I'm not your fucking wife."

He opens his mouth again, but nothing comes out. For the first time, I see it. Real fear, clear as day, hollowing out his expression. For a second, I feel powerful. Almost.

He swallows again, his gaze locked on mine, his voice too calm. Clinging to the last scrap of confidence he has left.

"We can resolve this," he says quietly.

I stare at him, my heart pounding so hard it makes my ribs ache.

Adrian doesn't look away when he speaks. After a moment, he says, "Doctor, please take a swab and a vial of blood."

I tense all over. "What?"

"Blood and saliva," Adrian repeats, discussing a lab sample instead of my body's current condition. "I want it compared to her DNA from her genetic testing. Immediately. The testing was done by Dr. Nelson in Chicago."

Why did Eleanor do genetic testing? Did she question her identity before?

My stomach flips and my skin goes cold. The doctor steps closer, carrying a small black case. I flinch back against the pillows, but Adrian doesn't let me move any further. His hand comes down on my thigh, a silent warning not to fight.

"I hate fucking needles," I whisper.

"You'll be fine," Adrian murmurs, not unkind. "Just hold still."

Turning my face away, I squeeze my eyes shut as the doctor ties a band around my arm. My pulse pounds at the pinch of the needle. I breathe through my teeth, trying not to gag at the hot sting when the vial starts to fill.

"Almost done," the doctor says quietly. When he finally pulls the needle free, I let out a breath I didn't know I'd been holding, but then he's tilting my chin back, holding a long cotton swab to my lips.

"Open, please."

I glare at Adrian, but he doesn't react. His jaw stays set, his green eyes locked on mine in silent challenge. Slowly, I part my lips. The swab scrapes across the inside of my cheek. They're going to test me like a lab rat, like I'm the one who has to provide proof. My stomach knots. He already faked my license, stamped my birthday on Eleanor's ID to make me fit her life. What's to stop him from forging this, too? Still, I cling to the hope that it'll prove what I know. I'm not her.

The doctor packs up his kit near the foot of the bed and glances between us. His tone is calm, but edged with quiet authority. "It may take a few weeks for the results, but I'll call as soon as I have them."

Adrian gives a short nod. "Thank you."

I don't look at either of them. My gaze stays fixed on the blanket, because if I meet Adrian's eyes, I might scream.

"I'd recommend taking a break from the games for a while," he says. "Her body needs time to recover. And so does yours."

What does his body need recovering from?

Adrian nods, subdued. "Understood." He walks the doctor to the door, murmuring words I can't make out. When the door closes, silence follows. For a minute, it's me, the IV, and the ache in my bones.

Then he's back. Moving slowly, he comes to stand beside the bed, approaching as though he's afraid I'll snap. Relief spreads across his face, barely hidden, radiating off him in waves. I didn't notice it before, but now I see it in his eyes. He really thought he might've killed me.

"Ellie," he says softly. "A bath will help. The warm water should soothe your body. The swelling won't last if we get ahead of it."

I roll my eyes. "Fine."

I'm only agreeing because I'm in pain and desperate for relief.

He nods and sets a glass on the nightstand. "And take these." He presses two pills into my palm. "It's for the pain. You'll feel better in twenty minutes."

I won't feel better that quickly. Probably not for days, or even weeks.

He waits, searching my face for permission, to help me, to touch me, to repair damage he can't undo. It's the calmest I've ever seen him, almost an apology he doesn't have words for. I hate how soft his voice sounds, like nothing happened. But I can't move because of the pain. I stare at the pills in my hand, feeling hurt and numb at the same time. I know I should take them. My body's screaming for relief. Every inch of me feels carved open. But I don't move.

Adrian's watching me. His expression shifts, subtly to disappointment. "Take it, Ellie. It'll only help."

His voice is soft enough to almost fool me into thinking he cares the way normal people do.

I hesitate just enough for his jaw to tense. Then I nod once and reach for the glass. A full-body release shudders out of him, relief washing through him because I'm not fighting for now.

"Good girl," he murmurs. Then adds, "I'll be back. Don't go anywhere."

I don't answer because I can't go anywhere. He disappears into the bathroom, and I stay perfectly still. My body feels like it's been through a war, and Adrian fought on both sides. After that, I don't know if I'm supposed to be angry, terrified, or too exhausted to care. But what I do know is everyone leaves him. And I will, too.

54

ADRIAN

I'm so fucking tired. Not of her, never of her, but of hearing her say she's not my wife over and over again. She says it like she believes it. She's said it enough that another man might start to wonder. But not me. I don't doubt she is.

When I look at her—pale, bruised, silent—I feel relief that the test will settle it. Not because I need proof, but because she does. When the results come back, she won't be able to pretend anymore. She'll have to face the facts. That she belongs here. With me.

I help her into the tub, careful with every touch. She winces when the water hits her skin—no surprise. She's welted, bruised by everything I gave her. I slide in behind her, the heat soaking into both of us. She holds herself tight, stiff, even with the meds taking the edge off.

I press my lips to her shoulder, grab the sponge, and wash her back and arms with lavender soap. This isn't how it should've gone. I should've fed her. Made sure she drank something before the punishment.

She was already weak when I threw her out—no food, no water, no care. Just rage and a door slamming behind her.

That's on me. But not entirely. It wasn't the punishment that made her black out. It was the weight of everything. The build-up. Her fragile body hit a threshold because I let rage run wild and I pushed her too hard, too fast. I'll never do that again. But I can't lie to myself. It terrified me but also thrilled me. And now I can't forget it. But seeing her pass out was the moment I admitted to myself that I love her. Fiercely. Irrevocably. Not in the way other men do. But in the way that means she's mine forever. The way you love something you've built with your own hands.

The way she screamed, the way her body trembled when I held her. That wasn't performance. That was surrender. And I'll never go that far again. At least that's what I tell myself.

I pull her closer, her back against my chest. She stays still, neither leaning in nor pulling away. I press a kiss to her neck and whisper, "You mean so much to me. I'll tell you that every day."

Because I will. If I can't take back what I did, I'll bury her in reminders of how much I love her and what she means to me. Even if she never says a word back.

When the water cools, I lift her out and dry her gently. She doesn't look at me, or speak. But I know she isn't shutting me out, she's processing. Sorting through everything I gave her tonight. The pain. The confusion. It's all blurring together, and now she's untangling it the only way she knows how—by pulling back. It isn't rejection. It's her way of trying to feel calm again. She just needs rest.

I'm going to make it right. When she's feeling up to it, I'll take her out on the boat. And when she's recovered, we will go on a vacation. Somewhere even brighter with sun. Far from this house where we can pretend we never hurt each other the way we did. The only thing between us will be the love we share.

When I settle her into bed, her back is to my chest and my arms wrap tightly around her, but she doesn't soften or relax the way she usually does. But I'm not worried. One day, she'll curl into me again, not because I ask her to, but because she wants to. It's only a matter of time. Because even in the silence, she's still here and mine in ways that don't need words. Every time she feels the sting on her skin, she'll remember who cleaned her wounds and held her close because care binds tighter than chains. And by the time she realizes it, we will be stronger than we were before, because by then it'll be too late. But tonight, her in my arms is enough for now.

55

MAREN

I lie still in the dark, wrapped in Adrian's arms, and I don't know what to feel. My body aches in a dozen places—my wrists, my thighs, my back—but that's not what keeps me awake. It's the confusion twisting inside me like a slow burn.

I'm relieved the punishments are on hold. Doctor's orders. I should feel safe with that. I should be able to breathe easier. But I don't.

What hurt even more, what I can't get past, is what he said. Trash. Fuck-up. He called me that like it was nothing. Like it had always been waiting on his tongue. That hit harder than a cane ever could. But I'll never admit it. Not to him. Not even to myself, not out loud.

At least this test will show him the truth—that this was all one big mistake, and he'll finally let me go. Or maybe I'll use it to blackmail him. Tell him if he ever wants to keep his perfect reputation intact, he'll pay me to disappear. I could go to the press. Show them everything he did to me. The thought makes my stomach turn, but I hold on to it anyway, like a rope I might need to climb out of this.

I stare at the ceiling, my heart a quiet throb in my chest, and then I hear his voice—barely above a whisper. "I'm sorry."

Did Adrian just apologize to me? I must be hallucinating from these pain meds.

"I'm sorry for throwing you out of the house," he says again, slower this time. "And for what I said. You're not trash, Ellie. You're my treasure."

He doesn't apologize for the punishment itself. He never will. That would mean admitting it was a mistake, and he doesn't have that kind of self-awareness. Still, to know he's capable of feeling remorse is baffling.

My throat tightens, but I stay still.

"You know how I feel," he murmurs.

I don't know how he feels about me. He probably doesn't even know.

"I was angry. I shouldn't have let it get that far."

I regret what I said to him, but I won't apologize. His reaction was to try and tear my body apart. I could've died tonight. And I don't want to face the fact that he could've kill me. Or worse, that for a moment he wanted to.

He waits, but I don't say anything. He doesn't seem to expect me to, though. He holds me the same way he has been, like all is forgiven, like my silence is a natural part of this marriage. And maybe it is. Maybe this is what apology looks like in his world—raw, understated, half-swallowed—but real in its own broken way. I don't trust it. But I don't leave, either. Not that I could, even if I tried. I'm not free here and never will be.

So maybe that says everything. Or nothing at all.

56

MAREN

Several days blur passed in a haze of bruises, painkillers, and his constant presence. On the first day, I barely register anything. Just warmth pressed against me, his voice low, his hands careful in ways that almost don't feel real. The next few, I drift in and out, aware of him hovering, feeding me, dosing me, keeping me in his arms, as though letting go would undo me completely.

After a week or maybe two, the fog clears enough to notice he hasn't left my side. Not once. No rules laid out on the bed. No corrections, no punishments. Just care. Baths, food, whispered apologies I don't answer. And tenderness that I can't tell if it's an act, or if he's finally showing me a version of himself I wasn't meant to see.

That's what unsettles me most. The pain's fading into background noise. It's the softness that keeps me awake. Because I don't know if it's change, or if a trap.

I wake slowly, blinking against the morning light spilling through the curtains. My body's stiff, sore in ways I expected and in some I didn't. But I'm warm. Wrapped in something solid and steady.

Adrian.

He's still here. Usually he's gone by the time I open my eyes, already halfway through some meeting or workout, or pretending not to watch me on the cameras. But this morning, he hasn't moved.

He's still holding me. One arm draped across my waist, his hand resting against my stomach like it belongs there. His body is warm, still, and when I turn my head just slightly, I meet his gaze. His green eyes are softer than they were last night.

"Good morning, beautiful," he murmurs, his voice low with sleep. He leans in and brushes a kiss against my lips. It's gentle, almost...sweet. Too sweet for what we are. Too soft for what we've been.

Before I can decide what to do with the sudden tenderness, he smiles faintly and says, "Let's go out on the boat today."

Part of me wants to recoil—ask what the catch is, brace for what's underneath—but another part of me? The part that hasn't stopped shaking since the basement? That part sees the opening.

Because if I can learn the boat and the water...Then someday I can drive away. Maybe one day I won't just be waking up in his bed, wondering who I am. Maybe I'll wake up free.

I nod, just once, and offer a small smile. It's not much, but it's more than I've given him in days.

"I'd like that," I say quietly. And I mean it.

Not because I trust him. But because the boat means possible escape. Distance from this house and all the walls that close in when he's angry, or too quiet, or too much. It means an opportunity. And maybe a little peace.

His thumb brushes across my side. "Once you learn, maybe you can take over the driving. Let me sit back and relax for once," he says, his voice teasing but warm.

I swallow and meet his eyes, something uncertain rising in my chest. "Why now?" I ask. My voice is thin, wary.

His smile doesn't fade. "Because I'm finally ready," he says simply.

That makes me smile a little more. The image of him lounging while I steer feels impossible, absurd...and yet part of me wants it. Wants the freedom and the control. Wants him to trust me with something.

He watches me, pleased. "I have plans for us next weekend, too."

My stomach tightens at that.

He grins slightly. "It's a surprise," he adds. "But you'll love it."

I don't ask what it is. I don't say I already know he's planning something elaborate, he always does.

I nod again, quietly. Because for now, playing along is safer than pulling away.

And maybe it'll get me closer to the exit. Or somewhere that feels like mine.

We eat breakfast outside on the deck, the sound of the water soft below. No commands, schedule, or pressure. And he didn't pick out my clothes this time. He always does—dresses, skirts. But this morning? Nothing. Just me in what I wanted. Comfortable. My own choice. And he's dressed down too—casual, barefoot, a t-shirt hugging his chest like he's not trying to impress anyone, not trying to dominate the moment.

He smiles at me again, that same quiet, warm smile, like I'm a dream he still can't believe he gets to wake up next to. It throws me off more than his punishments ever did.

This...tenderness. It's not a tactic. Not polished or practiced. It feels real. And that makes it worse. He reaches across the table and takes my hand in his, his thumb rubbing slow, rhythmic circles along the back of it.

"I'm so glad," he says softly, looking at me like I'm the calm after a storm, "I get to spend the rest of my life with you."

I glance down at our joined hands, then back at him. "That's a long time," I whisper.

That's terrifying, being stuck here for life, with him. No more bartending, my dreams of owning my own bar gone. My life will revolve around him, and his wants and needs. My life purpose will be to please him. And I never wanted this. Didn't choose this.

"Not long enough," he says.

I don't know what to say. Why is he being this way? So tender. So sweet. Is it because for one terrifying moment, he thought I was gone and realized what that would mean? Or is it because he lost control, really lost it, and now he's relieved? Like some part of him needed to snap just to let go of everything he's always held back?

Or maybe it's something darker. Maybe it's because he watched me break, scream, cry—and still stay. I watch the way his jaw moves when he thinks I'm not looking, the tiny twitch in his eyebrow when I hesitate before answering.

Maybe it's all of it. The fear. The release. The power. All tangled together into this strange, quiet version of him I don't recognize...but can't stop watching.

And in that moment, I hate that I like it. But I do.

But part of me wants to ask when the DNA results will come back, to know how close I am to everything breaking again. I don't, though. As soon as I ask, this calm will be over.

Later, when we're out on the water, the wind soft on my face and the sun warm against my skin, I keep my shirt buttoned and my shorts pulled low on my hips, even though the boat's mostly private. No one else is around—not today—but I'm still covered.

The fabric scrapes over a welt, and I flinch, but I don't

adjust it. I'd rather the pain than the reminder of what's underneath.

The bruises won't fade for days, maybe weeks. The welts are still raw. No one would understand. I don't even understand. Why I'm still here? Why didn't I run when I had the chance? Why do I keep listening to him, as if his words might make the pain mean something?

But I'm here. Sitting beside him on this boat, the engine humming low, the water glittering like nothing happened at all. I'm wearing sunglasses to hide my reactions to the pain.

He stands at the wheel, relaxed, one hand resting casually on the throttle, the other lifting to brush his hair back from his face. Then he turns to look at me with a softness I don't expect.

"You know, maybe I can start delegating more at work."

I glance at him.

"I know you hated that I was always working. And maybe you were right. Maybe I need to let go of some of it. I want to spend more time with my gorgeous wife."

He looks at me like he means it. He believes in what he's saying. And it hits me, and I smile. It's small. I don't even mean to. But it's there.

"I'd like that," I hear myself say.

What the hell is wrong with me? Why am I smiling? Why am I letting this feel good?

Because softness is the most dangerous thing he's ever given me, it makes me think I can trust him. Makes me want to.

He gives me that million-dollar smile—perfect white teeth, sunlit skin, eyes soft in a way that still looks brand new. And it's real. Not calculated or controlled. Not part of the push and pull. It's just him. Happy. Proud. Mine. And in that moment, I hate that I like it. But I do.

57

MAREN

The next several days drift by with a quiet that feels almost unreal. Adrian doesn't hover, but he doesn't leave, either. He's relaxed in a way I've never seen before, like he's taken off some invisible armor he always wore too tightly. He lingers close in ways I've never seen from him— bringing me coffee on the deck before I even ask, brushing my hair back when the wind blows it across my face, laughing at something I said without catching himself.

It feels like a dream. The good kind. The kind where I'm allowed to wake up slowly. Where sunlight spills through open windows, and there's music playing in the background instead of silence and tension, where I get to choose what I wear, what I eat, what I say.

But dreams aren't real. Maybe he thinks that to keep me, he has to let me think I'm free. Maybe something in him finally clicked—that locking me in a gilded cage doesn't make me his, it makes me a prisoner counting the days until I can escape. Hopefully, he gets that now. But the question that won't leave me is this:

When will the version of Adrian I survived crawl back into

his skin and remind me this isn't real—that this is grace, not change? And how long can I pretend I'm not watching for the fall? Because even in peace, I never stop looking over my shoulder.

"I want to show you something," he says suddenly, standing and holding out his hand.

I hesitate, shifting, and my shirt scrapes over the welts on my back. Pain shoots sharp across my skin, but I keep my face neutral. Then I take his hand. He leads me through a part of the house I've never been. We pass hallways I've ignored, doors I've never bothered to open. The place is too big, too endless, and I've kept to the same few rooms because that's all I could stomach.

He pushes open a door and flicks on a light.

It's designed as if it's a parlor with a bar. Dark wood shelves lined with bottles, glassware gleaming, and leather stools tucked beneath the counter. A hidden lounge, like something out of another life.

I stare. "I didn't even know this was here."

His eyes stay on me, not the room. "Can you make me a drink?"

I raise an eyebrow. "Seriously?"

His mouth curves into a slow grin. "Yeah. Show me how you'd serve me if I was just another guy walking into your bar."

I circle behind the bar. The polished wood under my hands feels familiar in a way that tightens my chest. This bar has everything. A bartender's dream. My dream. For a second, I almost forget where I am. I used to picture a space like this as mine—neon signs over the door, music humming low, regulars leaning in while I poured their stories as easily as their drinks. Freedom in glass and wood. My freedom.

Now I'm behind someone else's bar, in a house I never chose.

I scan the bottles lined up on the shelves, the soft gleam of glass under the parlor lights, and it's too easy to fall into the rhythm. The only thing pulling me back is the tug in my muscles, the reminder of welts hidden under my clothes—marks that don't belong in this world I used to know.

"What'll it be tonight?" I ask, slipping into the voice I used to wear at work, smooth and steady. "Old fashioned? Manhattan? Something strong to take the edge off your long day?"

Adrian leans forward, resting one elbow on the counter. "Surprise me," he says, his voice low, amused, watching me with a focus that makes my pulse kick.

I smirk, slipping into the persona that used to pay my bills. I grab bourbon, bitters, sugar, and orange peel—my hands moving fast, fluid. Ice clinks against glass, liquid pours, the shaker rattles in my grip. I don't hesitate. Not once.

I pour, setting the glass down in front of him with a practiced smile. "Drink's on the house tonight."

He laughs. He picks up the drink, but doesn't take a sip right away, too focused on staring at me.

Heat rises in my face. "Careful. You keep staring at me like that, I'll have to cut you off."

He grins wider, setting the glass down with a soft clink. "You could never cut me off. I'd buy out the whole bar just to keep looking at you."

I snort, reaching for another bottle. "Spoken like a man who doesn't know when to close his tab."

He chuckles again, softer this time, shaking his head like he's in disbelief. "You're teasing me."

"And you're eating it up."

He doesn't deny it. He tips the glass back, savoring the drink, and when he sets it down, his eyes are still locked on mine. "You're intoxicating," he says, and for once, I don't think he means the drink.

I reach for another bottle, the glass cool in my hand, and a sharp tug in my wrist makes me flinch. His eyes flick down, catching the way I wince. He doesn't smirk or tease—just studies me, gaze darker, more intent, like the bruise itself keeps him locked on me.

I force a smirk, masking the twist in my stomach. "You sound drunk already."

"On you," he says without hesitation.

I should step back. End this. But I don't. Because part of me wants it to last forever.

58

MAREN

I stretch out on the couch in my sitting room, staring at the ceiling. I don't bother tearing the place apart to find more of Eleanor's journals. She wouldn't have written down an escape plan, and even if she had, following it would be useless. Adrian already knows every move she made. If I want a chance at getting out, I have to find my own way.

"Ellie," Adrian calls from the hallway, his voice easy, almost light. "Start packing for our trip."

I pull the door open, meeting his eyes. "Okay," I say, keeping my voice steady. But as soon as I stand in front of the open closet, reality hits me like a wall. I don't know where to begin, because he's always chosen for me—dresses, shoes, lingerie I never asked for. Things that matched his idea of who I'm supposed to be, what I'm supposed to look like on his arm, in his house, beneath him. Now the decision's mine—and I don't know what to choose, because if I pick wrong, there's no one to blame but me.

He pokes his head in the door with a smile. "Tropical."

I nod, trying not to look confused. "Got it."

He doesn't check what I'm packing or step inside to swap

out my choices, doesn't critique them with that quiet look he always used to give when something wasn't "appropriate."

He smiles. "I can't wait to see you in a bikini." And then he disappears again.

I trail my fingers over fabric, pausing on floral dresses and swimsuits I didn't even realize were here because he never let me wear them without his approval. I pick the only bathing suit that looks like something I'd choose—black, modest, with a neckline that doesn't beg for attention. I toss everything into the suitcase, piece by piece, careful but unsure.

I stand there staring at the half-packed suitcase, wondering what the hell is happening—and how long this strange, dream-like freedom will last.

The plane is sleek, spotless, and quiet—unnervingly so. There's no engine hum loud enough to drown out my thoughts, no chatter, no announcements. Just polished wood, leather seats, and Adrian beside me, calm like he's done this a thousand times.

Of course, he has a private jet. I've never been on a plane while fully conscious. I grip the armrest tightly, trying to keep my breathing steady, but it's no use. My stomach is in knots, and my pulse won't slow down. The leather is smooth under my palm, too cool against skin that's already clammy.

Adrian notices. "Why are you afraid?" he asks, his voice is even but curious, not mocking.

I keep my eyes on the floor and answer honestly, even though I don't want to. "Flying scares me."

He shifts, turning more toward me, and reaches for my hand. His fingers wrap around mine, warm, firm, grounding. "It's safe," he says. "You'll be fine. I promise."

I swallow, still staring down. "I don't know."

His thumb brushes my knuckles slowly. "You trust me, don't you?"

I don't look up or answer because the truth is too complicated. Maybe a part of me did because I'm alive, I don't worry about bills, starving, or working. He does take care of me even in his own twisted way, but now I don't trust him at all.

He threw me out of the house over an argument, and then punished me so severely that I blacked out. I almost died. It was a harsh reminder that being with him is like walking on thin ice, and anything can make him want to break you.

After a moment, he exhales like he's decided for both of us. "I'm right here," he adds, giving my hand a gentle squeeze. And even though my chest is still tight, and the fear hasn't left me, I nod. Because somehow, with him sitting this close, I can almost believe that I will be.

Hours later, the plane lands softly on a private strip by the coast, and my stomach knots all over again.

I press my forehead to the window, scanning the water, the trees, the endless blue. "Where are we?" I ask. He doesn't answer right away. Just a faint curve of his mouth, like the question amuses him.

"Somewhere no one can bother us," he finally says.

"Is it your island?" I push, needing something more than silence.

His hand finds mine, firm. "It's ours." The words shut the door on anything else I might ask.

The beach house is massive and private. Not as sprawling or cold as the estate, but still bigger than I imagined, glass windows, wide-open space that smells like salt and money. It sits right on the water, the waves close enough to taste in the air. No staff, no hovering eyes. Just us. Adrian made sure of that.

He said only a private chef and a housekeeper stays nearby, and they come and go quietly. No one to witness, no one to interrupt, no one to hear me if I ever screamed.

When we arrive, someone wheels in our luggage, but Adrian doesn't let me take a single step past the door. Instead, he lifts me into his arms like it's tradition. I let out a soft sound, startled, but not enough to stop him. My sun hat tilts from the motion, and I clutch it to keep it from flying off.

He carries me across the threshold, grinning as if this is all part of a dream he's had planned for years. "You look perfect here," he murmurs, his voice low against my ear.

As soon as we're inside, he sets me down gently on the cool tile and tugs me in for a kiss. It's firm, warm, and laced with possession hiding under vacation skin. Then he pulls back just enough to murmur, "You're so sexy," and his hand slides down to grab my ass.

He sounds like he believes it, like the bruises don't exist.

I freeze, glancing over my shoulder toward the open door. "Adrian," I hiss, low, looking around to make sure no one saw.

He just smiles, because there's no one watching. No one but him.

"You have no idea how much I've been looking forward to this," he whispers, his thumb brushing the waistband of my shorts. "Just us. No interruptions."

I nod, my limbs already heavy from the flight, the heat, and the quiet softness of this strange, new version of him. He takes my hand and leads me upstairs to the bedroom.

It's huge—airy, white, soaked in golden light from the floor-to-ceiling windows. But it doesn't feel like the estate or a museum. It feels lived in. Less curated. It doesn't suffocate. It feels...possible.

For a few seconds, I almost let myself pretend this is a normal trip. Just two people escaping the city. No secrets. No bruises. If I close my eyes, I can almost believe this bed is mine. I picked it and paid for it. That there's no cage waiting if I disappoint him again.

We lay down on the massive bed together, and I sink into the cool sheets with a breath I didn't realize I'd been holding.

"I love it here," I whisper.

He smiles, watching me like he already knew I would. "Good."

After a long moment, he shifts closer, his voice low against my hair. "I've missed you. The real you. Not the one who fights me so hard."

I don't answer because I'm not combative, he's the reason why I fight him.

He sighs, content. "I like when you're like this...calm."

We don't speak for a while.

Later, the chef arrives—someone polite, quiet, local. He's clearly been briefed to keep things minimal and casual. He comes into the kitchen, greets us, and then asks me a simple question.

"What would you like to eat tonight?" he asks.

I freeze. The words catch in my throat, as if I didn't under-stand. I blink at him, confused not because it's hard, but because no one's asked me that in weeks.

I stumble, glancing at Adrian, but he doesn't answer for me. He just waits, letting me speak for myself, watching me—care-ful, observant, noting every flicker of hesitation. Maybe he's waiting for me to relax, or maybe he wants to see how far this illusion of choice will carry me before I realize nothing's really changed.

"I—I don't know," I admit, my voice small. "What do you recommend?"

The chef smiles, easy. "I can make something light with potatoes, grilled fish, vegetables, and bread. We caught every-thing this morning."

I nod quickly. "Yes. That, please."

Adrian's voice comes softly behind me. "Good choice."

The chef leaves to get started, and I sit down slowly at the table, feeling something strange twist in my chest. It's not fear.

It's not anger. It's the feeling of being given a choice and not knowing what to do with it.

A part of me wonders if I could run. Walk out the door, down the sand, disappear before he notices. But I've seen how secluded this place is, miles of private coastline, no neighbors, no roads. Even if I tried, where would I go? I have nothing left. And now I'm not sure who I am when he's not telling me.

59

ADRIAN

She still looks to me when someone asks her a question. She hesitates, searching my face like she's waiting for an answer before she gives one. She wants my permission. But I don't step in. I don't tell her what to eat. What to wear. What to say. I'm giving her what she asked for, even if she never said the words out loud.

Choices. Because maybe I've been suffocating her. Not out of malice...but to keep her. To make sure she wouldn't leave. But all I was doing was pushing her closer to the edge.

Now? She's different. Still cautious. Still watching me. But not on edge. Not flinching when I touch her. She's just herself. Calmer. Softer. And I'm loving it.

She walks across the kitchen barefoot in shorts and a loose tank, hair still damp from her shower, and there it is—her wedding ring. On her hand. Not because I told her to wear it or because I reminded her. She just put it on. Because she wanted to. I watch her as she leans against the counter, talking to the chef about drink pairings like he belongs here, in this house, in this life. With me.

And I can't lie—not even to myself. I'm hard just watching

her. We haven't had sex in a while. I gave her time. She needed it. Her body was still recovering, her mind, too. I didn't rush her. I let her set the pace.

But tonight?

It's time.

I don't want to punish her. I don't want control. I just want her on top of me, soaked and moaning, reminding me that I still make her come undone.

It's not about reclaiming power. It's about feeling her wrapped around me, nails in my shoulders, her body saying what her mouth won't.

It's time I fuck my wife.

And this time, I want it slow. But I really want it hard.

I go to her and wrap my hand around her wrist, pulling her gently toward the bedroom without saying a word. She looks up at me, searching for something in my face, but I don't give her time to ask. It's been too long. I need my wife. When we reach the doorway, I push her back against the wall and kiss her hard. She gasps into my mouth, her hands landing on my chest, but she doesn't try to stop me. I peel her tank over her head, drop it on the floor, and push her shorts down her hips. She's already breathing faster. Already softening.

I drag my palm between her thighs, feeling the heat there, and press my fingers against that spot I know she can't resist. Her hips jerk, her breath catches, and she moans, high and sweet. God, she's fucking melting for me, just like I knew she would. I lower my mouth to her chest, licking a slow line over her nipple before sucking it between my lips. She arches, her fingers twisting in my hair. I pull back enough to watch her face as I rub her harder.

"You feel that?" I growl, my voice low against her skin. "How wet you already are? You missed this. Missed me."

Her eyes flutter shut. Another moan slips out, helpless.

I smile and kiss her throat, tasting her pulse. "I'm going to fuck you so slow you'll forget every reason you thought you needed to stay away. You're mine, Ellie. Every last inch."

I watch her swallow, her lips parted like she wants to say something—maybe a protest, maybe a plea—but nothing comes out. She's too busy feeling. That's exactly how I want her.

I kiss her again, deeper, slower this time, letting her taste how much I've missed this. My hand never stops moving, my fingers circling her clit in tight, steady strokes that make her hips rock against my palm. Her breathing turns ragged, and when I pull back to look at her, her cheeks are flushed, her eyes glazed. Beautiful.

"Look at you," I murmur, sliding my mouth along her jaw. "Already shaking for me."

She whimpers, her head tipping back against the wall. I slip two fingers inside her, slow but firm, and feel her clench around me. My cock throbs so hard it hurts, but I don't rush. I want to feel her lose every ounce of control first.

I drag my free hand up to cup her breast, thumb brushing her nipple until she arches into me. "Say it," I breathe against her skin. "Say you missed my hands on you."

She shakes her head, but her hips roll into my touch, chasing more.

I curl my fingers inside her, pressing right where she's most sensitive. Her gasp is sharp, helpless. "Say it," I repeat, my voice rough. "Say you missed being fucked by your husband."

"I—" She tries to catch her breath, but it's useless. Her body's already giving me every answer I need. She's soaked, her thighs trembling, her pulse wild under my mouth.

I lean in, licking the hollow of her throat. "You're going to come for me, Ellie. Right here against this wall. And then I'm going to take you to bed and make you come again."

Her hands clutch my shoulders, nails digging into my skin. I love that. I love how she holds onto me like I'm the only thing keeping her upright.

I rub her faster, feel her hips stutter. "That's it," I whisper, my lips brushing her ear. "Don't fight it. You're mine. You've always been mine."

Her moan breaks, high and desperate, her body tightening around my fingers as she comes.

I hold her there, working her through it, watching every flicker of pleasure cross her face. Perfect.

When her breathing finally starts to slow, I pull my fingers free and bring them to my mouth. I suck them clean, holding her gaze the entire time. She watches, flushed and silent, her chest still heaving.

I step back just enough to pick her up, her legs hooking around my waist on instinct. She doesn't fight me. She doesn't look away.

I carry her to the bed, laying her down in the center of the sheets. She looks so beautiful like this—hair spread over the pillow, skin warm and pink, her thighs still trembling.

I strip off my shirt and climb over her, bracing my weight on my hands as I lower my mouth to hers. The kiss is slow this time, savoring every soft sound she makes. My cock drags against her thigh, and I shudder, barely holding back.

"I'm going to take my time with you," I tell her, my voice low and rough. "You deserve that. We both do."

And when I finally sink into her, slow and deep, I feel her breath catch in my mouth—and I know she feels it, too. This isn't a punishment. This isn't about control. This is me, reminding her how much she loves me.

She gasps when I push all the way in, her body arching under mine, her hands flying to my arms like she needs something to hold on to. I stay there for a moment, buried to the hilt, savoring the heat and the way she clenches around me.

"Fuck," I breathe against her neck. "You feel perfect."

I kiss her there, slow, tasting the salt on her skin. She shivers, her fingers flexing against my biceps. I move one hand to her cheek, tilting her face to mine so I can see her eyes. They're wide, soft, still glazed with that dazed surrender I can't get enough of.

"Look at me," I murmur. "I want you to watch me while I fuck you."

Her breath hitches, but she doesn't look away. She can't. She's caught in it, same as me.

I start to move, slowly at first, just enough to feel her body tighten around me. Her mouth parts in a soundless gasp, her brows pulling together like she doesn't know whether to moan or cry.

"That's it," I whisper, my voice hoarse. "Take it. Let me feel you."

I thrust again, deeper this time, and she lets out a soft, broken sound that goes straight to my cock. I bite back a groan and set a slow rhythm, dragging every inch of me out before sliding back in. Her nails scrape my shoulders, and I swear I feel it all the way down to my spine.

I lean in to kiss her, slow and searching, letting her taste every ragged breath. When I pull back, she's trembling.

"You look so fucking beautiful like this," I say, brushing my thumb over her lip. "You have no idea what you do to me."

Her eyes flutter shut, but I don't let her hide. I catch her chin in my hand and keep her gaze locked to mine.

"Say you want me," I tell her, my voice low, rougher than I mean it to be.

She hesitates, her breath coming in little shudders. I thrust again, slow and deep, and her lips part in a helpless moan.

"Say it."

"I..." She swallows, her voice catching. "I want you."

It's not loud, but it's enough to break something in me. My control frays at the edges, heat and need crashing together in my chest. I kiss her hard, my hand sliding between us to find her clit. The second I touch her, she gasps into my mouth, her hips jerking up to meet mine.

"That's it," I growl against her lips. "I want you to come on my cock. I want to feel you fall apart for me."

Her breathing turns ragged, her body tensing beneath me as I rub her faster, my thrusts getting rougher, deeper. Every time I drive into her, her breath stutters, her nails digging in harder like she's trying to ground herself.

"Please," she whispers, her voice breaking on the word.

"Please what?" I rasp, never stopping. "Tell me."

Her eyes open, wide and desperate, and she looks at me like I'm the only thing she can see.

"Please...don't stop."

A groan tears out of my throat, raw and guttural. I slam into her harder, my fingers circling her clit relentlessly.

"I won't," I promise, my voice rough. "You're going to come for me, Ellie. Right fucking now."

Her whole body seizes, her mouth falling open on a strangled cry as she comes. I feel her clench around me, tight, and wet, and perfect, and I don't hold back. I keep moving, fucking her through every trembling wave, watching her unravel beneath me.

When she finally goes limp, I press my forehead to hers, my body still moving slowly and deeply. I kiss her again, softer this time, letting her catch her breath while I chase the edge. I've been holding back.

"God, I love you so much," I whisper against her mouth, the words slipping out before I can stop them.

And when she doesn't flinch or pull away, when she lets me stay there, buried in her—she's mine. And I'll never let her forget it.

60

MAREN

He just said he loved me. He's never said those words before. Not once. He told me he didn't believe in it, and now he's telling me. It doesn't feel real. It feels as if something slipped out of him by accident, a confession he didn't mean to say out loud.

And I'm terrified that I like hearing it too much, that some broken part of me wants to believe he means it, because if he loves me, maybe all the awful things he's done will somehow make sense. Maybe it means I'm not just a project he needed to conquer or a stand-in for someone he lost.

I try to pull away, just enough to clear my head, but he grips me tighter, his arms locking around my waist, holding me in place as if I'll disappear if he lets go.

His eyes search mine, careful and unblinking, looking for something—gratitude, relief, the same confession he just gave me. Something to make this moment neat and redeemable.

I give him nothing. His smile falters, just for a second, before he smooths it over. His gaze drops to the sheets as if he's bracing for me to tell him he's lying. He kisses my temple again, softer this time, as if he can convince me this is safe.

"Say something," he says, low, the softness now edged with desperation.

I swallow. My throat feels raw, my heart beating so hard it hurts.

"You said you didn't believe in love," I whisper, my voice thinner than I want it to be.

He lifts his head, meeting my eyes. "Don't act so surprised."

"I'm not surprised. Just...confused."

"I changed my mind," he says quietly. "There's no other way to describe how I feel about you."

I shouldn't care why. I shouldn't give him the satisfaction of hearing me ask. But the word is stuck in my throat anyway, pressing harder the longer I look at him. If he loves me, there has to be a reason. Maybe if I hear it, I'll finally know what it is he thinks he sees in me.

"Why do you love me?"

His gaze doesn't waver. "Because before, you kept yourself locked up. I could never tell if what you gave me was real or just what you thought I wanted. But now you don't hide. I see you. All of you. And I'd take that over a wife who only gives me silence."

For a second, I almost believe him. No one's ever wanted the parts of me that fight back. He makes it sound like that's why he loves me. And some part of me is pathetic enough to want that to be true. But it isn't love. It's him twisting everything so I can't win.

I close my eyes for a second, steadying the rush of thoughts. He said he loved me with the same mouth that called me trash. The same voice that told me I'd never leave. If this is love, I don't know what hate would look like. I look at him, searching for any flicker of doubt, but he's certain. He believes it. I can tell he's expecting me to say it back now, to let him feel better about admitting it, to convince himself this is mutual. But I won't say it unless he forces me to.

"You've told me you love me plenty of times," he says, softer. His gaze stays locked on mine. "Do you mean it when you say it?" His voice is quiet but urgent, like he needs the answer to make sense of everything.

I swallow, searching for the right lie, the one that will keep this from exploding into something worse.

"Sometimes," I whisper.

His jaw tenses, and his eyes narrow just enough for me to see the crack in his calm.

"Sometimes?" he repeats, his voice low. "You're my wife. It should be all the time."

I lift my chin a fraction, my voice unsteady but clear. "You never said it until now, so I don't feel bad."

His mouth hardens, and for a second, I see anger, then disappointment.

"You knew how I felt," he says, the softness draining out of his tone.

I open my mouth, trying to hold on to something rational, something that makes this feel less inevitable. "You said you didn't believe in it."

"That was months ago. I show you how I feel every day," he snaps.

The color drains from my skin. Months ago. I've been here for months. It can't have been months. But the days blur together here. Maybe it has. Maybe I've already lost more time than I realize.

He settles back onto the pillow and exhales like he's convinced himself this is enough, this is proof that whatever he's decided we are must be real.

He never loved his actual wife. But he loves me. And that might be worse. Because if he loves me, he'll never let me go when the test confirms I'm not her.

I need those test results. I need proof that this was all one big mistake. That I'm not the woman he thinks he loves. That

I'm not Eleanor. Because if I don't have undeniable proof to show him, I'm afraid of how far this will go.

I don't say anything for a long time. He shifts closer, his hand smoothing over my hair like he thinks it's done. Like I'm settled. Like all that's left is sleep.

But the question crawls up my throat, anyway.

I swallow, my voice dry and flat. "When will the DNA results be ready?"

His hand pauses. Then he moves it again, slower this time, as if pretending he didn't hear the strain in my voice.

"Soon," he says quietly. "Dr. Chen will call as soon as he has them."

I nod, even though he can't see it in the dark. My heart thuds against my ribs, a dull, steady ache.

He exhales, a breath meant to be reassuring. "Don't think about it tonight."

I stare at the ceiling. "I am thinking about it."

Something flickers in his eyes—a thin crack in the calm he's tried so hard to build.

"It doesn't change anything," he says, softer but firmer now. "You're still mine. You always will be."

"It does change everything," I whisper, my voice raw.

His hand stills against my side. "Say this story is true," he murmurs after a moment, so quiet I almost think I imagined it. "Say you weren't my wife. Do you think I give a shit at this point?"

I blink, caught off guard by how serious he sounds. "Wouldn't you want your actual wife? Not...a stranger?" I ask, my throat tight.

He exhales, and when he speaks, there's no hesitation or softness. Just the truth, the way he's decided it.

"I'd rather take my chances on the stranger. Because she left me."

I swallow, my mouth dry. "And if she came back?"

His reply is instant. "I'd say she's a deranged woman who looks like my wife."

My stomach turns. This can't be real. He doesn't care; he'd rather have me than his wife.

"The results don't matter. I'm not letting you go. So if that's what you're hoping for, you need to get that idea out of your head."

He goes quiet, and for a second, I think he's finished. But then he adds, softer, "I realized I loved you since you've been back. The woman who left me...she isn't the version of you that I love."

I turn my face deeper into the pillow, letting my eyes drift shut. He holds me tighter, as if he can keep me here with the force of his arms alone. No matter how close he pulls me, it doesn't feel safe. It feels like a cage I'm pretending is a bed.

This makes the nightmare even worse. He won't let me go because he loves me. He's silent for a while. I almost think he's falling asleep. Then he speaks again, low and confident, the way he always does when he thinks he's right.

"Isn't life better with me than scraping by living as a nobody bartender?"

My jaw tightens. I don't turn around.

"I'd rather be a nobody bartender than be your wife," I say, my voice steady even though my hands are shaking under the pillow.

He exhales, sharp and frustrated. "You're just saying that out of fear. You've always been afraid to be vulnerable."

"And you aren't?" I whisper.

His hand flexes against my hip. "I have my faults. But I'm trying to be a better husband. I've given more of myself to you then anyone else."

I laugh, and it comes out cracked and ugly. "Yeah? You whipped me to a pulp. That's love to you?"

His fingers dig in. "You will accept my version of love. And you'll fucking love me for it," he says, his voice low and lethal.

That's the real Adrian. This sweet, patient man is an act to get back in my good graces. But he was never there. My chest goes tight. I can't stand the heat of him pressed against me, the seriousness in his voice. I shove the covers back and swing my legs over the edge of the bed, my heartbeat slamming in my throat.

"I can't right now," I say, my voice shaking.

He sits up behind me, his hand closing around my wrist before I can stand. His grip isn't bruising, but it's unmovable.

"Get back in bed. And lay in my arms like a good wife," he says, low and cold.

"I won't take orders from you," I snap, my voice louder than I mean it to be.

Surprise flickers in his eyes, then it darkens. He lets go of my wrist and stands, rising to his full height until he's towering over me.

"If I hear another word of this, I'm having you hospitalized. And they'll see how insane you really are."

"I'd rather be hospitalized than around you," I whisper, my throat raw.

His jaw tightens. He stares down at me, breathing hard, his jaw tight as stone. "Don't tempt me, Eleanor," he says, each word clipped and dangerous.

He's not bluffing. He would seriously have me locked away, convincing everyone I'm the crazy one. He has the money, the lawyers, the influence. If he says I'm unstable, they'll believe him.

DNA is the only hope I have left. Proof I'm not her. Proof this is all a mistake I never asked to be part of.

His gaze softens, though it doesn't reach his voice. "I don't want to fight with you," he says quietly, almost like he's disappointed. "I took a chance and told you how I feel, and this is how you respond. By telling me you don't want to be my wife. After I told you I loved you."

My pulse thuds against my ribs, and I hate how small I feel under the weight of his disappointment.

I lift my chin, even though my voice comes out thin. "What did you expect me to say?"

"I expected you to care." His tone sharpens, frustration seeping back in. "I expected you to understand what it meant for me to say it. I've never said those words to anyone."

I swallow, my throat tight. "That doesn't make it real."

His eyes flash, and for a second, I see the version of him that put me on my knees in the basement. The one who didn't care how much I screamed.

"Everything I feel for you is real." He takes a step closer, and I take one back. He doesn't stop. "You think I would go this far —give you everything, let you see parts of me no one else has— if I didn't mean it?"

"You don't get to use love as a reason for everything you've done to me," I whisper.

He exhales, long and ragged. "You're right. I don't."

His hand comes up, fingers brushing my cheek in a touch so gentle it makes my stomach twist.

"But you're wrong if you think you'll ever be free of me. Even if that test comes back saying you're someone else, it doesn't change what we've been through. What you are to me."

I shake my head, my eyes stinging. "You can't just decide that."

His thumb strokes under my eye, catching a tear before it falls. "I already have."

I look at him, and something hollow opens in my chest.

I'm playing a losing game. He doesn't care about me. He doesn't love me. He's just manipulating me. He wants me to stop fighting, to stop challenging, to be a broken doll. One who agrees and does whatever he says. He doesn't want a woman to love. He wants one who never leaves. And he's made it so I can't ever leave.

61

ADRIAN

I get up. I don't even look at her as I leave the bed, walk out of the bedroom, and keep going until I'm outside on the deck. The night air hits my skin, sharp and cold, but it doesn't do a damn thing to calm me down. She makes me want to drown a bottle of scotch just to shut off the noise in my head.

I'm furious. She has no idea what it cost me to let those words leave my mouth. *I love you.* The one thing I swore I'd never give to her, and she treated it like it was nothing.

I feel stupid. Stupid for giving her that power over me, stupid for believing even for a second she'd hear it and finally understand what this is.

She's using it against me. I told her I loved her, and instead of saying it back, she told me she only means it sometimes, that she'd rather be a nobody bartender than my wife. That she'd rather rot in some shit hole alone than be here in the life I built for her.

And all the while, she's secretly hoping she can prove she's not my wife. So she can leave the first chance she gets. She doesn't get it. No matter what she does, no matter how many times she tries to tear this down, she's not leaving. I've given her

everything. Security. A home. My loyalty. My fucking heart—
and she still looks at me like I'm the monster under her bed.

No matter what I do, it's never enough for her. I could give
her the world, and she'd still stare at me like I'm someone she
needs to survive, not someone she could ever love. And maybe
that's why I hate this feeling so much.

Because part of me would have done anything to hear her
say she loved me back. For half a second, when she didn't say it,
a hollowness opened up in my chest. It felt too close to fear of
rejection. The thought that even if she stays, she'll never really
want to.

I shove it down. That kind of weakness is why she thinks
she can defy me. I'm done letting her believe she holds the
cards here. Part of me wants to drag her back home tonight,
lock her in the basement, and chain her up until she learns
some goddamn gratitude. But I won't.

Not yet.

This trip was supposed to be a reset. A clean slate. I'm not
going to let her ruin it. But I'm not going to let her keep running
her mouth, either.

The second those results come in, I'm done entertaining
this. I'm going to shove the proof in her face until she can't
pretend anymore. Then she's going to look me in the eye and
say she knows she's mine. And when she says it, she'll mean it.

I don't want to punish her for this. I don't want to hurt her.
Not tonight.

I want her to understand that whatever she thinks she feels
—fear, hate, whatever lies she tells herself—none of it matters.
Because at the end of the day, she's mine. And if she can't say it,
then I'll fuck it into her until her body says it for her.

It's not about reclaiming power or proving I'm right. It's
about reminding both of us of what this is. I gave her time. I
gave her space. I let her think she had a choice. But I'm finished
pretending.

Tonight, I'm going to leave her and let her spiral. When we get home, I'm going to put her on her knees and bury every thought she has about leaving. And when she's shaking and spent, she'll remember exactly who she belongs to.

Me.

Always me.

62

MAREN

I can finally breathe. Adrian left me alone, and even though he's furious, at least he knows where I stand, that I'm not pretending anymore. That I won't smile, and nod, and act like a wife in love just because he whispers, *I love you* against my skin. I don't want to be with him.

I want to be free of him. And for the first time in months, I sleep. Because I'm not performing, not trying to soften my edges so he doesn't break me again. Just existing in my skin, even if it means he hates me for it. And maybe it will.

I don't see him until the next morning. Sunlight filters through the curtains, warm across my face, and for a moment, I almost forget where I am. But then I hear his footsteps.

He comes to my side of the bed, watching me like he's waiting to see if I'll bolt.

"Get up," he says quietly. "Come sit at the table."

My stomach knots, but I do it. My legs feel too thin under me as I cross the room.

He's already set out two chairs, a sheet of paper resting neatly between them.

I sit, my heart thumping against my ribs, and he slides the

paper closer. "Your DNA results," he says, his voice flat. "I thought you'd want to see the proof yourself."

I look down. The words slam through me: *99.99% match*. For a second, the letters don't even register. My eyes skim over the lines, but my brain won't process them. I can't believe it. I search the page for a flaw, a smudge, a name spelled wrong, anything, but nothing.

"No." I shake my head, my voice cracking. "No, you're making this up. This is forged. You have the money—you could do it."

"They're real." His tone doesn't waver.

I grip the edge of the table so hard my knuckles ache. My mouth is so dry I can barely swallow. It feels like the floor dropped out from under me.

"This doesn't prove anything," I whisper. "You could've bribed them—"

"They're real," he repeats, firmer.

I stare at the paper again, willing the letters to rearrange themselves into something that makes sense. Something that isn't the worst-case scenario. But there it is—*99.99% match*.

I squeeze my eyes shut, but it doesn't help. It just makes the nausea swell sharper in my chest. My head spins, a thousand questions colliding all at once. I open my eyes, and he's watching me with patience that feels worse than anger. He's waiting for me to accept it and fall in line finally.

"What the hell is going on?" My voice is thin, almost child-like. "What are you doing to me?"

He crouches in front of me, grabbing both my hands in his. "I didn't alter anything," he says, low and certain. "You're my wife. But you already knew that."

I start crying. The tears come hot and fast, my throat closing around a sob I can't swallow. The results in black ink says that everything I remember about myself is wrong, and the harder I push it away, the tighter it sticks.

"This isn't possible," I whisper. "I wouldn't forget marrying you. I grew up in foster care. I had no family. I never met you."

"That's not true. We met at the restaurant you worked at, and you know it."

Am I delusional? Or is this fake and he wants to make me doubt everything?

My voice breaks. "If I married you by choice...what the fuck was I thinking?"

He exhales slowly, the tiniest crack in his composure. "Now we can put this to rest. You're my wife. You don't need to hold on to this delusion anymore. I had the blood and swab taken from you. It was compared to the DNA test you took before. It was a match. I had no doubts."

He keeps holding my hands, as if his grip alone will keep me from slipping away.

63

ADRIAN

I should've taken her to see a fucking psychiatrist. I just delayed it because I don't trust her to talk to one and attempt to use it to leave me, but I can't keep denying how much she needs it. The way her eyes dart across the paper, like she's searching for some escape hatch. Like if she stares long enough, the words will rearrange themselves into the lie she wants to believe.

She looks...devastated. Completely undone by being confronted with the truth. And I don't understand how she can look at evidence this clear and still insist she doesn't know me.

I didn't alter anything. I'd never do that. Does she think I'm the kind of man who would snatch a stranger off the street because she happened to look like my wife?

The thought makes my jaw clench so hard it aches. Does she hate me that much? I know I'm far from perfect. God knows I've made mistakes. Her face crumbling like she's realizing she's trapped forever with the worst possible person? That's fucking painful in a way I can't describe. I've done nothing but take care of her. I've provided for her. I've given her stability, a home, and security most people only dream about.

And emotionally, I've tried. I've done better since she's been back. I've been present, affectionate, and patient in ways I never used to be.

Yes, I have a kink that includes punishment. And yes, I went too far last time. But it's part of us—part of what we've always shared. She responded to it. She came apart in my hands. She always does. So how can she sit here and look at me like I'm her captor instead of a husband trying to save our marriage? Like none of this ever meant a damn thing to her?

I want to shake her. I want to drag her onto my lap and make her say that she loves me and wants to spend her life with me. I should've never told her I loved her. I don't know what the hell I was thinking. Maybe I was drunk on the way I came so hard after days without touching her, the way she looked when she finally gave in. I lost all reason and said something I never should have.

And I did it because I expected her to be happy. I expected her to soften, to look at me and tell me she loved me, too, even if I'm flawed. Even if I'm not gentle the way she sometimes wants me to be.

But that didn't happen. Instead, she's devastated. She's looking at those test results like they're a death sentence, crying like I'm the worst thing that ever happened to her.

And the longer she sits there with her face in her hands, the more the anger simmers in my chest. I'm her husband. I'm the man who's done everything for her. I've given her a life most people would kill for.

What a fucking way to spend our vacation—her sobbing at the kitchen table because she can't stand the fact she's married to me. And the part that makes it worse?

She doesn't even realize what this does to me. How can she take the smallest thing—like me saying I love you—and twist it into proof I'm the villain she's decided I am?

I'm not perfect. I know that. But I'm here. I'm trying. And she still looks at me like she'd rather be anywhere else.

I rake a hand through my hair, jaw clenching so hard it hurts. I could walk out. Give her space to come to terms with it. But part of me wants to shake her, to make her see that she's not some innocent bystander in this. That she's my wife, whether she likes it or not. That nothing she says or does is going to change the fact that she belongs here—with me.

And if she can't handle that?

She's going to have to learn.

Because no matter how much this hurts, no matter how much her denial feels like a blade between my ribs, I'm not letting her go.

Not now. Not ever.

64

MAREN

I'm Eleanor Montgomery. Somehow, impossibly, I almost believe him when he says the results are real. The way he looked at me—cold, certain—he wasn't lying.

So what does that make me? Deranged? Broken? I didn't make up an entire life. We both agree that I worked at the Rusty Nail as a bartender before he kidnapped me. But before that is a dispute. I look up at him, wiping my face with the back of my hand.

Any softness in those green eyes—any hint of the man who called me beautiful and whispered I love you against my skin—is gone. He's furious.

Good. Maybe that will finally be the thing that makes him want to get rid of me. He takes a step forward, towering over me, his jaw tight.

"Now that this is put to rest, I expect you to move on from it," he says evenly. "I expect you to start acting like my wife again. Like the woman you were before you decided to play these games."

I swallow, my throat raw, my pulse thudding so hard it almost drowns out my thoughts. I'm not convinced he didn't give me false results. But if we are married, then we can divorce. At least I can get something out of this marriage, I don't even remember.

"I want a divorce," I whisper.

His eyes widen, and in the span of a breath, his hand comes down hard on the table, rattling the glass.

"That's not fucking happening, Eleanor."

His voice is low and lethal, vibrating through me. "And if you mention leaving again, I will lock you in that basement for months until you admit you're fucking mine."

That will be hell. I stare at him, my chest heaving, and something brittle in me finally cracks.

"There's the real Adrian," I whisper, my voice shaking. "The one who doesn't know how to love or care for anyone."

He flinches, just for a second, before his mouth hardens. "I know how to love," he says, his tone rough. "I'm capable of it."

I swallow back the ache in my throat and meet his eyes. "Who are you trying to convince? Me...or you?"

He goes still, breathing hard, and for a moment, he doesn't say anything.

Then his lip curls, and his voice drops into a low, dangerous calm. "Eleanor, you know what?" he says quietly. "Fine. You can have the divorce."

My pulse stutters.

"But I will make it a long, miserable process. So get ready to go to fucking war."

I lift my chin, my voice coming out hoarse but steady.

"Bring it on, asshole."

His nostrils flare, and he steps closer, towering over me like he thinks his height alone will make me back down.

"You know what pisses me off?" he asks, his voice low, vibrating with contempt. "You were a starving artist when I met you. I gave you a life you didn't deserve."

Something sharp twists in my chest, disgust and disbelief warring with the last shred of fear.

"You can tell yourself whatever you need to," I whisper. "It doesn't make it true."

His mouth tightens. "Sometimes I regret doing any of it, picking you. Bringing you back. Giving you everything."

"Then maybe you should've left me in that bar," I say, my voice shaking. "Because all you ever did was chain me to you and call it love."

His jaw clenches so hard I think he might snap. But he doesn't. He stares at me, breathing ragged, eyes bright with rage and hurt. And for once, I don't look away.

He stares at me, his jaw flexing, like he's trying to decide if he's going to yell or drag me out the door.

Then his voice drops, quiet but ice-cold.

"Pack up. We're leaving."

I stiffen, my pulse thudding hard against my ribs. "What?"

"You don't get rewarded with a vacation," he says, each word clipped and final. "We're going home."

Home.

That house isn't home. It's a fortress, a prison, full of cameras in the corners and locks on every door.

Here, at least, there's space. No staff. No alarms I can't disarm.

I stand there, my hands curling into fists at my sides, trying not to let him see how badly I don't want to go back.

My throat feels raw, but I force the words out, anyway.

"I'm not leaving," I say, my voice low but certain. "I'm staying here. You can go back to that prison, but I won't."

His head snaps toward me, eyes narrowing, the papers crumpling slightly in his hand.

"You will," he says evenly. "Or I'll drag you out of here myself."

I lift my chin, my pulse hammering. "Then that's what you'll have to do. Because I'm not leaving."

For a second, we stare at each other—two people locked in a standoff and neither of us is willing to break. He watches me, his jaw tight, his eyes cold and furious.

His voice cuts through the silence, soft and steady, as if he's explaining something simple to a child. "You think you can stay here, play house on this island? Fine. But understand what that means." His mouth curves, but it isn't a smile. "There are no stores. No neighbors. No one coming to help you. Everything you eat, everything you touch, I have brought here."

My hands curl tight at my sides.

"I'll leave you with water. That's it. You'll watch the fridge empty, the cupboards go bare. But I'll keep the electricity on for you. You'll starve in the middle of all this luxury, and you'll remember exactly who you need to survive. You'll be on your knees begging me to take you back home. And when I do, it won't be a happy reunion."

My stomach twists, bile rising hot in my throat. The picture he paints is too clear. I see myself pacing this kitchen while the food rots away, every day weaker than the last, no one coming, no one even knowing I'm here. He's stripped the island bare with his words until all I can see is how easily he could let me waste away.

I shake my head, but it does nothing to clear the image. He says it so calmly, like he's already thought it through. The worst part is knowing he means it. Out here, nothing belongs to me. Not the food in the fridge. Not the bed I sleep in. Not even the ground under my feet.

My voice scrapes out before I can stop it. "You'd do that to me?"

For a moment, something human flickers in his eyes, not softness, not mercy, but a fracture, like he's raging a war inside himself. I see the part of him that wants to be the man he promised me, straining against the part that will burn me down just to keep me. His jaw tightens, the muscle jumping as if he's forcing the decision out through gritted teeth. Then he answers, quiet but certain. "Yes. I would."

The word slices deeper than the threat itself. My chest seizes, heat climbing into my throat until it burns. I wanted him to deny it, to tell me I was wrong, even if it was a lie. But he didn't. He would starve me, strip me down to nothing, just to prove I can't live without him.

A sound slips out of me, half sob, half breath, and I bite it back hard enough to taste iron. My knees want to give out, but I lock them tight. If I sink now, he'll think he's won.

I force myself upright, though my legs tremble. My voice comes out thin but steady. "Then do it. Leave me here. See how long I last without you."

His eyes darken, and he just watches me, fury tightening every line of his face. Then his mouth twists into something that isn't quite a smile.

"You're so defiant," he says at last, his voice dropping to that low, dangerous register that always used to make my stomach flip. "I can't wait to punish you for this."

I laugh, sharp and hollow. "Good luck. You won't ever touch me again."

He exhales, a ragged sound that makes something in his expression crack. He reaches for me so fast I barely react. Spins me around. Presses me into the edge of the table. The edge bites into my hips, the pressure sharp, jarring. I brace my palms against the wood, but my hands are shaking.

His mouth finds the side of my neck, lips hot against my skin. I suck in a sharp breath, my body stiffening, and then heat rushes through me in a way I can't stop. He presses harder into me, his chest pinning me forward, and I feel him hard against me through the thin fabric of my nightgown. My nipples tighten, my thighs tremble, and shame burns hotter than the air in my lungs.

His hand slides down, slipping under the hem of my night-gown. My stomach lurches as his fingers part me, bare and exposed. I jolt, a sound catching in my throat when he finds wetness there.

"There it is," he murmurs, low against my ear. "You fight me with your words, but your body tells the truth. You love me. And your body does, too."

And then he pulls back, leaving me shaking.

I don't answer. I can't. My hands slide off the table, legs giving out beneath me. I sink to the floor, knees hitting the hardwood as his words echo in my head. My skin still burns from where he touched me, like my body is siding with him now, betraying me in the worst way.

He crouches beside me, silent, and sets the folded sheet of paper at my knee. The lab's logo stares up at me, with the result spelled out in black and white. The proof that should have set me free. But it didn't. It trapped me.

And now no one will believe me.

65

ADRIAN

This wasn't supposed to happen. It wasn't supposed to escalate like this. She looks at me the same way she did when I called her trash, furious and betrayed, like she'd rather burn this whole house down than ever let me touch her again. But underneath that fury I catch a flicker of satisfaction, because she knows she got what she wanted. She pushed until I snapped, and I gave it to her. I can see it in her eyes now, the triumph of knowing she can still get under my skin, still drag the monster out of me with nothing but her defiance.

She thinks that makes her strong, convinced she's going to win this war she started. All I can think about is how badly I want to fuck it out of her, whip it out of her, tear the fire out of her mouth until there's nothing left but the truth of how she feels when I'm inside her. She thinks I want her broken. She's wrong. I want her fighting, clawing, spitting, because every time she does, I get to break her again.

I try to steady myself, force the heat back down, but it's useless. My hands shake. My voice would, too, if I tried to speak. She's crying now, barely holding herself together on the floor, and I stand there, watching. Not because I feel guilty. Because she's never looked more breakable. More mine.

I wanted to do this differently. Be patient. Prove to her I could be better. But patience never kept her. Love without fear is useless. She doesn't need the man I promised her. She needs the one who can cage her.

Right now, all I want is to break down that wall she's hiding behind, force her to look at me hungry, needing, wrecked, and know she can't deny what we are together. I want her on her knees, and this time, I won't let her get back up until she remembers exactly who she belongs to.

"I hate you," she whispers, her voice raw.

I lean in, my mouth to her ear. "No. You love me. That's the one thing you can't change."

Her chin lifts, eyes wet but burning. "You'll never hear me say it, because you've made me your prisoner."

My smile spreads, slow and cruel. "Then I'll build you a steel cage of your own. And you'll stay on your knees until you say whatever I want."

The color drains from her face, panic flickering in her eyes before she can stop it, and the sound of her breath stuttering between a sob and a choke seals it. Heat floods through me, my cock already hard, because I know she believes me. She should. And when she drops her gaze, just for a second, it's enough. Fear is honest. Fear means she understands exactly who owns her.

She doesn't get to walk away from this marriage. Vows aren't words. They're chains. And I'll bind her with mine until the day she dies.

THANK YOU FOR READING

If you enjoyed *Falsely Yours*, please consider leaving a review on
Amazon or Goodreads. Your feedback helps other readers
discover the book.

Scan below to join the Scarlett Witherspoon newsletter for
updates on future releases.

Or visit:
scarlettwitherspoon.com

ABOUT THE AUTHOR

Scarlett Witherspoon writes fiction rooted in emotional intensity, psychological tension, and complex character dynamics. She left her career in IT to pursue writing full-time, teaching herself the craft through countless late nights. Her debut novel, *Falsely Yours*, launched the Forever Yours series and established her signature style.

She lives in Denver, Colorado, with her husband and their two Cavalier King Charles Spaniels, who keep her company through every draft.